KU-224-072

YOU DRIVE ME CRAZY

YOU DRIVE ME CRAZY

Carole Matthews

headline

Copyright © 2005 Carole Matthews (Ink) Ltd.

The right of Carole Matthews to be identified as the Author of
the Work has been asserted by her in accordance with the
Copyright, Designs and Patents Act 1988.

First published in 2005
by HEADLINE BOOK PUBLISHING

1

Apart from any use permitted under UK copyright law, this
publication may only be reproduced, stored, or transmitted, in
any form, or by any means, with prior permission in writing of
the publishers or, in the case of reprographic production, in
accordance with the terms of licences issued by the
Copyright Licensing Agency.

All characters in this publication are fictitious
and any resemblance to real persons, living or dead,
is purely coincidental.

Cataloguing in Publication Data is
available from the British Library

ISBN 0 7553 0994 4 (hardback)
ISBN 0 7553 0995 2 (trade paperback)

Typeset in Bembo by Palimpsest Book Production Limited,
Polmont, Stirlingshire
Printed and bound in Great Britain by
Mackays of Chatham plc, Chatham, Kent

Headline's policy is to use papers that are natural, renewable and
recyclable products and made from wood grown in sustainable
forests. The logging and manufacturing processes are expected
to conform to the environmental regulations of the country of origin.

HEADLINE BOOK PUBLISHING
A division of Hodder Headline PLC
338 Euston Road
London NW1 3BH
www.headline.co.uk
www.hodderheadline.com

To Steve

Edwin Jack Stevens

Who was everything a Dad should be.

16 January 1922 – 20 August 2004

Chapter One

'Divorce?' I give the man sitting opposite me my most reassuring smile.

He looks up, a surprised expression on his face, and glances round to check that I'm not talking to anyone else. 'Me?'

I nod.

'Er . . . yes.'

'Me too.' I shrug as if it's a massive coincidence that we're both sitting in a solicitor's waiting room looking stressed.

At this point I must say that I have seen the inside of solicitors' offices far too many times in my short and otherwise uneventful life. This one is more beige than usual – the only relief provided by funky red chairs which add a splash of vibrant colour to show what a trendy firm they really are. For the prices they charge I'd fully expect to see golden thrones in here for all the clients. Still, this is *only* my second divorce, for which I suppose I should be truly grateful these days. I didn't even want one divorce, so, to me, having two almost tucked away under my belt seems to be bordering on careless.

I'm leafing aimlessly through a pristine copy of one of those glossy, give-away magazines that's choc-full of adverts for smart little boutiques I've never heard of and couldn't afford even if I had. The magazine is called *New Style* and it makes me wonder why I haven't got any these days – style, that is. Why is it that models in catalogues can stand there posing in a simple oatmeal roll-neck sweater and faded bootcut jeans and look utterly fabulous, whereas in the same ensemble I cannot?

I stop pretending to read and take in the rest of the waiting room. Tumley & Goss, solicitors to the soon-to-be-impoverished, are not known for their meticulous time-keeping when it comes to appointments and I'm sure if they could manage to work out a way of charging their clients for waiting time, then they would have done so by now.

I turn my attention back to the man opposite me. He is also pretending to read *New Style* magazine and is making a worse job of it than me. His knees are jiggling nervously. First time. I know these things. I, Anna Terry, am an expert in the psychological profile of the occupants of solicitors' waiting rooms. Personal injury claims are usually a doddle to pick out — especially the ones that involve those NHS-supplied grubby neck collars.

'First time?' I venture.

'Yes,' he says, abandoning the *New Style* on the chair next to him. 'You?'

'Second,' I admit sheepishly. 'I feel like I'm in training for the Joan Collins award for services to marriage.'

I don't add that I've probably paid for all of these bright red chairs in the process — and a bit more. Like a couple of holidays in the Bahamas for each partner in the firm.

'I'm sorry to hear that,' he says, and he genuinely looks as if he is.

'The world is full of younger, blonder women with more comely bosoms.' There go my shoulders again, trying to shrug away the hurt.

My fellow divorcé risks a smile. And, if I were noticing these things, I'd say it was a very cute smile. 'You look very . . . *nice* . . . to me.'

'Nice.' I sigh over the word. 'It's not quite the same as being a wanton sex kitten, is it?'

'I suppose not.'

'Both of my husbands thought I was nice,' I go on. '"You're a nice woman, Anna," they'd say, "*but* . . ."'

'. . . "I'm running off with a wanton sex kitten".'

Now it's my turn to smile. 'You're very perceptive.'

Except that I don't know where my current excuse of a husband is at all. He just left. Without warning. I'd nipped out to the super-market to get some milk, and ten minutes later when I returned, Bruno had disappeared along with most of his shirts and his best jeans. That was it. He didn't leave a note. He didn't call. And, needless to say, he didn't send any money to feed or clothe the fruit of his loins. That was over a year ago and I've been trying to track him down ever since. Me and the Child Support Agency, of course.

'My wife ran off with a butcher,' my companion says.

'I expect it was the lure of free meat.'

'She's a vegetarian.'

'Oh.' I pull a suitably sympathetic face. 'Women can be strange creatures.'

'I expect men can be too,' he remarks as his mobile phone rings.

As he rummages for it, I study the posters proclaiming the sums that can be gained for those fortunate enough to suffer a personal injury that can be blamed on someone else's stupidity rather than their own. I could be a millionaire in moments if I fell over on a frosty pavement that the council had failed to grit, or tripped on some lumpy tarmac laid by a careless contractor. Perhaps if I take a tumble down the stairs on my way out and sustain a sprained ankle, Mr Tumley or Mr Goss might consider waiving my not insubstantial bill.

'Hello. Nick Diamond,' the man says into his phone.

Nick Diamond. Hmm. I try not to look as if I'm listening to his conversation, but of course I am.

'I'm fine,' he says, turning slightly away from me. He knows that I'm listening. 'It will all be fine. Really.' Then he lowers his voice. 'I'm fine, Mum. Really. Don't get upset. It's okay, I won't do anything silly. Yes, I know.' He lowers his voice further, but the waiting room of Tumley & Goss has superb acoustics and I have a trained ear for gossip. 'I won't say that. I'm in a public place, Mum. I'm going now. Bye. Bye. Yes. Bye.' He slides his mobile back into his pocket and with a loud tsk, he says, 'Business.'

'Oh.'

'You know how it is. Cut and thrust. This and that. International meetings.' Nick Diamond squirms in his seat. 'Pressure. Stress.'

'There's no need to explain,' I offer. 'My mum worries herself to death about me too.'

That is somewhat understating things. My mother holds me and my rather tortured love-life responsible for everything from her varicose veins to the angina she is not yet suffering from, but doubtless will one day all because of me.

My companion looks guilty. 'Are this lot any good?'

'If you mean will you have any money left at the end of it all then, no, they're not good.'

'I want to be fair about this,' he says with a shake of his head. 'I don't want to fight with Janine over money.'

'Don't you?'

He gives me a look that I'd class as self-deprecating. 'I'm not like that.'

I return an involuntary and altogether too cynical snort. 'You will be.'

'I believe you can get divorced without becoming all bitter and twisted.'

'But that's the fun part!' I tell him. He looks at me disbelievingly. You can tell this man is naive in the ways of the world. And, particularly, in the ways of marital disentanglement.

'It isn't in my nature,' he insists. 'I too had the "you're a nice man *but* . . ." speech.'

My heart sighs. 'Why do nice people always get dumped?'

'It's one of life's age-old mysteries,' he says. 'Like why is the coffee crème always the last chocolate in the box to be eaten?'

I laugh. And I realise that it's a very long time since I did that. Especially in a solicitor's office.

'Any kids?' Nick Diamond asks.

'No. No. No. Oh, no. None.'

'Me neither.'

I clap my hands together. 'Great. So we're both young, free and single.'

'I guess so.' And Nick sounds suddenly sad and alone. 'I would have liked them though. Children. A boy and a girl.' He looks slightly embarrassed at his confession. 'It's everyone's ideal, isn't it – except Janine's. She's a fitness fanatic – didn't want stretchmarks.'

'Who does? Kids ruin your figure.' I clear my throat. 'So I'm told.'

'I believe the comely bosoms are the first thing to go.'

We both giggle.

'I do hope they're not too much longer,' I say with a longing glance at the clock. 'I've got an interview with a recruitment agency this afternoon.'

'Career change?'

'You could call it that. I haven't worked for years.'

'Rich husband?'

'Er . . . filthy.' Never mind that Bruno never had two pennies to rub together and left me with even less. I can hardly tell my new friend that I'm a stay-at-home mum who spends her entire life looking after two rather hyperactive children when I have just denied their very existence. What sort of a mother am I, for goodness sake? At thirty-three I already feel like a raddled old one, I can tell you. I have borne Poppy who is supposed to be ten, but over the last few years she has clearly been ageing in dog years mentally. That makes her around fifty-six, which sounds about right to me. Connor is not quite two. He's destined to be a man and, therefore, will never, ever grow up at all.

'A life of leisure then?'

'Every moment of it.' I wish. Why can't I come clean and tell him that I'm a single mum struggling to hold her life together? 'But it means that I don't possess one single marketable skill. To be honest, I haven't got any inclination to work either, but now I haven't got any choice.'

'What about your settlement? Surely, your husband wants to look after you?'

'The only person Bruno has ever wanted to look after is himself,' I say. 'I'm currently trying to divorce him in his absence. He's done a runner.'

'I'm sorry to hear that.' Nick Diamond looks at me kindly. 'I'm sure you'll find something.'

'Yeah.' I fake a lightness I don't feel. 'I can't think of anything worse than being stuck in some pokey office all day.' Other than looking after kids all day, I mean.

Two secretaries simultaneously crane their heads out of office doors. They're wearing beige suits with red blouses to match the décor and have obviously not been availing themselves of the tips contained within the pages of *New Style* magazine.

'Mrs Terry. Mr Diamond,' the secretaries trill, and hover at their respective office doors through which we gain admittance to the inner sanctums – or the money-making centres as I like to call them.

We both stand up.

'Well . . .' Nick says.

'Well . . .'

'Nice to meet you.'

'Nice to meet you, too.'

Nick hesitates before he says, 'Maybe we could . . . No, well . . . never mind.' He casts an uneasy glance at the waiting staff. 'You've probably got a mad social whirl now that you're young, free and single again.'

'Yeah, yeah.' A bit of bravado for the secretaries who do look young, free and single and not like sad sacks who spend every night in front of the telly watching old Disney videos with nothing but a glass of cheap wine and a Mars bar for company. Nick's face falls and I suddenly realise what I've said. 'Well, not that mad.'

But I've missed my chance.

He holds out his hand and shakes mine, while the waiting secretaries start to tap their corporate feet. 'Good luck with your interview. I hope they find you a great job.'

Some hope. 'Thanks. Good luck with hanging on to your international business. And your shirt.'

We exchange a shy smile.

'Thanks,' he says. And we both take a deep breath. He seems such a nice man, I wonder how can he have deserved this? I watch him disappear into the office of his vulture – sorry, solicitor – before I too plunge headlong into the gritty and unpleasant world of divorce once more.

Chapter Two

I live in Milton Keynes, the fastest-growing city in the UK. It's a vibrant place that resembles a large slab of America set down amidst the green and gentle countryside of Buckinghamshire. I'm a bit of an anomaly here in that I arrived before it was a new city, when it was just a twinkle in a planner's eye and there was no grid system, no shopping mall and no housing estates, only fields and mud and cows.

I leave the heat of Tumley & Goss's offices – these people don't need to worry about the size of their heating bills – and emerge into the sharp, fresh air of Midsummer Boulevard. In the centre of the city, all the roads are perfectly straight, which ensures that every puff of wind is funnelled towards those unwise enough to be wearing a skirt in the middle of winter, i.e. me. Within seconds my knees are blue and frozen. I stride up the road, wrapping my coat around me, and eventually dodge into another stainless steel and glass building that typifies the architectural style here.

After the trauma of the solicitors', I'm not feeling very strong about subjecting myself to further humiliation at the hands of a recruitment agency. I've never been into one of these places before, but I feel intimidated enough by the banks of humming computers, let alone the rows of officious-looking women sitting next to them. They all have fake tans and look like they sit with their buttocks clenched all day. Also, they all look considerably smarter than I do and this is *absolutely* my best jacket. Not so much last season, though, as last century. When I get a super-duper status job, the first thing I'll do is rush out and buy a hideously expensive designer power suit. But from an outlet store, of course.

I give the receptionist my details, then sit down at one of the desks opposite the lovely Leone as I've been instructed.

'Hi.' She gives me a brief smile and it's clear that this is the full extent of her pleasantries. 'Name and address?'

I can manage that without too much trouble and duly reel them off. I even follow them with my phone number, without so much as a glitch, while Leone taps away.

She deigns to lift her eyes towards me. 'Previous experience?'

Does she want to know that I can churn out nutritious meals on a meagre budget with alarming regularity, or that I'm a dab hand with a vacuum cleaner, or that I can turn a hysterical, screaming child into an angel with only the help of a packet of M&Ms? Or should I just cut to the chase and tell her exactly how many men I've slept with? I'm afraid I'm not very experienced in that department either. I don't need to take off my socks to count the number of partners I've had – it's just one for each foot and both of them husbands.

'Jobs?' she says while I'm still pondering my reply.

'Oh. None.' Not in living memory, anyway. I'm not sure that a stint as an office cleaner or a supermarket cashier over ten years ago is anything to brag about in my current situation.

She ceases her tapping, abruptly. 'So you've no experience?'

A hush descends on the whole of the recruitment agency and I get the sense of tans blanching.

'Loads of it,' I say with as much bluff as I can muster. 'Just not in the work sense of the word.'

Leone loses the little smile she'd managed to produce.

'So you haven't brought a CV.'

'No,' I say. 'But I can do one. I've got a degree in Business Studies.' I hope she doesn't ask for proof of this as I actually did an NVQ in Business Studies at my local college. But it was very interesting and I came top in my class.

'That's rather like having a car but being unable to drive,' she points out.

'Oh come on.' My patience is skating on thin ice. 'There must be one job out there that requires no skill, no brain, no specialist equipment, but you can still make loads of money.'

Leone shows me her teeth. 'There is,' she says. 'But then it would be a pimp you'd require, not a recruitment consultant.'

It's clear that I am wasting my own and Leone's valuable time, so I get up to leave.

'Thanks,' I say. 'Thanks a bunch.'

If the government want to get single mums out of the home and working again – then they'd better do something about smug bitches like Leone. But, as we all know from the daily press, we single-parent families are the scourge of the nation, along with asylum seekers, beggars, drug addicts and the drivers of Vauxhall Corsas. I hope Leone has kids one day and they ruin her figure, and then her husband, who she still loves, leaves her to manage on benefits – that would wipe the smile off her pouty little face. And I hope that one day, when she is trying to drag herself up by her boot-straps, someone is as nasty to her as she's been to me.

But, obviously, I say none of this and start to slink out of the office instead, shame-faced and seething.

As I head to the door, she calls after me. 'Wait.'

She pulls a piece of paper out of her printer. 'There is one job . . .'

I take the piece of paper and scan it, trying very hard to look interested and not as if I'm about to cry. 'This looks okay,' I say. It doesn't really look okay, it looks beyond dire. But I am fast learning that beggars – and single mums – cannot be choosers. 'I'd definitely consider it.'

'Ah,' Leone says and takes the paper off me again. 'The thing is whether *they'd* consider *you*.'

Chapter Three

Nick Diamond rubbed his hands together, partly in celebration of being master of all he surveyed and partly because it was freeze-your-testicles-off cold. A corner used-car lot on a busy thoroughfare on the outskirts of the city was not perhaps much of an empire, but it was all his and there was a certain amount of pride in that.

Technically, the bank owned rather more of it than he did. But it would all be his one day – one day when he had paid off his astronomical debts. And, amid all the other doom and gloom of divorce, at least his solicitor had told him that he could hang onto his business as long as he signed over the house to Janine – his currently estranged wife. Which wasn't the fairest of deals, but it was the least painful option. As there were no children, the house wasn't classed as the family home – it was just a pile of bricks and mortar to be carved up between them as they saw fit. Anyway, he couldn't imagine himself living alone in a house that held so many memories of them as a couple. Nick patted the bonnet of an ageing Mondeo for comfort. His cars were a poor substitute for children, but currently they were all he'd got.

An elderly couple were doddering across the yard, weaving their way between the various cars, both stooped and frail-looking. They reminded him of his grandparents when they'd been alive and Nick cast a fond smile in their direction. He'd hoped that he and Janine would grow old and wrinkled together – but now that wasn't going to be the case. They hadn't even got as far as getting middle-aged spread together.

'Let me know if you need any help,' Nick shouted over to the old couple.

'We're just browsing,' the man said. His wife smiled pleasantly. 'If that's all right.'

'Of course,' Nick said. 'Take your time.'

It was heartbreaking. How could he sell a car to people like these who clearly were struggling to afford a vehicle at all? They both wore thin, threadbare coats and the wind today was biting. He wanted to take them into his office – a ragged, makeshift Portakabin at the back of the lot – and offer them hot sweet tea and slightly stale digestive biscuits. Guiltily, Nick jammed his hands deeper into the pockets of his snug North Face jacket.

He'd never envisaged being a car salesman, but then he'd never envisaged doing anything, really; that's probably why his career had lacked a certain amount of focus and drive. As a result, he'd wandered aimlessly through the wily world of estate agenting, he'd trodden water in the tedious world of export planning – which he never quite understood from the day he started until the day he was invited to leave – until several jobs later he had found himself in the marginally more distracting world of car sales. All those years of sitting rooted to *Top Gear* had paid dividends after all.

Nick had worked for three years in a main dealership selling expensive and shiny cars to high-end buyers with company budgets. Then, at the age of thirty – a dangerous time in a man's life – the lure of running his own business had presented itself in the rather dilapidated form of CHEEP AND CHEARFULL USED CARS (sic).

Janine had urged him to better himself and her vision of bettering himself had been passing up a decent salary, equally decent bonuses on a regular basis and a selection of shiny company cars, for the permanently impoverished and precarious state of the self-employed. The car yard had 'potential', Janine had assured him. Potential for what, he hadn't yet discovered. Other than the potential to be a bone of contention in their rapidly failing marriage. Still, all this lassitude towards his business was about to change. Now that he knew his car yard was secure for the foreseeable future, he could start to move forward. In a short amount of time, the word 'entrepreneur' would not be far from people's lips when they talked about Nick Diamond.

The elderly couple shuffled nearer to him, circling an ageing Rover that, rather like them, had frankly seen better days.

'Seen anything you like?' Nick asked.

'Yes,' the man said. 'I think we'll take this one.'

'Right,' Nick said. 'I'll get the keys and take you for a test drive.'

'No, no,' the man replied. 'I don't want to put you to any trouble. We just want to buy it.'

'But you must take it on a test drive.'

'Oh no,' his wife chipped in. 'We'd be too worried to do that.'

'You must,' Nick insisted. 'If you took it on a test drive you'd realise that the clutch needs replacing and one of the shock absorbers is shot.'

'Oh dear.' The couple exchanged a fearful look. 'That sounds very expensive.'

'It is,' Nick said.

'Well . . .' The man scratched his chin. 'My wife likes the colour, so I think we'll take it anyway.'

'Are you sure I can't dissuade you? There are other, much better vehicles.'

'No. We like this one.'

'Fine.' This felt like stealing sweets from a child. 'So how much are you going to offer me?'

'Offer you?' The couple swapped another worried look. 'We're happy to pay the price it says on the windscreen.'

'But that's outrageous,' Nick said. 'That's about five hundred quid over the odds.'

'Is it?' The man looked perplexed.

'It's daylight robbery, sir.'

'Things aren't like they were.' The old man shook his head. 'Business is business these days.'

'This is how it goes,' Nick said kindly. 'I overprice the cars and then you try to knock me down.'

'Oh.' The worried expression deepened. 'I couldn't possibly do that.'

'No. Really, you should. I fully expect it. Try to knock me down.'

The man's wife put her hand on his arm. 'Ron, you can't do that.'

'Please.' Nick could tell that he was beginning to beg. 'Knock me down.'

'Well,' the man said, 'if you insist.'

Without warning, the man cannoned out a scrawny fist and hit Nick squarely on the chin. It was like being hit by Frank Bruno or a speeding train, and Nick felt his legs buckle beneath him. A circle of birds was tweeting round his head. The couple stood over him smiling broadly.

'When exactly was the last time you bought a car?' Nick said, trying to massage his jaw back into shape.

Chapter Four

I'm sitting in my friend Sophie's kitchen, nursing a well-deserved cup of tea and a wriggling son. Sophie and I have been friends since forever, passing all the major milestones of our lives since primary school in amiable companionship. Our hissy spats have, thankfully, been few and far between. Now we live in neighbouring areas – me in Emerson Valley, Sophie in Furzton Lake. Close but not on top of each other, if you know what I mean. As children we lived in the same street, which would perhaps as adults be too close. If I'd had a sister I'm sure she couldn't have cared for me more than Sophie.

My friend has now been elevated from the level of best friend to something approaching sainthood as she has agreed to childmind Connor every day at no extra expense to myself while I try to rebuild my life – and is doing this despite having two monsters of her own to contend with. You simply wouldn't believe the depth of my gratitude. Sophie has offered me a lifeline when I was beginning to sink beneath the waves of debt and despair.

I lower my voice and cover Connor's ears with my hands so that my child doesn't hear my next confession. 'I told him I hadn't got any children.'

'Wishful thinking,' Sophie observed.

'What sort of a mother am I?'

'The usual sort,' Sophie said. '"I love them dearly, but if I had my time again . . ."'

'It's only the kids that are keeping me going,' I say rather shakily. 'I don't know what I'd do without them. They're my sanity.'

'And that is a truly scary thought.' Sophie sips her tea. 'So what was this man in the solicitor's office like?'

'He had "nice" stamped all over him.'

'Nice? More detail please.'

'Tall. Slim. Darkish. Well-turned out.'

'Well-turned out?' Sophie laughs. 'That's the sort of thing my mother says.'

I shrug. What else can I say about him? 'He wasn't heartbreakingly gorgeous. He wasn't pig ugly. He wasn't chisel-jawed. He didn't have predominant pecs. He was nice. Just nice.'

'Didn't you tell him that you don't do nice, you only do bastard?'

'I don't know what I told him,' I admit. And take another chocolate finger for solace. Connor immediately grabs it off me and pushes it up his nose. 'I went all weird. I've forgotten how to talk to men.'

'That's probably because you're normally used to shouting at them.'

I take the biscuit from Connor's nose and wipe it on my sleeve, before putting it back in the correct orifice whilst trying to convince myself that a certain number of germs are good for his immune system. 'I hate being divorced.'

'I hate being married,' Sophie says flatly.

And only part of her is joking. She's been with her husband Tom for ten years now, married for seven. And call me superstitious, but I'm convinced that the seven-year-itch is a very real phenomenon. I think it would be fair to say that they are not love's young dream any more. Even their home carries the air of a couple who have stopped caring. Everything is scuffed, shabby and very slightly dented.

'And the recruitment agency?'

'A deeply demoralising experience.' I purse my lips in dismay. 'Despite the fact that I've managed to survive until the tender age of thirty-three and am still of sound mind and body, and am capable of steering myself and my two children through the highs and lows of this existence we laughingly call life, I am fit for nothing in the employment market.'

'Nothing at all?'

'Well. One job. I've got an interview for it tomorrow. It sounds utterly miserable. The woman at the agency told me I should consider becoming a hooker.'

'There are worse jobs,' Sophie says sagely.

'Like what?'

'Divorce solicitor.'

'Ooo!' We both spit as if there's something very nasty in our mouths. Connor joins in – except there *is* something nasty in his mouth. A pile of soggy, half-chewed biscuit lands on my lap.

'I'd put recruitment consultant up there too now,' I say. 'She was such a cow. Looked at me as if I was your typical single mum – two divorces under her belt, two children by two different fathers, feckless woman.'

'You are,' Sophie says.

Technically, she's right, but it doesn't feel like that from my perspective. My first marriage didn't last as long as my unplanned and entirely unexpected pregnancy – the reason why the marriage took place at all. I was on the Pill, so it was one hell of a shock when, after missing a couple of periods, I realised that the reason I could no longer do up my jeans wasn't down to my increased chocolate intake.

My husband Steve *disappeared* just before our darling daughter Poppy *appeared* and I've never seen him since. To this day, I don't know why he left. We had no money, no home to call our own and a baby on the way – but is that enough reason to pack your bags and leave? When you're twenty-three, perhaps it is. I heard that he'd moved to Brighton and was doing casual work in the hotels there, but I have no idea if that's true. So it was down to me to bring Poppy up alone. And, unfortunately, this was long before the concept of 'starter marriages' and single celebrity mums was fashionable.

Bruno was a different kettle of fish altogether. We had a whirlwind romance followed by a hastily organised wedding. And you know what they say about marrying in haste. Well, it's true. I've certainly done a lot of repenting at leisure ever since. I met Bruno when Poppy was still a toddler, on a rare girls' night out with Sophie, having persuaded my mother to babysit. And I can rationalise it all now, but I'm sure I was just looking for another father for Poppy – though quite why I thought an irrepressible rogue like Bruno was good father material, heaven only knows. Maybe I should have suspected something was amiss when he proposed to me while he was drunk. I definitely have faulty wiring in my radar when it comes to spotting bad 'uns.

Our relationship was one that would be classed as 'volatile' if I were being polite; during a brief period of harmony when Bruno was more often in my bed than in someone else's, Connor was born. But Bruno never let fatherhood or marriage curb his natural instincts and, despite my fantasy of an idyllic family life, I was still left to bring up the kids alone.

'I felt so useless,' I tell Sophie. 'I had to do a cv. It was terrible. I just made up loads of stuff.'

'Everyone does,' states my friend, who hasn't worked either for the last few years. 'Don't lose any sleep over it.'

But I probably will.

'Still,' Sophie says thoughtfully, 'I'd consider becoming a hooker. I can't even give it away for free in this house.'

'Be thankful.' I jiggle Connor who is starting to get restless without the entertaining distraction of snacks to introduce into his body. 'If I ever want to find another man, it means dating again. I am *so* looking forward to going back on the giddy round of supper, snog and sex. Not! Sometimes you don't even get the supper.'

Why is it that some women get wined and dined and whisked away to exotic locations at the drop of a hat – and some just don't. The only 'wining' I've ever been on the receiving end of had an 'h' in it. This time I need a man who will feed the inner goddess in me. And as my inner goddess only needs chocolate on a regular basis, how hard can that be?

Sophie looks wistful. 'It sounds great,' she says. 'So exciting. Wild, reckless, abandoned.'

'It isn't.' I shake my head. 'It's nerve-wracking, expensive and horrible. You've just forgotten what it was like. Be thankful for what you've got.'

'A husband who's more emotionally attached to David Beckham than he is to me? Yeah, right.'

'Tom's not that bad,' I lie. He is, though. I like Sophie's husband as a person, but you couldn't really class him as a hunk of burning love. Tom treats Sophie as if she's completely invisible. She says she has to look in the mirror every ten minutes just to check that she actually is still there.

'I could dance round the lounge naked with a rose between my teeth and Tom wouldn't notice. He'd just tell me that I was blocking his view of the telly.'

Sophie does have a point. You can arrive at their house at any time of the day or night and find Tom fixed to the same seat of the sofa surrounded by remote controls and bags of crisps. Homer Simpson is more animated than Tom King. 'You're just bored with each other.'

'Ah, if only it were so simple,' she says enigmatically. 'So are you going to see the "nice" man again?'

'Nick,' I say. 'He was called Nick Diamond. And no, probably not. Unless we get simultaneous solicitors' appointments again.'

'Simultaneous anything would suit me these days,' she sighs. 'Still no contact from Bruno?'

'No. The solicitor said I should consider hiring a private detective to try and track him down.'

'Oh Anna.' Sophie takes my hand.

'Don't "Oh Anna" me or I might cry.'

'It won't be long before this is sorted out and you've got a fab new job and a "nice" new man.'

'Yeah. And in the meantime, I've got Cheeky Charlie hamburgers that need torturing.' I stand up, hitching Connor onto my hip even though he's far too big for me to be still carrying him. Men start playing the useless card very early. I kiss Sophie goodbye.

'Say bye-bye to Aunty Sophie.'

'Bye-bye to Aunty Sophie,' Connor lisps.

'I'll bring him round again tomorrow so that I can go to this job interview.'

'That's fine,' Sophie says. 'I'll be here. Same place, same shit.'

Chapter Five

Nick winced as the rim of the hot mug brushed against his swollen lip. He tested the sausage-like thickness of it with his teeth. Mr and Mrs Smith nursed their cups of tea too as they all stood and admired the cosy little car in front of them.

'This is a much nicer vehicle,' Nick said to the elderly couple. It was still a Rover, but a much newer model. 'It's as solid as a rock. There's a full service history. It has a state-of-the-art CD player . . .'

They both looked very confused.

'But maybe that won't bother you.'

Concerned, Mrs Smith asked, 'Will we be able to get Terry Wogan?'

'Yes, it has a radio. I'll tune it to Radio Two especially for you.'

The woman sighed with relief.

'It's got a full set of new tyres, and at that price, it's a steal.' Nick stepped away from Mr Smith. 'You won't need to knock me down again.'

Mr and Mrs Smith were visibly pleased. 'How do you know so much about this car?' the old fellow enquired.

Nick sighed. 'Because it's mine.'

'Oh, but we couldn't take your car, could we, Ron?' his wife piped up.

'I insist,' Nick said. 'It will last you a lifetime.' He looked at how frail they seemed. 'Probably longer.'

'This is very nice of you.' Mrs Smith patted his arm.

'I'm known for it.' He tried not to think how much this was going to cost him, but he hoped that when his own parents were similarly old and doddery that they'd find someone with a heart who wouldn't rip them off because they didn't know any better.

'Will you take our car in part-exchange?'

Nick followed Mr Smith's gaze to the heap of junk parked on the road outside the yard. There was no way that thing should still be on the road. It was a death-trap. Didn't they have a loving son tucked away somewhere to take care of them?

'Does it have a valid MOT?'

Mr and Mrs Smith gazed at him blankly.

He would never be able to shift this. The whole thing looked as if it were held together with string and prayers. He was going to have to pay for it to go to the scrapyard. 'Yes,' Nick said. 'I'll take it in part-exchange. I'll give you five hundred quid for it.'

Mr Smith's eyes lit up. Fifty was probably too much.

'So we have a deal?'

'Yes.' Mr Smith handed Nick his empty mug, pulled out a cheque-book and scribbled a cheque.

'I wouldn't normally take a cheque for this amount.' Nick chewed at his lip. 'Don't you have a credit card?'

Again they both looked at him without an obvious sign of comprehension. Back at home they probably had a video recorder they still couldn't programme either.

'This will take a few days to clear.'

Disappointment weighed them down. 'Oh,' Mr Smith said. 'We did so want to take it now. There is enough money in the account, isn't there, Elsie?'

Elsie nodded earnestly. 'We've been saving our pension.'

'Well,' Nick softened. 'I'm sure it will be fine. Can you put your address on the back, please? You can never be too careful these days.'

Mr Smith obliged and Nick handed over the keys, the log book and the vehicle's registration document.

'It's all yours now.'

'Oh, thank you.' Mrs Smith looked quite tearful as she too relinquished her cup. 'You've been very kind, dearie. And thank you for the tea.'

'You're welcome,' Nick said with a warm smile.

Mr Smith struggled to slide into the driver's seat and Nick went round to help Mrs Smith into the passenger side. He watched them as they drove slowly out of the yard, all smiles and waving madly, and along the street at a pace that would never induce a speed camera to flash.

Nick looked in dismay at the rusting pre-war heap that he'd been left with. He'd no idea how they'd managed to drive here in it. The bloody thing probably wouldn't even start. Somehow, he'd have to move it inside the yard or it was likely to get a parking ticket slapped on it – more expense.

'Hello, hello.' Nick's friend Sam crossed the yard towards him.

'Hi, Sam.' Nick turned his attention away from the problem car. 'What are you doing here?'

His mate was carrying two takeaway pizza boxes with two Styrofoam cups balanced on top of them.

'I have made enough money for one morning,' Sam said. 'Shall we stop the wheels of big business from grinding relentlessly forward and pause for an executive lunch?'

Sam was tall and handsome and supremely confident, and all of the things that Nick wished he would be in his next lifetime. He did something wonderfully flash in one of the posh buildings in the city centre and wore designer suits and drove a slinky new Porsche. Generally blokes hated Sam, while women adored him. Nick constantly felt as if he shrank in Sam's shadow, as much now as he did in their schooldays, but then his friend liked to play the protector and had been a constant source of support during his break-up with Janine. The fact that Sam had hated Janine anyway had made him particularly vociferous in his condemnation of her – which had made Nick feel better as he'd never quite found it in his heart to condemn her himself.

Nick fell in step beside Sam and they headed towards his office.

Sam took one look at the rust bucket for which Nick had just part-exchanged his own pride and joy – and nodded disdainfully in its direction. 'I think you've just been tucked up, mate.'

'The owners were old. They were poor,' Nick said in his defence. 'It would have been like ripping off my own grandparents.'

Sam gave Nick a pitying look.

'It's a classic car,' Nick went on.

'Right – classically awful.'

Nick sighed. 'Do you ever get the feeling I'm not cut out for big business?'

'Frequently.' Sam put his arm round Nick's shoulders and steered him round the puddles that had formed in the last shower of rain. 'What type of pizza do you fancy? Meaty Extravaganza or the girly seafood and sweetcorn bollocks?'

'I'll have the girly bollocks one,' Nick said. 'I'm off meat at the moment.'

Chapter Six

Nick balanced his pizza on his lap on a plastic garden chair, while Sam leaned back in the genuine leather-look armchair with his feet up on Nick's desk in the small gap his friend had cleared in the mountainous paperwork. The wind whistled through the gaps in the ill-fitting windows, causing the ragged curtains to flutter daintily.

'So tell me more.'

'She was nice,' Nick said. 'Pretty gorgeous, in fact. Blonde. Funny. Sophisticated. Single.'

'Breasts?'

'Yes. But not too much.'

'How can you have too much?' Sam said, chewing enthusiastically on his deep-pan pizza. 'What a result! Meeting a bird in your solicitor's office. Respect, mate.' He slurped at his cup of coffee. 'So when are you seeing her again?'

'Well . . . I don't want to rush into another relationship.'

'Which means that you didn't even get her phone number.'

'Not exactly.'

And that was another one of the many ways in which Nick and his closest friend differed. Sam would have had the lovely Mrs Anna Terry in his bedroom on the same night, whereas Nick was more of the slow-smoulder type. When, in the dim and distant past, he'd been on the dating scene, it had taken him on average around twelve calendar months to pluck up courage to ask a girl out. And that was only if she was known to be a character of loose morals and had already expressed an interest, via one of her friends, in being seen in public with him. The only reason he'd ended up with Janine was that she'd pursued him relentlessly throughout the courting process. Nick knew that he was not a natural predator.

He watched Sam rip into his meat-filled pizza. It was clear that his friend was.

'How are you ever going to achieve the status of lurve god when you let a golden opportunity such as this slip through your fingers?' Sam muttered through his tomato sauce.

'Don't you mean how can I ever achieve the status of lurve god when I'm back living at home with my two ageing parents in semi-detached suburbia, wearing stripy pyjamas and eating jam roly-poly every day?'

'You've got to move out of your parents' place, mate,' Sam said. 'Pronto. Come and live with me.'

'You have one bed, Sam. Both halves of it are usually occupied – one by your good self and the other by someone whose name you may or may not remember in the morning.'

'I could move the rowing machine out of the spare room for you.'

'Oh, that would be nice,' Nick said. 'I've always wanted to be a gooseberry. At least living at my folks' house I don't have to listen to them having conjugal rights through the walls.'

Sam smirked. 'I bet they still do it.'

'Oh, don't be ridiculous,' Nick snorted. 'My mother only did it once to have me and, by her account, found it very over-rated. My father's been having a tempestuous affair with his Flymo for the last thirty years.'

'What a life.' Sam licked his fingers thoughtfully. 'Do you think we'll ever be like that?'

'You won't,' Nick mused. 'You'll be like Mick Jagger – rocking and rolling on regardless even though you're about to draw your old-age pension. But very occasionally I see my dad fitting his grass box to his lawnmower with tender loving care and think that could well be me in a few short years.' Nick looked up from his pizza. 'You see, I *like* gardening.'

Sam tossed aside his pizza box. 'We've got to put a stop to this. Now.' He stood up to leave. 'Tonight, my friend, we are going out on the old razzle-dazzle-do.'

'No can do.'

'Pray why?'

Nick looked sheepish. 'Line-dancing.'

Sam started to laugh.

'Yes, I know. But I've promised my mum that I'd go with her.'

'Line-dancing?'

'Yes. Line-dancing.'

'This is more serious than I thought,' Sam said. 'There is such a thing as being *too* good a son.'

'I can't let her down,' Nick insisted. 'She's doing all my washing. And she's worried about my emotional well-being.'

'Line-dancing won't fix that,' Sam pointed out. 'There's only one thing that will.'

'A senseless shag isn't the answer to everything.'

'I think you'll find that it is.'

Nick sighed.

'Tomorrow night then.' Sam looked as if he wouldn't take no for an answer. 'And no excuses. I don't want to hear that you're going to the Flymo Appreciation Society with your dad.'

'Tomorrow's fine,' Nick agreed. 'Tomorrow's cool.'

'Great.' Sam rubbed his hands together in glee. 'There's a brand new, hot-to-trot, desperate divorcés and sex-starved singles club just opened. We will show it exactly what we are made of.'

Nick looked worried. 'I'm pretty sure I'm made of all things reluctant.'

'You'll be fine.' Sam brushed aside his concerns. 'You're just out of practice.'

'I don't want to practise on a desperate divorcée.'

Sam winked at him. 'But someone may want to practise on *you*.'

Nick's interest perked up a bit. Wasn't it time he started to cut his ties to his marriage and any hope that some tiny spark left in Janine's heart might be rekindled? There were butterflies in his stomach at the thought of dating again.

'I'm too old and too nervous for all this,' he protested. 'I liked being married.' And he had. Commitment and companionable cosiness was his natural state. Shame that Janine had grown tired of it.

'But you're not married any more, mate. It's over. Time to move on.'

Nick huffed unhappily and put down his pizza, unfinished.

'Polish up your Lurex dancing pants, my friend. Tomorrow will be the first day of the rest of your life.' Sam opened the door to the Portakabin, letting the breeze stir the unfiled papers. 'I'd better get going,' he said. 'Money to make. Hearts to break.'

Nick leaned on the door frame watching his friend stride out across the car yard. He wished he could be more like Sam. Self-confident, self-assured, self-centred and completely lacking in sensitivity.

Sam turned and pointed back at Nick. 'Tomorrow. Don't forget.'

'I'm not dancing with anyone with black roots or wearing white stilettos!' Nick shouted.

'We'll see,' Sam said, and jumped back into his shiny Boxter with a carefree wave. 'We'll see.'

Chapter Seven

Nick sat at the dining table in his parents' house and wondered how he'd managed, after what seemed like a startlingly short hiatus, to come full circle in his life and be back in his old bedroom and eating his mother's 1950s-style cooking once more.

'Come on. Eat up, Nicholas,' his mother urged. 'We don't want to miss kick-off.'

Nick groaned and surveyed the mountain of treacle tart that still graced his plate, despite his already having devoured a good half of the portion. He could feel his teeth decaying just looking at it. 'Mum, this is like having school dinners all over again. You do not have to make me a full-blown, stodgy pudding every night.'

'My puddings are never stodgy.' His mother trembled with indignation. 'Besides, your father wouldn't be without his treacle tart.'

'Janine was a health-freak, Mum.' And a qualified nutritionist. Nothing with calories, E numbers or taste ever graced their fridge. She used to resist every attempt by Nick's mother to cajole them into coming to dinner, because she knew she'd be forced to eat food that took eighteen days to digest. 'I'm used to living on stir-fried vegetables, yoghurt and tofu.'

'We'll have none of that talk in this house.' His mother shuddered at the very thought. 'That is not man's food. If Janine had given you roly-poly every night then perhaps you wouldn't be heading for the D.I.V.O.R.C.E. courts.' Monica produced a handkerchief from her sleeve and started to sniff delicately into it.

'Mum . . .' Nick placed a hand on her arm. 'We are not heading for the divorce courts. It's all being handled very amicably.'

'You mean that Janine has bled you dry and you've just handed it all over.'

'Mum . . .'

'Then why are you back in your old bedroom and she's still ensconced in your nice shiny house? Tell him, Roger.'

His father, otherwise intent on eating his treacle tart, looked up but said nothing. Nick looked round the room where he had eaten all his dinners as he was growing up. The sturdy, mahogany furniture was still the same, as was the sprigged-rose wallpaper. The carpet still clashed with it all horribly and he still wished that he'd had a sibling, or several, to help divert his mother's attention away from him.

His parents had been married for well over fifty years. Their Golden Wedding Anniversary celebration, a lavish sausage roll and Liebfraumilch affair, was but a dim and distant memory. They had the sort of stoic marriage that was fast dying out. Nick admired them for their tenacity and loyalty to each other, but could never quite understand why his father hadn't put his wife under the patio years ago. And he had often wondered, if his mother had been financially independent like Janine, would she have high-tailed it and run out on her husband too?

Marriage seemed to be an institution that no one respected any more – particularly not in Britain. This morning, the solicitor had gaily told him that the UK enjoyed the highest divorce rate in Europe and that the figures had now ominously slipped to the ratio of one in two marriages ending in failure. Nick was glad, in some bizarre way: at least he wasn't alone in his suffering.

'I get to keep the business, Mum.'

Monica snorted disparagingly.

'And I'm sure Janine will sell the house. Eventually. She said that . . . Phil,' he stumbled over the name of his wife's new paramour, 'Phil was having trouble getting a mortgage sorted out.' One of the other joys of being self-employed was that no one ever wanted to lend you money, unless you had enough in the bank not to need it.

'He seems like a right one,' his mother noted.

Nick paused with his spoon poised. 'How do you know?'

Monica looked embarrassed. Or as embarrassed as his mother ever got.

'Mum, you don't go into his shop, do you? Tell me you don't.'

'He does very nice stewing beef,' Monica protested. 'The best around here. And he's cheaper than that other chap down the road.'

Nick shook his head. 'I've heard it all now.'

Out of all the butchers in the world, his mother, bless her, chose to buy her meat from his love rival. Where was her loyalty to *him*? Nick felt like banging his head on the sturdy dining table.

His mother snatched away his bowl. 'Come on, or we'll miss "Achy Breaky Heart".'

Pushing away from the table, Nick stood up. 'I want to make one thing absolutely clear. I am *not* wearing a Stetson.'

25

Chapter Eight

I'm lying on Connor's bed trying to interest my son in the concept of sleep. I've been reading a story to him for the last hour and his eyes are finally starting to roll, whereas mine have been struggling to stay open for at least the last fifty-nine minutes. I came very close to bludgeoning him into unconsciousness with one of the myriad soft toys that he requires to comfort him in his night-time terrors. The poor little lad never had trouble sleeping before Bruno left and I can't help wondering whether the two things are related.

Just as Connor is dropping off, Poppy crashes through the door and flops down on his bed, making his eyes shoot wide open again.

'I'm bored,' she announces.

'You're too young to be bored.'

'Don't you ever get bored, Mummy? You never go out.'

'That's because I'm old and broke and have two whining children.'

Poppy pulls Doggy towards her and twiddles his moth-eaten ear between her thumbs. Doggy is the most revolting creature on God's earth. Any semblance to a real dog has long since been lost as all the stuffing has been tumble-dried out of him over the course of many years. Doggy was originally owned and almost loved into oblivion by Poppy before Connor formed a similarly unhealthy bond with him. Doggy has lost all of his fur, both his eyes and there's a gaping hole where his mouth should be. I have to handwash him now as one more trip to the washing machine would certainly mean curtains for this canine.

Last year Bruno and I took the kids on holiday to Devon – a rare and much-anticipated treat. When we arrived at the rather damp and gloomy cottage – that was, of course, all roses round the door in the brochure – we discovered amid high-pitched hysteria from both offspring, that Doggy had been left behind. That night, Bruno drove all the way back home to retrieve said manky animal to ensure that the rest of our holiday wouldn't be punctuated by

26

tearful scenes and sleepless nights. It was in the halcyon days when we were relatively happy and Bruno was going through a rare period when he would willingly have driven through the night to bring comfort to his wife and children. Though I have wondered in recent times if the Doggy incident contributed in some small way to our marital breakdown. But then I often wonder what caused it. Apart from his inability to face up to his responsibilities or stay faithful, of course.

As if reading my mind, Poppy pipes up, 'Have you heard anything from Daddy?'

By Daddy she means Bruno as he is the only father she has ever known. She knows that he isn't her real father – I went through the whole painful business with her when I thought she was old enough to understand, but she's never brought up the subject of her missing parent again. So until now I've managed to dodge the issue quite successfully. I dread the day she decides she wants to be reunited with her true dad, even though he's never shown the slightest bit of interest in her. Why does life have to be so complicated?

I snuggle down next to Poppy and Connor and stroke my daughter's blonde hair. She is the image of Steve – her real father – whereas Connor is dark, like Bruno. Both in colouring and char- acter, I suspect. 'No, love. I haven't.'

'Sometimes I miss him,' she says, sliding her thumb into her mouth.

'I know.' Sometimes I miss him too, but those times get less and less as the months go by. And most of the time, I'm heartily relieved that he isn't in our lives any more.

'Can I ring Stephanie?'

'You've spent all day at school with her and you haven't done anything since then. What have you got to talk about?'

'She's in love with Oliver Powell.'

'Ah, men.'

'I won't be long, Mummy. I promise.'

'Ten minutes. Max. Otherwise I'll have to rob a bank to pay the phone bill and you'll be taken into care.'

Poppy smiles and kisses me. 'You say the silliest things.'

'I want an early night, Poppy. I've got an important job interview tomorrow.'

My daughter skips out of the room.

'Well,' I say to no one in particular. 'A job interview.'

Poppy puts her head round the door. 'You'll get it, Mummy. You're well cool.'

My daughter disappears again to go and discuss the fledging love-life of Stephanie Fisher. As well as finding her real dad, I'm also dreading the moment when Poppy decides to fully explore her burgeoning interest in the opposite sex. She's only ten, for heaven's sake! But they're all getting engaged and pregnant by the time they're twelve these days, if you believe the media. I'm sure I was more concerned with dolls and playing leapfrog when I was her age. No such luck now. They all know far more than is good for them. I don't want Poppy to have a boyfriend until she's twenty-one at the very least. And preferably when she's moved away from home and then I won't have any idea what she's up to. I think the saying 'what the eye doesn't see, the heart doesn't grieve over' is very true when it comes to the relationships of one's own daughter. I'm sure I won't worry half so much over Connor. He'll no doubt be breaking hearts rather than getting his broken. Such is the way of the world.

Anyway, I can't think about this now – I'm too worried about my job interview.

Next to me Connor rouses. 'Story, Mummy.'

Opening the book again, I realise I'm in for another hour of ducks, dogs and goodness knows what else. Once I used to read all the stories in a very excited and animated way, but soon realised that this only served to keep the kids wide-eyed and attentive. Now I read them in the droning, monotonous tone that politicians save for Prime Minister's Question-time. I don't resent spending this time with Connor, but I did want to do some preparation for my interview, even though I have no idea what form that should take. I'll probably just iron a really, really short skirt.

Chapter Nine

The line-dancing class was held in St Stephen's church hall in Stony Stratford – a pleasantly sleepy market town on the outskirts of the city, not yet swallowed up by the relentless, encroaching development of Milton Keynes. Nick was pleased to note that the hall was dark, with the exception of a few paltry flashing disco lights that were covered in dust and looked as if they'd been in use by the groovers of St Stephen's church socials since the late 1980s. Surely in a room this dark no one would recognise him.

Alarmingly, when his mother took off her coat she was wearing a denim skirt and a blouse that bore more spangles and tassels than he'd previously seen in the environs of Milton Keynes and certainly at 43 Desford Avenue. If he hoped no one would recognise him, then surely his mother must, in her current garb, be unrecognisable too. Normally Monica Diamond favoured floral A-line skirts and pearls and court shoes with heels no more than an inch high. Cardigans were her favourite form of knitwear. However, now she slipped on a pair of white, fringed cowgirl boots that she produced from a Debenhams' carrier bag. Nick gazed with horror at the stranger in front of him. This was not the woman he knew and sometimes loved. Middle-aged suburban housewife meets Tammy Wynette was not a great look. Is this what his mother did to escape the stultifying boredom that was her life? Nick shuddered involuntarily.

Mrs Diamond, blissfully unaware of her son's thoughts, clip-clopped round the hall like John Wayne's ageing moll, greeting everyone as if they were longlost friends, while he knew that he was shuffling around behind her like a sulky child. And, in effect, that's exactly what he was.

Monica reached into a black bin bag at the edge of the dance floor, where some hideous cowboy-type country music was already in full throttle. Some other geriatrics, dressed in inappropriate Midwestern clothing, tapped out a few steps in preparation. His mother produced a musty, sweat-stained Stetson and brushed it down.

'No,' Nick said as she held it out to him.

'It won't hurt you to enter into the spirit of things,' Monica insisted.

'It will.' He could quite honestly say he'd never been in such pain. Except for the night that Janine had confessed her affair with Mr Bone the Butcher. That had been pretty painful too.

His mother shoved the Stetson onto his head. It was too big. 'It's too big.'

'It's fine,' Monica said. 'You look lovely.'

He seemed to remember she'd said the same thing about his school uniform the day he'd started at the local grammar. That too had been several sizes too big, bought on the premise that one day he would grow into it. Which he would have done if he'd gone to school until he was twenty-seven. The school uniform incident was the first time he realised that adults didn't always tell the truth. Now, as then, he knew he did not look lovely at all. He looked like a twat and, what was worse, he was fully aware of it.

With a certain inevitability, the strains of 'Achy Breaky Heart' came from the turntable, which was every bit as old and decrepit as its audience.

'Come on, darling. This is my favourite.' His mother took his hand and dragged him onto the dance floor.

'I have no idea what to do, Mum,' he panicked.

'Just follow everyone else,' Monica instructed.

Nick looked around. At least he could move quicker than most of them. His hips were a long way from arthritic, he thought smugly as he joined in with the toe-tapping and clapping, lurking at the back and on the end of a line. Halfway through his routine, when to his dismay he was getting breathless, an old dear in a fluorescent-pink cowgirl outfit sidled up to him. It looked as if the owner of a funeral parlour had advised her on her make-up.

'I didn't know you were Monica's son,' panted the wrinkled old lady with her red lips and black eyebrows as she looped around in front of him, giving sporadic claps. 'I hardly recognised you. My, haven't you grown?'

'When was the last time you saw me?' Nick puffed.

The woman paused in her heel-clicking to ponder. 'You were just starting school.'

'So I was five?'

'Ooo. Doesn't time fly?'

Nick smiled politely. 'Not when you're line-dancing,' he muttered to himself.

Chapter Ten

This is the only time of day I struggle with. It's bedtime and, as always, I'm wide awake. Throughout the day I'm so busy trying to make headway through my life, that I have no time to think about our predicament. But at night, through the wee small hours I toss and turn, balancing our meagre budget in my head and wondering what will become of us all if I fail to win the lottery again this week.

Poppy and Connor are both curled up beside me, thumbs in respective mouths. My daughter is doing some sort of dance routine even in her sleep, her tiny feet kicking erratically to some inaudible beat. That girl never stops dancing at any time of the day or night, and I hope she doesn't decide to turn this talent into a lucrative career in the only way I can at the moment imagine – scantily-clad and hanging upside down on a pole. This is not what I want for my child. Perhaps I'll try to afford ballet lessons for her, to encourage her away from the worst excesses of hip-grinding and pelvic-thrusting. The only dancing I can remember that was on television when I was her age was *Come Dancing* – an altogether more sedate affair, although sometimes the Latin-American team from Leicester South were downright lascivious. I expect even the programme title would be misconstrued nowadays.

My son, the indestructible Doggy pressed tightly to his face, is snoring wetly. Despite my nightly assertions that they really must sleep in their own beds, they invariably manage to wear me down and we all cuddle together in my double bed which, even though I protest loudly, gives me some jot of comfort. In my heart of hearts I know that there is nothing more depressing than sleeping in a double bed alone. And it has been some time since this bed has seen any form of sexual athletics. Since Bruno's last and most fleeting of visits, in fact. These days, as I've already bemoaned, my most passionate relationships are with cheap Chardonnay and chocolate.

I keep a photograph of my ex-husband on my bedside table and

I really don't know why. It's rather like keeping a thorn in your finger or wearing the same pair of shoes that repeatedly give you a blister on your heel. Partly, it's to remind my children that they do, indeed, have a father no matter how absent. And, I suppose, it's partly to remind myself what a bastard he is and how often he has let us down.

Reaching out, I stroke my finger down the glass that protects his smiling face from my household dust. He's a handsome devil and I guess that was always one of the problems – a lot of other gullible women find him attractive too. And, unfortunately, his wandering eyes were matched only by equally wandering extremities. He has left me more times than I care to recall and, fool that I am, I always took him back.

Poppy starts singing in her sleep. *'Hey, Britney, lose control.'*

'Ssh. Ssh.' I smooth down the wayward strands of her fine blonde hair and get a kick in the shins for my trouble.

I worry that they will grow up to be young offenders as, statistically, they're far more inclined to do so simply because their father can't keep his private parts in his pants. And, quite frankly, that seems just so unfair. If Bruno could have stopped chasing every available piece of totty and had stayed home reading every night to Poppy and playing football with Connor, they could grow up to be rocket scientists or accountants. Whereas Poppy is more likely to be a lap-dancer or an office cleaner and Connor will probably end up making pointless plastic components in a rundown factory somewhere. These are the things that keep me awake at night even though statistics shouldn't be believed. Isn't there some survey that says by the year 2023 everyone in the world will be Elvis impersonators? How can that be right? I don't even own a white spangly jumpsuit and can't see myself buying one just to become a statistic.

It's not that I don't have aspirations for my children, it just seems so much more exhausting to motivate them all by myself. Sometimes when I go to see Poppy's teachers at school, I feel as if they have written her off already simply because of her home circumstances. But she's hardly in a unique situation, is she? If you ask me, it's not that children from broken homes can't complete their lessons as ably as those from 'normal' homes – if there is such a thing – it's because teachers don't teach properly any more. Sitting around in groups, chatting away to one's heart's content is not what school used to be about in my day. And believe me, if Poppy's given the choice between learning something constructive and chatting with Stephanie Fisher about the latest shade of Pearly Girly eye-shadow, the Pearly Girly eye-shadow will win every time.

Maybe I should force myself back out into the big wide world and start looking for a replacement father for my children. Someone kind and gentle and generous. Someone with eyes the colour of a summer sky. Someone nice. Someone rather like the man I met in the solicitor's office today, in fact.

With that thought destined to keep me awake for another few hours, I turn Bruno's photograph face-down and, in the hope that it will drift across the ether to my feckless husband, say out loud, 'Where are you now, you bastard?'

Chapter Eleven

Nick's bedroom hadn't changed since he was fourteen and he wondered how he'd ever managed to be complacent about that. When all of his peers were painting their bedrooms black and listening to Deep Purple, his was still decorated with aeroplane motifs and contained a twee bookcase behind which at least he'd been able to stash his porn mags. His teddy bear, Georgie Best, still sat there to this day, smiling amiably, splay-legged amid the overspill of books on the top shelf.

Now that he'd returned he found it spooky, like some sort of shrine to all that he hadn't wanted to be. A few tattered football posters obscured the bi-planes and he remembered how mad his mother had gone when he'd Blu-Tacked them to the walls. Nick sighed to himself. His rebellions had always been small-scale, much as they were now.

He looked down at himself. For reasons best known to his mother, he was wearing a pair of his father's pyjamas. The sight of him, wrapped in nothing but a towel on the way to the bathroom, had been too much of an assault on her sensibilities. Maybe it reminded Monica rather too overtly that he was no longer her little boy. In defiance, Nick ripped off the top and threw it on the floor. He needed to get out of here soon, before his mother managed to mollycoddle out of him any will to operate as a fully functional adult in the real world. There was a gentle knock on the door. Nick groaned silently.

His mother popped her head round the door. 'Are you asleep?'

'Yes,' Nick said.

'It's only me.'

'Oh, and I thought it was Meg Ryan come to ravish me.'

His mother pushed aside his feet and sat on the end of the tiny single bed. 'Sometimes you have your father's mouth. Hot chocolate?'

He sat up in bed and his mother handed him the mug of chocolate, looking pointedly at the pyjama top discarded on the floor and avoiding her son's bare chest. Nick smiled at his small victory. 'Thanks, Mum.'

'You did very well at line-dancing. They all thought you were a nice mover.' Monica patted his leg beneath the covers. No duvets in the Diamond household, he was back to 'proper' sheets and blankets. Duvets were far too Scandinavian for his mother's tastes. He missed his own bed with its fluffy fourteen togs of goosedown. And he missed Janine sliding down next to him, curving her cool, firm body against his, more than anyone could know. 'You take after your mother.'

'Oh good.'

Monica reached out and stroked his hair. 'I worry about you.'

'There's no need to.'

'Mrs Bather has a daughter who's getting divorced.'

Nick feigned a yawn. 'Really.'

'I thought you might like to ring her.'

'Probably not.'

'You know that you need to start getting out and about again.'

Nick put his arms behind his head. 'I came line-dancing with you.'

'And that was very nice,' Monica said. 'But you know that's not what I mean.'

'Well,' Nick said brightly, 'you'll be delighted to learn that I'm going out with Sam tomorrow night. To the Hot Totty Club – or some such.'

'Oh.' His mother looked horrified. 'Will you be late home?'

'If I play my cards right, I might not come home at all.' Nick winked salaciously.

His mother whipped his hot chocolate away from him. 'Then you'd better get some beauty sleep.'

She stomped to the bedroom door and smiled at Georgie Best, sitting on the bookcase. 'Night night, Georgie Best.'

The door was clicked firmly shut. Nick looked over at Georgie Best, the most guileless teddy bear there ever was, and asked: 'How can I stay here without killing her?'

But, of course, Georgie Best had probably been bribed to be on his mother's side and remained shtum. Nick settled down in his bed. 'Night night, Georgie Best.'

Before he closed his eyes, Nick picked up one of his shoes and threw it at the teddy, knocking him off the shelf. He settled down to sleep laughing evilly to himself.

Chapter Twelve

'What are these?'

'Cornflakes,' my daughter says with a defiant note that I could, at this moment, quite joyfully smack out of her.

'And what are they doing here?' Here being under her bed – where, judging by the advanced state of penicillin cultures growing on the top, they've been for some time.

Poppy shrugs as if she's never seen them before in her life.

I wave the bowl at her in a menacing way. 'You could conduct scientific experiments into germ warfare with these.'

My daughter looks unconvinced. And unmenaced.

I discovered my child's slatternly tendencies this morning because we had no bowls left in the cupboard. Do 'real' families sit and have convivial breakfasts together or do they also start each morning with a screaming row?

'You will clean your room tonight, young lady,' I say in a voice that sounds more like my mother than I care to admit. I even wag my finger.

My daughter, unhappy that her slovenly behaviour has been uncovered, then proceeds to do everything at a pace that even the most reluctant of snails would have been pushed to match. There are times when I'm sorry that beating children isn't acceptable any more, because right now I can see the appeal in it. She knows that I am really stressed over this job interview which I am putting myself through entirely for their benefit, yet she is doing nothing to help. Every fibre of Poppy's being radiates that she hates me and it's times like these when I could really do with some support. I feel powerless to reason with her, and I'm sure that if I had someone else who would gang up on her with me then I'd have a chance of winning. Already, I'm dreading what it will be like when I catch her with her first drink, cigarette or boy.

'You can go without breakfast,' I snap. Which is not great punishment for my child as she eats less than a sparrow anyway and I

36

normally have trouble persuading her to eat, for which I blame every stick-like celebrity on television from Victoria Beckham through to Kate Moss. 'I want you dressed and in that car within five minutes.'

Which is all very well except that I've yet to get dressed myself. I am suffering agonies of indecision about my choice of outfit. Really, it couldn't be any worse if I were trying to find something within my limited wardrobe choices to wear to the Oscars. Because I spend my days in jeans covered in child-produced mank and goo – as my dear son has yet to grow out of the baby unexpected vomiting stage – there's a sad lack of chic little suits lurking in my cupboard. I have one black ensemble that I bought especially for Bruno's grandma's funeral five years ago, so that's what I'm going to have to wear. If there was ever a bad omen, that has to be one – going to a job interview kitted out for a cremation. Nevertheless, I wriggle into it, thanking God that I haven't had the money to indulge myself in luxuries and, therefore, haven't put on any weight since then. I just hope Connor behaves himself and doesn't puke on it or smear jam all over me.

This is the one day I needed to be on time and as I'm a firm believer in more haste and less speed being a great policy, I'm now running late. My job interview is only a ten-minute drive away from here normally, but in the rush hour it will take me more than twice as long. Poppy is sitting silently in the car, staring straight ahead by the time I load Connor in and we shoot off down the road, cocking a snook at the speed limit until we hit the first traffic jam. When I finally drop Poppy off at her school, she still isn't speaking to me.

'I love you,' I say, kissing her rigid face. 'Even though I don't like you sometimes.'

I'm convinced that you should never leave someone on a bad note, just in case something hideous happens during the day and you never have a chance to put it right. My daughter knows this. There's a defiant twinkle of victory in her eye.

'Wish your old mum luck at her interview.'

Poppy slams the car door which makes Connor cry. No chance. She sees Stephanie Fisher and runs over to her friend, no doubt to regale her with the tale of what a cow her mother is. Stephanie Fisher will, of course, be blessed with a perfect mum. And a wonderful dad.

Connor and I set off again, wildly weaving our way through the back streets until we get to Sophie's house. How on earth do I think I'll be able to manage to do this every morning if I get a job? I try to remind myself how wonderful my self-esteem will be when I manage to get off benefits and support us all with a wonderfully enlarged income that I have earned all by myself. And then this added stress and struggle will be well worth it.

With a quick glance at my watch, in the vain hope that time has conspired to help me for once and is running backwards, I grab a startled Connor from his car seat and race up the path to my friend's front door.

'You're late,' Sophie says as she opens it.

'I know,' I pant. 'I should just about make it.'

Connor, unhappy at being joggled about so soon after his breakfast, throws up on my shoulder.

'Oh fuck.'

Sophie snatches my child from me and pulls me into her kitchen, where she sets about scrubbing off the sick with a J-Cloth. Why, oh why was I blessed with a child who has a sensitive constitution?

'I might as well not go,' I wail.

'Nonsense,' Sophie scolds. 'You'll be fine.' She gets an air-freshener spray out of the cupboard and gives me a blast with the fresh scent of pine glades. 'Now, get going.'

I rush to the front door, followed by Sophie and Connor who is now wedged on her hip. 'Kiss Mummy,' I say as I steal a kiss from my icky son, before dashing off.

'Good luck!'

'I'm going to need it.' My son's lip is starting to wobble. 'Are you sure he'll be okay?'

'He'll be fine,' Sophie assures me. 'Say bye bye to Mummy.'

'Bye bye to Mummy.'

'I love you,' I shout to Sophie and Connor as I squeeze myself back into the car. I must do, I think, otherwise why on earth would I be putting myself through this hell?

With them waving madly in my rearview mirror, I cannon off down the road where not five seconds later I hit yet another traffic jam. Such is modern-day motoring in the UK, despite the government's much-hailed policy of trying to get us all back on public transport – which is pathetic because all the public transport is either stuck in traffic jams too or busy derailing itself. Apparently the average person spends six weeks of their lives just sitting in traffic – and it appears I'm rapidly turning into an 'average' person. I will arrive at my interview toothless at this rate, because I'll have gnashed them all out.

I need something to calm me down, but the radio is out of the question as someone ripped out the aerial many moons ago and I've never been able to afford to fix it. As I inch steadily forward, I turn up Connor's Postman Pat tape, in lieu of anything more adult or soothing, and practise deep-breathing. Unfortunately, the jolly old postman can't quite compete with Classic FM.

'Hello,' I try to smile. 'Anna Terry.' Too uptight. Relax the lips. Relax the lips. Easy. Easy. 'Hi. Good to meet you. Anna. Anna Terry.' Better. Much better. 'Hi. I'm Anna Terry.'

The clock catches my eye and I can't believe how time, traffic and life in general are conspiring against me. I wind down the window and shout into the logjam of cars, 'Get a bloody move on, you inconsiderate bastards!'

My voice is carried away on the chill morning breeze and I wind up the window again.

Postman Pat chirrups on relentlessly. I take ten deep breaths. 'Hi. I'm Anna Terry.' It isn't enough. I try another ten. 'Pleased to meet you. I'm so sorry I'm late.'

As a cacophony of car horns starts to sound around me, I rest my head on my steering wheel and try not to cry.

Chapter Thirteen

Nick paced up and down the floor of his office. As there wasn't a lot of floorspace in the office to begin with, the pacing wasn't particularly exhausting – nor was it relaxing him as he'd hoped. He'd already paced up and down in the car yard, tidying the 'For Sale' signs, making sure the tacky bunting round the boundary was all fluttering in the breeze, and that hadn't worked either. Plus it was cold today. This morning, the weatherman on Radio Four – his parents' favoured station – had announced that spring was on its way, but it wasn't immediately obvious that anyone had informed the elements. They were, as far as Nick could tell, still stuck resolutely on Winter.

Nick stopped at his desk. He rearranged his papers into tidier piles and moved the chair in front of it to a more jaunty angle. On the way to the car yard he'd stopped at the local greengrocer's and had bought a bunch of cheery flowers which he now fluffed up in the vase he'd pinched from his mother's kitchen cupboards. They provided a spot of much-needed colour in an otherwise bland and rather grubby landscape. Perhaps he should have borrowed a duster and some furniture polish too. Nick rubbed his hands together to calm himself. Was it warm enough in here, he wondered. During the colder months, it was a fine line between keeping warm and heating the street through all the gaps in the window frames.

Nick rotated his shoulders to try to ease the knots out of them. 'Hi,' he said to himself. 'Nick Diamond.' He held out his arm in an imaginary handshake. 'Too hard. Too hard. Ease back. Ease back.'

He had never imagined that finding staff would be this daunting, but the recruitment agency had warned him that young women these days wanted to work in PR and media or trendy wine bars, they weren't interested in rundown car yards with poor pay, terrible conditions and zero promotion prospects. Which probably meant that he was going to end up with a social misfit or a crazed psychopath as his trusty secretary. Still, he glanced at the CV on top of one of the piles on his desk: this resumé looked amazing so he was determined to put on a good show that would hopefully encourage this particular young woman to view him favourably. It also happened to be the only CV he'd received from the recruitment agency. Nick straightened his tie.

'Hi. Nick Diamond. Please sit down.' Nick indicated the rakishly positioned chair. He was considering whether he should move it again when there was a timid knock on the door of the Portakabin.

Nick straightened his tie again and headed for the door. When he pulled it open, he was vaguely alarmed to see the woman from the solicitor's office standing there looking attractively flushed, but rather sombre in a black suit. What did she say her name was? And, more importantly, how had she found out where he was?

'Shit.' Nick closed the door again. This was not good timing. He smoothed down his hair and straightened his tie for the third time. He went to open the door again, but all his limbs had involuntarily frozen.

There was a knock at the door again. This time considerably more forceful.

'Shit. Shit.' Before his courage deserted him, Nick wrenched the door open again.

'Hi,' the woman said.

'What are you doing here?'

'I've come about the job.'

'*You* have?'

'Why else would I be here?'

'I don't know,' Nick said.

'Perhaps I'd better introduce myself formally,' she said. 'I'm Anna. Anna Terry. And I'm *so* sorry I'm late.'

'Are you?' Nick glanced at his watch. 'I wasn't expecting you for another half an hour.'

A shadow crossed her face, but the anxious set of her shoulders relaxed a little.

'Can I come in?' She pushed past him into the office, which she surveyed with dismay. 'Is this it?'

'I'm afraid so.'

'It's nice,' Anna said with a forced smile.

'The last thing on earth you wanted was a job in a pokey office. And I quote,' Nick said. 'Unfortunately, they don't come much pokier than this.'

'I'm desperate,' Anna admitted with an unhappy sigh.

'Right.'

Not knowing what else to do, they stood and stared at each other expectantly.

'Aren't you going to interview me?' Anna said eventually.

'Oh. Right. Of course. You want me to interview you?'

'That was the general idea.'

'I've never had a secretary before,' Nick admitted. 'I'm not sure what to do.'

Anna smiled shyly. 'What sort of duties did you have in mind?'

Nick gave her an encouraging smile. Despite her bluff and confident demeanour, she seemed surprisingly vulnerable. 'Are you any good at making tea?'

'Not really.'

'Oh. Well, I am. I'll make us a nice cup while you take a seat.' Nick indicated the seat as he had during his practice run. Anna sat down, clutching her handbag to her knees.

Nick busied himself making the tea, while Anna tried to read what was on his desk upside down. He noticed that she'd hitched up her skirt to her thighs when she sat down. Was it him or had it suddenly gone very hot in here? Did men of a certain age start to get hot flushes? She was cute. Very cute. Even more cute than he'd remembered, and he was rather surprised how much he had remembered about her – although, in a typical bloke-type moment, he'd forgotten her name, if he'd even known it. Nick put the tea on a tray and carried it over to the desk. He handed a mug to Anna and also noticed that she nervously pulled her skirt back down to her knees before she took it from him.

'So,' Nick said. 'The recruitment agency faxed me a copy of your CV.'

He could have sworn he saw a gulp travel down her throat. Nick sat at his desk and picked up the piece of paper.

'A degree in Business Studies.'

Anna beamed back at him anxiously.

'Five years as personal assistant to Richard Branson.'

Anna's smile faded and she started to squirm in her chair. They both took in the crumbling office.

'Followed by a spell with Donald Trump in New York.'

Anna had slid down in her chair and was holding up her mug of tea as a barrier.

Nick smiled kindly at her. 'When we met at the solicitor's office, I thought you said you'd never worked.'

'I don't like to blow my own trumpet,' she said tightly.

'But you don't mind trying to pull the wool over someone's eyes?'

Anna stood up and took her CV from him. 'I should be going,' she said. 'Thanks for the tea. Mine is actually better than this.'

'Wait.' Nick sighed. For some insane reason he couldn't just let her walk out of the office like this. Surveying his own empire, he realised that he'd neglected it for far too long. Not that he expected Anna Terry to sweep in and turn him into Donald Trump overnight, but he did need someone to motivate him on to bigger and better things. It was strange, with Janine he'd classed that as nagging. But, it was true, this could be a great little business if he could get himself organised – or get someone else to organise him – and spruce it up. That wouldn't take a degree in Business Studies. Since he and Janine had split, he'd been walking round as if he was in thick fog – he barely even remembered the first few months, let alone had the wherewithal to run a company. Well, now it was time to bring back in a breath of fresh air. 'Have you ever used a computer?'

'I've got digital bathroom scales,' Anna retorted. 'They're a nightmare to fathom out. How much more difficult can a computer be?'

Nick laughed.

'I'm a quick learner,' she continued in a breathless rush. 'You could teach me.'

'Anna . . .'

'Look,' she said, 'I knew from the first time I met you that we had an affinity. We're kindred spirits, you and I.'

'Anna . . .'

'I need this job, Nick,' she pleaded. 'I need this very badly. Give me a week. I'll do it for a week and if I haven't got this place running like . . . like . . .'

'Like Donald Trump's empire?'

'*Exactly* like Donald Trump's empire,' she grinned, 'then you can sack me and no hard feelings.'

'Anna . . .'

'Please don't say no.' There were tears in her eyes. 'Please, please don't say no. I couldn't face that snotty woman at the recruitment agency again.'

'Anna,' Nick said patiently. 'You've got the job.'

Anna crossed the room, threw her arms round him and kissed him full on the lips. It took all of Nick's strength not to fall off his chair.

'I think I'm in love with you,' Anna said.

He could taste her lips on his — strawberries, cherries, all kinds of summer fruits. For whatever twisted reasons, he found the prospect of having Anna around the office on a permanent basis a very cheering thought. 'Eternally grateful will do.'

She clapped her hands in glee. 'So when do you want me to start?'

'The sooner the better,' Nick admitted with a rueful look at his paperwork. 'This lot isn't going to sort itself out overnight.'

'Tomorrow?'

'Why not?'

'Tomorrow it is then. Nine o'clock?'

'Let's make it ten,' Nick advised. 'I'm being dragged out tonight by my supposed best friend, Sam. This is my reintroduction to the world of the bachelor. We're going to a sad sack's singles and divorced club.' He pulled a rueful face. 'It will be full of desperate, ugly women of easy virtue with more children in tow than the Von Trapps.'

'It sounds great,' she said. 'Have a nice time.'

'I'll hate it,' Nick confessed. 'Every minute of it.'

Anna headed to the door.

'What about you? Are you doing anything tonight?' he asked.

'Me?' Anna snorted. 'No. Early night for me. I have to be bright-eyed and bushy-tailed. I want to impress my new boss.'

'You'll be fine. I've heard that he's a bit of a push-over.'

'Really? I've heard that he's a *very nice* man.'

'Don't believe all you hear,' Nick warned. 'You have no idea what a slave-driver I can be.'

'I'll see you tomorrow,' Anna said. 'And thanks again. I do appreciate it.'

'Yeah.'

'Nick.' Anna paused with her hand on the door. 'The Business Studies degree is for real.'

'Yeah?'

'Yeah,' she said proudly. 'Well, nearly. I did a two-year course at the local college. I did get top marks though.'

'I'm sure we'll put it to good use,' Nick said. 'And the bit about making better tea?'

'No.' Anna chewed her lip. 'My tea is terrible.'

Nick shrugged. 'You can't have everything in life.'

'No.'

'I'm sure we'll make a great team,' Nick said. 'I'll see you in the morning.'

Chapter Fourteen

I follow Sophie into the kitchen and my friend, knowing me as she does, heads straight for the kettle.

'No kids?' There is a distinct absence of deafening noise that gives me this hint. Nor does her kitchen look as if a bomb has recently exploded in it.

'I'd had enough,' Sophie admits. 'I've locked them in the cellar.'

'You haven't got a cellar.'

'Damn,' my friend says. 'Then Tom's mum must have them. You don't mind?'

'No,' I say. 'I'm in too good a mood to let a little thing like my best friend and supposed childminder offloading my only son onto her unsuspecting mother-in-law worry me.' I dump on Sophie, she dumps on Tom's mum. Sophie doesn't dump on me too often as she knows that my mum now lives too far away for me to chain dump on her. This is the way of our world. For all the use Sophie's husband Tom is, she might as well be a single-parent family. 'So,' I say, getting back to my theme, 'aren't you going to ask me then?'

'Hey!' Sophie cries. 'You got the job?'

I punch the air in the manner of First Division footballers after scoring a particularly nifty goal. Sophie joins me in a little victory dance.

'This calls for a celebration,' she declares.

'Absolutely,' I agree. 'Bring on the chocolate biscuits.'

'Nothing else will do,' my friend says and produces the biscuit barrel. 'How on earth did you swing that?'

'The job was at a local used-car yard and who should own it but the guy I met at the solicitor's office the other day. Nick.'

'Nick.' Sophie does a very poor impression of me being all simpering. 'He's the one who thinks you're a hot-to-trot babe with no children.'

'Yeah,' I admit. 'And he still does.'

'Ooo.'

'He also knows that I can't work a computer, make tea or do anything else that would be remotely considered useful in an office.' I still have no idea why he gave me the job.

'Did you offer to sleep with him?' Neither does my friend.

'No, I didn't.' Although, quite frankly, I would have considered it. 'I told him that we had an affinity.'

'And he understood what you meant?'

'Yes,' I say thoughtfully.

'My word. That's a good start.' Sophie pulls the lid off the tin of chocolate biscuits and peers inside. 'You know that he'll probably want to do unnatural things to you over his desk,' she says, selecting and biting a white chocolate wafer with relish. Her eyebrows wiggle enthusiastically. 'Fabulous! Can you get me a job there too?'

'I start tomorrow,' I say.

'Great! We can really celebrate tonight.'

'Tonight?'

Sophie puts her hands on her hips. 'Don't tell me that you've forgotten our wild night on the town.'

'Oh good grief. That's tonight?'

Sophie's face falls. 'Don't let me down. I've been looking forward to this for weeks.'

'I promised my new boss I'd get an early night.'

'He'll never know,' Sophie promises. 'Nice men who understand the meaning of the word "affinity" do not go where we are going.'

My friend struts her funky stuff. This should scare me.

'I don't know . . .'

'It's my one night of freedom, Anna,' she begs. 'One night without Tom. One night where I can pretend I'm not a married drudge with two demanding children and a terminally disinterested husband.'

'Well . . .' It's clearly not scaring me enough.

'I'll lend you one of my really tarty, glittery numbers with slits up to your bum.'

I give in. My friend can read me with the ease of Derren Brown. 'Go on then. You've twisted my arm.'

'You know you won't regret this,' Sophie says.

'Really?' I remark. 'And I thought we were going to have fun!'

Chapter Fifteen

Nick pushed in the last spoonful of some gargantuan pudding that his mother had served up following an equally gargantuan dinner. As soon as he moved into his own place, lettuce and yoghurt would once again feature heavily on the menu. He had never thought in his wildest dreams that he would miss cottage cheese. But then never in his wildest dreams did he think that he and Janine would be divorcing so soon after they'd said 'for ever'.

His mother smiled at his empty bowl. 'Good boy.'

'Thanks, Mum.' Nick untucked the tea towel from his neck – the one that Monica had insisted he wore to protect him from his own eating misdemeanours.

'See?' she said. 'All that fuss about wearing it and you didn't get a spot of custard down your nice shirt.'

'Yes, you're right. It was a marvellous idea. Truly inspired.' Nick glanced at his watch. 'Better get a wiggle on.'

His mother frowned. 'What time will you be home?'

'Late,' Nick said. 'Very late.'

'I'll wait up,' his mother offered as she cleared away the dishes from the table – whipping away his father's bowl before he had quite finished his last spoonful.

'Don't. I have a key.'

'Roger. Speak to him.'

His father looked up from where his pudding used to be and said nothing. His father usually said nothing. After a lifetime of nagging, his other parent had decided that silence was the best policy. In the good old days when Nick could remember his dad having an opinion, his mother had normally pointed out to him very forcibly that it was the wrong one. If you don't use muscles regularly they simply waste away and Roger Diamond's opinion-forming muscle had long since run to seed.

'Listen to your father.'

Nick bit back the riposte that *she* never did and instead said, 'I'll be fine. You worry too much. I'm all grown up – I can handle myself.'

His mother's eyes started to fill with tears. 'You look lovely.'

'Thank you.' Let's hope that some of the loose women I'm about to encounter also think so, he thought.

Monica sniffed into her handkerchief. 'And so vulnerable.'

'Mum . . .'

'Just promise Mummy that you won't talk to any strange women.'

'That's the whole point of the exercise. According to Sam. The stranger the better.'

'Tell him, Roger.'

Nick and his father exchanged a glance, but still his father failed to impart any pearls of wisdom for a son going out into the world.

'What are you two going to do tonight?'

'Your father's going to wash the dishes while I watch *Who Wants To Be A Millionaire?*' Monica then looked at her husband as if to indicate that *she* rather wanted to be one.

Perhaps it was as well that he was going for a wild night out with Sam – this could easily have been him and Janine in a few years and he wondered when his wife's discontentment had first started. But then Janine wasn't a nightclub sort of person either – there were too many calories in wine, for one thing. He wondered how she spent her evenings with her new man and then realised that he really didn't want to go there.

'Don't . . . DO NOT . . . wait up,' he instructed his mother. 'If I see one single light on, I'll keep asking the taxi to drive round until it goes off.'

'Your father could come and pick you up.'

'I'll get a taxi.'

'You are a silly billy,' his mother chided.

Nick kissed her on the cheek. There was no doubt that she could drive him to distraction, but she was his mother and due to her excessive ministrations he'd enjoyed the sort of cosseted childhood that only seemed to exist these days in Enid Blyton books. It was only as he reached adulthood that he grew familiar with the term 'disappointment'. Up until then his summers had been idyllic affairs spent with Sam in a neverending round of sunshine, cycling, swimming, Spam sandwiches and home-made lemonade. In fact, life had been pretty perfect until girls had been introduced to it – for that he had Sam to blame too. His best friend had even orchestrated the losing of his virginity with Patricia Kemp, and insisted on a blow-by-blow account of the event – something that Patricia never forgave him for, particularly after Sam shared his deflowering with all of Form 5B. And now he was going to let his mate loose on his love-life once again. Would he never learn?

Out in the hall, Nick shrugged on his jacket. Were these the right sort of clothes to be wearing to a nightclub? Shouldn't he perhaps have rushed out to Ted Baker's and bought himself some trendy gear, or would that have spoken of ageing divorced man trying too hard?

His father followed him, closing the dining-room door behind him. He put his hand on Nick's shoulder. 'I wanted to talk to you man to man.'

'Fine,' Nick said. Wasn't it a bit late to be doing this? Wouldn't the type of information that fathers gave to sons have been a lot more useful at the age of fifteen rather than twenty years later?

'If I were you,' Roger whispered confidentially, 'I'd grab hold of the first bird I laid eyes on and I'd shag her senseless.'

'I'll bear that in mind,' Nick said.

His father clapped him on the back and headed for the kitchen. Nick watched his retreating back in amazement.

He stared at himself in the mirror. 'Let's hope for my sake that it's Kylie Minogue then and not old Mrs Hooper next door.'

There was the beep of a horn and Nick checked out of the window to see his taxi pull up, which was very timely. Nick shot out of the door before his parents could inflict any more emotional damage on him by way of their own version of helpful advice. Next to the taxi and waiting patiently in the street was the battered wreck that he'd somehow acquired from the elderly couple. Even though he felt a complete heel leaving it behind, and seemed to have developed some sort of unhealthy emotional attachment to it, there was no way it could be described as a babe magnet. Any self-respecting woman would take one look at this and run a mile. Mind you, any self-respecting car dealer would have done so too. Tomorrow, he'd have to pick himself out something more suitable from the car yard. Perhaps he'd let Anna choose it for him. The thought made him smile.

He bounded to the taxi, just as old Mrs Hooper was doddering out of her front door to put her milk bottles on the front step.

'Hello, young Nicholas,' she called out.

'Mrs Hooper!' Nick gave her a friendly wave as he disappeared into the taxi. 'Just my bloody luck,' he muttered under his breath.

Chapter Sixteen

I'm lying in the bath trying to psych myself up for my night out with Sophie. I can't remember when we last went to a nightclub together, so I've actually forgotten what psyching myself up involves. When Sophie and I were younger we used to spend the entire day preening and grooming ourselves in preparation for the night's activities. And look where that got me. Two absentee fathers and a permanent cash-flow problem.

'Aren't you too old to be going to a disco, Mummy?'

'Yes,' I say to my darling daughter. 'And I'm so pleased you pointed that out to me.'

I am also trying to prepare myself spiritually for a night on the tiles to the accompaniment of a drum solo by Connor. And much as I love my child, I cannot pronounce him musically gifted. Poppy is dancing along to it. Sophie and I used to scrub up to the sounds of A-Ha, KC and the Sunshine Band and Bananarama. It used to take us three hours and as many cans of Silvikrin hairspray to get our hair to the required stiffness to be seen out in public. I used to try to look like Kim Wilde, while Sophie – for reasons best known to herself – strove to resemble Sheena Easton. When I look back now they seem such stress-free times and I never imagined that this was how my life would unfold. Then again, I did envisage myself married to Morten Harket or one of Duran Duran. Preferably John Taylor. Boys. They have always been my downfall.

'Stephanie Fisher's mother doesn't go to nightclubs.'

But then Stephanie Fisher's mum is a boring fart who bakes her own sponge cakes and makes up her own party bags. I do not voice this opinion as I don't want my daughter to grow up not respecting her elders – even when they're unutterably dull.

'Aren't you pleased that I still want to have some fun?'

Poppy considers this. 'I could teach you a dance routine so that you won't embarrass yourself.'

'Go on then.' Anything to keep her quiet. Although I fully intend to embarrass myself tonight as it may be a long time until I get the chance to do so again. We're going to some hideous office worker meat-market establishment with overpriced drinks and the music blaring out so loud that you can't hold a conversation and I think I might be dreading it. Isn't this a true sign that I'm getting old before my time?

'Connor, play "Oops I Did It Again!"' his sister instructs. Connor never misses a beat or even changes it, he just does it louder. A lot louder. 'Oops I Did It Again!' seems to have exactly the same tune as 'Old MacDonald's Farm'. Funny, I'd never noticed that before. I give up on trying to relax and sink down into the foam of my cheap Tesco's own-brand bubble bath. I crave designer bubble bath – Jo Malone or someone – with the scent of tuberose, and skin cream that's stuffed with vital sea minerals and flakes of gold at £110 a tub. This is how I want my life to be.

My daughter launches into a series of spins and jerks and unseemly gyrations for one so young. I really must do something about her Spearmint Rhino-style dance tendencies and I should bill *Top of the Pops* for all the dents in my furniture and walls caused by them. As it is I'm going to have to feed beans on toast to my offspring for the rest of the week to fund this extravagance. And, as Connor's drumbeats set up a pounding in my head, I wonder whether it would be too soon to ask Nick for an advance on my wages.

Chapter Seventeen

When Sophie bounced into the lounge, Tom, Ellie and Charlotte were sitting in a row on the sofa watching some celebrity trying to run 100 metres on *Superstar Sports*. To say that they were glued to the television would be an understatement. Extra-strength Evostick wouldn't have held them there as firmly. Not one of them looked up in her direction.

'Da-dah!' she bellowed to try to elicit some response.

Ellie and Charlotte reluctantly tore their eyes away from the puffing 'C'-list fame junkies. But not Tom — her husband's eyes stayed firmly fixed to Nell McAndrew's exuberant bouncing breasts.

Her children, both bathed and in their black and white cow-patterned pyjamas, looked absolutely adorable. Ellie sucked on long blonde hair while Charlotte, not yet having much hair, sucked on her dummy. Her husband, unfortunately, looked less than adorable. He was slumped on the sofa in a tracksuit that had seen better days — in fact, she was sure she'd banned it as 'gardening only' last summer. His stubble made his face look grey and his hair needed a good cut.

'Do I or do I not look like a woman who could tear a man limb from limb and eat him alive?'

'Yes,' Ellie said. Which was about all the input she could expect from a three year old. Charlotte, one, clapped enthusiastically.

Tom eventually looked up. 'Yeah,' he said before turning his attention back to the television.

There was only so much domestic lethargy she was prepared to blame on the pressure of Tom's job. The British worked, on average, the longest hours in Europe, if you could believe what you read in the newspapers — and, in that respect, Tom was no exception. He'd been in the same grinding job for the last ten years, pushing through the ever-increasing traffic every day to repair office computer equipment that had invariably been bathed in coffee, hit with something hard or had not been switched on in the first place. It was destroying his soul — and their marriage. The antipathy he felt for his work —

or any kind of work, it seemed – was bleeding out into their everyday lives. At the age of thirty-five, instead of going out and finding a better, more stimulating job, he was wishing his life away until retirement. Well, there was no way he was going to wish *her* life away too.

Sophie put her hands on her hips. 'Did you know that being a wife and mother is a valued occupation in some countries?'

'Where?' Tom mumbled.

'I don't know,' Sophie admitted. 'But I think we should move there.'

Most of their rows these days focused on the fact that, in Tom's words, Sophie had the 'life of Riley' staying home and looking after the children while he had to go out to work as the breadwinner. But wasn't that what the idyll of family life was all about? It was all very well for emancipation, but did most women really want to juggle a demanding job and an equally demanding home? She wanted to stay at home and look after her children. What was so wrong with that? You only had to look at how ragged Anna was running herself and that was before her job had even started in earnest.

And Tom might complain about his lot – frequently – but all he had to do after his hard day was sit upright long enough to eat his dinner and then slump in front of the television. Her hard work didn't stop until she fell into bed too exhausted to speak, let alone do anything else. Which was just as well because there hadn't been an awful lot going on between their sheets for a very long time. She could count on one hand the number of times that she and Tom had cosied up together since Charlotte was born. Conversely, she'd run out of fingers and also toes to count the number of pointless arguments they'd had in the same period.

Sophie found her handbag. It was time she was out of here. She thought about kissing Tom and then changed her mind.

'See you later,' she said.

Tom sighed. He'd objected to babysitting, but how much more difficult was it to watch television with two children than it was without them? 'Yeah.'

Sophie went out into the hall and grabbed her jacket. Before she put it on, she regarded herself coolly in the full-length mirror by the door.

'You are looking gorgeous,' she said to herself. Well, if not exactly gorgeous then certainly half-decent. Nothing that shifting a few pounds and a face-lift wouldn't sort out.

Sophie held back her cheeks. It took years off her. 'You sexy beast,' she growled. 'Grrr . . .'

Suddenly a wave of uncertainty washed over her and she stared at herself levelly. 'You *are* a sexy beast,' she said. 'And don't let your husband or anyone else convince you otherwise.'

Chapter Eighteen

I'm ready and sort of raring to go. But I'm sure that a few glasses of my old friend Chardonnay will help to get me in the mood. I hardly recognise myself as I've dragged one of my ancient sparkly numbers from the back of my wardrobe – right next to the funeral suit, funnily enough – and have found some ridiculous strappy shoes that even Poppy thinks are 'well cool'.

Both of my children are, miraculously, in their nightclothes – a feat not often attained without hours of persuasion. But, for once, something has gone smoothly. The babysitter has also arrived. I hate leaving my kids with other people and I know that I'll have a constant battle with my conscience not to ring home on my mobile phone every ten minutes to check that they're still breathing. If you don't go out very often you definitely get out of the habit.

The babysitter is called Vicky and she's been recommended by a friend who I meet most often in Poppy's school playground. She's reputedly very good, although I'm not sure what being very good involves for a babysitter, other than making sure the children in your care are still alive by the time the roustabout parents arrive home sozzled. Vicky has, however, arrived with her boyfriend which I'm not too sure about, and he's called Lee which makes me deeply suspicious. Everyone I have ever known called Lee has been a lecherous troublemaker with more arms than an octopus. I also remember what I used to get up to when I could persuade anyone to let me babysit for them with boys called Lee. They are both sixteen and yet somehow I've decided that it was a good idea to put some Bacardi Breezers in the fridge for them and have even splashed out an extra three pounds on a pizza from Iceland. How stupid am I? Vicky and Lee are what used to be called 'canoodling' in my day. Their thighs are making micro-movements against each other and they think that I can't tell – but I'm missing nothing. They look like they can't wait to get down to it. Already I am regretting that I'm going out at all.

'You look very pretty, Mummy,' Poppy pipes up.

'Thank you, darling.'

'Are you going to find us a new daddy tonight?'

You don't know how much it makes my heart ache to hear this.

Vicky and Lee giggle. I'm going to put that pizza back in the freezer. I want to tell them that they should have more ambition in their young lives than just to explore the contents of each other's underwear. There is a whole world out there. They should be planning to travel the world or climb mountains or go to university. But then I'm a fine one to talk. I was absolutely no different at their age. The pinnacle of my dreams was to find some harassed parent who would pay me handsomely so that I could have some relative privacy in which to snog my boyfriend to death for a few hours.

'I think it's very unlikely.' The type of men I'm likely to meet at this nightclub are the sort of men I should be avoiding like the plague. But then where do financially constrained women of my age and lowly status go, to find decent men? I scowl at the aforementioned babysitters. 'I won't be late.'

Vicky nods at me.

'In fact I'll probably be quite early.'

Vicky nods at me again – this time there is more insolence in the tilt of her head. Lee sniggers.

'I might only be gone for a short while. I could come back at any moment.'

Vicky looks unconvinced.

'Bed at nine.' I look directly at Vicky. 'Them,' I say, pointing at Connor and Poppy, 'not you.'

My babysitter sighs.

'Be good.' I turn to Poppy and Connor. 'And you two.'

Feeling as if I'm already being entered on the Social Services register for further investigation, I head for the door.

Behind me, I hear Vicky muttering, 'Let's all put our tongues out at Mummy.'

But I can't rise to the bait, otherwise I'll never have a social life ever again.

Chapter Nineteen

Nick and Sam climbed out of the taxi and crossed the road towards the nightclub. Above their heads a vivid red neon sign flashed FIFTY PER CENT, no doubt a jolly allusion to the fact that 50 per cent of marriages in the UK now ended in divorce – a statistic Nick was more than aware of, thanks to his kindly solicitor.

The club was in the busy theatre district of the city, squeezed in between an overflowing Pizza Hut and TGI Friday's. Already, the pavements outside were thronging with half-dressed women who were oblivious to the cold and the fact that their thighs weren't necessarily flattered by short skirts.

Nick could feel himself backing away. 'I'm hyperventilating just thinking about this.'

Sam wedged his hand under Nick's elbow and steered him towards his doom. 'Nick. If you were a baby seal, I'd have clubbed you to death by now.'

'Sam, my dear friend, it's approximately fifteen years since I've been in a nightclub. I hated it then.'

'Relax,' Sam said. 'It will be great.'

'What's your definition of great?'

'Lots of women. Very little clothing.'

'I'm not sure I'm ready for this, Sam.'

His unsympathetic friend yanked him through the door of FIFTY PER CENT and paid their extortionate entrance fee, while Nick quaked in his shoes. They walked through a set of double doors and down a narrow staircase into the darkest room Nick had ever seen. It was painted dark red and black and was how he imagined the entrance to hell would look.

Nick gasped as he looked round the room. There were tarty women everywhere.

'There,' Sam said, 'that's not so bad, is it?'

Nick looked stunned. 'I see *divorced* people,' he breathed, sounding like something out of the *Sixth Sense*.

Sam clapped him on the back. 'Well, get used to it, old chum. You're one yourself now.'

He headed towards the bar, towing Nick along in his wake. Nick hated to admit this, but he was terrified to lose sight of his mate. Various unsavoury women gave them the eye as they passed. Nick could feel himself breaking out into a cold sweat. Was this the sort of terror that his social life held from now on? He hoped to goodness not.

'Smile,' Sam hissed in his ear. 'You look like a psycho-killer.'

'I can't,' Nick hissed back. 'I've got lockjaw.'

'They won't bite.'

'They will.' Nick scanned the women nervously. 'I can tell they will.'

At this point he was beginning to wish that he'd listened to his mother. Sam had reached the bar and ordered them two beers.

''Ello, darling,' a particularly scary woman said to them, eyeing Nick up and down as if he were a piece of meat.

Nick jammed himself up against his friend in fear.

'Will you stop it,' Sam snapped.

'I want to go home.'

'We've only just got here.'

Nick grabbed Sam's arm.

'Let go of my arm.'

Reluctantly, Nick let go and Sam brushed his arm down, frowning darkly. 'You don't think your divorce has affected your self-esteem, by any chance?' he demanded.

Nick sighed. 'Sorry.'

Sam sighed too. 'Uncle Sam will look after you. Have I ever got you in trouble before?'

'Yes,' Nick said.

His friend looked wounded. 'Just the once.'

'And Janine never let me forget it.' He wondered what his wife would feel if she could see him now. Pity. Probably pity.

'Well, there's no Janine now,' Sam said briskly. 'Your ex-missus is playing Happy Families with Mr Bone the Butcher.' Sam swept his arm expansively to take in the dance floor of the club. A dozen chubby, half-dressed women bounced around to the music in front of them. It was too depressing for words. 'There are, however, some very lovely girlies here tonight for your delectation.'

'Where?'

'Do you know your problem?' Sam said. 'You're too fussy by half.'

'They've all got arms like welders.'

'See what I mean?' Sam shook his head in dismay. 'Next you'll be wanting them to have all their own teeth and hair. Use your imagination.'

It was no good, he was going to have to give himself a good shaking and pull his life together. Sam was a great friend, trying to get him out and about again, but what Nick really needed was someone to sit down and talk to him about what had happened as he was still trying to make sense of it himself. He couldn't discuss it with his parents as . . . well . . . it just wasn't the sort of thing you talked to your parents about. Especially not his mother. And Sam wasn't a talking type of person either. Sam had always been a great believer in the adage that actions speak louder than words. And his particular choice of action was to show the world that you didn't care and bounce back as quickly as possible.

Sam pointed across the dance floor. 'Those two aren't too shabby,' he said hopefully.

Nick followed his friend's finger. On top of a table far across the room his new secretary, Ms Anna Terry, and a friend were doing some sort of suggestive Britney Spears dance routine. Nick felt himself do a double-take.

'Don't they look like a bagful of trouble?'

'They do,' Nick agreed.

'Wouldn't you like to spend a little time with them?'

'I think it might well be on the cards.'

Sam looked puzzled.

'Come on then,' Nick said.

Sam's beer stopped halfway to his mouth. 'What? Now?'

'Yes. Let's strike while the iron's hot.'

Before he thought better of it, Nick marched off across the dance floor towards Anna. Too shocked for words, Sam scurried behind.

'What's the hurry?' he called out. 'You know the saying about fools rushing in.'

'That's exactly what you wanted me to do just a moment ago.' Nick strode ahead of him until he stopped in front of Anna and her friend, who gyrated on, completely oblivious to their audience. Sam and Nick watched them, both faintly agog. Nick hadn't learned about this particular talent during the course of their interview, if you could call it that, and he wasn't quite sure how he could best employ it in an office situation, but he was awfully glad that his new secretary could move like that.

59

'Hi,' Nick said after a few moments of unbridled admiration. Beside him, Sam was dying a thousand deaths.

Anna looked down and ground to an abrupt halt. 'Hi,' she replied, hurriedly pulling down the hem of her dress to hide her rather attractive knees.

'So this is your quiet night in,' Nick noted.

'And this is your sad sack singles club?' Anna grinned and Nick helped her down from the table. 'I don't make a habit of this,' she told him.

'Shame,' Nick said. He didn't think he'd ever been quite so pleased to see anyone.

Anna's friend had now stopped dancing too and Sam put his arms round her waist and lifted her down.

'Would anyone like to put us in the picture?' Sam said.

'This is Sam,' Nick obliged.

'And this is Sophie,' Anna added.

'And this is Anna,' Nick said to Sam. He noticed that his friend still hadn't taken his hands from around Sophie's waist. 'Anna's my new secretary. She's going to turn my rather rundown car yard into a thriving empire even though she can't type and can't make tea.'

'So, who cares?' Sam gave Anna his best smarmy look, before rubbing his hands together. 'Can we buy you two ladies a drink?'

'Isn't mixing business with pleasure a really bad idea?' Anna said.

'I think under the circumstances,' Nick answered with a smile, 'that it's absolutely essential.'

Chapter Twenty

I can't believe that even before I've set foot in Nick's office as an employee, he probably already has me down as a slapper and a lush. Still, he doesn't look overly concerned about it. In fact, he seems to be quite enjoying himself. I just hope that he doesn't sack me in the morning.

I must be getting old as I've decided that nightclubs are truly hideous places filled with forty-year-old men trying to pick up nineteen-year-old girls. The moment I saw Nick's face in the crowd I was filled with an amazing sense of relief. What was going to be ordeal-by-Sophie has turned into a very pleasant evening – if only we could hear each other speak. Time is marching on and I must think about getting home to the babysitter before she loses her virginity. But of course, I can't voice this to Nick as he is still blissfully unaware that I am shackled with – sorry, the mother of – two children who are currently in the care of someone who is probably incapable.

The music slows to a scary pace. I hate this time in nightclubs as it always leaves me in a terrible quandary. What's worse – not to be asked to dance at all and to have to lurk on the edges of the dance floor or to rush off to the ladies to sit out the slowies – or be asked to dance by some hideous monster who will maul you and quite probably push a stiffy into your groin?

'Would you like to dance?' Nick says.

He doesn't look like a natural mauler. 'I don't think I've ever danced with my boss before,' I say.

'Not even Donald Trump?'

I can't help but smile. 'Ivana wouldn't let me.'

'Then let's consider this our first office outing.' Nick leads me to the dance floor and takes me in his arms. I can tell he's not entirely comfortable with this and neither am I. It's a long time since I've been in this close proximity to a man and I can feel an invisible barrier around me. There's a lot of air space between our bodies and

I'm quite grateful for that. However, my dear friend Sophie has no such inhibitions. She is currently draped all over Nick's mate, Sam. They are looking very cosy together as they smooch on the dance floor, tightly welded together, and I wonder will she regret a surfeit of strong drink by tomorrow morning. In comparison Nick and I move stiffly in circles – and not the sort of stiffly I alluded to earlier, I hasten to add. He has lovely eyes; even in the smoky atmosphere they're managing to look clear and kind.

'Thanks for taking me on, Nick,' I say, more to ease the silence between us than anything else. 'I'm sure I'll be able to help you.'

'I'm sure too.'

'You're very vulnerable running that yard on your own.' We edge nearer to Sophie and Sam. I might be tempted to give them a kick as Sam's hands have slid down onto my friend's bottom and she doesn't seem to mind in the slightest. And I rather think she should. 'I was reading in the paper the other day that there are a couple of conmen going around secondhand car dealers in the area.'

'Really?'

'They're buying up nice cars with dodgy cheques. It's a scam they've been running for years.'

'Don't tell me.' Nick rubs his chin. 'They're a sweet and inno-cent pair of old dears.'

'You read the paper too?'

For a moment his face looks as if it might contort in agony and then he smiles, tapping the side of his nose knowingly. 'Call it busi-nessman's intuition,' he says.

I can feel myself relax in his arms and I think that maybe Nick is a lot more shrewd than he looks.

Chapter Twenty-One

Outside, the cold shock of air hit Nick like a slap. A breeze had picked up, and discarded newspapers, polystyrene boxes and Coke tins skittered noisily along the road. Why was no one capable of disposing of litter thoughtfully any more? Nick started every day by clearing up all the rubbish from outside the car yard that had been carelessly thrown on to the streets at pub turning-out time. Was there anyone left who had pride in their country? It appeared not.

Anna stood awkwardly beside him. He could have kissed her and that was a very strange feeling, as he hadn't thought he'd ever want to kiss anyone again after Janine. It wasn't necessarily that he'd been overwhelmed by lust for his new assistant – even though there were definitely a few lustful thoughts straying in there – it was more in gratitude for the fact that he hadn't had some ageing, fat-bellied bruiser foisted on him by Sam in the interests of curing his current state of celibacy. Plus he couldn't think of a nicer way to avoid that than being with Anna.

He looked over at Sam. His friend was currently entwined around the rather comely Sophie. Sam had never found his bachelor status a problem. Although they were friends, the two men couldn't have been more different. For as long as he could remember, Nick had always wanted a settled family life, two kids, family saloon, brick-built barbecue, top-of-the-range Flymo, and he couldn't say it was because of the fantastic example that his parents set. Perhaps some people were born with the marriage gene and some weren't.

If that were true, then Sam was one of the people whose marriage gene was definitely missing. Even though they were both now fast approaching the horrors of middle age, Sam still showed no inclination to live any differently than he did when he was nineteen. He was, even now, unfeasibly delighted if he managed to take home a different female every single time he went out. Nick, quite frankly, had no idea where his friend found the necessary stamina – although he didn't have Mrs Diamond's stodgy puddings to slow him down as Nick did. He must move out of his parents' house as soon as humanly possible, there was no doubt about that. But even if he did, he couldn't imagine himself wanting a string of different women gracing his bed. Not even if they'd agree to.

While he was thinking about all this, they were standing there getting cold. Anna shivered in her thin coat. There was a certain fragility about her that made him feel protective. Sam and Sophie started to head off towards the taxi rank and, obediently, Nick and Anna followed.

When they all reached the rank, Sam turned and spoke. 'Sophie and I are going to get a taxi together.'

Anna looked concerned, as well she might. She pulled her drunken friend to one side. 'Are you sure you're going to be okay?'

'I'll be fine,' Sophie slurred. 'I'll see you tomorrow.' And she lurched back towards an equally sozzled Sam.

'See you, mate!' Sam shouted at Nick as he gave him a wave goodbye. Then he winked lasciviously at him as he bundled Sophie into the waiting taxi.

Anna frowned as the cab sputtered away. 'I should have gone with her.' She chewed at her fingernail. 'Can she trust your friend?'

'Absolutely not,' Nick said.

The ridges in Anna's forehead deepened with anxiety. 'I knew you were going to say that.'

The next taxi in the queue pulled up by the side of them. 'As we've been abandoned by our respective mates, shall we share too?'

'Can I trust you?' Anna said.

Nick opened the door for her. 'With your life,' he answered rather sadly.

Chapter Twenty-Two

The taxi pulls up outside my front door and, like the slow-dance scenario, this is another potentially embarrassing moment. Shouldn't I have grown out of this by now? I do hope that Nick remembers that we are only professionally linked – no matter how cute I might find him – and doesn't attempt anything that involves lips, tongues or intimate contact on any level. I also hope that my children are soundly tucked in bed – some hope. Or, at least, that they're not peering out of the windows.

I have a lovely little home. Nothing grand – just a small, modern terraced place. But it's smart and in a nice area. My parents bought it as an investment for my future when I was first starting out, in the dim and distant days when property was relatively cheap round here, and that's the only reason it's survived the vagaries of my love-life and the clutches of two husbands. I pay my parents rent for the privilege – via the Department of Health and Social Security, of course.

The taxi is warm, the company is good and I don't want to leave, but while the going is still good, I slither away from Nick. 'I'll see you in the morning then.'

'Bright-eyed and bushy-tailed. Nothing less.'

'I'll do my best.'

'It's been a great night,' Nick says. 'Thanks.'

'Do you think my new boss will realise that I've been up half the night drinking and dancing and will give me the bullet?'

'Maybe one, but not the other.'

When I'm safely out of the door without further fear of physical contact, I say, 'It's been fun. Goodnight.'

'Goodnight.'

'Where to now, mate?' the taxi driver asks over his shoulder.

Nick reels off his address, before giving me a final glance. 'Bye.'

I wave as he leaves. Then I watch the taxi putter off down the street, wondering whether Nick had expected to be invited in for coffee. He didn't look too disappointed. Or maybe he was dreading me inviting him in for coffee, I don't know. I'm out of practice at reading the signs. This is one of the worst things about divorce, apart from the financial impoverishment – it throws you back into situations that you'd long since hoped you'd escaped.

Anyway, apart from the fact that it would blow my cover as a young, free and single babe, I couldn't invite him back in for coffee as no doubt my babysitter is now getting low down and dirty on my three-piece suite.

I make as much noise as I possibly can opening the door, and stamp into the hall, rattling the keys in the lock. I even wait outside the lounge for a moment, coughing a loud theatrical cough, before going in. Vicky and Lee are sitting next to each other very chastely on the sofa watching something with Jonathan Ross in it on the television. The empty Bacardi Breezer bottles and a couple of dirty plates grace the coffee-table, showing that the pizza has been devoured. Of my young ones, there is no sign.

'Hi,' I say. 'Okay?'

Vicky nods. She's probably the chattiest person alive when there isn't an adult in the vicinity.

'Been good?'

Vicky nods again. 'Yeah.'

'And the kids?'

Both my babysitter and her acned boyfriend glower at me. Perhaps I'm being unfair – not everyone can be tarred with the same brush. They could have just sat here all night holding hands, couldn't they?

'The kids are fine,' Vicky mutters.

'Good, good,' I say hastily and root in my purse for some money.

I hand it over to Vicky who is already shrugging into her coat and heading for the door. Lee ambles out behind her.

'Well, thanks,' I say brightly. 'Thanks very much.'

As they reach the door I spy something peeping out from beneath one of the cushions. I pull it out, being careful not to touch it any more than I absolutely need to.

'Here,' I say to Vicky before she can escape. 'You might be needing this.'

I extend the finger over which the offending article is hooked and return the cheese-wire thong to its rightful owner.

Haughtily, she snatches it from my grasp and rushes out without so much as a word of apology. I have to smile to myself before vowing that my daughter will never, ever be allowed to babysit for anyone.

Chapter Twenty-Three

Nick could see that his mother's bedroom light was still on from halfway down Desford Avenue. It was shining out like a beacon from his past. Too many times as a teenager, he'd been in this situation. As the taxi drew nearer to the neat, detached house, he could also see his mother resplendent in her floral nightdress peering out of the window into the darkness.

It was some ungodly hour in the morning and his parents didn't do ungodly hours. They were pitched into the heights of anxiety when the BBC moved the nine o'clock news to ten o'clock as it would interfere with their beauty sleep. Heaven only knows what they did to make themselves so tired.

Nick leaned forward to speak to the taxi driver. 'Can you drive round again, please?'

The taxi driver looked at him as if he was mad but, as requested, he drove away, looped round the block and after a few minutes approached the house again. This time there was no light on in the window.

Nick grinned. 'Yes!'

The taxi driver sighed with relief.

'Cheers, mate,' Nick said. The taxi stopped outside the house. Monica's bedroom light snapped on again.

'Bugger!'

The driver rested his arm on the back of his seat. 'Divorced and living back at home with your mother?'

'Temporarily.'

'Been there, done that.'

'Then you will realise you are currently preventing a murder from taking place.'

'Round again?'

'Yep.'

The taxi driver eased the cab away from the kerb as his mother's head poked between the curtains.

★   ★   ★

Nick realised that he'd dozed off. He roused as the taxi slowed down for the tenth time.

'We'll win this bloody battle,' the taxi driver said, looking a bit sleepy himself. He screeched to a halt outside Nick's parents' home which was in darkness. The light snapped on again.

'Right, that's it!' the taxi driver cried, and jumped out of his cab. Nick sat bolt upright as the man stormed up the path to the front door and opened the letter box. 'Go to bloody bed, will you? Then we can all get some sleep! There's no way he's coming into this house until it's in complete darkness! I'm going to go round one more time.'

The taxi driver stomped back up the path and got into the cab. Nick wondered if he was going to have to go through this every time he went out. And what if, heaven forbid, he ever wanted to bring anyone home with him? He put his head in his hands. There was no way he could go on like this. Blood would be shed. The sooner he took himself off to the jolly old estate agent's and started the search for his own place, the better.

'Thanks, mate,' he said to the taxi driver.

'It's okay,' the man said, steam coming out of his nostrils which Nick couldn't entirely attribute to the cold night air. 'My mother was exactly the same. Drove me nuts.' He pulled away again. 'We'll give it one last twirl.'

The light in Monica's bedroom clicked off.

The sky was brightening the next time they circled round the road and came slowly back towards number 43. Heading towards them, trundling and clinking along his delivery route, was the milkman. The taxi driver pulled up outside the house. Amazingly, the light in Monica's window stayed switched off.

'We did it,' the taxi driver said triumphantly. 'We bloody well did it!'

Nick sagged with relief. He would like a few hours' sleep before he had to go into the office and meet Anna all over again. Despite the fact that he was half-frozen and stiff as a board from being cramped in the back of the cab, a warm feeling surged through him at the thought of spending the day with his new secretary.

The taxi driver high-fived Nick. 'Go and get some sleep, mate,' the man said. 'You deserve it.'

At that moment, Monica's light snapped back on.

The two men sighed in unison. 'This is ridiculous,' Nick said. 'Do you want to come back to my car yard, mate? It's not far. I'll make us some tea.'

'Why not?'

'Just a mo'.' Nick wound down the window and leaned out. 'Hey, mate!' He flagged down the milkman. 'Give us a couple of pints, please.'

The milkman obligingly handed over a couple of pints. Nick paid him.

'Right, we're set,' Nick said. 'I've got some cornflakes in the office and there's a place just next door that does great bacon sandwiches. It should be open by now.'

'Sounds good to me,' the taxi driver said. 'I'm Bill, by the way.'

'Nick.' They shook hands. 'I'm sorry about all this.'

'No worries,' Bill said. 'There's a principle at stake.'

The taxi pulled away again and as they drove down the road, Nick looked back to see the front door open and his mother's head stuck out. 'Nicholas! Nicholas!' he heard her shout.

But Bill was right. There was a principle at stake. He only hoped there was a clean shirt in the office that he could put on before Anna arrived.

Chapter Twenty-Four

I'm sitting behind Nick's desk and if you saw me you'd instantly know that I was suffering from the most monumental hangover.

'More coffee?' Nick says.

I nod. Even though I feel paler than pale, I could seriously fall in love with this man. He has the patience of a saint and a deftness of touch with a kettle that I haven't seen in a long time.

He hands me yet another cup of strong, black caffeine reviver. 'I see I'm going to have to increase my office beverage budget.'

'I won't make a habit of this,' I promise, trying not to notice the wind that is howling through the gaps in the windows and whipping round my ankles. What I wouldn't give to be in my jeans, thick socks and trainers rather than my smart suit, woefully thin tights and stilettos. 'Last night was definitely a one-off. I have decided that the short skirt and strong alcohol combination is a bad idea at my age.'

'Shame.' My new boss smiles at me over his own cup. 'You're fun when you're tipsy.'

I scan the piles of paper heaped up in front of me – trying to keep my head still and just move my eyes. Movement, today, is going to be restricted to the more minimal kind. 'This isn't a great start to my making a major impact on your empire.'

Nick shrugs and sits down in the garden chair opposite me. 'These things take time. Just sit and absorb the atmosphere.'

My boss and I both look round at the mildew-speckled walls.

'We need to talk about my role.' I put my hand to my head, mainly to reassure it that I'm not going to subject it to anything worse.

'We do?'

'You know,' I say, 'I really don't see myself as a secretary.'

'Is that because you have absolutely no secretarial skills?' Nick teases me.

'Not entirely.'

'So what do you want to be?' Nicks asks. 'Managing Director? Chief Executive? Vice President of Paper Clips?'

'I see myself more as your Executive Assistant,' I say. 'And Business Advisor.' I think I'm quite possibly still drunk.

'Oh, right.'

'I can help shape your business,' I assure him. 'Really I can.' I glance outside the window at the wind-battered cars and I can see so much potential here. Like most male-run businesses, it is definitely lacking a woman's touch. 'You need to move towards the future.'

'Aren't we all doing that anyway,' he notes, 'without any help?'

'I can draw up strategies and mission statements,' I say without adding 'possibly not today though'.

Nick looks vaguely alarmed. 'I'm not sure me and my old bangers are ready for this.'

'Trust me.' I knock back my coffee with a shudder. 'You won't feel a thing.'

I hand over my cup for yet another refill as the office door bursts open. A young, attractive woman dressed from head to toe in a Juicy Couture tracksuit stands there puffing and panting. She has a personal CD player plugged into her ears and Nick looks so taken aback that I'm sure this can only be one person.

'Can I help?' I say brightly as Nick stands there clutching our empty coffee cups.

The woman's head snaps round to face me. Now it's her turn to look taken aback.

'Hello, Janine,' Nick says into the uncomfortable pause. 'What are you doing here?'

'Jogging,' Janine says. 'I'm running the London Marathon.'

'Again?' Nick remarks.

'Again,' she answers crisply. 'I need to put in some miles.'

She can't keep her eyes from straying towards me. And, quite frankly, she doesn't fool me. There are a dozen different parks and lakes that Janine could choose for a session of convivial jogging. We have 250 kilometres of cycle and running tracks that meander through woodland and fields right in the centre of Milton Keynes, and there's absolutely no need for her to risk carbon-monoxide poisoning by pounding the pavements anywhere near Nick's car yard. *And* it's raining. Do people in Juicy Couture tracksuits really jog in the rain? I don't think so. I back this up with the fact that she isn't wet. I am used to deceit on a grand scale and can spot the telltale signs a mile away. Whereas Nick – it appears – cannot.

'I thought I'd just pop in to say hi.'

71

'Why?' Nick says. And I can't help but smile, so I bury my head in a pile of papers and pretend to look busy while trying to get my eyes to focus. My ears have no trouble focusing, of course – even when Janine lowers her voice.

'I'm still your wife,' she hisses.

'Only for the next few weeks,' Nick says pleasantly. 'I've signed the divorce papers.'

'Nick,' Janine murmurs tightly. 'I'm trying to be civil about this.'

'So am I.' A perplexed look has settled on Nick's brow.

Janine gives me a pointed glare, indicating that she doesn't want to talk about this with anyone else in the room. Particularly not someone who she doesn't know.

Nick follows her stare. 'Oh,' he says. 'This is Anna. Anna Terry.'

I stand up and join Nick, presenting a consolidated front. I don't know why I'm behaving like this, but she's irritating the life out of me just by being here. And I think I'm safe in assuming that the feeling is mutual.

Janine is beautiful. Her hair bounces in a pert, little dark bob, and she has a figure that would cause most women to want to stab her. I'm no exception. But she's brittle and has tight little lines around her mouth even though I'd say she was younger than me and I'm a knackered old hag with two kids to wear me down. Try as I might, I can't imagine her and Nick as a couple. He's far too nice for her.

I hold out my hand and, reluctantly, Janine shakes it. Dry as a bone. 'I'm Nick's Executive Assistant and Business Advisor.'

'My . . . Executive Assistant,' Nick echoes uncertainly. He looks blankly at me.

'And Business Advisor,' I prompt.

'And Business Advisor.'

Nick and I smile happily. Janine, however, looks distinctly put out.

'When did this happen?' she asks.

'Er . . .' my boss says.

'Ages ago,' I inform her. 'We're going international.'

'Oh,' Janine says. 'That's good. Very good.' She doesn't look as if she thinks it's very good. 'I'm pleased for you.'

'Is there anything else we can help you with?' I put on my most pleasant and helpful face even though it's a huge effort to get my features to comply as they are still in a state of alcoholic reluctance.

'Er . . . no,' Janine says. 'No.' She looks to Nick for some sort of input, but – bless him – he remains completely impassive. Or perhaps he just had too much to drink last night as well.

'I'd better be going then,' Nick's wife says. 'Pavements to be pounded.'

'Yeah,' Nick replies. 'Nice to see you.'

Janine looks as if she's about to say something else and then changes her mind. She gives me a freezing stare that says I might have just won a battle, but that I should be in no doubt that this is a war. And I wonder why a woman who has so recently left her husband for someone else should be feeling so malevolent towards someone she clearly views as competition. Even though I can safely say that I'm not.

'Keep in touch,' Janine says to Nick.

'Yes. You too.'

Without bidding me farewell, Janine turns on her heel and leaves.

From behind the safety of the holey curtains, I watch her jog out through the car yard, dodging the puddles with an expert weave. And then I see her glance back at the office and slide furtively into the driver's seat of a BMW that's parked just a little further down the road. Inside, I smile the smug smile of the terminally right. That's my kind of jogging too.

'Well.' I pull a thoughtful face at Nick. He suddenly looks sad and I can hardly bear to see it in him.

'I wish you were my lawyer,' he says quietly.

'So that's the woman who's a stranger to stretchmarks?'

'Mmm.' Nick nods.

'Does she often just pop in to say hello?'

'Never.' Nick rubs his chin, confusion written large on his face. 'That's definitely a first.'

'She wants you back,' I say.

'Don't be silly.' Nick laughs at the very suggestion.

'She does. Women know these things.' I try to put on my most sage voice, but the effect is spoiled by it coming out as a dehydrated croak. I won't tell him that I've just seen her getting into a car and all the jogging thing was complete bollocks. 'Perhaps the size of the butcher's chopper is losing its attraction.'

'It's been done,' Nick sighs. 'And every joke you can think of about sausages.'

'Oh,' I say. Still, I'm sure I'm right. Mrs Jogger's Nipple looked far too put out to be classed as an impartial observer. Why else would she have hauled her arse over here without good reason? 'Shall I put the kettle on again?'

'I'll do it,' my lovely boss insists. 'You look decidedly peaky.'

I sit down behind the desk again and it's all I can do not to lie down on it and go to sleep. Both of the kids were in my bed when I finally got to it and, consequently, as they'd already staked their claim, I ended up sleeping on slightly less than five millimetres of mattress.

Nick does wonderful things with a jar of Instant Nescafé again.

'I'm sorry that I didn't invite you in for coffee last night,' I mumble. 'It just didn't seem . . . well . . . appropriate.'

'No,' Nick agrees. 'You're probably right.'

He looks like he might have been up for coffee, which makes me slightly nervous as I might well have been up for it too.

'Still, we're making up for it now,' he adds, busying himself with the mugs. 'So,' he says over his shoulder. 'We're going international, are we?'

I grin at him. 'In the fullness of time.'

'As it happens,' Nick says, 'I have an important meeting with a Japanese businessman tomorrow. I'm going to discuss the future of the car yard with him. Despite the outwardly shabby appearance, I do have big plans for expansion.'

'I should come along too.'

'I was afraid you'd say that.'

Nick walks over to me, concentrating on not spilling the coffee. Although, goodness only knows, coffee spills couldn't make the state of the carpet any worse. I watch his brow furrowed in earnest and he sticks the tip of his tongue out of the corner of his mouth as he approaches the desk. He is such a nice man that it does strange things to my insides, and that's not what I want at all. I want this to be a serious proper job and not to have a schoolgirl crush on my boss in the manner of my daughter and Stephanie Fisher. Nick hands over my coffee and, despite all my resolve, I give him a quick peck on the cheek.

For the second time today Nick looks taken aback, as well he might. I'm a bit taken aback myself.

'So you're coming with me?' Nick says.

'You wait and see,' I tell him. 'I'll be your biggest asset.'

Chapter Twenty-Five

Sophie sat up in bed, sheet wrapped round her, feeling very self-conscious. Sam, sharply dressed in a black designer business suit, came and sat down next to her and stroked her hair.

'I have to go,' he said. He gave her a lingering kiss, pulling gently on her lips. His finger hooked inside the sheet and toyed with her breast. Sophie felt another surge of pleasure – and there'd been plenty of them last night. More than she could remember for a long time. 'But I'd like to do this again.'

'It's too difficult, Sam.' Sophie shook her head. Even once had been sheer madness. 'I don't know how I'm going to explain this as it is.'

Sam lived in a smart apartment in a flash development in Campbell Park – all chrome and glass and black slate floors, with a price tag to match. She had no idea what the rest of the place was like as they'd headed straight to the bedroom when the cab had dropped them off. But in here the atmosphere was one of unbridled sex. It was sleek, masculine and even the clichéd black silk sheets somehow managed to look cool.

Sophie looked out of the window at the view of the park, the rolling hills, the woolly sheep dotted around even though they were still in the heart of the city. It was as far away from her cramped, terraced, toy-strewn home as she could possibly imagine. A home where she could hear the nextdoor neighbours arguing through the flimsy walls and where they could probably hear her and Tom's ever-increasing ding-dong rows too. Blushing at the thought, Sophie hoped that Sam's neighbours hadn't been able to overhear them last night. She trailed her hand over the crumpled silk and thought of her own ten-year-old BHS flowery nightmare of a duvet cover. Whatever happened after this, some things had to change.

Sam meanwhile trailed his fingers down the sensitive skin of her arm and looked at her with dark, beguiling eyes. There was no doubt that he was an extremely handsome man and although he was slightly older than her, he very definitely felt like toy boy material – younger, firmer, wilder – whereas Sophie felt older than time itself. His lips traced the outline of her neck. 'I had a lot of fun.'

'Me too.' Sophie huffed regretfully. He was freshly shaved and smelled of expensive, musky aftershave. She wanted to kiss him again and realised that she was storing up memories as this was all they were ever likely to have. 'Sam, I've never done anything like this before.'

'Haven't you?' he grinned. 'I have.' And he winked at her.

Sophie slapped him on the arm. 'Be serious.'

'I am,' he said. 'You're one in a long line of married women whom I've lured back here to my love-nest to have my wicked way with.'

Sophie felt her face fall. 'Am I?'

'No,' he said. 'You're the only one. I promise.'

But she wondered whether she could really believe that. She couldn't imagine he was short of willing women to keep his black sheets warm – married or otherwise.

'Come on. Let me drive you home,' Sam said. 'It's on my way.'

Her house was nowhere near on his way. Sam worked in one of the financial institutions that had moved their head offices out of London to enjoy the benefit of the lower leasehold prices in the new city. He did something that sounded exciting and important – although, if she was truthful, she couldn't remember exactly what. She wondered if she'd think of last night every time she drove past his office.

'Best not,' Sophie said.

Sam stood up, reluctantly. 'Enjoy the facilities.' He nodded towards an en-suite shower room.

'Thanks.' It was early, but she'd have to get a move on. She had children to feed, chores to do and a husband to make excuses to. Thank goodness that Anna's son was going to Tumble Tots with one of her other friends this morning as she had no idea what she would have told Tom if Anna turned up with a screaming Connor under her arm and there was still no sign of her.

'Don't rush off,' Sam said. 'I want to think of you here while I'm working. Although if you're going to go through my stuff the minute I'm gone, then all the compromising photographs of my ex-girl-friends are in a shoe box in the left-hand side of the wardrobe.'

Sophie grinned. 'What do you take me for?'

Sam kissed her passionately. 'A very beautiful and sexy woman.'

He let go of her hands and headed to the door. 'You know where I am if you change your mind,' he said. 'Ring me anytime you can.'

'Yes.' And she knew that she never would.

Chapter Twenty-Six

I've managed to motivate myself out of my stupor and am actually doing some work. Nick is looking more terrified than grateful that I've rallied, but I think this is because I've now got all of his papers spread over the office floor, with a view to sorting them out. Admittedly, at the moment, it all looks rather worse than when I started, but I'm sure that's going to be a temporary state of affairs.

I could get quite into this work lark, really I could. What would I be doing if I was at home right now? Probably ironing and watching *Countdown* under the false pretence that it was keeping my brain stimulated and thinking which UFO (unidentified frozen object) I could get out of the freezer and transform into something wondrously nutritious for dinner.

Everything has been quiet at the car yard today, which isn't great for business, I know, but at least it's given Nick and me time to get to know each other a bit better. I know that he's living back at his parents' house and is hating it. I know that he didn't intend to be in secondhand car sales and can't quite work out why he is. I know that he desperately wanted children and was very much in love with his wife. And I know that Janine must have been absolutely mad to leave him, but I suspect that if she's got half a brain she's thinking that too.

Why couldn't I have met nice men like Nick on my tortured wanderings through the world of love? And why is it that women who do meet nice men, invariably leave them for bastards? Is not life constantly cruel?

To shake me out of my musings, the phone rings – but we both have a bit of trouble locating it as it's buried under an avalanche of paper. All of which is perfectly well organised, I must point out. It just doesn't look as though it is.

Finally, I find it. 'Nick Diamond International,' I say with a smile at Nick. 'How can I help?' It's Janine and she tells me that rather curtly in my opinion. 'Mrs Aerobics Arse,' I mouth to Nick.

With a reluctant puff, he takes the phone. 'Hello, Janine,' he says brightly.

I give him the thumbs-up.

'Yes. Yes. Yes,' he says.

Damn – this gives me no idea what the conversation might be about.

'Yes. Yes. Yes,' he continues. 'Yes. Yes. Yes. Bye then.' And he hangs up. Then he says nothing.

'I'm your Executive Assistant and Business Advisor,' I remind him after a suitable interval. 'That means you've got to tell me everything.'

Nick is staring into the middle distance. 'She wants to see me. Tonight.'

'And you said yes?'

Nick shrugs. 'What else could I say?'

This does not look good, I think. Not good at all.

Chapter Twenty-Seven

The taxi took forever to arrive at Sam's apartment. Of course, in this day and age none of the children walked more than 100 metres so all the local cabs were booked for the school run. Sophie had tried phoning Anna's house, but her friend must have already left for work and her mobile phone wasn't responding. Though exactly what she was going to tell Anna, she wasn't quite sure. However, that was the least of her worries. First she had to face her husband.

After a nail-biting journey, the car eventually pulled up outside Sophie's house. Hurriedly, she paid the driver and then got out looking very furtive. Conspicuous in last night's glittery extravaganza, she braced herself to face the music. Dodging past Ellie's dolls' pram, which had been left outside in the garden, she rushed up to her front door and, as she was fumbling with her key, it opened. Her husband Tom was standing there looking furious.

'Thank God,' he exploded. 'You're back!'

'Tom,' she started, 'I can explain—'

'Don't tell me.' Tom held up his hand. 'You got pissed and crashed out at Anna's.'

'I . . .' Sophie stopped dead in her tracks, her jaw slackened. 'Yes.'

'The kids haven't had their breakfast yet,' Tom complained. 'And I'm late. I'm off. See you later.'

And with that he shot past her and jumped into his company car.

Sophie stood and watched as he roared off down the road, not knowing whether she should be relieved or disappointed that her husband wasn't particularly interested in where she had spent the night. Or should she feel more guilty that he was so trusting of her? Or was it simply that he couldn't envisage another man finding her attractive? Why were life and love always so damn complicated? If she'd stuck to her guns and become a nun as was her calling at the age of eleven, then none of this would have ever happened. She rubbed her hands over her face.

Ellie came to the door. She was wearing her ballet tutu, fairy wings and had the hair of a mad witch. 'Mummy,' she whined, 'I'm starving.'

And she could empathise with that. Although it was a bit of love and affection rather than food for which Sophie hungered.

Chapter Twenty-Eight

At six o'clock, the end of a very slow and tedious day, Sam popped his head round the door of Nick's office. He recoiled in horror – only some of it staged – when he saw the devastation of Nick's filing system spread out all over the floor. 'Bloody hell – what happened here?'

'Anna did,' Nick said.

Sam threaded his way through the paper trail and took up residence in his usual place in Nick's chair, feet on Nick's desk.

'She's organising me,' Nick said.

'That's what they call it these days, is it?' Sam made a steeple of his fingers.

Whatever 'organising' involved, it had been very pleasant having Anna here today, Nick decided – for company more than anything. Being self-employed was all very well, a cosy little unit to take on the world, but the reality was that he spent most of his time alone staring at four walls waiting for a customer to deign to turn up. A bit like the latter stages of his marriage when he'd stared at four walls waiting for Janine to deign to come home. Nick sighed inwardly and wondered when the pain would ever stop. Every time he thought that he was starting to move on, Janine bowled up again out of the blue and sent his emotions into freefall once more. He had no idea why he'd agreed to see her tonight, or even why she wanted to see him. It would probably involve a conversation about money, solicitors and divorce as they were the only things they talked about these days. Still, he had nothing else to do. And how sad was that?

'Where's the lovely Anna then?' Sam would have no such inner turmoil if he'd had a wife who dumped him. He would have simply erased her from his personal radar and would have bedded every available woman in the county of Buckinghamshire and beyond in order to purge his soul. It sounded like a great idea, but Nick just wasn't like that. No matter how much he wished that he was.

'I sent her home early,' Nick explained. 'She looked terrible. That woman had one hell of a hangover.'

'I'm sure she did,' Sam remarked dryly.

'It was a good night,' Nick said. Which had been a nice surprise, because it was fair to say that he would rather have eaten a plate of his own toenails than have gone there in the first place. And meeting Anna again – in relaxed circumstances – had been even more pleasant than that. He wondered if she thought so too. 'I enjoyed it.'

'Me too.' Sam smirked. 'So did you and Anna . . . ?'

'Did we what?'

'My friend, has it been so long that you need me to draw you a diagram?'

'Oh that,' Nick said distractedly. 'Of course we didn't. I hardly know her. Although I realise that isn't a good enough reason for some of us.' He looked pointedly at Sam. 'And now she's my "Executive Assistant and Business Advisor" – apparently. You should never mix business with pleasure.'

'There'd be no such thing as conferences if that was the case,' his friend observed. 'Do you know that the average British worker spends five hours of every working day flirting?' Sam grinned. 'The rest of the time he wastes.'

'Well, I can hardly class myself as the average worker,' Nick said. 'The subtle art of flirting has always eluded me. The only time I ever winked at a woman in a pub, I got decked by her brick-built boyfriend who was standing behind her. The thought of going out there in the wide world and getting involved with the opposite sex again terrifies me.'

'You can't live with your mother for the rest of your life, Nicholas.' Sam wagged a finger at him. 'I thought there might have been a little flirting going on last night. A little chemistry. I know about these things.'

'Anna might be a fine-looking woman – extremely fine – but my relationship with her will remain purely platonic.'

'And do you know why that is?' Sam said. 'Because you are both sad puppies who are frightened to get involved.'

'And tell me,' Nick replied, 'when did you last have a serious girl-friend?'

'Yesterday, as a matter of fact.'

Nick, in his plastic garden chair, sat upright. 'Yesterday? With Sophie? With Anna's friend, Sophie?'

Sam nodded in confirmation.

'But she's married. With several children.'

'Two.'

'How many do you need to make it a really, really dreadful idea?' Nick shook his head.

'Anyway,' Sam looked indignant, 'who told you how many kids she has?'

'Anna, of course. We've had a girly, gossipy day together.'

'How nice for you.'

'Jeez, Sam.' Nick shook his head. 'Even for you, this is a classic. A married woman with multiple sprogs. This calls for some emergency beer.'

Nick crossed to the tattered fridge that graced the corner of his office and extracted two cans of Stella Artois from the six-pack that was always kept in there for extreme circumstances. And this could certainly be classed as an extreme circumstance. He handed a can to Sam and they ripped them open.

'I've got it bad,' Sam said, taking a slug of his beer.

'Yes, but you'll get over it in a week. You always do.'

Sam looked serious. 'Not this time.'

'*Especially* this time,' Nick said. 'This is a lots-of-people-getting-hurt scenario. This is potentially more business for my lawyer. And, believe me, he *so* doesn't need it. This, my friend, is a very, very bad place to be.'

'I'm glad you're happy for me.'

'Sam, the world is full of ridiculously attractive *single* women. You know several dozen of them already. Intimately.'

Sam sipped at his beer and Nick realised that his words were falling on deaf ears. 'This is the flipside of what happened to me, Sam,' he tried. 'And it feels terrible. Truly terrible. Don't do this to another man. Maybe he's a nice guy who doesn't deserve it.'

'And maybe he's a wanker who does,' Sam said immediately. 'Do married women sleep with other guys because they're happy?'

Nick winced with pain.

'Sorry, mate,' Sam said, slightly shamefaced. 'I didn't mean anything by that.'

'No,' Nick said. 'But you can see why it rankles.'

'This is different.' His friend was dismissive. 'Entirely different. Besides, we're all adults.'

'Yes, you are.' Although Nick thought it was questionable at the moment, given their behaviour. 'But what about the kids?' he tried.

'I love children,' Sam insisted. 'I've *always* wanted to be a dad.'

'Since when?'

'Yesterday,' Sam and Nick said in unison.

Nick knew that he was on a hiding to nothing. Once Sam had made up his mind he was impossible to sway. He could only hope that Sophie had more sense than his dunderheaded friend and that this wouldn't finish with blood up the walls and a custody battle. He looked at his friend and told him: 'Your idea of *always* is like one of Kylie Minogue's skirts, mate. Way, way too short.'

Chapter Twenty-Nine

Sophie and I are sitting at her kitchen table and we each have a wriggling child on our knees that we're jiggling for all our worth. Sophie is doing a 'go to sleep' jiggle for Charlotte, whereas I am doing 'galloping horsey' jiggle in a vain attempt to entertain Connor who is clearly bored witless by my futile efforts. The only effect of all this jiggling is to make me feel nauseous. Still, I only have fifteen minutes before I need to collect Poppy from school and to find out whether she hates me or not today. As always, it could go either way.

'He let me come home early because I didn't look very well,' I say.

'He noticed you were sick?' Sophie looks amazed. 'He noticed you were *alive*?'

'Yes.'

'This bloke isn't for real,' Sophie says. 'Anyway, you do look knackered.'

'So do you.'

Sophie, for some reason, avoids my gaze. 'How was your first day at work?' she asks.

'Exhausting,' I confess. 'I really wanted to impress Nick, so that he'll keep me on.'

'We are still talking about work?'

'I wanted him to think that I was dynamic and driven,' I huff into the ether, 'but it was all I could do to stay upright. I should never have let you lead me astray. I'm going to get an early night tonight – *and* make the kids stay in their own beds so that I've got somewhere to sleep that's not like hanging onto a ledge.'

Sophie shifts Charlotte to her other leg. Her jiggling is vigorously renewed. 'This is looking very promising.'

I shake my head. 'He's too nice a man for me,' I say. 'As you well know, I only do idiots, bankrupts, philanderers and perverts. And he doesn't seem to be any of those. Anyway, I think he's still emotionally attached to his wife.'

'I do wish you'd stop reading self-help books, Anna. You're beginning to talk like one.'

Connor's patience at being penned on my lap is running short and I need to start hitting the road. 'How did you get on last night?' I ask as I finish my tea. 'Did the lovely Sam return you relatively unmolested?'

'Oh. You know how it is,' Sophie says.

I halt abruptly in my preparations to leave and I can feel my eyebrows form an involuntary frown. 'I would if you weren't being so cagey.'

The front door slams and a moment later Tom comes into the kitchen and tosses his coat onto the nearest chair. 'Ah,' he says, addressing me. 'The other reprobate surfaces. I hope she didn't keep you awake all night with her snoring. I can't stand it. She makes the walls vibrate.'

I laugh, because I really have no idea what else to do. Tom goes through to the lounge and I note that he hasn't spoken to Sophie or kissed her or generally, in any way, acknowledged her existence. Do all relationships end up with this kind of benign indifference as their linchpin? What a depressing thought.

Sophie looks at me shame-faced.

I check that Tom is well out of earshot, but lower my voice nevertheless. 'You didn't come home last night?'

Sophie shakes her head.

'Not at all?'

My undoubtedly insane friend shakes her head again.

'Are you mad?' I don't think I even need to ask the question.

Sophie nods her head.

'And you weren't even going to tell me.' I can hardly believe this. Sophie tells me everything. We've never had any secrets between us – or at least I thought we hadn't. 'What would have happened if Connor hadn't been able to go to Tumble Tots? What if I'd brought him round here instead? Why didn't you phone to warn me that you were being a complete idiot?'

'Idiot!' Connor says, clapping his hands in glee.

I lower my voice further. 'What would you have told Tom then?'

My friend lets her daughter slide from her knee and puts her in her high chair. She goes over to the fridge and takes out a packet of cheap sausages and plonks them down by the cooker. Tonight's fare, no doubt. Then she slams on the grill.

'It was a one-off,' Sophie says. 'And it was stupid. Okay?'

86

'You're telling *me*!' I shout at her in a whisper.

Sophie turns to look at me. 'Yes, I am,' she says. 'And I want it to go no further.'

'Are you going to see him again?'

I can see that my friend is struggling. Her knuckles are white where she's gripping the work surface, her back muscles are tensed. I might not be able to condone this, but I don't like to see my friend hurting either.

'Sophie?'

'No,' she snaps. 'Of course I'm not.'

'Good,' I say softly. 'I'm pleased to hear it.'

Sophie turns to me and her face is bleak. 'Anna,' she whispers, 'it may have been an incredible risk, but I had a lot of fun last night . . .'

Tom's voice breaks in from the lounge. 'What time's dinner, Soph?'

Both Sophie and I cringe.

'. . . and I get precious little of that in this house,' she says.

Chapter Thirty

Yet another mealtime had trundled around with a certain amount of inevitability in the Diamond household. It was no wonder Nick had been tempted to stay late at the office drinking with Sam. He still couldn't believe that his friend – who had the choice of all the unattached women on the planet – had chosen a married woman. One with children to boot.

His mother put some sort of huge steamed pudding on the table. Nick felt as if he was about to be ill. Some of his digestive discomfort could be blamed on the 'date' with Janine he was anticipating later that evening, but there was no way he was going to admit to Monica that it was his ex-wife who was putting him off his food.

'Just a little bit, Mum,' he said. 'The tiniest bit you can imagine.'

'This is comfort food,' his mother said firmly. 'And if anyone needs comfort food, you do.'

'It's heart-attack food. I can feel my arteries narrowing just looking at it. I've lost at least ten years off my life since I moved back home.'

'You are silly.'

Ignoring his pleas, his mother dished up two huge portions and handed them to Nick and his father. For herself, she took the tiniest bit imaginable.

'Did you have a good time last night at the . . . *nightclub*?' his mother asked with a shudder.

'Fabulous,' Nick said while trying to bolt down his pudding.

Monica fussed with her hair which was never a good sign. It meant there was an awkward question coming. 'Did you meet anyone nice?'

'No.' Nick shook his head. 'I met a woman called Mandy who's a mud-wrestler from Macclesfield. She definitely wasn't nice.'

His mother looked horrified.

'Strong thighs,' Nick elaborated. 'But very dirty fingernails.'

Monica cleared her throat. 'And are you seeing her again, darling?'

'Tonight.' Nick glanced at his watch. 'In fact, I'd better dash. She's not the sort of woman you'd want to upset.'

'Roger, say something!'

'Is there any more roly-poly?' Roger said.

Nick finished his pudding and then rushed towards the door. 'See you later.'

'Bring her home for dinner, darling,' his mother shouted after him. 'Tomorrow. Mummy wants to meet her.'

As he closed the door behind him he heard his father say: 'Mud-wrestler, eh?' There was a note of admiration in his parent's voice.

'Roger!' his mother snapped. 'You've got to take a firmer hand with that boy. He gets more like you by the minute.'

Nick grinned to himself as he shrugged on his jacket. But he knew that his mother would be even more horrified if he knew who he was really going to meet tonight.

Chapter Thirty-One

Nick met Janine at the Old Boot pub which was in a fairly nondescript village outside Milton Keynes consisting of a few terraced cottages, a church that was far too large for its now meagre congregation and a new housing estate that looked exactly like the sort of place The Stepford Wives would move to if they ever tired of Stepford. And the pub. The pub where he and Janine had celebrated their five wedding anniversaries in fairly low-key style. Perhaps if he had whisked her away to Paris for a weekend of passion instead, they might still be married.

Mind you, it was a nice pub. One of the few that was resisting modernisation and was clinging to its horse brasses and low beams and traditional pub grub rather than the new rash of watering-holes that couldn't decide whether they were wine bars or restaurants or nightclubs or branches of Habitat. This was not the sort of place that would start serving Thai food on a Tuesday night simply to attract a more trendy crowd. He'd no idea why Janine liked it here really, since she was the sort of person who would go somewhere that served Thai food on a Tuesday night. Perhaps she didn't like the Old Boot at all and it was something else he'd been deluding himself about all along.

He put her glass of mineral water – no ice, because ice in pubs was unhygienic – down on the table in front of her. She sipped it unenthusiastically. Despite the fact that his wife was clearly uncomfortable, she looked fantastic. As always her hair shone and her skin glowed and she wore some sort of clingy black jumper that looked very soft and showed off all her curves. And Janine had plenty of curves. All of them in the right place. She was a very good advert for her chosen profession. Nick wondered if he was still in love with her. Would he be this anxious if he didn't care any more? No, he wouldn't and of course he cared. You didn't spend seven years with someone and just stop caring overnight. Well, at least, he hadn't. He couldn't vouch for Janine, who seemed not to care much at all, really.

'So,' she said eventually, 'how's life at home?'

'Oh, terrible,' Nick replied. 'I need to get my own place soon or I'll go mad.'

'Your mother?'

Nick nodded. 'How my father hasn't hacked her into small pieces with his Strimmer by now is a mystery. He could plead extreme human suffering in defence.'

Janine let her hair fall forward and she looked at him under her eyelashes. 'Does she know you're seeing me tonight?'

'No.' Nick grimaced. 'The less my mother knows the better. Actually, she thinks I'm indulging in high jinks with a mud-wrestler from Macclesfield.'

Janine raised her eyebrows.

'It's a long story,' Nick said.

'She'll find out,' Janine observed. 'She's probably bugging you.'

'Oh yes,' Nick sighed. 'She's definitely doing that.'

Janine toyed with the sheet of cardboard that comprised the menu. 'Have you eaten?'

'I'm living at my mother's,' Nick said by way of reply.

'Of course. You'll have eaten enough for ten people.'

'Twenty,' Nick said, patting his stomach. 'But don't let it stop you.'

Janine pushed the menu away. 'I'm not hungry,' she said. She pursed her lips as she looked at him. 'I've not had much appetite recently . . .'

Oh my goodness, Nick thought. Please don't let her be here to tell me that she's pregnant! Do women go off their food when they're pregnant or do they eat more? He really had no idea. But that would be the cruellest blow, if he found out that Janine was pregnant by Mr Bone the Butcher. He felt his back break out in a cold sweat and slurped some of his beer to distract himself.

'You know,' Janine said, 'I'm glad that we can still be friends.'

'Well, otherwise it would be a waste of all our years together.' He relaxed slightly as there was no announcement yet. 'And we had some good times.' Nick smiled wearily at his wife. 'Actually, I was still having them.'

Janine flushed. 'I'm sorry it ended up like this.'

Nick shrugged and tried to look indifferent. 'It's the way of the world now.' Get fed up with your old one, move on to the new one. Mobile phones. Cars. Fridges. Partners. It's all the same. No matter that, with a spouse, you've made all sorts of solemn promises to the contrary. All it takes is a few thousand quid, a couple of pieces of paper to say that it was really all a big mistake and that you didn't actually mean it, and your conscience can be clear again.

'There are times when I miss you, Nick,' his wife said. 'Phil's not like you at all.'

'I thought that was the main attraction.'

'I think we've all been very adult about this.'

'Oh yes,' Nick said. 'Very adult.' Only adults could behave so bloody stupidly.

Janine hesitated as she slid her hand across the table towards his. Nick looked at it in amazement. Did she expect him to take it? Better to be on the safe side and hold on to his glass.

'Nick.' She sighed a little exasperated and barely audible sigh. 'Sometimes I wonder if we were too hasty?'

'We?'

She bristled slightly. 'This isn't all my fault.'

'No.'

Janine put on her head girl's face. 'People don't leave perfect marriages, Nick.'

'No,' he agreed. 'But sometimes they give the other person a chance to fix what's wrong.' And Janine hadn't given him a chance at all. She'd just announced that she'd met someone else and asked him to leave. He still really had no idea what had gone on and perhaps that's why there hadn't been any closure for him as there was a sad lack of tawdry details to pin on her. Quite how Vegetarian of the Year came to be hooked up with a butcher was anyone's guess. And that's all Nick had been able to do as his wife had remained tight-lipped – and rather self-righteous – about the exact nature of her affair.

'Is that what you wish we'd done?'

'It doesn't really matter now, does it?' he said. 'We've both moved on. You're happy with Phil. And I've got an imaginary mud-wrestler.'

Janine retracted her hand. 'You seemed to be getting on very well with Anna.'

'Yes,' Nick said enthusiastically. 'She's great. A real asset to the business.'

'Really?' Janine countered. 'I thought she had one or two more obvious assets.'

Nick feigned innocence. 'I hadn't noticed.' But he had, and Janine knew that he knew that she knew he had.

Chapter Thirty-Two

I am sitting on my sofa enjoying yet another glass of cheap Chardonnay. At least I have the excuse now that it is comfort after my stressful day, rather than drinking out of sheer boredom. On either side, I'm propped up by Poppy, Connor and a variety of stuffed toys including the manky old Doggy. We're watching re-runs of *Fame Academy* which has my daughter enthralled. Connor is dozing and is viewing through hooded eyes, which means he'll be awake half of the night again. In this house we like to get our money's worth from our television licence.

As I watch all the hopeful, fresh-faced youngsters being put through their paces on the screen, I wonder if I can channel my elder child's fondness for the performing arts into something lucrative. From the way she currently shuns academia she's not going to keep me in my old age from her earnings as a barrister. She's singing along to all the lyrics and I only wish she could remember her times tables with equal ease.

I hate to admit this, but I'm exhausted after my one day at work. It's not physical tiredness, but mental overload. This is the first time in months that I've had to spend any length of time in conversation with another adult. If Nick had wanted to chat about Girls Aloud, Beyoncé Knowles, Destiny's Child, Blue, One True Voice or how Gareth Gates is so cool that it's like unreal, then I would have been on safe ground. Any form of sophisticated adult discourse is going to take a little more practice, I think. I am, however, rather proud of myself that I am no longer a scourge on society and am now a gainfully employed member of the human race once more.

The *Fame Academy* teachers rant on. It seems as if everyone these days wants to be a star, a celebrity or at the top of some sort of tree without actually having to put in the groundwork. Whereas I, on the other hand, am really going back to basics. As one of the teenagers on screen is winding herself up to a screaming tantrum – I think this is where my daughter learns the excesses of her behaviour from too – the telephone rings. Sophie is the only person who ever rings me and I hope that she's calling to tell me that she's had time to think about her unseemly episode with Sam and that she has, indeed, come to her senses.

'Hi, Soph.'

Sophie's dulcet tones do not trill back at me.

'Hello. Hello?'

Nothing.

'Nick? Nick, is that you?' He's the only other person I can think of who might ring and I do hope he's not phoning to sack me after I have just summoned up the courage to put a tentative toe out into the big wide world again. 'Nick?'

The phone goes dead. Strange.

'Who was it?' Poppy says, still giving the television her full attention.

'No one.' I give her a puzzled shrug.

She turns to me and there is a hopeful smile on her face that tears my heart into little pieces. 'Do you think it might have been Daddy?'

'Daddy?' I want to say, 'Why on earth would it be your father?' but there is a flash of unbridled joy in Poppy's eyes that I can't for the life of me wipe away with cruel words about her errant parent.

Her face settles into a disappointed frown. 'He never phones us any more,' she complains. 'Do you think he's forgotten all about us?'

I pull my daughter to me and she reluctantly submits to a hug. 'I don't know, Poppy Poppet,' I say. 'I really don't know.'

Chapter Thirty-Three

Nick and Janine stood awkwardly by their cars under the orange glow of a streetlight at the edge of the pub car park – not least because Janine's smart BMW and Nick's battered old wreck were in sharp contrast to each other.

'Thanks,' Janine said. 'That was really nice.'

'Yeah,' Nick agreed and wondered whether it really was. He still wasn't entirely sure of the purpose of their meeting. There'd been no haggling over money, no announcements about impending pregnancy, thank goodness. Nothing more, on the surface, than a few pleasant beverages between friends. The subject of their divorce had pretty much been skirted around altogether. He looked at Janine who appeared small and vulnerable in the darkness. It seemed impossible that someone who had been his love, his life, his wife was the same person as this stranger standing in front of him. 'So what do we do now?' he asked.

'Let's see how things go.'

And what was that supposed to mean? Why did women always want men to be skilled in the art of advanced mindreading? 'I've not had that many ex-wives,' he said lightly. 'I'm not sure what the protocol is for saying goodnight.'

Janine looked coy.

'Should I give you a friendly peck on the cheek or what?'

'You could do,' his ex-wife said. 'If you liked.'

Nick leaned down and kissed her tentatively on the cheek. Despite the fact that she'd kicked his heart around until it resembled a deflated football, he still missed the smell of her and the feel of her. It was depressing sleeping alone in a single bed, thinking of his wife cuddled up in their comfortable double divan with her new man. Had their marriage really been bad enough for them to end up like this? He'd always thought that love was like a river, sometimes little more than a gentle meander, other times a raging torrent and, occasionally, during periods of drought, it could dry up and disappear entirely.

But it was always there, mapped out on the landscape. He hadn't expected Janine to try to erase it as if it hadn't existed at all.

Wasn't the point of getting married that you vowed to stick with each other through thick and thin, and that if the going got tough you didn't run into the arms of the first man who waved his prime beef in your direction? Nick liked to think that if the tables had been turned and he was the one tempted by an affair, that he'd have said no. He'd loved Janine too much to have done that to her. And he had hoped she'd felt the same about him. Perhaps it was the betrayal of that loyalty that hurt more than the actual physical act of adultery.

Janine reached up, brushed his cheek with her fingers and then kissed him tenderly on the lips.

'Does Phil know that you're here?' Nick asked.

'No,' she admitted quietly.

'Then you'd better go,' he advised. 'He'll be worried.'

Janine turned towards her car. 'I'll phone you.'

'Yeah.'

He watched as she slid into the driver's seat, gunned the engine and drove off into the night. With a heavy sigh, Nick headed for his battered old wreck. He'd never understand the workings of a woman's mind in a million years. He touched his lips where Janine had kissed him. There were faint stirrings of feelings that he was trying very hard to ignore. He wasn't sure what he'd expected from tonight, but he definitely hadn't seen that coming.

Chapter Thirty-Four

I'm in my comfiest pyjamas and I'm planning to take solace by cuddling up with a hot water bottle tonight – such is the excitement of my life. Before I can retire for the night, I'm scouring my wardrobe for something suitable to wear for my business lunch tomorrow with Nick. Ha! One day as an employee and I'm already doing super-dooper power meetings in swanky restaurants. Except that it's such a long time since I've been to a swanky restaurant that I'm all out of swanky-restaurant-type clothes. I chew at my lip. My idea of fancy dining recently has been three glasses of wine at the local pub with Sophie followed by a greasy kebab on the way home.

Bruno's clothes are still hanging in the wardrobe. Well, most of them. He packed very lightly when he chose to depart from our lives with such haste. I should throw them away or take them to a charity shop, but it's like a bereavement – I can't bring myself to clear them out and finally admit that he isn't coming back. Not that I'd want him now. There was too big a trail of devastation in his wake for me ever to go back there.

I thought I'd never stop crying when Bruno left for the first time. I felt as if all my insides had been sucked out and there was a big vacuum where the real me used to be. I considered buying a packet of cigarettes – even though I don't smoke – and stubbing them out on my arms just so that I'd feel something other than numb. Then he left again and I cried less and didn't have the urge to buy cigarettes. When he left for the third time, I was all cried out. But it didn't make the pain any less – it just proved my tear ducts were worn out from overuse. I'm sure I started a new medical phenomenon – repetitive strain injury of the waterworks. If Tumley & Goss could find my vanishing husband then I'm sure they could sue him for me.

The Buddhists have a saying that a heart is meant to be broken as that is how it learns to open up. Well, my heart has been broken often enough to have blown it wide apart. But quite frankly, my heart is very wary now. And rightly so. It has a little fence of barbed wire around it to keep trespassers out. I think it's simply had enough of people crashing in, tramping round without due care and then leaving a mess behind them. And I can't blame it.

I caress the sleeve of one of Bruno's shirts. It was my favourite, bought by me as a birthday or Christmas gift – I can't remember which now. I always loved him in that shirt. Holding the fabric to my face, I inhale his scent. Musky, manly, a faint trace of his usual aftershave and cheap Tesco's softener. Sometimes we were good together. I let the sleeve drop and feel a stab to my bruised heart. And sometimes we weren't.

I slip into bed, pulling up the duvet under my chin, still without having made that all-important what-to-wear decision. It will have to wait. I'm ready to sink into sleep.

My door crashes open and Poppy comes in struggling to carry a dazed and very sleepy Connor in her arms. 'We thought you might be lonely,' she says.

Smiling wearily, I give up my share of the duvet. Poppy and Connor climb in next to me and we all snuggle down. I wonder if there will come a time when I can conceive of sharing my bed with anyone other than two wriggling children. I catch sight of a photograph of my ex-husband grinning widely at me. I decide to turn him face-down. Tomorrow morning, first thing, I'm going to throw him in the bin and see how he likes *that*!

And with that cheering thought, I turn off the light.

Chapter Thirty-Five

It's the sort of winter morning that is clinging to its sparkly coating of frost, making my teeth chatter. And I really would stop to admire the glittering scenery if it wasn't so damn freezing. As I get out of the car outside Sophie's house, I can see my breath which is coming in ragged pants due to the battle I've already fought just to leave home before noon with two dressed and fed children.

Tom's car isn't in the drive, which means that he's already left for work. And it's pathetic, because I feel guilty about seeing him even though I'm only the hapless alibi for Sophie's marital misdemeanours. Even from the safety of the garden path, I can hear Charlotte screaming the place down in the sort of ear-piercing shriek that only one year olds have mastered to perfection. I don't know if Sophie will even hear the doorbell over the noise.

She does and pads to open it with her mobile phone in her hand which I note and she guiltily avoids my gaze. I hope she's not thinking about Sam. It would be madness – particularly with this din in the background. He'd think she was phoning from feeding-time at the zoo.

To add to the chaos, Ellie is stomping round the kitchen blowing a red plastic trumpet as if she was auditioning for the Brighouse and Rastrick Brass Band. Sophie looks as if her eardrums are about to burst and her spleen is about to vent and possibly her blood is about to boil; either way it would make a horrible mess on the kitchen floor. More bloody clearing up. Mind you, I'm a fine one to talk. I too am looking flushed and harried and am sporting Connor on my hip who is looking pale and sick.

'You're early,' Sophie says.

'Ulterior motive,' I admit, casting a glance at my son. 'He puked up in the car.'

'Give him to me,' Sophie sighs and relieves me of my wan child.

'I'll make it up to you,' I promise.

'How?'

'I don't know,' I say, 'but it will be something utterly wonderful. Just wait until I get my first pay day.' Then I screw up my face and try to give her a pleading look. 'I need another favour.'

'Go on.'

'I'm accompanying my new boss to a business meeting with an important Japanese client.'

My friend looks suitably impressed.

'So? Have you got something fabulous for me to wear to a posh lunch?'

'Of course,' Sophie says. 'My wardrobe is bulging with designer outfits. Do you prefer Armani, Versace, Burberry or maybe an interesting little number by Stella McCartney?'

We both start up the stairs towards Sophie's bedroom. 'Anything that you've bought in the last ten years will do,' I say. 'I'm desperate. Even the moths are refusing to eat my clothes.'

Sophie takes in my funeral suit. 'The first thing you must do with your pay cheque is go shopping. And I don't mean for your wretched kids.' Teasingly, my dear friend shakes Connor, who is promptly sick on her. 'Cheers.'

She then flings open her cupboard and gestures to the contents with a flourish. 'Help yourself to whatever,' she says, holding my son at arm's length. 'I'll go and give myself and this young man a scrub-down.'

'You're an angel,' I say.

'Not always,' she replies darkly as she disappears.

Hurriedly, I drag off my suit and rifle through Sophie's clothes until I find a gorgeous red suit with a slinky, slit skirt that she must have worn for some wedding or another. My friend is a little more rounded than I am and certainly possessed of bigger tits. But it doesn't look too bad and there'll certainly be room for a large lunch without the need to undo my waistband.

I'm going through her shoes trying to find something to match, when Sophie comes back into the bedroom. My son is looking all shiny and as if butter wouldn't melt in his mouth.

'You're a good boy.' I kiss him softly on his head. 'Or you would be if you'd stop throwing up for ten minutes.' A surge of panic goes through me. 'I don't know if I can leave him while he's like this.'

'Go to work,' my friend says firmly. 'It's your second day. This is the sort of crisis that working mothers have to take in their stride every day. He'll be fine. Aunty Sophie will look after him.' She pulls a funny face at Connor, who obligingly giggles. 'By the time you've had a couple of glasses of wine with your lunch you'll have forgotten that you even have a child.'

'I love you.' I give Sophie a kiss on the cheek. 'What would I do without you?'

'Go out looking like a bag lady.'

On cue, I present my new look to her.

She looks at me admiringly. 'Fab,' she says. 'I hate you, Anna Terry. I'm sure I've never looked as sexy in that suit. You'll knock Nick's eyeballs out.'

'I'm really worried about this,' I admit. 'I want it to go well.'

'Of course it will,' Sophie assures me. 'You'll have them both eating out of your hand.'

'And now I'm going to be late,' I say.

'Take these.' Sophie dives into the wardrobe, rummages around and then pushes another couple of suits into my arms. 'You might need them.' I stuff my feet into a pair of her shoes and then we both rush out, hurrying down the stairs.

'Have fun,' my friend says.

'I have big plans for this car yard,' I announce.

'And for Nick too?' My friend attempts to look coy and fails.

I lower my voice. 'And what about you?' I ask. 'I take it you haven't phoned lover boy?'

'No.' She mimics my voice.

'Good girl,' I say, kissing her and my son again. 'You know it makes sense.'

'It makes me a bloody dull housewife,' Sophie complains.

'Promise me you'll be sensible.'

'I'll be sensible,' Sophie says as I dash out of her front door. 'Killjoy.'

The cold air hits me like a slap after the cosy warmth of Sophie's house. I throw her suits into the back of the car. How I wish I were staying here to drink tea and eat biscuits and watch mindless morning television. But I know that really isn't true – it's just a momentary feeling of panic. I so want to make this job work out for me. For us all. 'Wish me luck,' I breathe nervously.

'You won't need it,' Sophie shouts after me. 'It'll be a breeze.'

Chapter Thirty-Six

Nick's mobile phone rang at six o'clock in the morning. No one rang him at six o'clock in the morning. No one. Not ever.

When he'd struggled out of bed and managed to find his phone, snuggled on Georgie Best's furry lap, he was even more surprised to discover that it was Janine at the end of the line.

'Hi,' she said. 'I didn't wake you?'

'No,' Nick said, suppressing a yawn which made his eyes water. 'Why would I be asleep at this hour?' It was barely dawn outside. Grey fingers of light teased at the curtains.

'Sorry,' his wife offered. 'I'm out running at the moment. I wanted to clear my head.'

'Oh good.' His own head was a bit fuzzy, but nothing on God's earth would persuade him out of bed at this hour to try to jog it away. He favoured the idea that a nice cup of tea and a hearty breakfast would do the same trick. Although Janine had always resorted to jogging during times of stress.

'It was good to see you last night.'

'Yes,' Nick said.

And then there was a gap that went on for far too long, filled only by the sound of Janine's puffing breath. Nick hopped about from foot to foot. His parents had always been frugal with the central heating and even though they were getting older there seemed to be no discernible change in the habit. The ancient carpet was rough beneath his feet.

'Nick,' Janine said. 'Can you meet me at Willen Lake?'

'Sure.'

'I mean now.'

'Oh,' Nick said. 'Why?'

'There are things I want to say to you,' Janine intimated. 'Things that I can't say on the phone.'

Things that, presumably, she couldn't have said in the cosy warmth of the pub last night.

'I hardly slept a wink,' she continued. 'I need to see you.'

'Okay.'

'Get here as soon as you can,' Janine urged. 'I'll be waiting in the car park.'

'Fine.' Nick wondered whether he should shower and shave or whether he should save time and go for the Neanderthal look. 'You're not going to tell me you're pregnant, are you?'

Janine sounded horrified. 'Whatever makes you think that?'

'Nothing,' he said. 'I'll be there in five minutes.'

It was more like twenty-five minutes by the time he arrived, but only because it had taken him longer to creep out of the house than he imagined. He never realised that his parents had so many creaky stairs and he was in no great rush to explain to Monica why he was sneaking out of the house into the cold, cold dawn. Then, before he could drive off, he'd had to squirt the car with a liberal application of de-icer to melt the hard frost.

Thankfully, there were very few cars on the road at this hour in the morning and the roads were all long and straight, so it didn't require much in the way of thought to get from one side of the city to the other. As he swung off the main road and down to the lakeside, Janine's BMW was the lone car parked in the bays next to the sailing club and the leisure centre. She was huddled inside and as he locked his own car, he could hear her radio blaring out. And the amazing thing was, he was starting to prefer his parents' choice of Radio 4 as a way to wake up rather than the incessant, shrill babbling of Radio 1. A sure sign he was past his prime.

As he walked towards her, shivering with cold, she got out of the warmth of her car and came towards him.

'Do you still jog every morning?' Nick said with a shudder.

'Yes,' Janine said with a smile. 'Mostly. And I still call it pleasure.'

Perhaps he and his wife hadn't been quite as compatible as he'd thought. He'd rather go line-dancing than jogging – as he'd so recently proved. However, he thought it best not to divulge this information to Janine.

'Shall we walk?' she said.

Nick thought it would be preferable to sit in a nice hot car, but instead he heard himself say, 'Yes.'

They set off towards the lake. The sky was washed out and barely blue, dotted with heavy grey clouds which reflected the grey bobbled expanse of water. A group of sturdy Canada geese wandered aimlessly across their path, looking hopefully for any crumbs of bread to tide them over the frugal winter months, and Nick felt sorry that he hadn't thought to pinch some bread out of his mother's kitchen to ease their plight.

Walking next to each other, Nick and Janine kept a suitable distance – near but not quite touching. They passed the children's playground and the ice-cream hut that was boarded up for the winter and Nick noted that they were the only people mad enough to be out strolling at this hour. Just a short time ago he would have taken his wife's chill fingers in his warm hands and rubbed them back into life or put them into his pocket alongside his own. For someone so fit, she had dreadful circulation. She'd always liked sticking her cold feet on him in bed. Despite the ungodly hour of the morning, she still looked immaculate, perfectly groomed, complete with make-up. She didn't look, as he did, as if she'd just fallen out of bed. He hadn't even combed his hair and his stubble scratched uncomfortably. If he felt like death, he probably looked even worse. They walked the gravel path that skirted the edge of the lake in silence.

'I didn't sleep a wink last night,' Janine finally said.

'You said.'

'I had a lot on my mind.'

He'd slept like the dead. But then he always did. Sleep of the just, Janine used to say. Nothing to trouble his conscience. He used to think it was a positive thing. Now he just wondered if he simply wasn't capable of appropriate emotional responses. Should the meeting with his wife last night have kept him tossing and turning until dawn too? It hadn't and maybe that did tell him something.

Janine stopped in her tracks. 'Nick,' she said crisply. 'I can't think of any other way to say this . . .'

Nick felt his heart speed up and he wasn't sure if it was with expectation or terror. He wasn't really sure that he wanted to hear what Janine was so eager to say.

'How do you feel about giving it another go?' The words tumbled out, tripping over each other. 'Giving *us* another go?'

Nick's mind went numb.

'I want to stop the divorce proceedings,' Janine rushed on. 'I think we might have made a mistake.'

We?

'I want you to come back, Nick.' There were tears in his wife's eyes and Nick was sure that it wasn't just down to the biting wind blowing across the lake. 'I want us to try again.'

Janine's eyes pleaded with him. If only he could make himself speak, but he was struck dumb. Wasn't this what he had hoped for? All those months crammed back into his old bedroom, hadn't he dreamed of his wife saying these very words? (That and 'Phil's shite in bed', of course.) Now, however, he was more confused than ever.

Chapter Thirty-Seven

The office floor is still covered with mounds of paper, but I'm sitting at Nick's desk, working my way slowly but surely through one rather large one. Most of it is stuff that could be archived away by now. It's clear that Nick doesn't regularly springclean his filing system – or that there's even a system to it.

Nick, on refreshment duty yet again, stirs the tea wistfully.

'So,' I look up from the papers. 'It sounds as if you're getting back together.'

Nick shrugs noncommittally. 'Looks like it.'

He comes over with the tea and sits down on the garden chair in front of me. His face bears a mournful look. I abandon any attempt at sorting this mass of invoices into some semblance of order.

'You could sound a bit more enthusiastic,' I suggest.

'I am.' Nick accompanies his statement with an unhappy little huff. 'It's just a bit of a shock. One minute I was married, then the next I was getting divorced. Now it appears I'm not again.'

'So she's given Mr Bone the Butcher the flick?'

Nick takes a thoughtful sip of his tea. 'Not exactly.'

'How "not exactly"?'

'She doesn't want to rush it,' Nick says. 'I'm going to stay at my mum's house for a bit longer.'

I can't help but raise my eyebrows at this.

'She needs to find the right moment to break it to him gently.'

'Did she offer you the same courtesy?'

'Another "not exactly" there, I'm afraid.'

'Mmm, I see. So you still get to sleep in your dodgy old single bed at your parents' house, while Meat Man continues to sleep with *your* wife in *your* double bed in *your* four-bedroom detached desirable residence?'

'For the time being.'

'So where's the benefit for you in this arrangement?'

Nick frowns. 'I'm not sure yet.'

I give a derisive snort. 'This sounds exactly like one of my ex's scams. Bruno managed to convince me that our relationship would be stronger if we had an "open" marriage. Which effectively meant that he had carte blanche to go out and screw around every night while I got to stay at home and look after the k . . .' I feel myself flush '. . . cat.'

Nick looks surprised. 'You've got a cat?'

'Not any more,' I say hastily in my attempt to brush over the secret parts of my life. 'It cleared off the day after my husband did. They were both the same species. Un-neutered Toms.'

We laugh together. 'It's nice having you around the office,' Nick says.

'It's nice being here.'

'I rushed to get here this morning,' he admits, a faint blush staining his cheeks. Good grief, I adore men who blush. There are far too few of them around. 'It's a long time since I've been so enthusiastic about coming into work.'

I'm not sure what the implications of this frankness are, but I did think he was looking a bit bedraggled this morning. In a rather cute way, it has to be said.

'I think we can achieve great things together,' he goes on.

'In the office?'

'Where else?' he says.

Where else, indeed.

'So . . .' He sighs again and hugs his cup against his chest. 'What shall I do?'

'I am the last person to give out relationship advice,' I say. 'I am to relationships what Sweeney Todd was to tasty meat pies. My current tally amounts to Bastards – two points, The Lovely Anna – nil points.'

'Are you sure it isn't in your job description that you're supposed to sort out your boss's personal life as well as his filing?'

'I haven't got a job description.'

'If you were to have one,' Nick says, 'I'd put that in.'

'You're on your own with this one.' I don't want to be blamed for anything that may or may not go on between Nick and his wife. Even though I feel like telling him exactly what to do. And that would involve fleas and ears and the lovely, pouting Janine not being very happy.

'I want to give Janine time to sort this out.' He gives me a rueful gaze. 'Time is one thing I've got plenty of.'

'Nick,' I say. 'Has anyone ever told you that you're far too nice for this world?'

Chapter Thirty-Eight

Sophie sat on the sofa watching more daytime television. Her life revolved round programmes featuring Dale Winton and David Dickinson, with a bit of Gloria Hunniford thrown in for good measure. Her existence had become so puny and pathetic that she was developing a crush on Richard Madeley, for heaven's sake.

Connor, Charlotte and Ellie were all curled up on the cushion next to her fast asleep. A merciful moment of respite in an otherwise relentless onslaught of babble. Mind you, it had taken an hour of pounding packet cake mix into submission and subsequently decorating the walls and resulting burned cakes with green icing sugar and silver balls. Wouldn't it have been nice if she could have just tucked a little bit of hash into a couple of them? That would have got her through the afternoon in a more mellow frame of mind. But gone were the days when she could have dallied with recreational drugs. The only drugs that she was likely to indulge in now were prescription ones for treating depression. It made her depressed just to think about it.

Some participants in an inane quiz show were being interviewed by an orange-coloured, gay host who'd had too much plastic surgery. 'And what are your hobbies?' the presenter asked one of the contestants brightly.

'And what are your hobbies, Sophie?' she echoed. 'Me?' She put on her best girly voice. 'I like nothing better than to spend my days getting unsightly stains out of my friend's children's clothing. And, of course, watching crap quiz shows.'

The quiz-show contestant on the screen held down a top City job, worked for several charities, ran marathons, baked all her own cakes and probably sewed all her own sequins on. And we all believed that. So why would she be on a downmarket daytime quiz if her life was so damn fulfilling?

Sophie looked longingly at her mobile phone. Would one little call hurt? Just one little call to brighten an otherwise endlessly dull day. A day that dragged on until lunchtime and then dragged just a bit more until it was time for the kids' tea. Was this what her life was reduced to? She'd envied Anna dashing off this morning to her fab little job and her equally fab little boss. Not least because her friend had looked an awful lot better in her red ensemble than Sophie herself did. And when did she last have the occasion to dress up in a smart suit? Not in living memory, that was for sure. Now that all of her friends were hitched, she only had the odd christening or remarriage on the horizon to look forward to.

She was sure that her brain cells were atrophying too. There were days when, if there was a lull in the decibel level, she was convinced she could hear them shrivelling up and dying, one at a time.

With a nervous nibble at her lip, she picked up her mobile phone. Her fingers lingered over Sam's number – which had already been committed to memory. Some things her brain was all too capable of remembering. As she punched in the first number, Connor whimpered next to her and then promptly threw up again.

'Come on, sweetie.' Sophie gathered him up, being careful to keep her charge at arm's length, and shuffled him through to the kitchen. 'I'm obviously destined to go through the rest of my life clearing up after helpless men.'

She sat him on the draining board next to the sink and doused some kitchen roll in warm water and wiped Connor's face. 'You're a lovely child,' she said to him. 'But you do, unfortunately, remind me of your father.'

Connor giggled in response.

'I just hope you don't inherit the worst of his excesses,' she continued. 'Or you'll give some poor woman a lot of grief.' She turned her attention to his sticky hands. 'Let's hope for your mummy's sake, poppet, that your daddy doesn't ever turn up again.'

'Daddy,' Connor echoed.

'I hope that's all you understand,' Sophie said to him. She tickled the child under the chin with a piece of the kitchen roll. 'Now, how would you like a nice Uncle Nick instead?'

Connor clapped his hands together.

'Better?'

'Sweets,' Connor said.

'Yeah. You're better.'

Sophie carried him back into the lounge and cuddled him on her lap. Within minutes he'd fallen asleep again. The quiz show had finished and there was nothing on the other channels to stop her mind from wandering. Soon her own children would be waking and needing the next round of feeding. It was now or never. Before she had a chance to think better of it, she punched in Sam's number.

Chapter Thirty-Nine

Anna had taken off the jacket of the rather smart red suit she was wearing and Nick thought that the sheer black blouse she was wearing beneath it was just the sexiest thing that had ever been seen in this office. He'd been trying to stop looking at her all morning. And this was not good behaviour for a man who might be on the verge of being married again. But it was a very sexy blouse. You'd have to be blind, not just married, not to notice it.

His Executive Assistant and whatever else her title entailed had abandoned the filing, deeming it too boring – which was a shame because it was still all over the floor – and had moved onto the computer which she was tapping at painfully slowly, one tortured key at a time. Nick couldn't help but smile. What she lacked in business acumen, she made up for in sheer determination and the fact that she was utterly delectable certainly didn't detract from her talents. She ran her tongue round her lip in concentration, peering at the screen, and it was doing appalling things to his anatomy. Nick thought it was due to the fact that he was back in his teenage bedroom that his hormones had decided to revert to type too. Perhaps Sam would take him back to FIFTY PER CENT to find a dogfaced divorcée who would be grateful to get laid. But then if he was going back to Janine, he shouldn't even be thinking like that.

It was true that he'd felt rather more enthusiastic about coming into the office this morning than he had in months – maybe years. He'd been in so much of a rush to get to work on time that he'd bolted his bacon-and-egg breakfast, earning him another admonishment from his mother. Monica believed in having the Atkins Diet and something that might be called Carbo Crazy all on one plate. The mountain of food lay heavily in his stomach.

He'd managed to get back into the house after his early morning meeting with Janine without his mother noticing – which was something approaching a miracle as she rarely missed a trick. Though, throughout breakfast she'd given him searching sideways glances. It was a good job she'd managed to hold her tongue and hadn't quizzed him about his supposed date with the mud-wrestler. She'd have got more than she'd bargained for.

Nick glanced at his watch. 'We'd better go,' he said. 'My business contact, Mr Hashimoto, is a stickler for punctuality and I need to impress him.'

Anna gave up with the computer. 'They're very particular about good manners in Japan, aren't they?' She shot him an anxious look. 'You're sure you don't mind me coming?'

'No. No,' Nick assured her. 'It'll be great.'

Getting up, Anna smoothed down her skirt and, thankfully, slipped on her jacket again. He might actually be able to focus on his business meeting if his assistant remained fully clothed. Anna pushed her way through the papers on the floor.

'Do you think we might get on with the filing reorganisation tomorrow?' Nick asked.

'Maybe,' Anna said dismissively. 'I'm prioritising. I thought my first job should be to set out the mission statement for the company.'

'Can the first thing on the mission statement be "let's put all the filing back in the cabinets"?'

Anna took his arm and steered him towards the door. 'You worry too much.'

Nick grabbed his briefcase as they passed it.

'Do you need to go for a wee-wee before we set off?' Anna said.

Nick blinked back his surprise. His assistant flushed a nice shade of beetroot. 'A wee-wee?'

'I thought it might be a long way,' Anna croaked.

'It is,' Nick said. 'We're going into London. To Nobu – Mr Hashimoto's favourite restaurant.'

Anna looked horrified. 'I knew we were doing posh, but not that posh! Are you sure I look all right?'

'You look fine to me,' he said, clearing his throat. 'More than fine.'

'Thanks.'

Out in front of the car yard, Nick's battered car stood waiting. Anna took one look at it and turned to him. 'Let's take mine,' she said. 'It's in marginally better condition.'

'We could take one of these.' Nick gestured at the rows of cars.

'We've no time to take off all the stickers now.'

'Right. But tomorrow I will get a better set of wheels, I promise.'

'You have to think of your image,' Anna advised. 'You should drive something smart.'

'You're right.' This was the new business-savvy Nick now and he kept forgetting. 'We could upgrade your car too. It's a bit of a heap. There's a nice little Corsa over there you can use instead.'

'A new car?' Anna looked as if she might have a heart-attack.

'Would you like that?'

'I'd be eternally in your debt.'

'Good,' Nick said. 'It runs well. Very reliable. We have to think about your image too. Let's sort it out tomorrow.'

'Tomorrow,' Anna repeated with a dazed nod before glancing at her watch. 'We'd better get going.'

'You know?' Nick said. 'I think I will do a wee-wee after all.'

'Good call,' Anna agreed. 'I'll go and get the heap warmed up.'

Chapter Forty

It took three rings for Sam to answer his direct line, but that was still plenty of time for Sophie's nerve to have deserted her. Despite her promises to Anna and to herself, she just had to speak to him one more time. Just once more. That was all.

'Sam Felstead.' His voice sounded clipped and formal. She could imagine him in his smart city office in his smart city suit and it was a very different vision from the one she held from her night of passion with him.

Sophie glanced at the children asleep behind her. 'It's me,' she said uncertainly.

'And which particular me would that be?' There was a soft, teasing note in his voice.

'Me from the other night,' Sophie said, twisting her hair in her fingers. 'This is a really, really bad idea.'

'No, it's not,' Sam whispered into the phone. 'It's not even lunchtime and I'm missing you already.'

'I just wanted to say thanks.'

Sam laughed. 'You're welcome. The pleasure was all mine. Well . . . not *all* mine, I believe.'

Sophie sighed. 'You're a great guy, Sam.'

'So meet me for lunch.'

'Lunch?' It was Sophie's turn to laugh. Lunch usually consisted of some abandoned fish fingers whilst balancing a child on her hip. 'I'm not the sort of woman who does lunch.'

'Maybe you should be,' he suggested.

Sophie hesitated. She would love to be the sort of woman who nibbled at baked goat's cheese, who ate rocket salad with tender asparagus tips and a sprinkling of balsamic vinegar. Instead, she had become the sort of woman who bought boxed pizzas in the bargain frozen section at the supermarket and married them perfectly with nothing more exotic than chunky potato wedges. She'd forgotten what it was like to eat food that couldn't be dipped in tomato ketchup.

'One hour,' Sam pleaded. 'That's all it will take. One tiny hour out of a whole day. It isn't a lot to ask for.'

Next to her, Charlotte stirred. He might as well have asked for the moon. 'Sam . . .'

'Live dangerously for once.'

Sophie looked up at the television. On the screen there was a washing-powder advert playing away to itself, expounding the virtues of having ultra-white towels in order to make your family love you more.

Some minor celebrity held up a packet of said powder. 'As every housewife knows, there's no greater joy in life than giving your towels the Ultra-White glow.'

There were a lot of things that Sophie could think of that would give her greater joy in life than anything involving washing powder. And one of them was currently on the end of the phone. Her stomach lurched.

'Lunch,' she nodded. 'Let's do lunch.'

Chapter Forty-One

Getting into the car, I pull the Postman Pat tape out of the cassette player and fling it into the back seat. Wee-wee? I ask you, what was I thinking of? I must not address my boss as I would my two-year-old son. Repeat this several times. Particularly as boss does not *know* about two-year-old son. I could beat my head against the steering wheel at my own stupidity. How will Nick ever trust me to run his business with him if I can't even control my own vocabulary?

I have jammed a coat hanger into my aerial socket so I can now pick up a radio signal – albeit a crackly one. It's scary to think that, even in this state, my car is better than Nick's. But soon that's to change. I'm going to have a new one! I feel like doing a happy dance. A new job, a new car – all I need now is a new man. I make my subconscious avoid looking in Nick's direction. My life is going onwards and upwards. I am one of the upwardly mobile career go-getters, not a downtrodden single parent! Hurrah!

Flicking the dial to Radio Two, I listen to the traffic reports. Nick gets into the car and we don't mention the wee-wee thing and I don't ask him if he's been and whether he did number ones or number twos or tell him off for not washing his hands. Nor do I warn him that I won't stop for him to go again en route or issue instructions about wearing his seat belt, but instead we set off towards London in companionable silence. The M1 motorway is jammed as normal so we decide to take the more leisurely route down the A5 through Dunstable and head out that way.

The icy morning has given way to a bright, sunny day and through the windows of the car, the sun feels warm and comforting on my skin. I hate the long stretch of winter and would love to emigrate to warmer climes if I didn't have two children to consider.

Nick settles back into the passenger seat, his eyes heavy, and already I'm so comfortable with this man. He's so nice that it's very hard not to like him. You'd have to have a very cold heart to be able to

116

hurt him – like Janine, of course. Even though I've only known him for a few days, I know that it is absolutely the wrong thing for him to go back to her. He would be much better off with someone who would nurture him – like me, for example.

'You're a very good driver,' Nick says.

'Thanks.' Here's hoping that he feels the same when we hit the London traffic. It's so long since I've driven into London that my confidence is a bit wobbly. When I was younger, I wouldn't have thought twice about this. Why is it that the older we get, the more nervous we become? Is it simply that we're fully aware of the pitfalls that lie ahead of us rather than blustering through life with the exuberance of youth? Oh, and I must remember to keep all words beginning with 'f' out of my exhortations to other road-users.

Still, for now, we are travelling sedately through country lanes. All the fields are ploughed, brown and waiting for their spring colour. Nick and I exchange what can only be classed as a shy glance.

'This is nice,' he says. 'Is "chauffeur" on your job description too?'

'I guess so.' I give him a smile. 'Ooo! Look! Tractor!' Before I can stop myself, I point into one of the fields we are passing.

Nick gives me a long sideways glance and I can feel myself colour up.

'Yes,' he says thoughtfully. 'A big red one.'

'I like tractors,' I say tightly.

I can't read the expression on Nick's face, but there's definitely some amusement in there. 'Me too,' he agrees.

I concentrate on the road and try not to notice that Nick is looking at my legs as I drive. And as soon as we get to this restaurant I'm going to cut out my own tongue.

Chapter Forty-Two

Sophie knocked more loudly at the door, just in case Tom's mum was hiding. In the buggy Charlotte and Connor were screaming even more loudly while Ellie stood listlessly rubbing the toe of her clean shoe into the muddy borders of the garden created by a particularly wet winter.

Sophie jiggled the pushchair maniacally. Feeling her desperation rising, she bent down and shouted through the letter box. 'Margaret, are you in? It's Sophie!'

The front door of the adjoining terraced house opened and Mrs Fox, Tom's mum's neighbour, came out in her hat and coat. 'Hello, love.'

'Hi, Mrs Fox.' She noticed that the woman took in her smart appearance. 'Do you know where Margaret is?'

'Oh.' The neighbour rubbed her chin. 'I think she went out shopping. Not that long ago. You've only just missed her.'

That was not what she needed to hear. 'Damn.'

'Are you going somewhere nice, love?' Sophie was done up to the nines in full war-paint, freshly spruced hair and best coat, whereas normally she'd be round at Margaret's in her scruffy old jeans and jumper. Only the harassed look was the same.

'I was,' Sophie huffed. 'I'm supposed to be meeting a friend for lunch.'

'Oh dear.'

Sophie brightened. 'You couldn't keep your eye on this lot until she comes back?'

Mrs Fox looked suitably horrified – even though the screams had now died down to the odd snivel or two.

'Oh no. Oh no.' The neighbour backed away in fear. 'I'm just off out myself.'

'Thanks,' Sophie said miserably as Mrs Fox scuttled away as fast as her little legs could carry her. 'Thanks a bunch.'

Glancing down at her watch, Sophie's heart sank. Sam would be sitting waiting for her now. She could see the baked goat's cheese and rocket salad beckoning. 'Now what do I do?'

'McDonald's,' Ellie shouted, clapping her hands together excitedly.

Sophie sighed heavily. 'That wasn't quite the plan, sweetheart.'

Chapter Forty-Three

Nobu is just so sophisticated that I could bite off my own legs. I have never been anywhere quite like this before. I can't even describe what the décor is like because I'm so overwhelmed that all my senses have gone numb. But it's all classy – so terribly, terribly classy. Steel, chrome, frosted glass. My heels clonk on the wood floor. That's the best I can manage.

The place zings with animated chatter and we give our name to the host and head to the bar. Needless to say, all the stools are occupied by beautiful people wearing beautiful clothes who are laughing gaily at the tinkling conversation of their unutterably beautiful companions. I am the only person in the entire place wearing a red suit. Everyone else, it seems, favours black as their colour scheme and I feel like a Christmas tree decoration. I'm the only one who doesn't fit seamlessly into their surroundings.

The nearest I have ever come to a venue like this is reading about it in *OK!* magazine or seeing pictures of David and Victoria Beckham emerging from it in *Hello!* These people look like they pop in here for lunch every day of the week and I realise that, on the whole, my life has been very small and very dull. I am a stranger to designer clothes, wasabi and crème fraiche. I can feel myself vibrating with terror and excitement in equal amounts. Nick looks completely unfazed. He is scanning the bar, looking for Mr Hashimoto.

'Good,' Nick says, rubbing his hands together. 'We're here before him. We can have a drink and relax.'

Relax! Is he mad? 'I'm driving,' I say. 'Just a mineral water for me.' The further I stay away from strong drink, the better. I remember what happened last time.

Nick orders a ginger martini – speciality of the house.

'Try just a sip.' He offers his glass to me. Our fingers touch around the stem and Nick blushes slightly. The drink is delicious and I'm glad I'm abstaining from alcohol otherwise I suspect I could have knocked half a dozen of these back in a row. I notice that he doesn't wipe my lipstick mark from his glass.

We find a seat while we wait and Nick says, 'I want this to go perfectly. Mr Hashimoto is looking to set up a dealership. He wants the land that I own and I want his money *and* a partnership.' He looks at me with earnest eyes. 'This is very important to me.'

I smile through my nerves. 'So no pressure then?'

Nick laughs. 'Just be yourself,' he says. 'You'll be wonderful.'

And now is the time to put that to the test as Mr Hashimoto arrives, all bows and smiles. My knees wobble alarmingly as we stand up to greet him.

We're sitting at our table – a prime spot by the window overlooking the spiky winter trees along Park Lane – and Mr Hashimoto is a charming and convivial companion, but the atmosphere is a little stilted. The menu is terrifying and, not surprising for a Japanese restaurant, everything is Japanese. And because everyone who comes here obviously knows all there is to know about Japanese food there are no helpful little explanations to aid the terminally ignorant like myself. I don't know what the difference is between tempura or sushi or sashimi – but I expect at least one of them is raw. Nor do I have a clue what kushiyaki or nasu miso might involve. It's as incomprehensible as the winscrollrop.e.42 messages that the office computer keeps sending me before the screen and my mind both go blank. I scan the menu again looking for something – *anything* – vaguely familiar. I do know what teriyaki sauce is, but only because Uncle Ben does a jar of it and I still haven't tried it. Bruno was never into oriental food and any leanings I might have had to develop a palate for exotic food have been knocked out of me by my children's distinctly unadventurous diet.

I must be staring blankly as Mr Hashimoto leans over and says to me, 'Can I help you with your choice?'

'Yes, please.' My voice is barely audible. 'I've never eaten Japanese food before.'

'Never?' Mr Hashimoto laughs. 'Then this is a very good place to start. You like fish?'

'Oh yes.' Captain Birdseye does a wonderful cod in breadcrumbs. Knock it together with some Tesco Oven Chips and you can't go wrong. Good grief, I'm such a pleb. I must start buying the BBC *Good Food* guide.

'I recommend the black cod,' our important business guest says.

'It is their signature dish. Sublime.' Mr Hashimoto puts his fingers together and kisses them to show me just how sublime it is.

And because I recognise the word 'cod' I agree to try it. Nick smiles reassuringly at me. He's so laid back even though I feel I'm making a complete arse of myself. Does nothing ever rattle this guy? He reels off his own order like a man who's been here several times before – and maybe he has. Like everyone, he probably has little secrets. I didn't have him down as an urbane man about town, but you never know.

Nick and Mr Hashimoto chat about the car business while I sit there and try to look intelligent and like I have a clue what they're talking about. How can I get back into the habit of polite chit-chat? Did I ever *have* the habit? Gossip with Sophie is not quite the same thing. I have been living my life in a childcare cocoon with relatively little adult interaction and I hadn't realised that in my attempts to provide a good home for my kids, all my grown-up neuro-transmitters and stuff have become rusted up. This is all a bit too much for me after one day back in the big bad world of commerce. I look around surreptitiously and wonder if anyone else here is suffering a crisis of confidence. No one else looks as if they are, but you can never tell from outward appearances, can you?

The room is filled mainly with people who look like business associates rather than couples. I wonder how many are here because they're fighting for their jobs or are here because of an illicit office union. I wonder how many of them are as carefree as they seem. There's a portly, balding man who must be pushing sixty with a girl who looks barely nineteen over in the corner. She's fawning all over him, running her hand up his thigh – I'd say they were definitely business associates. She is the type that charges by the hour.

There are a couple of minor celebrities too. The sort of actors you see in *Holby City* and *Casualty*. I've never been in the same room as a celebrity before – not even a minor one. Except, of course, when they're on the telly and I'm sat watching it. It's true that they never look as impressive in real life, but if I'm not careful I could still find myself staring. Wait until I tell Poppy that her old mum has been hobnobbing it with soap stars. Still, knowing my darling daughter, she'll be deeply unimpressed by anything I do.

My thoughts travel to Connor and I wonder if he's okay with Sophie. I've barely had time to think about him all morning. What sort of mother am I, that I can swan off to lunch while my child is ill? A working mother, I guess. And the sooner I get used to it, the better. No more sports days, no more carol concerts, no more school plays, no more poetry recitals with lisping children spouting on for three hours about trees – hey, there is a God after all! I get a pang of guilt. Perhaps I should nip to the loo and check my text messages.

But just as I'm summoning up courage to excuse myself from the table, our food arrives and my black cod does indeed look wonderful. Mr Hashimoto has some sort of steak of exquisite proportions arranged artistically on his plate. Nick has something involving huge prawns. The waiters depart and with polite smiles we all pick up our cutlery. I'm starting to relax now, but I would still die for another sip of Nick's martini. However, I am a professional businesswoman now and must remain sober and righteous and upright at all times.

'So, Anna.' Mr Hashimoto smiles at me. 'Tell me, how long have you been working with Nick?'

'Well . . .' I say. The noise level in here is rising and I lean forward to hear him better. 'It's a relatively new development . . .'

A horrified look spreads over Mr Hashimoto's face and his eyes travel to his plate.

I continue, only slightly abashed, 'All part of the plans for expansion . . .'

I glance at my new boss for reassurance, but Nick too is frozen with horror. I follow his gaze and my throat closes up immediately.

Without realising what I was doing, I have started to cut up Mr Hashimoto's steak for him. Slicing it into little bite-sized pieces, just like I would for Connor. My knife grinds to a halt mid-cut.

'Oh my word,' I breathe. 'I'm sorry.' I look to Mr Hashimoto, then to Nick, then back to Mr Hashimoto. 'I'm so very, very sorry.'

I try to shuffle the steak back into one piece. My two male companions are too stunned to move. They sit like statues, staring at the chopped-up steak. This is probably the social equivalent of baring your arse to a priest.

I can feel my eyes welling up with tears. 'This is considered a very great honour where I come from,' I say weakly and put my knife back onto my own plate.

Mr Hashimoto shakes himself out of his reverie and regains his composure. 'Oh?' He tries to form his face into a mask of politeness. 'And where is that?'

'Milton Keynes,' I say.

I turn my agonised face to Nick, hoping for some kind of support, but he is still sitting there, in a catatonic state, with his eyes and his mouth wide open.

Chapter Forty-Four

Through the window, Sophie could see Sam sitting alone at a table, sipping a large gin and tonic, talking on his hands-free mobile and browsing through the menu. Before her courage deserted her, she crashed through the door, bringing a hiatus to the relaxed atmosphere, a full stop to the tinkling jazz piano. Sam looked up – as did all the other diners in the restaurant.

Sophie caught sight of herself in the mirror. The immaculately groomed hair had gone for a burton in her frenzied dash down the street. The look of calm sophistication had, once again, failed to displace her normally harried frown.

Sam stood up. His eyes were the size of saucers. 'Sophie,' he said.

Sophie looked down at the pushchair. Charlotte and Connor were fighting over a stuffed yellow duck. She pulled her whining daughter forward and Ellie clung to her legs, completing the presentation of her miniature entourage. It was way past their normal lunchtime and they were all getting fractious – Sophie included.

Sam's mouth fell open.

'This is the reality of my life, Sam,' she said bleakly.

'Well.' He rubbed a hand through his hair, making it even more heartbreakingly dishevelled. 'We'd better get a bigger table then.'

The slightly perturbed waiter moved them to a large table in the corner, well away from the main crush of diners. This was not a restaurant used to entertaining children, that was clear. It was an upmarket Italian place that normally catered for businessmen and the well-heeled and everyone else who existed beyond her budget.

Heads turned as they were ushered to their new seating. But Sophie was glad to be pushed out of the way – she had no desire to be sitting on full view in the window with Sam. Tom's mum was in the city – what if she'd walked past? That would have taken some explaining and she'd already used up one of her nine 'explaining' lives.

The two babies were fastened into highchairs and they'd managed to find a booster cushion from somewhere for Ellie. Sophie was fussing to get them settled in their seats, meaning that she could avoid looking at Sam. When she finally finished her mother hen routine and looked up, her lunch companion was grinning at her.

'I'm glad you came,' he said.

'How can you be?' she whispered, surreptitiously gesturing at the children with her head.

'As you said "this is your life".' Sam looked sanguine. 'If I want to be involved in it I have to accept your commitments, your children too.'

'I would like to point out that these aren't all mine,' Sophie said. 'One of them I only borrow on a daily basis.' And then she bit her tongue as she remembered that his friend Nick had no idea that Anna herself was the mother of two rather robust offspring. 'And you can't become "involved" in my life. This is a one-off, Sam. It has to be.'

'You said that before.'

'And I meant every word of it.'

Sam ignored her imploring look and put on a particularly guileless expression.

'At the time,' she added with a lame smile.

'Shall we order?' Sam said.

'This lot will eat anything as long as it involves pizza,' Sophie remarked as she scanned the complicated menu of grown-up food. No Happy Meals or free toys in here.

'The baked goat's cheese is very good,' Sam said as he ordered for them all.

Even with the baked goat's cheese of her dreams on offer this still wasn't the type of lunch she'd envisaged. Quiet romantic lunches with her illicit lover weren't even on the cards for her. Illicit lover? Is that what Sam was? Certainly the pornographic video that kept replaying in her head was fairly convinced that he was. It was true to say that she'd never been touched as Sam touched her – not in a long, long time. Her insides lurched just thinking about him. Her sex-life with Tom could, at best, be described as desultory. It was not an adjective she could apply to Sam. She looked across the table at him. He was a skilled and surprisingly sensitive lover, and her skin shivered just to think about it. To the casual observer they probably looked like a happy family unit enjoying lunch together. If only they knew. She sighed quietly. Sam's foot found hers under the table. It offered pathetic comfort, but at least it was comfort. Her face softened. Even with three little pairs of eyes and ears monitoring their every movement, it felt so good to see him again, to know that their one night together wasn't just meaningless sex to him. He wanted to see her. He wanted to be with her. Even with three kids in tow.

'Why are we doing this?'

'Because we are two irresistible forces drawn together,' Sam suggested. 'Something like that.'

'It's wrong,' Sophie murmured.

'What?' Sam spread his hands. 'We're having a convivial lunch surrounded by kids. What's wrong with that?'

'Because it's not the kids I'm thinking about,' Sophie admitted.

'Me neither,' Sam agreed and his hand found hers, hidden from sight by the voluminous white tablecloth. It was warm and gentle. He lowered his voice. 'Are we ever going to get to spend time alone together?'

'No,' Sophie said.

'If we really want this to happen,' Sam said as he squeezed her fingers, 'we'll find a way.'

'We won't,' she insisted.

'There'll be highs,' he said as if she hadn't spoken. 'And there'll be lows.'

'There won't, Sam.' Sophie fixed him with an earnest look. 'There won't be anything. There can't be.'

'So what are you doing here?'

Sophie smiled reluctantly. 'Indulging in some temporary insanity.'

'Sounds good to me,' Sam said.

And it sounded very dangerous to Sophie.

Chapter Forty-Five

We're standing outside Nobu, bidding fond farewells to Mr Hashimoto who seems to be sufficiently recovered from his ordeal by inappropriate mothering. We watch our guest get into a taxi and wave his goodbye. It's late in the afternoon and the traffic is already starting to build up for the long, slow journey homewards. The light is fading, bringing on the winter night and the temperature is plummeting fast. The pretty white fairy-lights are sparkling on the trees outside the Dorchester Hotel, bringing a year-round festive touch to the sophistication of Park Lane.

Nick and I turn away into the side street where the car is parked and walk back to it in silence. My boss waits with his hands stuffed in his pockets while I unlock it and we slide inside. He has a grim look on his face. I sit in the driver's seat and grip the steering wheel, staring straight ahead.

'So,' Nick says. 'How many children do you have?'

'Two,' I confess.

We sit in silence for a few minutes longer while I contemplate the mess I have made of Nick's important business lunch. 'I should have told you,' I say. 'I know I should.' I hang my head. This is very hard for me to admit. 'But I wanted to pretend I was something I'm not.'

Nick massages his temples. 'Which is?'

'I wanted you to think I was a sexy, single woman with no commitments.'

'Two out of three isn't bad.'

I sigh miserably. 'I was frightened that if you knew I was really a hopeless divorcée with two kids in tow that you wouldn't give me the job.'

'You told me you weren't a secretary,' Nick reminds me, 'but I still gave you the job.'

'That's because you're too nice,' I say.

'No.' Nick turns in his seat to look at me. 'It's because I had an ulterior motive.'

Now it's my turn to be puzzled.

'That skirt you came in was ridiculously short. I quite liked the idea of having it around the office. Especially with you in it.'

'So you're just a randy old lech after all?'

Nick grins. 'I've been called worse. I just can't remember when.'

I put my hand on Nick's arm. 'I can't believe I behaved like such an idiot this afternoon. Not when it was so important to you.'

'Of course, Mr Hashimoto now assumes that I'm sleeping with you.'

'I'm so humiliated.' I bury my head in my hands. 'What must he think of me?'

'I don't know,' Nick says, 'but he told me that I have rather good taste.' My boss starts to laugh and I can't help but join in even though I still feel like a prize plonker.

'Did I really cut up his meat for him?'

'Yes,' Nick says, 'you did.'

And we're both gripped by a fit of the giggles. Nick shakes with mirth and tears stream down my face. I can't remember laughing like this in a long time. A couple passing by the car window look in and smile at us.

When I get myself under control, I say, 'I'm sorry, Nick. I'm really, really sorry.'

'If it's any consolation, Mr Hashimoto thought you were charming,' he says. 'Completely scatty, but utterly charming.'

'And what do you think?' I nibble nervously on my lip. If I was Nick, I'd probably fire me.

'I'd have to agree with him.'

'I'll settle for that.' I sound shaky. 'You're not going to give me the sack?'

'No,' Nick says. 'You're far too entertaining to have around. Besides, it's a sound business proposal and Mr Hashimoto is an astute man. I hope the deal will still go ahead.'

I breathe a sigh of relief. 'I hope so too.'

I want to kiss him or do something to show my appreciation. Instead we both sit there for a moment doing nothing, then we exchange a shy smile and I start the car engine and ease my way out into the weight of London evening traffic.

Nick settles back in the passenger seat. 'So,' he asks. 'When do I get to meet these kids of yours?'

Chapter Forty-Six

Two long and traffic-filled hours later, I pull up outside Sophie's house. Nick is still sitting beside me. It's pitch black already and I can't wait for the end of these long winter nights.

'Are you sure you want to do this?' I ask.

'Of course.'

We get out of the car and walk to Sophie's door. I'm sure the air between us is getting more crackly all the time and I find it quite disconcerting. I wonder if Nick has even noticed. He looks down at the space between our arms and I think perhaps he has.

I knock at the door and wait until Sophie answers, Charlotte balanced on her hip. Her eyebrows rise in surprise.

'You remember Nick,' I say.

'Barely,' Sophie admits dryly. 'Although I have heard a lot about you since.'

Thanks, Sophie. 'Well,' I say as we go inside, 'Nick's heard a bit more about me too. He's here to meet the kids.'

'Mad fool,' Sophie tells him brightly.

We all go inside. Whatever Sophie has been doing today doesn't involve housework. We pick our way past an expectant basket full of ironing and through a minefield of abandoned toys until in the lounge we find a row of children sitting mesmerised on the sofa as they watch cartoons on the television.

'These two are mine,' I say as Connor launches himself off the sofa and cannons into my legs. Despite it being the middle of winter, my child is clad only in his vest. I'm sure he has naturist leanings as he strips off at the drop of a hat or perhaps Sophie is just fed up with him throwing up on his clothes. 'Say hello to Nick.'

'Hi,' Poppy says, sucking her hair. She is too cool to care who this man is with her mother.

'This is my boss,' I explain.

'Oh.' No. Still can't impress that one.

'Hi,' Nick says shyly.

'Hello!' Connor shouts at the top of his voice.

'Hi.' Nick bends down to Connor's level and is duly rewarded for his trouble.

'Doggy!' Connor exclaims and hands Nick his filthy, ragged excuse of an animal. To his credit Nick does not recoil in horror as he rightly should. To be handed Doggy is to be handed the equivalent of a drool-soaked tennis ball that has enjoyed a lengthy stay in a friendly Labrador's mouth.

Ellie sidles off the sofa and leans against my leg, sucking her thumb. 'We had our lunch with Uncle Sam today.'

Nick stops doing doggy-type things with Doggy. I look at Sophie, pointedly, over the children's head. What is it they say about out of the mouths of babes? 'Uncle Sam?'

While Sophie cringes, Nick mouths to me, *'My Sam?'*

'Did you, sweetheart?' I say to Ellie.

'He's nice. He puts chips up his nose,' she tells us.

Resignedly, Nick nods in confirmation. *'My Sam.'*

'I think Mummy and I should just have a little talk.' I signal to Sophie that she should dump Charlotte and join me for a private tête-à-tête in the kitchen. 'Will you excuse us for a minute, please, Nick?'

For a moment, he looks panic-stricken.

'Are you all right holding the fort?'

'Fine,' Nick says rather tremulously. 'I'll be fine.'

'Poppy – help Nick to look after the babies,' I instruct.

'Yeah,' my daughter replies in a voice that sounds far too like Vicky the Bonking Babysitter for my liking.

I hustle Sophie out into the kitchen and I hear Connor cry, but I don't care. Nick will have to cope. I close the kitchen door.

Chapter Forty-Seven

I face Sophie, leaning my back against the door to stop any unwanted interruptions by marauding children. I can't help it, I'm furious with Sophie and I can feel my face reddening.

Before I utter a word, Sophie heads me off at the pass. 'It was lunch,' she says. 'Nothing more.'

'Where did you go?'

'Some swishy little Italian bistro in the city.' Sophie folds her arms defiantly. 'For once in my small, tedious life, it wasn't McDonald's. So I didn't get to rip his clothes off in the ball pit.'

'It did cross your mind though?'

'Of course it did,' Sophie snaps. 'But any rolling around in the hay that I might have fantasised about was severely curtailed by having three kids in tow. One of which was yours.'

'You took the children to meet him?'

'What choice did I have?'

'You could have chosen not to go at all.'

Sophie turns away from me and picks up the basket piled high with ironing. She slams it on the table and pulls out the ironing board, screeching it across the floor. The iron gets similar treatment – it's banged onto the ironing board and the plug goes into the wall so forcibly that I'm surprised the plaster doesn't crack.

I try to soften my voice. 'Why are you doing this, Sophie?'

She yanks a tiny dress out of the pile and starts attacking it. 'Because I'm bored, Anna. Bored shitless.' The dress gets thrown to one side and she yanks out one of her husband's shirts. 'I'm bored with Tom. I'm bored with the kids. I'm bored with me.' She continues to bang the iron up and down. At this rate it'll be in pieces before she gets to the bottom of the basket. 'And someone has come along who thinks I'm funny and sexy and doesn't see me as just another useful domestic appliance.'

'That's all very well for you,' I say, 'but you have no idea what it feels like to be on the other side of this.'

Sophie hangs her head, but continues crashing the iron backwards and forwards. 'No,' she says quietly.

'That's because Tom, however boring he is and however unappreciative, isn't an adulterer.' My voice is tight. 'He might not be demonstrative. He might not make the bedsprings bounce any more, but at least you know where he is every night.'

Sophie won't look up at me.

'He's loyal,' I say. 'And he's here.' My throat tightens further. 'And he's never ever laid a finger on you.'

Sophie bangs down the iron. She's breathing heavily and I can't read the swirl of emotions crossing her features. 'And suppose that isn't enough any more?'

'It has to be,' I say.

'So I'm supposed to be grateful that we have a joint bank account and he doesn't use me as a punch bag?'

I feel myself wince at her words. And, for a moment, Sophie looks remorseful.

'You don't know Sam,' I press on. 'He probably has a different woman every night.'

Sophie sets her jaw again and gives me a steely stare. 'He isn't like that.'

'You don't know that for sure,' I say. 'One night of lust isn't worth ruining lives for. Stop it now while you still can. Before you're in over your head.'

Sophie leans on the ironing board. All the fight has gone out of her and she lifts tearful eyes to mine. 'I think it may already be too late for that.'

But the sound of Connor emitting an ear-splitting scream stops me from finding out any more as both Sophie and I rush back into the lounge.

Nick is holding Connor at arm's length. He turns towards us to show that my dear little bare-bottomed son has weed all down the front of his nice suit. My boss gives me a weak smile. 'Is this considered a great honour where you come from too?'

Sophie and I burst out laughing and I rush to Nick's aid, scooping my terrible terror of a tiddling son from his arms.

132

Chapter Forty-Eight

Nick and Anna stood by her car door outside the yard. Poppy and Connor were safely belted up in the back of the car while the dulcet tones of Postman Pat belted out from the cassette player. Anna chewed at her fingernail.

'I'm worried about her,' she confessed. 'Is Sam reliable?'

'About as reliable as the cars in this yard.' Nick waved expansively at the rows of old jalopies.

'That bad?' Anna said with a tut. 'What can we do?'

'I'll have a word with Sam,' Nick promised.

'Can you talk some sense into him?'

'I've never managed it before,' Nick admitted.

'Same with Sophie. Everything I say goes in one ear and straight out of the other without pausing at the grey matter in between.' Anna sighed. 'I can hardly blame her though. She's given me plenty of advice over the years that I've ignored at my peril.'

'It's always easier to give advice than to take it,' Nick said comfortingly. 'Don't be too hard on yourself. At least you're trying to protect her.'

'Yeah.' Anna fiddled with her hair.

It was late and the night was cold and black. More than likely it would be frosty overnight which meant scraping all of the car windscreens in the morning. Nick felt cold just thinking about it.

'I'd better get back,' Anna said, seeming reluctant to go. 'I've got fish fingers to incinerate.'

'More fish?'

Anna laughed. 'Thanks for today. I hope I didn't F.U.C.K. up completely.' She mouthed the spelling of the swearword, casting a guilty glance at her daughter as she did so.

'I'm sure it will be fine.' Nick hoped to goodness that it would be. After the initial shock, Mr Hashimoto had seemed to take the fact that Anna was keen to interfere with his food in good spirit.

And he supposed it could have been a lot worse. He looked down at the dark stain on his suit.

'I'm sorry about the suit too,' she said.

'That's okay,' Nick said. 'I'm sure the dry cleaners have had to deal with worse.'

'I'll pay for it,' Anna insisted. 'Just give me the bill. It's the least I can do.'

'Don't worry,' Nick said. He pulled out an envelope from the inside of his jacket-pocket. 'I haven't done the paperwork and stuff yet,' he admitted. 'But as it's the end of the week, here's your pay for the last couple of days.'

Anna took the envelope gratefully. 'Oh Nick,' she said. 'You don't know what this means to me.'

'That you can pay for the dry cleaning of other men your children wee on?'

'It's my first step back on the ladder of independence.'

'I think you'll find independence is a treadmill rather than a ladder.'

'This is a very symbolic moment for me.' Her cheeks flushed.

'Then I'm glad to be sharing it with you.'

'I do appreciate you taking me on,' she said. 'And not being too mad when I embarrass you in front of important clients . . .' She stopped in her tracks. 'Why am I always grovelling to you, Nick Diamond?'

'No idea,' Nick said. 'But I quite like it. If you want to do a penance, then just make sure that all my filing goes back into those things they call filing cabinets. All neat and orderly.'

'Of course I will. First thing on Monday,' she promised.

'And your kids are great,' Nick said. 'Not fully house-trained, but great nevertheless.'

'They are good kids.' Anna cast a tender backwards glance at them, obviously full of pride for her offspring. 'They have to put up with a lot.' She looked suddenly vulnerable. 'With them not having a dad around . . . and all that.'

'He must be mad,' Nick observed. 'If they were my kids I wouldn't be able to stay away from them.'

'Well, their father doesn't seem to have the same attachment.'

'Why don't we go out for the day with them?' Nick suggested before he could think better of it. 'We could go tomorrow. To London or the seaside or somewhere.'

'What about the car yard?'

'I'll close for the day,' he said. 'It's one of the few perks of being the boss. Business is dead. No one will miss me for a few hours.' He could tell he was babbling. 'If you're not busy . . .' he tailed off. Of course she'd be busy.

'No,' Anna said. 'Hugh Grant was going to pop in for lunch, but he's tied up in rehearsals for his new movie. I guess I'm free after all.'

'Right,' Nick said. 'Fine. Any preference as to where we go?'

Anna shook her head. 'It's a long time since my kids went anywhere outside of Milton Keynes. Anything beyond the end of our road will be an adventure.'

'Good,' Nick said. 'I think we'll go back down to London. What about the Tower?'

'Sounds good to me.'

'I'll organise something.'

'Nick,' Anna sighed. 'You really are too good to be true.'

'I'm not,' Nick corrected. 'I was supposed to be having lunch with Nicole Kidman, but she's busy too.'

'Amazing that,' Anna observed.

'So you see I'm only offering to take you all out because I'm suddenly at a loose end and I just hate it when that happens.'

'Mmm. A day out with a couple of bratty kids or lunch with Nicole,' Anna mused. 'I can see how that would be an adequate substitute.'

'It was only going to be sandwiches at the car yard with Nicole,' Nick offered. 'Nothing fancy.'

'Then we'd love to spend the day with you.' Anna still looked uncertain. 'This won't cause problems with Janine?'

'Why should it?' he asked. 'We're two friends – and business colleagues – having a day out together. With your children. I'm hardly going to try to ravish you in front of the Crown Jewels.'

Although now that he came to think of it, that was a rather nice idea. What was he thinking of? It must be the surfeit of ginger martinis affecting his brain. It was going to be a fun day out with Anna and her kids. No strings. No romantic overtures. No hearts and flowers. No holding hands. Nothing like that.

'It'll be fun,' Nick said with conviction. 'We can talk about business in the car if it will make you feel better.'

Anna kissed him on the cheek. 'You are a very nice man.'

'I'll see you tomorrow then,' Nick said. 'Meet me here at ten o'clock.'

He might be a very nice man, but there was no way he wanted his mother seeing him set off for the day with Anna and her kids. Particularly if he was going to break it to her that a reunion between him and Janine might be on the cards. Monica would read far too much into it and, as it was, he wasn't sure how much he should read into it himself.

Chapter Forty-Nine

The day starts out in a shroud of thick fog. It hangs heavy in the dips of the road as, all crammed in Nick's car, we wend our way to London. The low-slung sun is a bright, white perfect sphere, like a 100-watt light bulb. To entertain herself, Poppy breathes against the cold windows and draws hearts with her fingertip in the patch of steam. Connor, bless, sleeps blissfully through the start of our adventure.

Nick and I sit shyly in the front seats, listening to happy, high-pitched Gareth Gates warble on the CD player — Poppy's choice. But as we whiz up the M1 and into Central London, the fog lifts, revealing a perfect blue sky. And I know that this is going to be a wonderful day.

We park up and jump on the Tube — another first for my children. Poppy is trying to be cool, but is shaking with excitement. It makes me realise how much they have missed out on over the last few years. I know that money can't buy you happiness, but it can buy you nice days out with your kids, which helps.

The majestic fortress of the Tower of London looms into view as we emerge blinking from the depths of Tower Hill Underground station. I was eleven when I last visited here — on a day trip with school — and that's longer ago than I care to remember. It doesn't seem to have changed much as far as I can tell, but then it has been standing here largely unaltered since William the Conquer knocked it together nearly one thousand years ago.

'Does the Queen really live here?' Poppy's voice is filled with awe.

'No,' I say. 'She's moved to somewhere that isn't as draughty.'

'I'd live here, if I was the Queen,' my daughter tells me. 'And I'd give all my money away to the poor people.'

Like us, I think.

Nick has already been pressed into service, pushing Connor in his buggy and I must say that he looks quite at home in that role.

I wonder if people watching assume that we're a family, and it gives me a warm glow to think so. It's so nice not to be struggling with the kids alone. Dirty Doggy has had to come along too and I've stressed the importance of his presence to Nick, who took the emotional responsibility for my son's stuffed toy in his stride.

Our first stop is to join a guided tour given by a Beefeater – an elderly gentleman in smart navy frockcoat and top hat, who launches into a vivid description of all the beheadings and torture that have taken place in the Tower over the years. Poppy is transfixed and, seizing on her rapture, the Beefeater coerces her into service – mimicking a particularly brutal beheading on my daughter's delicate neck (five chops of the axe) and all because the lady had fallen in love with the wrong man. How I can empathise with her! And there are times when I think I should have had my head lopped off to stop me doing the same stupid things over and over again.

Nick, Connor hoisted up onto his shoulders, is smiling benignly at my child on centre stage. I wonder will this man break my run of bad luck? Will the saying 'third time lucky' be true for me? I can hardly dare to think it, as life has left me feeling bruised in more ways than one. Our arms are close together, touching, and I want to put my hand in his, but I don't – and not just because I'm worried that he'll drop Connor. And then I have to remind myself that he's going back to his wife. That he isn't free. And that all these fanciful feelings are utterly, utterly pointless. That Happy Ever After is an illusion. I try not to dwell on the fact that Janine is a spoiled cow who doesn't deserve a lovely husband like Nick.

The Beefeater pretends to hold Poppy up by her pony tail, proffering her severed head to the appreciative crowd. The tourists cheer enthusiastically and Poppy giggles more than a corpse should. When she is returned to us, Poppy breathes, 'I want to be an actress when I grow up.'

I'm not so sure that she needs to wait until she grows up, as every day there seems to be some sort of drama. We sweep on through the ancient, walled courtyard past Traitor's Gate, the White Tower and the infamous Bloody Tower to the pretty expanse of Tower Green complete with its row of wonky, black and white Tudor houses. Connor, who has largely eschewed the value of speech, leaving his big sister to explain all his requirements to a waiting world, carries on a running commentary to Nick in his own unique scribble language while the dear man ums and ahs in all the right places. Conversely, Nick and I haven't chatted much at all – we seem to be content being quiet in each other's company. Either that or he's regretting being here at all. But I don't think so. He's too smiley and relaxed and I think I should chill down to his level and not keep worrying that my children are going to say something inappropriate at the wrong time (Poppy) or wee on him again (Connor).

We finish our guided tour at the Jewel House and queue up along with a steady stream of Americans, Germans and an assortment of European races to view our Monarch's treasures. On a Disneyland-style conveyor belt, we're whisked past a breathtaking and priceless collection of crowns and sceptres with diamonds the size of your fist. While Connor falls asleep in his buggy, Poppy's eyes grow wide.

'I want to be a princess,' she intones.

I'm glad my daughter is beginning to understand the value of ambition. Frankly, I'll be grateful if she turns out to be anything other than a lap-dancer. As I've discussed earlier, this is where all her talents are currently leaning. I hope she is listening and learning.

'Lunch,' Nick suggests when we're back out in the fresh air again and he whisks us all over to the Armoury Café – a pine extravaganza complete with heavy beams decorated with pikes and guns and broadswords. The décor may be medieval, but the prices are definitely twenty-first century. We find a table and, threatening Poppy with another beheading if she fails to look after her brother properly, Nick and I head off in search of food. We queue up – again – alongside the display of pre-wrapped sandwiches and cakes while we wait for our orders of chips.

'This is very kind of you,' I say.

'Nonsense.' Nick dismisses my thanks with a wave of his hand. 'It's great to have the excuse to come down here. I'm having a marvellous time.'

'You're a natural with the kids.'

'Well,' he says bashfully, 'it's a novelty, I suppose. If they were mine, I guess I'd be shouting at them like all parents seem to.'

I touch his arm. 'I don't think so.'

Four plates of chips arrive before he can reply and we stack them up amid the paper cups of Coca-Cola and the chocolate cookies – and if my kids are fat and spotty in years to come it will be all my fault.

We head back to the table where Poppy has taken Connor out of his buggy and has found him a highchair into which he's now happily strapped. There are times when I adore my daughter. They are few and far between, but today I'm so proud of her that I forgive her all her usual pre-teen-type transgressions.

Nick sits down and I play mother, doling out the plates of food. 'Say thank you to Nick,' I instruct them. This must be costing him a small fortune, but he insisted that he wouldn't take a penny from me.

'Ta!' Connor shouts from his chair.

'Thank you,' Poppy says, already slathering her chips in tomato ketchup.

'And thank you from me,' I say as I sit down, reminding myself that I must not attempt to interfere with his food.

Poppy examines a chip, blowing on it in case it's hot. 'Nick . . .' she says in a considered manner.

He looks up from his plate expectantly. 'Yes?'

I hope that she's going to ask him an intelligent question that proves she's been paying attention to her surroundings and has appreciated the educational value of her visit. Both Nick and I are all ears.

Poppy cocks her head to one side. 'Do you think that one day you might like to marry my mummy?'

But no. This is the inappropriate speech moment.

Nick flushes. But not half as much as me. 'I'm already married,' he stammers.

'Oh.' Poppy frowns. 'Henry the Eighth had six wives. Couldn't you get rid of this one and get married again?'

So she had been paying attention to some things.

'Not really,' he says in a croaky voice. 'That only works if you're a King.'

Or a movie star. Or a single mum.

'Oh.' My daughter digests this and then returns to her chips. 'Shame.'

I want to tell her off or apologise to Nick, but words refuse to come to my aid, because really I couldn't have put it better myself.

Chapter Fifty

'I am married,' Nick said to himself. He repeated it over and over, letting the phrase knock around inside his brain. 'I am married.'

The trouble was, he didn't feel as if he was married any more. It was true that he'd agreed to go back to Janine – it was just that somehow, somewhere, it hadn't quite computed into his cerebral wiring.

They'd left the Tower soon after lunch and had walked down the Embankment to the skating rink in the sumptuous courtyard at Somerset House. Connor was safely ensconced in the bright warmth of the crèche for an hour while they headed for the tent that housed the rental skates. It had been difficult to leave him, even for a short amount of time. Not that Connor had cared – when his eyes had lit upon a vacant plastic car he was off without a backwards glance.

It was also hard to watch Anna and Poppy giggling as they put on their hired skates preparing to take to the ice and think that they would never be a couple, a family. He wanted more than to be on the periphery of their lives and had to remind himself that he couldn't be.

Nick sat on the damp bench next to Anna and surveyed his skates with dismay. It had been his idea to go skating and it was a great one, but he hadn't reckoned on having to put his feet inside steaming boots that had already seen half a dozen pairs of sweaty feet that day. With a shudder, he took off his shoes and jammed his feet inside, trying to ignore his revulsion. This was awful and it made him think that if he couldn't bear to wear ice skates that were still warm, how would he feel about getting back into his wife's bed. He pushed the thought away. This had been a great day so far and he didn't want to ruin it by thinking bad thoughts about Janine.

'Okay?' Anna asked with a smile. Her cheeks were pink from the cold and as she stood up she tottered unsteadily on her skates.

Nick reached out and grabbed her hand. 'I've got you,' he said.

Anna flushed a deeper pink. 'I've never been any good at this.'

'Give me a minute.' Nick finished lacing his boots and jumped up. Hmm, his boots very nearly fitted. It was a long time since he and Sam had gone ice skating together, but he used to be reasonably good at it. Ignoring the crush injury he was sustaining to his toes and the fact that he was probably catching verrucas and athlete's foot at the very least, he tiptoed forwards. 'Let's give Torville and Dean a run for their money.'

'Who are Torville and Dean?' Poppy said, wobbling towards the door.

'There's one thing about having kids,' Anna advised him, 'they always make you feel your age.'

And then some.

He took a tighter grip on Anna's hand as she stepped out gingerly onto the ice. The rush of freezing air took their breath away, making them gasp. Poppy gripped hold of the side rails and eased herself out through the crowd of skaters, too independent to need to hold someone's hand. Thankfully, her mother was more than willing to accept his help. Nick wasn't exactly steady on his feet, but it was all coming back to him. He might not get the judges holding up perfect tens, but at least he was comfortable being upright. The ice was hard and rutted and Nick had to concentrate on shepherding them both along.

Anna grinned at him, before doing three little tottering runs. 'This is fun.'

And it was. There was nothing quite like behaving like a kid again to strip away the cares of adulthood. Plus the setting was picture-perfect – the rink was bounded by torches flickering with orange flames, nestled in the crook of the ornate stone building, classical music playing from hidden speakers. The ice was thronging with all ages wrapped in colourful hats and scarves against the cold.

Anna's hand was hot and small in his and it made him feel big and protective. It was a feeling he liked. With Janine he always seemed to feel inadequate. They made it halfway around the ice before Anna said breathlessly, 'I need a rest!'

So he steered her towards the rail and as he pulled her out of the stream of skaters, she pressed up against his chest, panting hard. Her nose was as red as her cheeks, her lips pinched with the cold. She looked up at him, mouth slightly apart in a smile. It would have been so easy to lean forward, just a fraction, the tiniest fraction, and kiss her, just brush his lips gently against hers. Nick lowered his head.

Poppy, face set with determination, crashed into their legs and the moment was broken. 'This is way cool,' she declared.

'You're doing well, sweetie,' Anna said, kissing her daughter on the top of her head as she teetered away again.

Nick's lips itched to kiss someone too. Someone who was standing right in front of him.

Chapter Fifty-One

I don't want this day to end, even though I'm tired and have realised that I'm never going to make the ice-skating team at the next Winter Olympics. Connor is exhausted too. His head has drooped forward in the pushchair and I suspect he'll sleep in the car all the way home – which, of course, means that he'll be awake for half of the night. Poppy, as always, has more energy than the Duracell Bunny and is dancing along telling Nick who is considered cool and who is not. They're both eating hot roasted chestnuts from a greasy paper bag, bought from a street vendor by Charing Cross station – a rare sight these days.

Nick turns round and hands one to me. I nibble on the soft centre and study the back of his head thoughtfully. Poppy has slipped her hand in his and I know how nice that feels. And I wish that he could be a permanent feature in our lives, that days out like this were marked regularly on our social calendar, instead of it being pocked only by dentist's appointments and school parents' nights.

We're heading back through Trafalgar Square to catch the tail end of the celebrations for Chinese New Year – the Year of the Monkey. Paper lotus flowers float in the fountain and all the lamp-posts and NO LOADING AT ANY TIME signs are hung with lucky red Chinese lanterns. The discordant sounds of Chinese opera come from the main stage and there's a dragon dance taking place down by the big black statues of the lions. Nick buys both Poppy and Connor a small paper dragon on a stick which they wave enthusiastically. Night is closing in and the lights are coming on across the city. London looks beautiful and exotic, as if it's a set in a Richard Curtis film.

'We should be getting back,' Nick says.

I take his hand and squeeze it tightly. 'Nick, this has been really, really great.'

He squeezes back. 'We must do it again,' he says. 'Soon.'

And we exchange a look that says we both know that we can't.

Chapter Fifty-Two

Anna finished strapping a sleeping Connor back into his car seat. Poppy kissed Nick shyly and said, 'Thank you for a lovely day out.'

Then she skipped away and slid into the passenger seat.

They were back at the car yard and it was past Connor's normal bedtime. Anna stopped fussing with her car and came back to stand in front of him. She hesitated and then reached up and kissed him tenderly on the cheek. 'That's for being a very lovely man,' she breathed.

And before he could say anything else, she jumped back into her car and drove away. Nick touched his face where Anna had kissed him, feeling himself break into a spontaneous grin and he walked back to the cold, dark Portakabin with a definite spring in his step.

His heart was lighter than it had been in months. He felt he'd had a glimpse of his destiny – family man and provider. And he knew who he wanted it with. If only things were different. Anna's kids were great and they'd provide him with a ready-made family to make up for lost time. But if he was going to make a go of it with Janine then he had to put any such thoughts behind him. However, that would be easier said than done.

Nick was in the office in the light of his wonky desk-lamp, carrying out a final check before calling it a night, when – as if summoned by his thoughts – Janine walked in.

'Hi,' she said.

Nick jumped a mile. 'Good grief,' he said. 'You nearly gave me a heart attack.'

'I was waiting for you to come back,' she said tightly.

And Nick wondered how much of the scene with Anna she had witnessed and why she hadn't made her presence known earlier.

'Have you been out all day?' she went on.

'Yeah,' he said, offering no further information.

'Somewhere nice?'

'Yeah.' It was quite a realisation that it was no longer any of Janine's business what he did with his days and, for the first time in his life, he resented telling her.

'How are things?' she asked.

'Much the same as they were yesterday.'

'Not quite,' Janine said with an expressive exhalation of breath. She looked down at her feet. 'Phil's gone.'

'Gone?' Nick couldn't keep the surprised tone out of his voice.

'He's moved out.'

'So soon?'

'It's over between us,' she said with a sob. She came and wrapped her arms round him, squeezing tightly. He wasn't quite sure where he should put his hands any more. The back that had once been so familiar that he knew every vertebra was suddenly like that of an alien being. This didn't feel like a person he'd ever touched before. 'You can come home, Nick.'

'Home?'

'Home,' Janine echoed.

Wasn't home now his old bedroom in his parents' house? It certainly wasn't the place where Janine had been living with her new man. Nick realised that he'd been drifting aimlessly for the last six months, not really knowing where his roots were. And now he'd got what he'd always dreamed of. Mr Bone the Butcher out on his ear and him, Nice Nick, back in his own home and in his own bed with his own wife. But something had shifted and he couldn't quite put his finger on it. Was it because he'd begun to realise that Janine wasn't the only one for him? Maybe he had plans of his own that no longer fitted his estranged wife's view of life. He looked beyond Janine's shoulder and into the car yard as she nestled into his shoulder. For some strange reason he was glad that she couldn't see his face, because he wasn't awfully sure whether his expression would have been happy or sad.

Chapter Fifty-Three

Nick and Sam stood at the back of the car auction beyond the rows of blue plastic chairs, huddling into their coats. The auction was held in a huge hangar with both ends chopped off, so that the wind was funnelled perfectly through the space. But at least it meant they didn't choke on the exhaust fumes.

This wasn't Nick's favourite way to spend a Saturday evening, but sometimes needs must. He was supposed to keep his finger on the pulse of the motor industry, et cetera, and this was the most miserable of all ways of doing it – standing round, freezing your knackers off with a couple of grand stashed in your back pocket on the off-chance of finding something to stir the blood. It was nine o'clock and he wondered what Anna was doing now and whether he might have been doing it with her. Still, he needed to find some wheels of his own to replace the rusting heap that he'd been conned into buying from the old couple. The sweet old couple who'd bounced the cheque on him. Plus he needed to see if there was anything interesting to replenish the stock at the car yard. He'd been surprised when he rang Sam, as an afterthought, to find him at home alone and not entertaining a member of the opposite sex on a Saturday night.

A few minutes later he'd collected Sam and they shot up a couple of motorway junctions to where the auction was held, which made Nick feel less guilty for closing up the car yard during the day. He let his mind drift as he drove. He'd really enjoyed himself with Anna and the kids. If this was what family life was like then bring it on – he wanted more of it. Much, much more. He wanted his own son to swing on his shoulders. His own daughter to spoil with glittery clothes and silly hair braids.

The auction was packed, as usual. A crowd thronged round the auctioneer's podium and around the main car lane. But there was a motley range of vehicles going under the auctioneer's hammer, nearly as motley as the shaven-headed, leather-jacketed punters poking around them. The auctioneer was having to use his best patter to drum up some interest in the buyers. He was gabbling as fast as a horse-racing commentator, building up a head of steam to encourage someone to part with a few quid for a long-dead Vauxhall Vectra.

Nick always liked Sam to come along with him to these things, but goodness knows why. He spent the entire time worrying that Sam was going to nod in the wrong place or overtly pick his nose or scratch his ear, and without meaning to they'd end up buying some rusting Austin Allegro or a top-of-the-range Merc or a fleet of clapped-out Mondeos or something infinitely worse than he was driving already.

After an hour of hanging around in the cold without feeling moved to make a purchase, they'd abandoned ship and had taken solace in eating a greasy burger from the café just outside the huge shed where the auction was taking place, while trying to keep one eye on the proceedings through the vast open doors. Now they were sampling the exquisite tea of Frying Fred, and gripping the plastic cup was the only thing that was keeping Nick's hands warm.

He hated to admit this, even to himself, but the main part of his enjoyment today had been spending some time with Anna again. She was funny, feisty and, just below that fragile protective shell, a very warm person. Only a few days as his Executive Assistant and Business whatever-it-was-she-wanted-to-call-herself, and already he wondered how he would manage without her around. Was that a good sign or a bad one? Her smile lit up his very drab office. And it looked as if that was the only place he was going to be seeing her from now on. The thought of Anna made Nick remember his promise to talk to Sam about his affair with Sophie.

Before his nerve could fail him, he said, 'It's not like you to be hanging out on a Saturday night, mate.'

'No,' Sam said. 'I was catching up with some DVDs I'd been meaning to watch. *Matrix Reloaded* was crap, by the way. I don't know what these women see in Keanu Reeves.'

'You weren't planning to give the wee lassies of Milton Keynes the benefit of your company?'

'No,' Sam said.

'Unusual.'

'There's only one woman for me now,' Sam said flatly. 'You know that.'

'Sophie?'

'Who else?'

'But you haven't seen her?'

Sam examined the contents of his cup. 'She has commitments. As you well know.' He gave Nick a rueful look. 'It isn't easy for her to get away. I have to accept that.'

'So you're going to sit at home every Saturday night with Keanu for company?'

'No,' Sam said. 'I'm here with you.'

'This is one step away from joining me at my mother's line-dancing classes. You'll be asking if you can come along next.'

To his surprise, Sam didn't look overtly worried by the prospect. Nick could hardly believe this was his friend talking. Sam wouldn't normally hang around waiting for someone if they were even half an hour late, and now he was putting his thriving social life on hold for the odd crumb of attention from a married woman.

'Anna thinks you shouldn't hook up with her again.' They threw the remains of their tea into a nearby rubbish bin and squeezed through the crowd to the front of the auction.

A dilapidated example of a Ford Capri chugged in. There should be one of those make-over programmes for cars as this poor beggar could certainly do with an overhaul, Nick thought. It had been a fine beast in its day – a sure-fire vehicle for pulling the birds. Not that he'd ever owned one. And maybe that was the problem. If he'd paid more attention to his mode of transport earlier on in life, perhaps the course of true love would have run more smoothly for him.

'Really,' Sam said, clearly disinterested in Anna's opinion. 'And what do you think?'

'I think she has a valid point.'

A VW Passat with a crumpled rear end but a genuine low mileage failed to meet its reserve – the ultimate indignity to be suffered by a car. Where to next? The scrapyard, probably. Nick almost felt compelled to buy it. He was going to have to toughen up. When he and Sam had walked round outside before the start of the auction, weaving through the endless rows of cars due to go under the hammer, he'd felt a sadness welling in him. Here they were in their masses, the unloved, the abandoned, the dented, their owners having already moved on to something bigger, brassier and with more horse-power without a backward glance.

149

'Doesn't it matter to anyone that I might actually love this woman?' Sam's voice pulled him back to the auction in hand.

Nick shrugged. 'I expect her husband might be interested.'

The hammer fell. Another poor bastard sold off cheaply. The next car wouldn't start and who could blame it. Could the reluctant Renault sense its fate? A burly mechanic wheeled in a bright yellow battery charger on a trolley, furtled under the bonnet and gave the car the full benefit of its volts. It roared into life. Nick sighed to himself. Perhaps if he slipped the guy a fiver, he'd apply the jump leads to his deadened heart.

'I don't give you advice on your relationships,' Sam said tightly.

'That's because I don't have any.'

'Well, maybe you should.'

The car stood in front of them sputtering and coughing asthmatically. Nick studied his feet. 'I'm afraid that sort of thing is out of the question from now on.'

Sam shook his head. 'It's time you moved out of your mother's clutches.'

'I am,' Nick admitted. 'Tomorrow.' He rubbed at the puddle of oil on the floor with the toe of his shoe. 'I'm going home. To Janine.'

Sam looked suitably stunned. The hammer went down on the Renault. The car was revved up, smoke billowed and puffed from the back of it like an old boiler and it went out to start its new life. Probably as a lethal, unlicensed taxi somewhere.

'Mr Bone the Butcher got the chop,' Nick continued. 'Mr Nick the Nice Guy – the true and faithful husband – is back on the game board.'

His friend didn't look overly pleased for him. 'Tell me you're joking, mate.'

'No, I'm not.'

'Are you insane? How can you do this?' Sam asked. In rather too loud a voice, Nick thought. 'Your ex-wife is a complete cow. She always has been.'

Heads swivelled in their direction. Even the auctioneer looked up. Nick gave them a sickly smile and after a few tut-tuts the heads swivelled back.

'She speaks very highly of you too.'

'She left you for some other bloke.'

'Can I, at this juncture, point out that there's a certain irony in your argument.'

'You can't go back to her,' Sam insisted. 'I won't allow it. You and Anna are made for each other.'

'Made for each other?' Nick was amazed. 'Did I hear you right? Is this the same man who last week wouldn't date anyone who didn't wear crotchless knickers?'

Another car was driven in. This one seemed sound. He couldn't get a clear view of it, but the engine sounded reasonably sweet. The bidding started way too high though.

His friend looked defiant. 'So?'

'And now you understand the concept of "soulmates"?'

'People change,' Sam said. 'I've changed.'

The bidding was at a silly level. Had someone lost their mind? There was no way this car was worth so much.

'Well, maybe Janine has too,' Nick said. 'I have to give her a chance.'

'Bonkers, mate.' Sam pointed at his head. 'That's what you are.'

The heads swivelled again. A heavily tattooed man turned to them and said, 'Can't you two carry on your lovers' tiff at home and give us all a bit of peace?'

Nick held his hand up. *'Sorry,'* he mouthed.

The auctioneer crashed his hammer down and the price brought a gasp from the seasoned punters. Some idiot had bought the car at a ridiculously inflated price. 'Sold to the gentleman at the front with the complete cow as an ex-wife,' the auctioneer shouted and he pointed to Nick.

Him, it appeared. The crowd around them cheered.

'Jeez,' Nick hissed. 'Is that what I've bought?'

'It would seem so.'

Nick looked at it with the bleakest of looks. Now he was giving it his full attention, he could see that it looked familiar. The car was driven past them. Oh good. He'd just bought back the car the old folks had conned him out of.

'Isn't that your old car?' Sam asked.

'No,' Nick said shiftily. 'But it does look a bit similar.'

'This is the car that you let those old folks pinch off you.'

'No.'

'Yes,' Sam insisted.

Nick sagged. 'They might have been conmen, but they were still old and frail and unloved.' And what was even worse, they had wanted to nick a cheap car and Nick had persuaded them to take a more expensive one.

'You've obviously developed an unhealthy attraction to lame ducks, my friend.'

Over the tannoy, the auctioneer said, 'Can the gentleman who bought the last car please come to the podium and pay for it now.'

Nick dug into his back pocket for his money. Now he was not only going back to his old life, but he was going to be doing it in his old car. 'Oh bugger,' Nick said.

Chapter Fifty-Four

Sunday morning cooked breakfast was an institution at number 43 Desford Avenue. It had been since Nick was a teenager and only managed to crawl out of his bed once ten o'clock had been and long since gone. The passage of time was slow at his parents' home and they had yet to embrace the newfangled concepts of low-fat cereals, yoghurt and fresh fruit as adequate sustenance with which to start the day.

The smell of sizzling sausages and bacon twitched his nostrils and took Nick back to a time when trying to eat enough food had been his only worry. Despite his long, lean frame his stomach had constantly fretted over where its next meal was coming from and, as a result, he ate every one as if it were his last. This Sunday morning he'd been awake since dawn, staring at the aeroplanes on the wall and wishing that he could catch one to somewhere, *anywhere*.

His mother put down the huge fry-up in front of him and instantly his appetite deserted him. Monica and his father sat down too and tucked in. Nick toyed with his food.

'There's no one at home to Mr Faddy Pants,' his mother said.

'Sorry, Mum,' Nick said. 'It looks lovely.' In an artery-clogging sort of way. 'But I'm really not that hungry.'

'Nonsense.' It was a concept his mother didn't understand.

Nick put down his knife and fork, steeling himself for the next conversation. 'Mum,' he said. 'I'm moving out.'

Monica's sausage stopped on the way to her mouth. 'Not the mud-wrestler from Macclesfield,' she said. 'Please tell me it's not her. Roger, talk to him.'

His father distracted himself with his scrambled eggs.

'I'm going home,' Nick said.

'You are home.' Monica abandoned her breakfast. 'This is your home.'

'No,' Nick sighed. '*Home* is where Janine and I live. And I'm going back there today.'

His mother looked flabbergasted. 'You're going back to that woman?' She shook her head. 'I'd rather you did take up with the mud-wrestler.'

'Thanks.'

Monica puffed herself up to full indignation. 'She'll let you down again. Once you do it the first time, it gets easier. Look at . . . look at . . . *Liza Minnelli.*'

'Janine is hardly Liza Minnelli.'

'More's the pity,' Monica snapped. 'At least that woman can sing. I've heard Janine doing karaoke.'

His mother had never, ever heard Janine doing karaoke. *He'd* never heard Janine doing karaoke. Janine didn't do karaoke.

'What happened to Mr Bone the Butcher?'

'Gone.'

'Gone?' Monica bristled again. 'I hope he's not moving out of the area. Where will I go for my neck fillet?'

'For heaven's sake, Mum. There must be other butchers.'

'He may have been a philandering no-good, but he has very tender lamb shanks.'

Nick put his head in his hands.

'I can't believe this,' his mother continued. 'What am I going to tell them at my line-dancing nights out? I've called that woman not fit to burn for the last six months.'

'Tell them you have a very loyal son,' Nick said. 'I took marriage vows, Mum. And believe it or not – although it flies in the face of fashion these days – they're important to me. I want to stick by them.'

His mother looked unmoved.

Should it matter to him to try again, just because he'd stood there in front of all their friends and family in some ridiculous morning suit that Janine had decreed the height of fashion and that he'd loathed, and made all of these promises? Promises that he'd carefully considered, promises that he wanted to make. It didn't seem to matter to most people. But then he wasn't most people, and he had to admit that no matter what everyone else thought about the suitability or not of his match with Janine, it mattered to him. He sounded too defensive when he said, 'Everyone makes mistakes.'

'And this is yours.'

'I thought you didn't want me to be divorced?'

'I don't,' Monica said. 'But nor do I want you to be married to someone who doesn't treat you very nicely.'

His mother started to fill up with tears.

'Don't cry,' he said. 'You should be happy for me.'

Monica pulled out a hanky and sniffed into it.

'Mum.' He took her hand and appealed to her. 'I'd rather go with your blessing.'

'And I'd rather you went with two sausages and three rashers of bacon in your tummy,' she said, whipping his plate away from him. 'It looks as if we're both going to be cruelly disappointed.'

Chapter Fifty-Five

'I am *not* buying you a nurse's outfit.' I'm going to be very firm about this.

'I was just *looking* at it,' Sophie says in a voice that would suit my ten-year-old daughter better. Reluctantly, she puts it back on the rack.

We are in one of those user-friendly, high street sex shops designed for modern women. It's slap-bang in the middle of the city centre and I just hope that no one I know saw me come in here. I never thought that I was a prude, but I'd prefer to get half of this stuff through the post in a plain-brown wrapper – and preferably not from our regular postman who is a very nice chap and would be shocked. It's Sunday and, of course, the shopping centre is jammed and I don't want to walk round Milton Keynes with the sex shop's name emblazoned on a carrier bag. What if I bump into one of the neighbours? Or even worse, Nick!

Sophie and I are shopping together and I'm supposed to be treating her to something lovely with my hard-earned cash from the last few days. When I checked the envelope Nick had given me there seemed to be an awful lot of money in it, compared to the time I'd actually worked, and I'm starting to get a swirly stomach every time I think about how kind he is. Which is not good. It is a job. He is my boss. I must be professional about this.

Despite our lovely day out yesterday, I must not become emotionally attached to him. I think I'll write it out a hundred times like the lines you used to get in school. *I must not become emotionally attached to my boss. I must not become emotionally attached to my boss.* Even though he is rather lovely.

He's so good with the kids – despite never having been a dad. He's a natural and it's a sin that his miserable, skinny wife Janine can't see that. Or maybe she can and chooses to ignore it. And I must remember, all the time that I'm thinking fondly of him, there aren't just the two of us in this equation. He might well be going back to her, for heaven's sake. It's definitely on the cards. And where does that leave me? *He is still emotionally attached to his wife.* I must write that out a hundred times too, to get it through my thick skull. Just because he wants to take me and my kids out for a fun day it doesn't mean that he wants to whisk me down the aisle. I have been an unwitting participant in an eternal triangle too many times to ever enter one willingly. And Nick isn't like that either. I know that he loves Janine. He must do, to consider going back to the cheating old bat. I sigh to myself. Still, it would be nice for the kids to have a dad like Nick. Even when Bruno *was* around he didn't come close to being great father material.

'Why don't you get one?' Sophie suggests, nodding at the skimpy outfit.

'Oh yeah.' By the time I've finished playing nurse to my kids all day, the last thing I'd want to do is dress up for some bloke in the same role. That also goes for the French maid's outfit and the serving wench get-up. Why do all male fantasies seem to revolve around women being subservient? Then I look over at the dominatrix section with its array of rubber bodices, whips and studded dog collars and think that maybe they don't.

We manoeuvre our pushchairs round the display of rainbow-coloured vibrators, earning ourselves a glare from the svelte and rather surly-looking assistants. There's a big, pink 'soft feel' vibrator that professes to be 'realistic' – heaven forbid. I'd book into the nearest clinic if I were a bloke and had an appendage that looked even remotely like that. At least Sophie isn't trying to coerce me into buying one of these. Although in my current celibate state, I could probably make better use of it than the nurse's outfit.

'Can I get one of these then?' Sophie whines. I look at her in horror. She's picked up something called The Rampant Rabbit. It's pink and horrible and not like any cute lop-eared rabbit I've ever seen. 'I saw something just like this on *Sex and the City.*'

'I don't think the city they had in mind was Milton Keynes.'

'We're broad-minded, sex-starved girls too,' my friend points out. 'We have a lot in common with Carrie and chums. Perhaps one of these would perk us up too.'

'You can speak for yourself.' I shudder as my eyes fall on The Purple Penetrator on the shelf next to it. I turn Connor's pram away from the display and lower my voice. 'I don't need perking up. And neither do you. Besides, I would have no idea what to do with one of these.'

Sophie gives me an incredulous look. 'Anna!'

'How would you keep it clean?' I can feel myself cringing.

'Just give it a rub round with some anti-bacterial cleanser.'

'Euw! I can just see you peeling potatoes with this sitting on the draining-board next to you.'

'You have no romance in your soul.'

'I do,' I insist. 'That's why I don't want sex with a plastic toy.'

Sophie picks up another deadly weapon. 'What about this one then?'

'This one' is called The Maximiser. It's twenty-three centimetres long according to the packaging and I've no idea how big that is in real money. It looks flipping enormous. I'm one of these people who are stuck resolutely on feet and inches and can't do metric at all – particularly not in vibrators. I wonder if my daughter and her friends will discuss men's anatomies in the future in centimetres. 'My word, Stephanie, he's a good twenty-three centimetres!' It just doesn't sound right, does it?

My daughter has been banned from entering this emporium of cheeky delights – mainly because she probably knows more than her mother about some of the gear in here. She is sitting outside running up her mobile phone bill, talking to Stephanie Fisher – not about metric wotsits, I hope – with a Coca-Cola from McDonald's as a bribe.

I smack Connor's hand as he reaches for a box of chocolate-flavoured sweets fashioned as nipples. 'Don't touch anything,' I warn him as I steer him quickly away from the chocolate willies. This experience could scar him for life. I should have left him outside with Poppy.

My friend is still drooling over strangely shaped sexual aids.

'Come on. How would you ever hide one of these from the kids?' I ask. 'They'd manage to get hold of it and then Ellie would whip it out of their toy box just when you had visitors, brandishing it for all to see.'

'True,' she says. 'And when am I ever going to find any privacy to use it?'

Sophie reluctantly puts them back on the display and, with a sullen sigh, leaves the vibrators behind. But now her attention turns to the lingerie section and she's soon fingering some ridiculously tiny piece of lacy frippery that's supposed to be a pair of knickers. Picking up a pair from the rack, I try to work out which bit goes where. They look desperately uncomfortable. Undoubtedly sexy –

if you find having a piece of dental floss up your bottom a turn-on. Hastily, I put them back. They look suspiciously like the pants Vicky the babysitter was – or wasn't – wearing. Personally, I haven't worn underwear like this in years and I'm not sure that I'm the poorer for it. There was a day, long gone, when my figure would have been flattered by this sort of lingerie, a day when my hips used to jut out like the ends of coat hangers beyond my tiny belly. But now my rounded 'mummy tummy' protrudes way beyond my hipbones and my bottom has spread to the comfort-seeking proportion of big pants and eschews any form of lace as an unnecessarily scratchy adornment.

'Why this sudden interest in minuscule lingerie?' As if I need to ask.

'No reason.' Sophie shrugs.

Ellie amuses Charlotte by wrapping her from head to toe in a scarlet feather boa.

'I thought it was all over with Sam? One off, silly mistake, et cetera . . .'

My friend remains ominously silent.

'You're not getting these for Tom?'

Sophie gives me a black look. 'Perhaps I'm getting them for myself.'

And maybe that's true. 'I could kill Tom for paying you so little attention,' I whisper to Sophie. 'But even though I could kill him, I'm not sure that I can be a party to buying his wife saucy undies to wear while entertaining her new lover.'

Sophie's body tightens. 'Your morals always were better than mine.'

I go and hug my friend. 'I don't want us to fall out over this,' I say, 'but I've already been an unwitting alibi for you and I just don't feel comfortable doing that.'

Sophie squeezes me back, but it's a bit half-hearted.

'If I thought any of this stuff would help to save your marriage I'd buy it for you like a shot,' I say. 'You know I would. But I can't pay for it if I think it's going to help you move further away from Tom.'

'Then maybe if I'm going to wear it for myself, I'll buy it for myself,' Sophie says defiantly, whipping all manner of frillies from the racks.

'Don't be like that.' My mouth downturns. 'I want to spoil you,' I say. 'You've been so kind. I wouldn't be able to do this job if it wasn't for you.'

Sophie grins and holds up her very dubious retail choices.

'I'd rather buy you a Kate Spade handbag,' I offer.

She jiggles a leopard-print basque at me.

'I want you to know that I'm doing this under protest.'

My friend holds up a black lacy camisole to her chest. Oh my word, it would barely cover her . . . Well. 'I don't even want to picture you in these,' I say, imagining exactly what kind of mischief Sophie could get up to while wearing them.

We go to the desk to pay for her purchases. 'Why don't you get something for yourself?' she asks me.

'And when am I going to wear anything like this?' I hold up the leopard-print number.

'At the office,' Sophie grins. 'You could give Nick a nice surprise over his desk.'

'You're perverted,' I say. 'He's far too nice to succumb to such obvious charms.' Although I admit I do get some sort of unhealthy flash of Nick and me doing unseemly things amid the piles of filing. Mmm . . .

'Go on!' Sophie nudges me in the ribs.

Maybe I will just treat myself to something silly. To mark my first pay-packet – for no other reason. I snatch up a tiny black, see-through thong trimmed with marabou feathers. Surely this would tickle anyone's fancy? 'This is ridiculous.'

'Now all we have to do is find you a reason to wear it.'

'Chance would be a fine thing,' I huff.

The cashier rings up our purchases and puts them into bags with the name of the shop all over them, so that no one can be in any doubt what we've been buying.

'Mummy, look what I've done!' We turn round to find that Ellie has locked Connor to his pushchair with a pair of pink, fluffy hand-cuffs. My son, rather than looking perturbed, is smiling broadly. Oh, my word.

'Where's the key? Where's the key?' Sophie demands, panicking.

'I don't know,' Ellie says.

Oh, my word. 'Can you help us?' I say to the surly assistant.

Boredom writ large on her face, she reaches into a drawer and then saunters over to the buggy with a key. Perhaps people come in here and find their children clamped into their merchandise on a regular basis. The assistant unlocks my child from his shackles. Then, and only then, does Connor start to cry. I wonder if this says anything about what his future predilections will involve?

'Come on,' I mumble. 'Let's get out of here.'

And we grab our bags stuffed with salacious goodies and our wailing children and run laughing for the door.

Chapter Fifty-Six

From the sex shop we engage in an altogether more wholesome pursuit and take the children to the local park to play on the swings. The weekend ice-cream van is there, despite the chilly day, and we feed them Mr Whippy ice creams that they proceed to wipe all round their smiling faces and down their nice clean clothes. Poppy has managed to prise her mobile phone from her ear for five minutes and has been put in charge of the littlies. While they make themselves sick on the roundabout, Sophie and I squeeze our adult-size bottoms onto child-size swings and rock backwards and forwards, enjoying our own ice creams.

The sky is a brilliant clear blue which belies how cold the day is. We both huddle into our coats and I wish my kids would wear gloves but they won't. Why do children never feel the cold? They're running round, coats gaping open, noses frozen red without a care in the world. I wish their lives could always remain so simple. I hug myself to keep warm and dwell on the fact that they really enjoyed yesterday and I could tell that they liked having Nick around. Me and them both. I gaze out over the park, trying to blot out any semblance of a Happy Families fantasy. The trees are bare and they look as if they're shivering in the breeze. The once-colourful leaves they shed last autumn are slowly turning to black slime at their feet.

'Nothing from Bruno?' Sophie asks.

'No.' I shake my head. 'Although I do keep getting some weird, hang-up phone calls. I half-wonder if it is Bruno at the other end. I suppose it could be any kind of nuisance caller – it doesn't have to be a missing husband.'

'I'm glad he's gone,' Sophie says.

She doesn't really need to tell me that. There was hardly any love lost between them even when he was around.

My friend swings backwards and forwards. 'Is this how we saw ourselves living our lives when we were at school?' Sophie looks over to me. 'Wasn't I going to marry Simon Le Bon?'

'I think that was me,' I point out. 'Although I always secretly preferred John Taylor.'

'Oh.'

'He's fat now,' I say.

'Simon Le Bon?'

I nod.

'Not fat,' Sophie objects. 'Rounded. Cuddly. He was always cuddly. Well-covered.' She swings herself higher. 'I still wouldn't say no,' she adds. 'And look at us. At least Simon's still living the high life. He's probably got a yacht or two in the South of France, a villa in Spain. What have we done with our lives?'

'You've got Ellie and Charlotte.'

'Is the random process of raising offspring really all that it's cracked up to be?' she asks. 'Would we have had children at all if we'd known what it really involved?'

'I wouldn't be without them now.'

'That's hardly the same thing, is it?'

We watch them twirl round on the roundabout, giggling maniacally as Poppy spins them madly, carefree and cosseted. I love my kids, but it's such hard work that maybe Sophie is right. I have submerged my own life for them to live theirs and I wonder is it all worth it. When will I get my reward for such selfless love? Do they really appreciate how much I work and worry for them? I know that I only ever started to understand what my mother had gone through for me when I had kids of my own. But on the days that I feel like nothing more than a driving, feeding and washing-up machine I do think I might have been better off remaining child-free, travelling the world, living in a hippy commune, that sort of thing. Then I look at Connor aimlessly inspecting the contents of his nose and my heart squeezes for him.

'I wonder, if I'd married Simon Le Bon, would he have only wanted to make love to me once every blue moon?' Sophie muses. 'Do you think we'd be at it every night if I'd married a pop star?'

'Well, I suppose us plebs always assume that famous people are having so much more fun than us,' I say. 'So I would imagine you'd have been at it at least three times a week.'

Sophie looks wistful. 'Three times a week.' She stares at her feet. 'With Tom we're down to about three times a year. Two birthdays and one Christmas Eve. Even Valentine's Day has dropped off the agenda. It's not enough.'

'Bruno was always very keen,' I shrug. 'It wasn't quantity we lacked.' But there was a certain quality missing. 'I usually felt very pressured.'

I gaze off into the distance. It never seemed to matter how tired I was or what had been going on in our daily lives, Bruno still expected his conjugal rights. An old-fashioned term, but then Bruno was a very traditional type of male in some ways. And I usually gave in to him – laid back and thought, if not of England, then of the sundry domestic chores that were waiting for me. I never felt especially loved by our love-making, more as if I'd been used as a convenient receptacle. It's ironic: here's Sophie complaining about how little interest her husband has in her and yet I would quite happily have had a husband who took much less interest in me. There was very little in the way of curling up together in companionable sleep. Bruno was either all over me or not speaking to me. I can't imagine Nick being like that. But then I'm imagining what Nick would be like in rather too many situations.

'There's certainly something to be said about having the bed to myself,' I sigh to Sophie. 'Well, apart from two wriggling children and an assortment of soft toys.'

'If there's anyone who should have given up on their marriage long ago it's you, Anna,' my friend says. 'I have very little to complain about in comparison.'

'Don't I keep telling you that?' I reply with a smile.

'It was fantastic being with Sam.' She pulls a wry, unhappy face.

'*Was* being the operative word.'

'Yeah.'

I put my hand on Sophie's arm and give her a squeeze. 'You'll forget him in time.'

'I don't want to forget him,' she declares. 'No one has ever made me feel like that before. And now that I know what it can be like, should I settle for anything less?' She looks to me for an answer.

'Store the memory away,' I say. 'Use it to try to move on in your own life. Get kitted out in those sexy undies.' I flash a look at our respective carrier bags. 'They may work wonders for Tom.'

'All very sound advice,' my friend agrees miserably.

'Have you tried talking to Tom about how you feel?'

'Have you ever tried giving a worming tablet to a reluctant cat?' Sophie enquires. 'You have the same sort of struggle, the same sort of success.'

I laugh. 'He never has been much of a talker, has he?'

'And now he's not much of a doer either,' Sophie notes ruefully.

164

'Are you sure it's not just easier for me to trade him in for a new one?'

Our children, tiring of entertaining themselves, come running over and cannon into us. Poppy dumps Charlotte in Sophie's arms and my friend looks down at her daughter's flushed cheeks with a smile. 'I think we both know the answer to that one,' I say.

'Come on,' Sophie says. 'We'd better get back.'

'Are you doing anything tonight?' I ask her.

'No,' my friend says. 'Another wild night in with *Heartbeat* and cheap booze. You?'

'Same,' I say wearily. 'I might paint my toenails.'

Sophie heaves herself from the swing. 'What extraordinarily exciting lives we lead.'

At this moment, I can't disagree.

Chapter Fifty-Seven

Nick's suitcase stood open on the bed. Very slowly and deliber-ately he was folding items to fit into it while taking in the contents of his room. With a heavy sigh he decided that it wasn't much to show for thirty-odd years on the planet.

There was a gentle tap on the door and behind him, his mother entered the room.

'Hi.'

Monica also took in the room and he wondered what was going through her mind.

It was sad. This shouldn't be how he was living – running back to his parents' nest just because his life was falling apart. He should be settled now, with children of his own to worry about, not coming back to mess up his parents' retirement plans and sponge off their hospitality. But life had changed since Mr and Mrs Diamond's day. The average age of a bridegroom now was thirty, that of a bride twenty-eight. That made the average age of a divorcé somewhere around thirty-five, didn't it? Or was that being far too cynical? People didn't exactly rush down the aisle in droves nowadays. The number of couples getting married was at an all-time low. Most of his friends had lived at home into their twenties – KIPPERS all of them. The latest social stereotype – Kept in Parents' Pocket, Eroding Retirement Savings. Most of them had married in their thirties and most of them were still married, albeit some of them were hanging on by a thread. You'd think if people were waiting longer to tie the knot, they'd have the sense to pick the right partner when they did – but having age on your side didn't seem to make it any easier. Still, having fled the nest, there was something terribly defeatist about returning to the bedroom of your childhood, even as a temporary measure.

Monica should have her own grandchildren to fuss over by now. Again, his friends were popping babies left, right and centre. None of this had convinced Janine to have broody thoughts. She looked at babies and thought that they looked like a lot of responsibility. Wasn't it supposed to be blokes who shied away from that sort of commitment? Nick took in his mother's stout figure, her determined jaw, and his heart went out to her. That's what he'd always wanted to give her – two fresh-faced, chubby-legged grandchildren that she could indulge to her heart's content. But neither of them had seen their wishes come true. Was it too much to hope for in life? His mother would adore having grandchildren like Connor and Poppy. Perhaps Janine would have a change of heart on the issue of children. It was one of the many, many things they needed to discuss.

His mother sat down on his bed. 'You're welcome to leave some things here,' she said. 'Just in case.'

Nick gave an empty laugh. 'You have that much confidence in me making a go of my marriage?'

'I just want you to be happy.'

He came and sat down next to her and put his arm round her, giving her a hug. For once, his mother, who was not generally a huggable type of person, leaned gently against him. 'I know,' he told her.

'Despite the circumstances, it's been good to have you home again,' she said quietly. 'We don't see enough of you.'

And that was also true, because Janine didn't like his parents very much. But then she didn't like her own parents very much either. 'If I'd stayed any longer,' Nick joked, 'I'd have had to take out life membership with Weight Watchers.'

Monica looked tearful and Nick squeezed her to him again. 'Thanks, Mum. You've been great.'

'Go on, silly billy,' his mother said. 'That's what mums are for.'

'I'll be all right,' Nick assured her.

'I hope so.' His mother patted his knee and stood up. 'But you know where we are if you need us.'

'I'm just about ready to go.'

'Are you sure this is what you want?'

'No,' Nick admitted. 'But I have to give it a try. I couldn't live with myself if I didn't.'

Monica walked to the door. 'You're a lovely person, Nick. And that's not simply because you're my son. I hope she looks after you this time.'

Nick hoped so too, but he thought it was better not to voice that thought just now.

'I'd better go and put the kettle on,' Monica said shakily. 'Otherwise your father will be complaining that I neglect him.'

His father never complained about anything and perhaps that was the key to a successful, lifelong marriage. One partner was the driving force and the other merely went along for the fifty-year ride.

When he was alone again, Nick took down Georgie Best from the light fitting where he was hanging by the neck from Nick's old school tie. He dusted down the aged teddy and smiled at him fondly. 'Sorry, mate,' he said. 'Nothing personal. I was just trying to make a point.'

Nick placed Georgie Best on the bed, propped up by the pillows so that he had a good view of the room. Then he closed his case and, with only a moment's hesitation, turned off the light.

Chapter Fifty-Eight

Tom, Ellie and baby Charlotte were lined up on the sofa watching television when Sophie came in shrugging on her coat.

'Out again?' Tom said without looking up from the inane programme flickering across the screen. 'The neighbours will think you've got a fancy man.'

'I need to pop round to Anna's,' Sophie explained. 'I won't be long. A couple of hours.'

Tom finally managed to tear himself away from the telly. 'I've no idea what you women find to talk about.'

'The inadequacies of men,' Sophie snapped back.

Without comment, Tom returned his gaze to the television. Sophie came over and kissed the girls. Charlotte, all snugly in her sleepsuit, glugged at her bottle of milk. Ellie, distracted, sucked on her thumb. She owed the girls more than this, she knew she did.

Sophie headed for the door, and then looked back, suddenly filled with guilt and regret. 'See you later.'

Tom grunted at her.

Fighting a wave of irritation, Sophie slammed the door. Outside she shivered in the cold air before jumping into her car. For a moment, she rested her head on the steering wheel and wondered for the millionth time today what she was doing with her life. When Anna rationalised her choices she made it all sound so simple. But it wasn't. Far from it. Starting the engine, she drove off down the street. There were days when she felt as if she could get in her car and drive for ever. Miles and miles. Never coming back. And when she reached the turning to Anna's road, where she should by rights be swinging the car off the dual carriageway, Sophie just carried on driving.

Ten minutes later, Sophie pulled up outside Sam's apartment. She sat in her car looking up at the bright lights which picked out Sam's window and her tummy turned at the memory of last time she was

169

here. Before she could have second thoughts, she was out of the car, across the road and pressing the buzzer marked *Sam Felstead*.

'Hi.' Sam's voice came over the intercom.

'Pizza delivery,' Sophie said. 'Ham and pineapple with extra cheese.'

'Come up.'

The door buzzed for her to enter. Sophie pushed inside and then ran up the stairs to the first-floor apartment where Sam was leaning languidly on the door frame waiting for her. Her heart was banging loudly and it wasn't just from running up the steps. It was a mixture of excitement and fear. Temptation and trepidation.

As she approached, Sam grinned and said, 'I don't like pineapple.'

'It doesn't matter.' She sounded breathless and slightly giddy. 'I haven't brought pizza.'

Sam wrapped his arms round her and pulled her into the hallway, kissing and undressing her before he'd even closed the door. He threw off her coat, unbuttoned her blouse and tossed it to the floor before unzipping her skirt and tugging it over her hips. Sophie sighed with pleasure, glad that she'd worn the leopardskin-print skimpies – though, no doubt, her friend Anna would be less than pleased if she knew.

Leaning against the wall, Sophie let her head arch back as Sam peeled off the leopardskin underwear, stroking and caressing her, his lips travelling over her body. Sophie trembled with desire – the undies might have been shortlived, but they were clearly worth it.

'I have never wanted anyone so much,' he murmured into her neck.

Sophie could hardly get her breath. 'This is absolutely . . . the last time . . . this can happen.'

'Absolutely,' Sam agreed as they sank to the floor.

Chapter Fifty-Nine

We've got the stero blaring out and Poppy is trying to show me some lascivious dance routine to a hip-hop or garage CD or something. My hips will never again be able to rotate like that. After bearing two children they are locked resolutely into seized-up mode – I think my pelvis is terrified that I might be mad enough to consider doing the whole birth thing again and is silently registering its protest. Whereas my daughter knows far too much about pelvic thrusting for a ten year old. I'm sure I didn't know about pelvic thrusting until I was at least twenty. I have pelvic thrusted for very few people in my life – a measly two at the last count – and look where that got me.

Poppy and I are both giggling and out of breath. Connor is giggling too although he's uncertain why. I hate to tell him that when he grows up he will be a white English male and will, therefore, be genetically incapable of dancing properly.

The next track starts and we take up our positions again, just as the lyrics take a turn for the worse.

Poppy looks puzzled. 'What is a loved-up bitch, Mummy?'

'Er . . .' How I dread this sort of question. Don't record producers ever consider these excruciating parental moments when they are doing their mixing or whatever producing a record entails? Don't they have children at home? Christina Aguilera and co will have a lot to answer for if they ever bowl up at my front door. At this point the phone rings and I can't tell you how relieved I am. Saved by the bell and all that. I just hope it's not another hang-up call.

'Hello.'

'Hi, Anna.'

'Hi, Tom.' Now I wish it was my mystery caller. Anyone other than Sophie's husband. I'm worried because Tom never calls me. Never. I thought he was physically unable to use a telephone. Something must be seriously wrong. 'Is everything all right?'

'Is Sophie there?'

171

'Er . . . Sophie?'

'You know,' Tom says down the line. 'Sophie your best friend. That Sophie. The one who said she was popping round to your place.'

'Yes. Yes,' I blabber. 'Sophie's here.' I know exactly where she is, if she's told Tom that she's here and she damn well isn't. I could murder her. 'Yes. She's here.'

'Can I have a word then?'

'Er . . .' Damn. Blast. Buggeration. 'She's in the bathroom at the moment. On the loo.' Too much information. 'Can I get her to ring you back in a minute or two?'

I can call Sophie on her mobile and hope to goodness that she answers it and then I can get her to ring Tom back.

'No.' Tom sounds crisp. 'You did say she was in the loo?'

'Yes.' My throat is nearly closing up. 'Do you want her to ring you?'

'It's okay. Don't bother.'

And Tom hangs up.

Sophie walked in the front door just as Tom was replacing the receiver on the phone. 'Hi,' she said. 'I'm home.'

They were all still lined up on the sofa watching television where she'd left them three hours earlier, despite the fact that the girls should have been tucked up in bed long ago. Sophie hoped that she didn't look as dishevelled as she felt. Three hours in Sam's bed had been like running a marathon for someone so out of practice.

'You've been longer than I thought.' Tom's tone was even more brusque than normal. 'I was getting worried about you.' He cast a pointed glance at the clock.

'You know Anna.' Sophie tutted and rolled her eyes at the ceiling for extra effect. 'She likes to chat.'

'Yeah,' Tom said.

Sophie peeled off her coat and threw it down. 'Who was that on the phone?'

'No one,' Tom said. 'Wrong number.'

'Oh.'

Ellie piped up. 'Daddy wanted you to get some chips on the way home from Aunty Anna's house.'

'I can go back out and get some if you want,' she offered. 'It won't take a minute. It's no trouble.'

She looked at her family and felt wracked with guilt. Vivid images of her and Sam together flashed before her eyes and she tried to block them out.

Tom stood up. 'I'll go myself,' he said. 'I could do with some fresh air.'

'Fresh air?' Sophie gave him a sideways glance. 'Since when have you needed fresh air?'

'Since now.' Tom shrugged on his coat and, without speaking, headed to the door and slammed out. Sophie chewed her lip worriedly.

I try to massage my frown away and having failed, replace it by biting my fingernail.

'Why are you telling lies about Aunty Sophie?' Poppy asks. 'She isn't here.'

I flop down on the sofa and rummage in my handbag for my mobile phone. 'Sometimes grown-ups do that.'

I punch Sophie's number which is programmed in. Her phone is turned off and goes straight to voicemail. I leave a cryptic message asking her to call me, but it's clear that I won't be able to warn her that Tom has rung. If she's determined to be an adulterer then she'd better start getting her act together and not use me as an excuse for her infidelity if she doesn't even bother to tell me.

'Isn't Uncle Tom worried?' And now she's dragging my daughter into her deception.

'Yes, he is.'

'Grown-ups seem to lie all the time,' Poppy observes. 'It's very silly if you ask me.'

'It is,' I agree. I hug my daughter to me. 'Very silly indeed.' Yet we all insist on doing it, don't we?

173

Chapter Sixty

His mother and father stood in the hall with him. All three of them looked uncomfortable beneath the gaze of overblown floribunda roses that smiled down from the wallpaper. Nick's suitcase stood at his feet. Monica's eyes were watery with welling tears.

'This is worse than sending you off to your first day at school,' she said, stroking the lapel of his coat.

'Mum,' Nick said. 'I'll be fine.'

His mother hugged him to her, clinging to him as if she was never going to let go. After indulging her for a few moments, Nick managed to prise her off.

'Roger,' Monica sniffed. 'Say something.'

His father extended his hand stiffly. 'Son.'

Nick shook his hand, leaving his father looking rather anxious. 'Thanks, Dad.'

Monica tossed her head in exasperation. 'You'd never believe he had Italian blood!'

His father with Italian blood? That was a new one. Nick picked up his case and headed for the door.

His mother held on to his sleeve. 'Call me when you get there.'

'I'll call you tomorrow,' Nick said.

'I'll put a hot water bottle in your bed just in case.'

'Don't.' Nick tried to sound firm. 'I'm staying.'

'I want you to know that you don't have to,' his mother said. 'I'll make up something to tell the girls at line-dancing.'

It wasn't the time to point out that not one of the girls was under seventy and he couldn't care less what his mother told them about his marital strife. Or that they were mostly all deaf and mad and would never remember the next day anyway. All that mattered was that he was going home and he was determined to make a go of it with Janine. 'Mum.' Nick kissed her on the cheek. 'Take care. I'll talk to you tomorrow.'

And he left before he too decided it would be much easier to stay.

Nick sat outside his marital home in his ancient car, motionless. He felt as battered and ageing as the vehicle he occupied. Too many miles on the clock. Too many scrapes. Too many bits not quite working properly. Too short on tender loving care and an affectionate owner. All his limbs were aching and his head and the space behind his eyes, and – if he were truthful – his heart harboured a dull ache too. He felt as if he was coming down with a cold, or flu or some other terrible lurgy. Maybe it would be wiser to go back home – home to his mother – and curl up with a hot water bottle and let her feed him chicken soup and perhaps come back to Janine tomorrow when he was feeling better.

All the lights were burning in his house and he watched Janine move about inside, flitting from room to room. It was as if he were a Peeping Tom, trying to catch glimpses of his own life. Had he really ever lived here? It all looked so alien. A cut-out home from *House Beautiful* magazine, rather than somewhere he had once put up his feet on the sofa. The last time he had been here was the day he was kindly invited to leave his marriage, and he had done so carrying the very same suitcase that he was now taking back into it.

The car was getting cold now that the heater was turned off – not that the heater worked properly when it was on, but at least it gave some promise of warmth. His arms were stiffening to the point of immobility; if he waited any longer he might not even be able to get out of the car. It was time to stop procrastinating, otherwise he'd be discovered by the postman on his morning round frozen to death at the wheel.

His mobile phone rang. That would buy him a few more minutes. He rummaged in his pocket to find it. Should he really be thinking like that? What advice would Anna give him in this situation? Maybe it was her calling. He checked the caller-identifier. No. It wasn't Anna. 'Hi, Mum,' he sighed.

'I just wanted to see if you were all right?'

'I'm fine.'

'How's everything?'

'Everything's fine.'

'And Janine?'

'I haven't spoken to her yet.'

'Why?'

'Because I'm still in the car.'

'Are you having second thoughts?'

Second, third, fourth, fifth thoughts. 'No.' His breath was steaming up the windows. 'I've got to go, Mum. Janine will be wondering where I've got to.'

'You'll always be my little boy.'

'Yes,' he said. 'And you'll always be my mother.' And some days that was a good thing and other days it was not so good. He ended the call before she managed to talk him into going back to Desford Avenue. It was times like this when he really wished he was a bastard. A bastard who didn't spend his life trying to keep everyone happy but himself.

He put his mobile phone back into his pocket – deep into his pocket before the temptation to ring Anna became too strong. He just wanted to hear her voice and, in the circumstances, that couldn't be considered a very good idea.

With a weary little huff, Nick got out of the car, heaved his suitcase from off the back seat and crossed the road. The night was clear and still. Frost was starting to glitter on the pavements. The perfect disc of full moon hung heavily in a cloudless black sky. Nick stopped on the garden path and looked at it. He was sure it should have been symbolic, but he couldn't work out why.

Turning away from the pull of the moon, he rang the door bell. After a moment, Janine came to open the door, her outline indistinct and watery behind the glass.

'Hi,' she said with a nervous exhalation.

'Hi.'

Janine smiled uncertainly and stood to one side.

Without looking back, Nick stepped inside.

Chapter Sixty-One

You'll think I'm nuts. *I* think I'm nuts! I lay awake all last night thinking about Nick. And I know all that stuff I said earlier about him being my boss and being still, for some reason, emotionally bound to his manipulative ex-wife – but sometimes I'm wrong. Sometimes these things are worth going for just to see where they'll lead, and if I don't do it now, I might regret it in years to come. I have wrestled back and forth with this all night – in between trying to wrestle some space in the bed from my dear, duvet-hogging children.

So now what am I doing? Apart from running late again, I'm tearing my wardrobe limb from limb trying to find something to wear that's on the one hand utterly sexy, yet on the other, demure enough for the office. I have settled on another one of Sophie's sultry suits again. This time it's a lavender number and under it I'm wearing a clingy black top: if I pull it right down and tuck into my big pants then it gives me a fab cleavage. Oh, and the push-up bra has been rescued from the back of my undies drawer. I drew the line at the marabou thong because I couldn't then achieve the cleavage effect as I'd have nowhere to tuck the top. Sexy it may be, but practical it is not. Plus, if I put tights on top of the thong, it would squash all the feathers. I'll have to wait until I've got tanned legs to wear it.

I've been too busy with my wardrobe choices to have time to feed my children this morning, so Poppy has been in charge of breakfast. Which more than likely means there are a lot fewer chocolate things in the cupboard than there were half an hour ago. Connor is bearing a tell-tale brown ring round his mouth which I swish away with a J-Cloth. I have no idea where she gets her concept of nutrition from.

Anyway, they are now both ready and waiting. Poppy is lying on the bed again looking bored. She hasn't mentioned phoning

Stephanie Fisher though I can see the question lurking at the corners of her mouth.

As I'm hopping about trying to jam my feet into heels that aren't co-operating, the phone rings and this could well be the afore-mentioned Stephanie Fisher checking what Poppy is wearing for school. I am one of these old-fashioned parents who would heartily endorse a return to school uniform rather than suffer this daily ritual of fashion comparison. I do not want my children to express them-selves via their school clothing. As it is I have to have regular inspec-tions for all signs of nail varnish, eye-shadow and lip gloss that are sneaked on against all school regulations.

'Shit, shit,' I say, forgetting that Connor repeats all of my obscen-ities at inopportune moments. 'Get that please, sweetheart.'

Poppy rolls over and grabs the phone.

'But if it's Stephanie Fisher tell her you've no time to get changed now,' I add. 'And if it's anyone we owe money to, tell them that I've emigrated.'

Poppy puts the phone to her ear. 'Hello?' There is a gasp of delight from my daughter. 'Daddy! Daddy! It's Daddy!'

Poppy is wide-eyed with delight. I am less so. Dashing over to the bed, I grip the phone. Within seconds my knuckles have turned white. 'Bruno?' I spit. 'Is that you?'

There's no reply and after a moment, I hang up.

Poppy's face falls.

I put my arm round her and pull her into my side. 'There's no one there, sweetie.'

'He said hello,' Poppy insists. 'It sounded like Daddy.'

Would my daughter recognise the sound of Bruno's voice after so long? I'm not sure that I would.

'It was Daddy, wasn't it?'

'No,' I say softly. 'I don't think it was.' I give her another hug. 'Come on, time for school. We need to get our skates on.'

Poppy stands up and she's all deflated and lethargic. 'Why does he never ring any more?'

'I guess Daddy's busy, sweetheart,' I offer. *Wherever the bastard is,* I mutter to myself.

Poppy doesn't look convinced, but it's the best I can do. 'Go on.' I pat her on the behind. 'Be a good girl, take Connor and put him in the car for me.'

When I hear my daughter unlock the front door and know that she's safely out of the way, I check the 1471 redial on the phone,

178

but find that the caller has withheld their number. Typical. There's not much else I can do.

With a frantic glance at my watch, I finally finish putting on my shoes and hop out after my children.

Chapter Sixty-Two

Nick and Janine sat at the small frosted-glass table in the middle of the kitchen amid the white glossy units and stainless steel appliances. It was a far cry from his mother's rustic carved-oak-and-frilly-curtains kitchen. Nick looked down at his bowl – so was the breakfast. He and his wife – and didn't that seem like a funny word now – were struggling manfully through bowls of assorted nut muesli topped with live, natural yoghurt. A glass of freshly squeezed orange juice sat on a steel coaster etched with a Chinese symbol that meant good luck or good health or something. There wasn't a sausage or anything else cholesterol-forming in sight. He coughed and it sounded too loud in the silence. It was as if he'd never sat at this table in his entire life before, as if this scenario had never formed part of his daily routine.

Janine smiled across the table at him, but it was a tight and uncomfortable attempt at joviality. 'Did you sleep well?'

'Fine.' He'd hardly slept at all. It hadn't gone down very well with Janine when he'd decided that he wanted to spend the night in the spare room rather than reclaim the marital bed. Nick sighed inwardly. Was he being too sensitive about all this? Shouldn't he be marching in victorious and staking his claim back in his home? Should he have taken Janine upstairs, thrown her on the mattress and made love to her like some sort of conquering hero? She'd looked as if she'd expected that, but unfortunately it wasn't his style. He'd barely been able to bring himself to glance at the double bed that he and Janine had shared – the same one that had been recently vacated by Phil the Butcher. He couldn't in all honesty feel happy about lying where another man had just lain. It was bizarre, but while he'd been away from Janine he'd quite successfully managed to block out any images of her with her lover. Now that he was returned to the scene of the crime, as it were, it was proving a lot more difficult to pretend that all of this had never happened. Somehow to be here again made it more raw, splitting open wounds that he had thought were healing quite nicely.

Plus, the bed might as well have been a concrete block compared to the squishy worn mattress of his childhood bed. Somehow he'd developed too many elbows and knees and his hips were more bony than he remembered. Janine was very keen on hard beds and he'd realised at three o'clock in the morning that he was less so.

Completing his ablutions had been fraught with difficulty too. Instead of enjoying seeing Janine bounce backwards and forwards to the bathroom in her skimpy black underwear, he'd been terrified of bumping into her in a state of undress. Once upon a time, every morning had been a friendly fight in front of the mirror, each one vying for space to brush teeth, wash faces, apply make-up – Janine, not him. If they were late they shared the shower, which usually made them even more late. Today he lay in bed frozen until he was sure that all the slooshing and splashing and scrubbing had finished. Only then had he felt safe to pad across the landing in his boxers and for the first time ever in his own bathroom, he'd locked the door.

'What would you like for dinner tonight?' Janine sounded strained. Was this what their conversation was reduced to?

Nick shrugged. 'As long as it doesn't involve some sort of heavy-duty sponge pudding, I don't mind.'

'I've got some nice lamb in the freezer,' Janine said.

They both looked up, realising the implications of this simple statement.

Janine's face was bleak. She mimicked her own voice, but made it sound truly pathetic. '"There's some nice lamb in the freezer".' She picked up her spoon and banged herself on the head with it. 'What are you thinking of, you stupid, stupid cow?'

'That's okay,' Nick said. 'I guess it's not going to be that easy, slotting back into each other's lives again.'

'No,' Janine agreed. 'I'm sorry. Really sorry.'

They both concentrated on their muesli.

'Lamb?' Nick said after a few mouthfuls of cereal. 'So, you're not a vegetarian any more?'

His wife looked at him sheepishly. 'Lapsed.'

'Oh.' How could he have expected that time had stood still for Janine too? She would have moved on, changed, evolved into a shape that fitted her new relationship. But becoming a meat-eater? That was like the Pope deciding he'd become an atheist. 'Maybe fish would be nice.'

'Fish,' Janine echoed earnestly. 'Yes. Fish would be nice. I'll get some salmon.'

Organic, no doubt. Fewer toxins. They picked up and sipped their fresh orange juice in unison.

'Salmon's okay?'

'Salmon's fine.'

Nick gave up with his cereal. It was clearly going to take some time to wean himself off his mother's succulent grilled bacon and yellow, fluffy scrambled eggs swimming in butter. 'Janine, why did you split with Phil?'

His wife also pushed her breakfast away from her. 'I don't really want to discuss that,' she said. 'I think we should forget the past and move on.'

If only it were that simple, Nick thought. When he'd left, Janine had refused to talk about the reasons for the breakdown in their marriage, she'd refused to consider counselling and, apart from the fact that she'd fallen in love with another man, he really had no idea what he'd done wrong. It wasn't going to be easy to make sure he didn't do it again, if he didn't know what 'it' was.

'Well.' Nick got up from the table. 'The wanton world of used cars waits for no one.' Remembering that now he hadn't got his mother to clear up after him, he decided he ought to take his empty bowl and glass to the dishwasher. 'I'd better get going.'

'Nick,' Janine said anxiously. 'Everything's going to be all right, isn't it?'

'Of course it is.' Nick went back to her and kissed her briefly on the lips. They didn't seem to fit together as easily as they used to. In six months apart the shape of your lips couldn't change, could they? 'It'll just take time.'

And hard work. And tolerance. And forgiveness. Nick never thought love would be perfect, but he didn't imagine it would be this flawed either.

Chapter Sixty-Three

At the King residence all hell was breaking loose. In the kitchen, breakfast television was blaring out from the portable set in the corner. Some woman in a leotard was jumping around like a thing possessed. Charlotte was crying so loudly that she was about to burst her lungs or everyone else's eardrums. Ellie, also at the top of her voice, was singing 'Baa-Baa Black Sheep' above the din. In the middle of it all Sophie was trying to concentrate on boiling eggs and producing perfect toast soldiers. She pushed the pinger to time the eggs for five minutes – if the yolk was too hard, Charlotte would scream even louder. And her darling child wasn't the only one who felt like screaming. Sophie sighed to herself – another jolly day in the family home. 'Fuck,' she muttered under her breath.

Tom came into the kitchen. He hadn't eaten any breakfast, but he was already dressed for work and was carrying his toolkit. They hadn't spoken yet this morning, but there was nothing unusual in that.

'I'm going to work,' her husband said.

Sophie could hardly bring herself to acknowledge him. Last night he had lain in bed next to her, making sure that he kept a good six inches between their bodies, his back, as rigid as wood, turned towards her. Sophie, in turn, lay on her back staring at the ceiling, seething quietly and thinking how different it was compared to how she'd spent the previous few hours.

'I'm going to work,' Tom repeated.

'Yeah. Yeah.'

'Any plans for today?'

Sophie spun round in surprise. 'Me?'

Tom shrugged.

'Yeah,' Sophie said. 'As a matter of fact, I've got a pedicure booked for nine. Then I'm playing tennis with Amelia, followed by lunch at The Ivy. I thought I might do a little shopping at Harvey Nics in the afternoon.'

Her husband did not look amused.

'Or I could stay here,' she continued, 'and look after the bloody kids all day.'

Tom's jaw set. 'See you later.' And he slammed out of the front door.

Sophie sagged against the work surface. For all that bluff and bravado, she now felt terrible. This was no way to conduct a marriage. She sighed wearily. But there was no way she could continue to live this half-life either. She was destined to spend too little time on this planet as it was to commit it to a man who wasn't the slightest bit interested in her any more. When had the rot started to set in? Was it when they'd had the children? Had the very thing that was supposed to unite them as a family, been a catalyst in driving them apart? They seemed to have very little in common these days apart from their two lovely girls. Now the children were the only cement in their rather shaky wall. Would it be easier to up sticks and start all over again? It was an even more difficult decision to stay when she knew that there was someone waiting in the wings for her with strong arms and a sexy body.

The smell of burning roused her from her reverie.

'Toast!' Charlotte shouted.

And two black, smoking pieces of bread shot out of the toaster. Sophie pulled out the smouldering remains and tossed them on to the bread board where they lay accusingly. Charred to the point of charcoal, not even a liberal coating of butter and strawberry jam could be employed to disguise their condition. Beyond redemption, Sophie decided. And, as she flipped open the bin to discard them, she wondered what else was.

Chapter Sixty-Four

Nick sat at his desk, surrounded by papers – piles and piles of papers. He no longer had any clue where their intended home might be. He pushed them to one side. There was still no sign of Anna, but then it was early. And he didn't want to examine the reasons why he was happier to come into the office an hour before he really needed to rather than stay at home facing Janine across the breakfast-table.

He needed to talk to Sam. Picking up the phone, he dialled his friend's work number. Sam would have been at his desk for hours. He was one of those people who measured his worth by the number of hours he spent at work. And, on that marker, Sam was very worthwhile.

Unusually, Sam's direct line rang for a few moments before it was answered by a colleague. 'Sam Felstead's phone.'

'Oh,' Nick said. 'Can I speak to Sam, please?'

'Sorry, Sam's not in today,' the woman said. 'He phoned in sick about a half-hour ago.'

'Sick?'

'I know,' she said. 'I've never known him to miss a day's work before. Can I help you?'

'No,' Nick said. 'But thanks. I'm just a friend. I'll give him a call at home.'

'Okay.'

Nick hung up and punched in Sam's home number. The answer-phone cut in. *'Hi, this is Sam Felstead. I'm currently out with Gwyneth or maybe Cameron. Catch you later.'*

'Mate,' Nick said. 'Where are you? The office said you were sick. Give me a call.' He replaced the receiver just as Anna came through the door.

'Wow!' Nick let out an involuntary exclamation. 'You look wonderful.'

'Thanks.' Anna smiled shyly. 'It's just something old I threw on.'

'Well, it worked,' Nick said. 'I'm not sure this office is worthy of you.' Good grief, she looked fabulous. All scrubbed and shiny like a new pin. 'Wait.' Nick frowned. 'You've not got an interview for a better job?'

'There isn't a better job,' Anna replied. 'Shall I put the kettle on?'

'No.' Nick held up his hand, vacating his seat. 'You make terrible tea. I'll do it. Come on, my Executive Assistant and Business Advisor, you sit here and carry on with our plans for world domination.'

Anna laughed and took her place behind Nick's desk while he headed for the wonky table with the kettle balanced precariously on it.

'I've been thinking,' Anna said. 'I've come up with some great plans for the new improved Nick Diamond empire. And none of them involve you making the tea.' She wagged a finger at him.

'Good,' Nick said. 'I could do with something to cheer me up.'

'Why?' Anna said as she started shuffling papers. 'Heard any more from the jogging monster?'

'Yeah.' Nick hesitated and Anna looked up from her task. He scratched at his ear even though it wasn't itchy. 'I moved back in with her last night.'

Anna was clearly taken aback.

'We're going to give it another go,' he admitted sheepishly. Why did he feel so terrible about telling Anna this?

'Good. Good.' Anna had flushed to the colour of the sexy red suit she was wearing when they went out to lunch last week. 'I'm pleased for you. Delighted. It's wonderful. Marvellous. Great. Fantastic. Great. *Really* great . . .'

She finally ran out of steam and adjectives, so they both stared silently at each other across the office.

'You don't think I should have done it, do you?'

'Take no notice of my ramblings.' Anna brushed a hand through the air in a dismissive wave. 'It's none of my business, Nick. She's your wife. It's good. Very good. It's . . .'

'Don't start that again,' he begged.

Anna stopped and her face crumpled. She even looked as if she might cry. Her voice was almost inaudible when she spoke. 'It's the right thing to do.'

'Is it?' Nick said, coming to sit on the garden chair opposite her. Anna's cheeks were still tinged with a blush and her eyes were teary and troubled. 'Then why does it feel so wrong?'

Chapter Sixty-Five

This time, Sophie had at least had the good sense to organise with Tom's mum that she would stay at home to look after the children for the day. After that, all good sense had departed out of the window.

It was just after nine o'clock when Sophie pulled up outside Margaret's house and unloaded her own two hyperactive children from the car plus a soundly sleeping Connor still fastened into his car seat from when Anna dropped him off earlier this morning. She struggled the dead weight of Connor up the garden path. How people ever considered having more than two children of their own was a mystery to her. Yet there were loads of families who had three, four, even more offspring. Imagine having IVF and giving birth to four at once. That was Sophie's vision of hell.

Margaret was waiting at the door for them and Sophie's heart squeezed painfully at the thought of deceiving this lovely woman who had done every single thing she could to help them as a family. Nothing was too much trouble for Tom's mum. Anything she could do to make their lives a little easier she did. Occasionally she'd turn up unannounced and clear the entire ironing basket for Sophie, and she'd usually arrive with some delicious cake she'd baked as she knew how much Tom liked home-made cakes. Sophie knew that too, but it still didn't tempt her to do wonderful things with eggs and flour for her husband's delectation. The only time she got involved in baking – and that was only the cake-mix variety – it was to keep the girls out of trouble for an hour or so. Tom's mother was a proper mother, the old-fashioned type with old-fashioned loyalty to the family. Sophie herded the children to the door, guiltily.

'How are my lovely girls?' Margaret cooed.

'Nana!' Ellie rushed into her arms, closely followed by Charlotte. Sophie trailed behind them and then as she approached, Margaret kissed her on the cheek.

'Come on in. Come on in. You'll catch your death out here.'

'I can't stay,' Sophie said. 'I have to be going.'

'Come in while I get them out of their coats,' Margaret insisted. 'Bring Connor in and put him in the lounge.' She peeped into his chair. 'Oh bless,' she said. 'He's spark out. I'll leave him in there until he wakes up.'

Even though Connor technically wasn't related to them Margaret had known Anna long enough to treat her kids like extended grand-children.

Sophie followed them all through into the hall. A cocoon of warm air enveloped them, fuggy and sleep-inducing, and Sophie reckoned that Margaret's central-heating thermostat must be set in excess of twenty-five degrees. The girls certainly weren't in any danger of catching cold here today. There was a hint of cinnamon drifting from the kitchen on a raft of baking smells. Tom's mum was the epitome of domesticity. Anyone wandering into Sophie's house couldn't hope for much better than the smell of something unpleasant rotting in the fridge. Grief, what a mess she was. No wonder Tom had lost interest in her when he'd been used to this sort of treatment at home. And it wasn't that Margaret had been a stay-at-home mum; she'd worked in a school canteen for most of her life. It was only in recent years that she'd retired and had time on her hands.

The girls were standing obediently while their granny stripped them of their coats. 'You look tired, love,' Margaret noted.

'Yeah,' Sophie agreed. 'I'm not sleeping that well.'

Margaret patted Charlotte on the bottom and sent her packing into the lounge. Ellie followed her. It was a typical grandma's house with patterned carpets and net curtains and every surface stacked with sparkling ornaments that Ellie and Charlotte were allowed to play with. Margaret kept a dressing-up box for them filled with old evening dresses and stiletto heels and glittering marcasite necklaces that had belonged to her mother. The children loved it. 'Is every-thing all right?'

Sophie tried a smile which didn't reach the required level of light-ness. 'Just the daily grind of life.'

'You definitely look peaky. It's nice that you're going to have some time to yourself today.' Margaret gave her a sympathetic glance. 'It's never easy with two little ones. They're a full-time job.' Her eyes followed her grandchildren into the lounge. 'Lovely as they are.'

'Yeah,' Sophie agreed. 'They're even lovelier when they're asleep.'

She followed Margaret into the kitchen where the older woman opened the oven door to check on the progress of whatever was inside. 'Gingerbread men,' Tom's mum informed her. 'I thought they could ice them later.'

Sophie smiled tiredly. 'You're a peach.'

Margaret frowned at her. 'What's the matter, love? Everything all right with you and Tom?'

'Fine,' Sophie said, avoiding her gaze.

'I know he's not the most communicative of men,' his mother said. 'He was just the same as a child. You could never get more than two words out of him.' Margaret put a hand on her arm. 'But he does love you, you know.'

'Yeah.'

'Why don't I babysit for you at the weekend?' Margaret offered. 'It's ages since you've been out together. You should go out somewhere nice for the evening.'

'I'll mention it to Tom.' Sophie could think of nothing worse than sitting across a candlelit dinner-table from someone who had nothing to say to her these days. It would be a waste of fifty quid.

'What are you going to do today?'

'Nothing much. A bit of shopping. Some lunch.'

'Who did you say you were meeting?'

Sophie had steadfastly avoiding mentioning anyone. 'Anna,' she blurted out under Margaret's enquiring eye.

'I thought Anna was working now,' Tom's mum said. 'Isn't that why you've got Connor?'

'Yeah, well.' Sophie shuffled uncomfortably. 'Anna's blagged a day off too. She dropped Connor off because she had to pop into the office for an hour.'

'Oh, that is nice,' Margaret said. 'You two girls have always been such friends.'

But Sophie wondered how much longer Anna would stay her friend if she kept incriminating her in her tortured love-life. If she was going to lie to everyone, she must start to brush up her stories and get them prepared in advance. Sophie nodded her head towards the door. 'I'd better get a move on,' she said.

'Yes,' Margaret agreed as she followed her out into the hall and to the door. 'Don't keep Anna waiting.'

'Bye, girls,' Sophie shouted and Ellie and Charlotte came bowling out to kiss her goodbye. 'Be good for Nana,' she instructed.

'Bye bye, Mummy,' Ellie and Charlotte said.

'Bye, Margaret.' Sophie pecked her mother-in-law on the cheek. 'I'll see you later.'

'You two girls have a lovely day,' Tom's mum said as they all stood at the door and waved her off. 'Don't you worry about us.'

But worry she would. Walking down the path away from her family Sophie felt like the biggest heel in the world, but she kept her bright smile pinned in place until she was safely in her car. Then she waved for the last time and drove off.

In her relief to be away from the stifling heat of Margaret's house and heading to her lover, Sophie failed to see Tom's car parked just down the road behind her. And she failed to notice him pull out and follow her, at a discreet distance, down the street.

Chapter Sixty-Six

I'm still reeling from Nick's announcement that he's moved back in with Janine, but I'm trying not to show it. This shouldn't bother me as I knew all along that he was still in love with her. But it does bother me, goddammit! I really thought that we were getting along well on Saturday and, I'll admit, in a coupley sort of way. I was sure there was a bit of a frisson between us, the type that I haven't experienced in a long time. It just shows that my super-sensitive love detector has gone wonky through lack of use. Oh well, back to the chocolate and Chardonnay for solace. And the truth of the matter is that I just ought to give up on the opposite sex. No wonder I'd rather have a bar of Dairy Milk than sex these days. At least after a bar of chocolate you know it's not going to turn round and ask, 'What's for dinner?'

It's a stinky horrible day – the sort of day that British winters do so well, where the grey of the sky matches the grey of the pavements and the sleeting rain is relentless. The landscape has blurred into one indistinguishable soggy mess. This is the price we're paying for having one of the longest, hottest summers on record last year. Somehow, I don't think there'll be a lot of people rushing out to buy secondhand cars today. Nick is kicking round the office, looking listless.

I have thrown myself into my work which involves trying to make the computer do the things I want it to do without resorting to tears. I'm also trying to do it without sticking out my tongue.

'You'll bite it off,' Nick says.

And failing.

I stop bashing at the computer and he perches on the desk in front of me on the one spare inch that isn't under the deluge of paperwork.

'You didn't say what you thought of me and Janine getting back together.'

'It shouldn't matter what I think.'

'I value your opinion,' my boss says.

'I'm not the world expert on these things,' I say. 'But maybe it's better to stay with the devil you know.'

Nick fiddles with the tired, leaky biros in the pen-holder. 'To be honest, Anna, one of the reasons I'm rushing back to Janine is that I'm frightened to death of going back on the market to find someone else to love. Who would want me?'

I don't answer that.

'If I could put myself on eBay that would be one thing,' he continues while the obvious stares him in the face. '*Male, loveable, slightly shop-soiled, heart possibly broken but could be restored with some well-placed tender loving care.* But doing the whole dating thing at my age? Well, it's not natural, is it? I shouldn't be out chasing women in short skirts.'

I look down at the length of my skirt and so does Nick.

'I want to be at home assembling childproof gates and taking my turns with bathtime. That's what I feel I should be doing.'

'It sounds very admirable,' I say. 'If a little unusual these days.' The kids thought he was wonderful too and haven't stopped talking about him since Saturday – which is heartrending. I'm trying to work my socks off to deliver them all manner of delights on a plate, and the one thing that I can't give them is the thing they need the most. A nice, homely father in their little lives.

'And what if the devil I know isn't interested in these things?' Nick asks.

I sigh at him. 'Then maybe the devil you know doesn't deserve you.'

He ponders this without speaking, but his face looks so sad that I'm sure he's not convinced this is the right thing for him. I admire him for his loyalty to Janine, but I for one am also a great exponent of misplaced loyalty.

'Speaking of devils we know,' I say, trying to change the subject, 'have you heard anything from Sam? I think Sophie was round there last night.'

'I called his office and he's off work sick today,' Nick says with a frown. 'Sam's never sick. His bloodstream is ninety per cent alcohol. Germs can't survive in it. I've called his flat too, but all I get is the world's worst answerphone message.'

'Maybe you should go round there,' I suggest. 'I don't think there are going to be coachloads out here today.' I flick my thumb towards the large puddles that are forming in the car yard amid the forlorn rain-streaked cars.

'You could be right.'

'I think Sophie's husband Tom may suspect something. He called me last night looking for her and that's just not like him.'

'Oh marvellous,' Nick says. 'As if I haven't got enough problems of my own.'

'I've tried calling her mobile, but my darling friend's not picking up. And she's ignoring my text messages.'

'I can't understand what Sam sees in her,' Nick admitted. 'It's not that she's not pretty, and she's got a great sense of humour.' He gives me a rueful glance. 'She laughed like a drain when Connor relieved himself on my best suit.'

I put my head in my hands. 'Don't remind me.'

'But he could have anyone. Really,' he says, as if to convince me. Maybe I look doubtful. 'Anyone – and without the complications that Sophie brings with her. It would be much more understandable if, say, he'd fallen head over heels in love with *you.*'

I try not to look shocked. 'Would it?'

My boss flushes to his hair roots. 'Yes,' he blabbers. 'Completely understandable. You're very . . . very agreeable.'

I can't help but grin. *'Agreeable?'*

'Yes. Very much so.'

'Remind me never to ask you for a character reference, Nick,' I tease. '"Anna is agreeable".'

He in turn looks flustered. 'Well, there are other things I could say but I'd probably better not.'

And I'm left wondering what they might be as Nick stands up and, appearing glad of the excuse to escape, announces: 'I think I'll jump in the car and shoot over there. Check on Sam. Make sure everything's all right. You'll be okay here on your own?'

'I'll be fine.'

'Anna,' he says, and then fidgets in front of the desk. 'I do like you being here.'

I try to ignore the wind whistling round my knees through the gaps in the desk and the tattered blinds and the beige walls pocked with Blu-Tack marks. 'I like it too.'

'If we do get the money from Mr Hashimoto, it won't be like this for ever. It will be bigger, better . . .'

'Less draughty?'

'And no mushrooms growing behind the filing cabinets.'

I hadn't noticed those.

'I won't be long,' Nick says as he grabs his jacket. 'See you later.'

I watch him plod across the windswept car yard, head down, collar up, and he hasn't even got into his car before I start to miss him. This is not good. Not good at all.

Chapter Sixty-Seven

For the second time in as many days, Sophie pulled up outside Sam's apartment. If this carried on – and in some ways she hoped it would – she would need to get the code to the private area of parking in the underground garage so that her car could be tucked out of the way of prying eyes. Although this didn't seem to be curtain twitchers' territory – unlike the road Tom's mum lived in.

Sophie had been sure to wait for her husband to leave for work this morning until she changed into smarter clothes. And she'd freshly washed her hair and taken care over her make-up – both unheard of in the King household on a weekday morning. But Sam was worth the extra effort. This was the sort of sexual relationship of which she'd always dreamed. One that involved passion and mild perversion and chocolate body-paint. Their appetites matched each other's perfectly. They say that sex alone can't make for a great relationship, but it certainly doesn't make for a great relationship if there isn't any at all. Take one important ingredient out of a cake-mix and it will fail to rise to the desired heights. Sophie decided that marriages were the same.

She buzzed at the door to gain entry to Sam's apartment again. Even that small act seemed exciting, as if she were going to be allowed into some secret place, and there was a new energy in her step as she raced up the stairs to his front door. She didn't notice as she slid inside the doorway that Tom had pulled up a little way down the road.

Her lover was waiting there for her, a dark shadow over his chin, still sporting bed hair and clad only in his dressing-gown. Not a ratty ten-year-old towelling affair like Tom wore, but a short, black number that showed his strong legs. His feet were bare whereas her husband had taken to wearing socks and slippers years ago. It looked like his sheets would still bear the warm imprint of his body. Sophie smiled to herself. Why did men never make the same effort with their appearance as women did? They were just as vain, just as worried about ageing as women were these days, but they never made the same connection with spending hours in front of the mirror to stave off the horrors that everyday living could inflict on a person. Their battle with face creams, tweezers and toiletries seemed cursory by comparison. Sam looked utterly gorgeous nevertheless.

'Hi,' he said, kissing her hard on the lips and pulling her towards him.

'I don't know what I'm doing here,' Sophie said when he finally let her up for air.

'Oh, I think you do,' Sam said with a grin, as he unbuttoned her coat and peeled it off her.

The apartment was immaculate, a minimalist palace of wood floors, leather sofas and bold paintings with blocks of bright colours. Little piles of bachelor nonsense brought the only homely feel to it – a PlayStation plugged into the huge plasma-screen television, an untidy pile of *GQ* magazines and newspapers, a bank of remote controls lined up on the glass coffee-table. This wasn't the sort of place she could imagine strewn with so many toys that you could barely see the floor. Sam wouldn't take kindly to crayon on the walls, whereas in her home it seemed to add to the general air of neglect.

As she was being showered with kisses, she glanced through to the kitchen. It was tiny and oh-so sophisticated. A sleek arrangement of steel and black granite. It looked as if a meal had never been cooked in it. Sophie couldn't imagine knocking together boisterous family meals in something that was more like a work of art than a working kitchen. There was a juicer, a cappuccino maker, a cocktail shaker lined up ready for use, all in fingerprint-free, gleaming chrome. They didn't look as if they'd ever been used in anger either. She wondered if Sam ever did his own cooking. There was so little she knew about him. It wasn't as if they spent what precious time she'd managed to snatch with him in deep and meaningful conversation.

Sam discarded her coat, tossing it onto the sofa, and started on the buttons of her blouse.

She felt a pang of guilt. What was she, raddled and wrecked housewife and mother of two, doing in a place like this? A pang of guilt twisted her insides. What was she thinking of? 'I'm wrestling with my conscience,' Sophie said.

'I'd rather you came and wrestled with me.' Sam pressed on with her disrobing. He eased her blouse from her shoulders.

'I'm married,' she said to Sam.

196

He put his hands on her arms and gazed into her eyes. 'This I know.'

Sophie stood there feeling self-conscious in her bra. 'I shouldn't be behaving like this,' she said. 'I've dumped the kids on Tom's mum today. I've left them with her while I'm out betraying her son. She thinks I'm having a well-deserved day off with Anna. I'm supposed to be shopping. Do you know how that makes me feel?'

'Terrible,' Sam said. 'And that's because you're a nice person.'

'I'm not nice,' Sophie said. 'How could I do this if I were nice?'

Sam flopped down on one of the leather sofas and cajoled her onto his lap, cradling her in his arms. He pulled her head down to his shoulder and stroked her hair. 'Marriage isn't like a puppy,' Sam said softly. 'It doesn't have to be for life any more.'

She sighed unhappily into his neck.

'People change,' Sam continued. 'Their needs change. You're probably not the same person you were ten years ago.'

'I'm not the same person I was ten days ago,' Sophie mumbled.

'You have one life to live.' Sam traced his fingers over her bare arms. 'Should you be forced to spend it with the wrong person simply because you signed a piece of paper saying that you would?'

'It isn't that easy,' Sophie said.

'I know.'

'You've never been married,' she said. 'Have you?'

'No,' Sam admitted. 'I've never even come close.'

'Then you can't understand this,' she said. 'Tom's a good man. For whatever reason, it just doesn't seem to be working for us any more. We've grown apart.'

'I love you,' Sam said.

Sophie's stomach lurched as if she were riding in a high-speed lift. She hadn't heard those three words for too long.

'This isn't just a bit of fun for me.' His fingers moved to her breasts, easing inside her bra. Her sexy, sex-shop bra that she'd chosen specially for him. It made her feel cheap. 'Well, not all the time.'

'I've got two kids.'

'And very lovely they are.' Sam dipped his head and kissed her throat.

'I should put them first.'

'Yes,' Sam said, 'but you should also consider your own needs. And Tom may be a good man, but he isn't meeting them.'

She couldn't argue with that. This was ridiculous, she'd felt dead for years and all it took was an hour in Sam's arms to make her feel as if she was alive again.

'Leave him,' Sam said. 'Come and live here.'

'You don't mean that.'

'Try me.'

'What would I do with the kids? Does this place even allow children inside?'

'There aren't any kids living here, but it doesn't mean they can't,' Sam said. 'It's right on the park. They'd love it.'

Would they? 'And what if you decide that it's not right for you, after all?' Sophie asked. 'What if you got tired of us? What if Ellie threw up on the sofa and Charlotte put jammy fingers all over your plasma screen? What if you came home to the screaming harpy that I usually am?'

'It wouldn't be like that.'

But it would, she thought, but didn't say it. It wouldn't be about us any more. There would be other people to consider. Other hearts to break. Would Sam really be able to cope with the grim reality that generally made up family life? Would he eventually move on, find someone else who suited his needs better, rather than feel trapped with the wrong person as he had just advocated she should do? Would he be there, steady and plodding, day in, day out as Tom was?

Sam's fingers travelled to the zip of her skirt and he slithered it down. 'We are wasting valuable time,' he whispered into her hair as his lips brushed over it. 'I want to make love to you.'

Sophie melted in his arms, surrendering to his kisses, swamped by desire. If only she had a little switch that could turn off her brain.

Chapter Sixty-Eight

Nick pulled up outside Sam's flat in his battered old car. He jumped out and slammed the door, watching in dismay as his hubcab fell off. Picking it up and banging it back in place, Nick vowed to sort himself out a new set of wheels as soon as he got back to the yard. He sprinted across the rain-lashed road and up to the front door, where he buzzed Sam's intercom.

'Hi,' Sam's disembodied voice crackled out.

'It's me, mate,' Nick said. 'And I'm piss-wet through, so be quick.'

The entrance lock clicked and opened. Nick pushed inside and plodded up the stairs shivering. What a God-awful day to be out on a mercy mission when he could have been cosied up in the office with Anna, indulging in some choccy biscuits and hot coffee.

Like Sophie, Nick also failed to notice that his every move was being watched by the man across the road, slumped down behind the wheel of his car.

As Nick approached Sam's flat, his friend opened the door. His hair was in a mess and he was still in his dressing-gown.

'What are you doing here?' Sam asked briskly, which Nick thought was a bit churlish.

'The office said you were sick,' Nick explained. 'And you never pick up your bloody answerphone messages. I thought you might have been collapsed on the floor in a pool of your own vomit.'

'What a pleasant thought.'

'You look all right,' Nick said, giving his friend the once-over. 'What's the matter with you?'

'Nothing,' Sam confided. 'I'm having a duvet day.' He winked and jerked his head towards the bedroom. Suddenly the penny dropped with Nick.

'Oh.' He huffed at Sam. 'So *that's* why you're keeping me standing in the hall.'

'Yes.'

'This is getting too complicated for me.' Nick shook his head. 'I think you *must* be sick – or insane.'

'I love her,' Sam said plainly. 'She loves me.'

Nick held up a hand. 'I don't want to get involved, mate.'

'Then why are you here?'

'Look,' Nick said, 'Anna's been trying to get hold of Sophie too. She thinks her old man might suspect something.'

'Trust me,' Sam said smugly. 'He's completely clueless.'

'Well, in my experience it isn't always the husband who's the last to know.'

Sam clapped his hand on Nick's shoulder. 'You worry too much, my friend.'

'And you don't worry enough.'

'Anyway,' Sam said, brushing the comment aside, 'how is it going with Janine? Is it like riding a bike – back in the saddle as if you'd never been away?'

'No,' Nick admitted. 'Not quite. It's more like walking on eggshells.'

Sam gave him a sympathetic look.

'I'm in the spare room,' Nick went on. 'I couldn't . . . It just seemed too . . . Somehow my side of the bed still seemed a bit too warm,' he finally settled on.

'Mate,' Sam said, 'you need my full attention. And I'm a bit busy right now.' He cast a longing look back to his bedroom.

'Right,' Nick said. 'Of course you are. Sorry. Look – very sorry. I just thought . . . I wanted to make sure you were okay.'

'I'm fine,' Sam insisted. 'Never better. But I'll call you. I promise. I'll give you a bell later and we can sink a beer or two.'

'Yeah,' Nick said, knowing full well that there was no way Janine would let him go out tonight with Sam. Tonight they were going to sit opposite each other in strained silence and have grilled organic salmon while they picked over the shreds of their tattered marriage. Beer and bullshit with Sam sounded like a wonderful alternative.

'Thanks, mate,' Sam said, ushering him towards the door. 'I do appreciate it.' But it was hard for him to disguise the urgency in his voice and the twinkle of lust in his eye. Sam was obviously dying to get back to his unfinished business and Nick supposed he ought to get back to his, now that he knew Sam wasn't in any immediate danger.

'I'll see myself out.' It was clear that he wasn't wanted. And, if there was one thing he could take, it was a hint.

Chapter Sixty-Nine

He needed to be out of here quick, Nick thought, before Sam and Sophie got down to it again. This might be a luxury apartment block, but the walls were probably as thin as any downmarket terraced house. As Nick was about to let himself out of Sam's front door, the intercom buzzed.

'I'll get it,' Nick shouted, but there was no reply from Sam. He picked up the internal phone. 'Hi.'

'Delivery,' a gruff voice said.

'Come up.' Nick pressed the button to unlock the main door. It was a good job he was here otherwise Sam would have been practising coitus interruptus once again. With a quick glance towards the bedroom, from which there was thankfully still no noise, Nick opened the front door to the apartment.

Before he knew what had hit him, someone literally *had* hit him. A fist cannoned out of nowhere and hit him squarely on the nose. Nick fell to the floor, clutching his face. Blood poured through his hands. It was the second time he'd been floored in as many weeks – something in his lifestyle had to change.

A man towered over him, rubbing his reddened knuckles. His face was white with anger and he was heavy-set and looked as if he was someone you shouldn't mess with. Nick's whole head throbbed with pain.

The man wagged a meaty finger at Nick. 'Stay away from my wife.'

'But . . .' Nick said, desperately trying to come round from his daze.

'I don't want any buts,' the man said. 'Just listen to me. Stay away.'

'Okay,' Nick said feebly. If this nightclub bouncer of a guy thought that he was Sam, then let him think that. Nick could protest his innocence, but then that would put his friend in line for a beating too.

The man marched off, slamming the door to the block of flats behind him.

Nick lay on the cold, tiled floor of Sam's hall and wished the pain would stop. So, he thought, his assailant was presumably Sophie's husband. Unless there were any more husbands out there looking for his friend, which was always a possibility. All sorts of bits of him hurt – even bits that hadn't been hit. A pleasant blackness was creeping in at the edges of his vision. 'Aargh,' Nick said to no one in particular.

From somewhere far away in a different world, he heard Sam's bedroom door open. His friend rushed out. 'Has he gone?'

'Mmm,' Nick muttered.

'Oh shit.' Sam came and knelt down by his head. 'That was Tom. Sophie's husband.'

'Really?' Nick wasn't sure if a word came out.

'Jeepers,' Sam was panicking. 'He's hit you!'

'Yes. He has.' If there was a degree in the bleeding obvious his friend could get an honorary one.

'Fuck,' Sam said. 'You're pouring with blood.'

Nick tried to push himself up. 'It's only a flesh wound.' The room spun round alarmingly.

Sam steadied him, heaved his dead weight onto his shoulder and half-dragged him through to the lounge. 'Tom must know about us.' Sam chewed his lip anxiously.

'I think that's a safe assumption.'

Sophie bustled in, trying to smooth down her dishevelled hair, belting Sam's dressing-gown round her.

'Hi, Sophie,' Nick managed as he lay prostrate on his friend's couch wishing he was anywhere but here in the middle of their not-so-secret love tryst.

'I'm so sorry that you've been brought into this,' she said tearfully, handing him one of Sam's small black hand-towels that she'd brought out of his bathroom.

'Is there anything I can do?' Sam asked.

'Stop shagging other people's wives.'

Sophie burst into tears.

'No offence meant,' Nick said.

'I was thinking of brandy or beer,' Sam said darkly. 'I've got some Stella in the fridge.'

'Is beer good for a broken nose?' It seemed like a good question.

'You think it's broken?'

How can I have been punched that hard and it not be broken, Nick thought. He said nothing, but he lay there with the feeling that this was the first in a horrible chain of events that would leave all of their lives changed irrevocably.

Sophie stood looking shamefaced on the periphery. 'I'd better get dressed,' she said sheepishly and disappeared back into the bedroom.

'I owe you for this, mate,' Sam said gratefully.

Nick let his eyelids grow heavy and fall shut. The room closed in, enveloping him, and the last thing he remembered saying was, 'Yes. You do.'

Chapter Seventy

I've been working frantically all day in between trying to call both Sophie and Nick to find out what the hell is going on. Neither of them have their mobile phones switched on – which is typical. We have all the technology in the world these days and it still fails at the first sign of human error.

It's late in the afternoon when Nick finally returns to the office. I watch as he steps out of the car and then take in the blood and the bruises that grace his countenance. My stomach turns over. I've seen this type of beating far more often than I care to remember. I abandon my computer and rush out to meet him.

'I met Sophie's husband,' he says by way of explanation.

'He hit you?'

'Yes,' Nick says. 'Rather hard.'

'But why?'

'He thought I was the philandering bastard Sam Felstead,' Nick says resignedly. 'An easy mistake to make.'

'I take it you were in Sam's flat.'

'Yes,' Nick says. 'Trying to make a sharp exit before your friend and mine got down to it.'

'How awful for you.'

'Yes,' Nick says again.

His clean white shirt is now spattered with crimson blood and it's crusted round his nose. The latter is the size of an apple and there's a vicious split on the bridge of it. Nick looks thoroughly and utterly pissed off.

'Come on.' I slip my arm round him. 'I'm great at tea and sympathy.'

Now I've got him reclined in his office chair and I'm on the garden chair next to him dabbing gingerly at his face with wet tissues. There is a cup of tea with two sugars in it – even though Nick doesn't take sugar. But isn't that what they do with blood donors to help them recover? It can't do any harm. Two rather soft chocolate digestives wait patiently on a plate next to him.

'Ouch,' he says and pushes my hand away. 'Don't we need raw steak for this?'

'No.' I resume my dabbing and Nick lets me. 'We just need friends who can keep their hands off each other.'

'That seems to be asking rather too much.' Nick tries to feel his nose. 'Do you think it's broken?'

'No,' I say. 'I have some experience of this. I broke my nose a couple of years ago.'

'Did someone else's husband punch you too?' Nick jokes.

'No,' I say sharply and then wish that I hadn't opened my big fat mouth. 'You'll be fine. A few days of swelling, a couple of good shiners. Nothing that a few painkillers won't sort out.'

Nick sighs. 'I could kill Sam.'

'You're lucky you didn't get killed for him,' I tut. 'I can't believe Tom did this. He's normally such a quiet man.'

'Ah,' Nick says sagely. 'It's the quiet ones that you have to watch.'

'I've tried calling Sophie,' I say worriedly, 'but there's still no answer from her damn phone. What did she say?'

'Not a lot,' Nick admits. 'But she got dressed pretty quickly. An unusual trait in a woman, if you ask me.'

'Maybe she was trying to head off her hubby at the pass.'

I give a last and rather tender dab at Nick's nose. His lip is split too where he must have bitten down on it. I give that a dab too, before I sit back and look at him. 'I think you should go home and rest. This has been a terrible shock for you.'

'Maybe we should both call it a day.' Nick eases himself up in the chair and sips his tea, wincing as the hot liquid hits his lip. I hand him two painkillers which he swallows obediently. 'The general populace will have to manage without used Renault Clios for a few hours.'

'Do you want me to drive you home?'

'No,' Nick says. 'I'll be fine. I slept for a few hours at Sam's place. When I woke up, Sophie had gone.'

'Hell,' I say. 'I wonder where she is?'

'Sam said she'd gone to face the music. He was worried sick,' Nick tells me. 'But if I were her, I may have thought better of going home and be round at your place.'

I give my lovely boss a kiss on the cheek. 'You're a very sensitive person.'

'Yeah.' Nick touches his nose. 'Some bits of me more than others.'

Chapter Seventy-One

Nick still felt anxious as he pulled up outside his own home. He sat and stared at it for a few moments, trying to stave off the feeling that it was someone else's house. His nose started to drip blood again, so he pulled himself together and got out. This could scar me for life, he thought, as he nervously scanned the road for signs of people who might want to hit him or otherwise do him harm. But there was no one, so he fumbled in his pocket for his door key only to find that it no longer fitted in the lock.

Instead Nick rang the bell and waited until he heard the patter of Janine's feet on the stairs. She came to the door and let him in.

'Good grief.' Her hand flew to her mouth. 'What happened to you?'

'You've changed the locks,' Nick said, his tone sounding more accusing than he would have normally liked.

'Sorry,' his wife said. 'I'd forgotten. My solicitor advised me to. I've got a spare key somewhere.'

Nick sighed and followed her inside. 'Welcome home, Nick,' he muttered to himself.

'Sit down,' Janine said, marching across the kitchen. 'I'll make you some tea.'

'I don't want tea,' Nick said. 'I've just had some. Anna said I need frozen peas for the swelling.'

Janine's lips pursed as if she'd sucked a lemon. 'And Anna's some sort of expert, is she?'

'Apparently so. She broke her nose a couple of years ago.' Although it looked far too cute to him to have ever been broken. He tried to shake the thought away as he wasn't sure he should be having it while he was in his kitchen, with his wife and in pain.

Abandoning the kettle, Janine sat down opposite him at the table. All his bones were aching wearily as if he was starting with a cold.

'Are you going to tell me what happened to you?'

Nick gingerly touched his injuries. 'Sam's having an affair with a married woman,' he explained, rather reluctantly. 'In a mix-up worthy of Shakespeare or some delightful French farce I got myself punched by her husband.'

'Oh my goodness,' Janine tutted. 'What a prat!'

'Me, Sam or him?' Nick asked.

'Him,' she spat. 'You can't just go around punching people.'

'Even if you think they're having an affair with your missus?' Nick rubbed at his stubble. That didn't hurt which was surely a good sign. 'He probably feels much better. He doesn't know that he decked the wrong bloke.'

'Well,' Janine bristled, 'I'm just glad that you didn't resort to that sort of behaviour.'

'Maybe I should have done.' Nick shrugged. 'It's a very effective deterrent. If I'd been having an affair with Sophie I'd have dropped her like a hot potato.'

'You can't mean that.'

Nick laughed, but it sounded humourless. 'Would you advise doing what I did? I let someone else take my wife from under my nose. Without an ounce of protest from me, he walked straight into my house, my bed and my life.'

Janine slid off her chair and came and sat on his lap. She put her arms round his neck. 'But that's behind us now.'

'Yes,' he said, but even to him it sounded lacking in conviction. Would it have made him feel better to have used Phil the Butcher as a punch-bag? He'd never know now. Suddenly, he didn't want to be with Janine or with anyone. 'You know, I think I'm going to have to lie down for a while. I can't cope with all this excitement.'

Janine hesitated before speaking. Her fingers teased through his hair. 'I could come up with you.'

Nick peeled her arms from around his neck and eased her weight from his lap. He tried a tired smile. 'Maybe not just yet,' he said.

Chapter Seventy-Two

Sophie is sitting on my doorstep in the darkness when I arrive home and she nearly gives me a heart attack as she steps out into the light above my front door.

'Where are the kids?' I ask.

'Connor and Poppy are in the car. It's a bit warmer in there,' she says. 'Tom's taken Charlotte and Ellie from his mother's house.'

'Was that after he punched Nick or before?'

Sophie puts her head in her hands and starts to cry. 'I'm so sorry,' she gulps. 'Is he all right?'

'He can be patched up,' I assure her. 'What did Tom tell his mum?'

'Nothing.' Sophie shakes her head. 'This is such a terrible mess.' She looks at me bleakly with her mascara-streaked face. 'What can I say?'

'Say it's over.'

I put my arm round Sophie and we both walk over to her car where Poppy, bless her, is huddled into her coat and is getting on with her homework under the faint glow of the interior light. Connor, as usual, is fast asleep. Poppy opens the door, stuffing her books back into her school bag, and comes to kiss me. She wraps her arms round me and hugs me, which is most unlike my daughter.

'Hey,' I say. 'I've missed you.'

'I've missed you too,' Poppy says. I don't know if she's picking up unhappy vibes from Sophie, but she certainly seems unsettled and I remind myself to spend some quality time with her later. Sophie hoists the sleeping Connor from his car seat. He stirs briefly and then settles back onto her shoulder and we all troop into the house.

We go through to the area of devastation that is my kitchen. One day, I promise, I will get up earlier so that I can make the beds and wash the dishes before I go to work and am not faced by a room that looks as if it's been hit by a tornado as soon as I walk in.

'Take a biscuit and a drink,' I say to Poppy, 'and finish your homework. I need to talk to Aunty Sophie.'

'Can I watch television while I do it?'

That girl knows how to bargain. 'Just this once,' I say, because quite frankly I don't feel strong enough for an argument. As instructed, Poppy helps herself to some orange juice and half a packet of cheap biscuits and then makes herself scarce in the lounge. The days are not far away when I'll be having to make myself scarce for my daughter's convenience, I fear. 'Keep an eye on Connor for me, sweetie.'

When she's gone, I make Sophie some tea while she sniffs into a pile of wet tissues. 'What if Tom wants a divorce?' she sobs from amid the clutter and used cereal bowls that litter my kitchen table. 'Where will I go? What about the children? What am I going to do?'

I sweep aside the worst of the debris with the back of my arm and plonk down the tea. 'Isn't it a little bit late to be thinking about all this?'

Sophie takes the tea and clings on to it like a lifeline. She lowers her voice. 'What if I can never see Sam again?'

I sigh at my friend. 'I guess that's the general idea.'

Sophie looks devastated and bursts into a fresh spate of tears.

'What did Sam say?'

'Not much,' Sophie admits. 'He's pretty shaken.'

'Sam is?' This stretches my patience. 'He wasn't the one who got punched on the nose.'

'I know.' Sophie is mortified. 'I'm so embarrassed. I don't know how I'll ever face him again. I can't understand what got into Tom.'

I stare at her open-mouthed. 'Probably the fact that someone else got into his wife got into him. You must have some sympathy for him.'

'I hate any form of violence.'

'Well, I'm not its greatest exponent,' I say, 'but maybe sometimes it's justified.'

Sophie gives me a direct stare. 'You really think that?'

I crumble beneath it. 'No,' I admit. 'No, I don't. But I do feel sorry for Tom. He doesn't deserve this, Sophie. However dull you think he is, he doesn't deserve this.' I reach out and take her hand. 'In his own quiet, undemonstrative way, I'm sure he adores you.'

Sophie hangs her head.

'Do you still love Tom?' I try to see some trace of it in her miserable face.

'I don't know,' she says. 'I'm frightened of losing him.'

'That's a good place to start from,' I suggest. 'And it's not Sam you need to worry about facing. It's Tom. Go home now and sort it out.'

Sophie has a last sniff into her tissue. 'Suppose he does want a divorce?'

'Then you've got some pretty fast talking to do.'

'You're right,' she says. 'I'd better get back and hear the worst.' My friend stuffs all the soggy tissues into her pocket and stands up. 'You know, this could actually strengthen our relationship.'

I give her my best puzzled frown. 'You don't really believe that, do you?'

'No,' Sophie says. 'But I can live in hope.'

And as she leaves to go and find out what awaits her at home, I don't tell her that I too have lived in hope and it's a vastly over-rated place.

Chapter Seventy-Three

Nick jerked awake. Janine was standing over him bearing a cup of tea and a sad smile.

He pushed himself up on his elbows and ran his hand through his hair. 'I thought it was someone coming to hit me again.'

'I've brought you a cup of tea,' Janine said.

'Ah. The great British answer to all forms of crisis.'

He gingerly examined his nose. It felt like a tennis ball sitting in the middle of his face and he wondered what colour it might be. The rest of him didn't ache quite as much as it had and his nose only throbbed intermittently rather than constantly. That must mean there was no permanent damage. Surely?

Janine sat down next to him on the bed. The proximity of his wife made Nick feel uncomfortable and he shifted up a bit to give her more room. He never imagined it would be so difficult to slip back into cosy intimacy. It was as if he grew an extra skin when Janine was around – a protective barrier to fend off unwanted boarders, just like the battleshields on the *Starship Enterprise*. He wondered whether it would be possible to ever let them fully down with her again.

Dark shadows stretched across the room. Janine switched on the small lamp on the bedside table which cast a soft light into the shadowy corners. This was a truly awful room. It was all gingham and flowers in shades of yellow and red. He felt as if he was sleeping in an overblown dolls' house. Cutesy pine furniture added to the effect. Janine kept it immaculate just in case they ever had people to stay over for the night or the weekend, but as she hated having people stay over, the room was never used. It was an empty shrine to their non-existent social life. It would have made a perfect nursery, but it never went down very well when he voiced those particular thoughts, so he kept quiet. He had a vision of himself being just like his father in a few years' time, unable to express any opinion other than one formed in his wife's brain. Did he really want this for his life? Mentally,

212

he shook away the image. Any physical shaking was way beyond his current capability. He must have slept for an hour or more, he guessed, judging by the onset of dusk. Rain pattered on the Velux windows and the wind whistled mournfully in the eaves. It had been a filthy day which was now morphing into a filthy night.

'How are you feeling?'

'Like I've been hit very hard by someone very big,' Nick said quietly.

'You don't look great,' his wife observed.

He certainly didn't feel it. 'What time is it?' he asked groggily.

'Time that we faced up to what's happening,' Janine said softly.

That made him sit up. 'Which is?' A heavy pounding started in his head.

'Nick.' Janine gave a sigh laden with disappointment. 'This isn't working, is it?'

No, it wasn't working and that was primarily because the woman opposite him, the woman whom he'd promised to have and to hold and to cherish above all things, now seemed like a stranger to him. He didn't think he'd moved on since he and Janine had split up. He thought he'd been stuck, stuck in his old bedroom, stuck in his old life. But he wasn't. In some small way, he'd moved on. Without noticing it, he wasn't the same person as he used to be.

'Give it time.' Nick avoided her gaze. He wanted to touch her hand, but somehow couldn't bring himself to do it. Would he ever trust Janine again? Would he ever feel secure in the relationship or would he always worry that she'd find someone else to replace him just as easily? Maybe a greengrocer might turn her head next time. Would the sight of a firm young cucumber make her wonder whether the grass would be greener elsewhere? It was a ridiculous thought, he knew that. But what *would* reassure him? He couldn't go through the rest of his life simply hoping that his wife would avoid all fresh-produce shops.

'I'm not sure that time is all it takes,' his wife said wearily. 'After all we've been through, I don't think we're going to be able to get back to the way we were.'

'We can't go back,' Nick agreed, 'but maybe we could go forward.' He forced his fingers to creep across the bed and find hers. 'We must be honest with each other.'

Janine took Nick's hand and squeezed it as she shook her head sadly. 'I've seen the way you look at me,' she said. 'There's nothing in your eyes for me any more.'

213

'I . . .'

Janine put her finger to his swollen, tender lip and hushed him. 'I've seen the way you look at Anna.'

'Anna?'

'We must be honest with each other,' she reminded him. 'You said so yourself.' Janine distracted herself by plucking at the duvet cover. When she looked up there were tears in her eyes and her voice was unsteady. 'And I wondered whether it's possible you might be in love with her.'

'I . . . I . . .' Nick sagged back onto his pillow. Honesty had to be the best policy. 'I have a horrible feeling you may just be right.'

Chapter Seventy-Four

Sophie stood outside her house. Her knees were shaking and she was terrified to go inside and face what awaited her. There was no way she could run away from this though, so she steeled herself and headed up the garden path.

As she went inside, Tom was standing in the kitchen and Sophie was stunned by the sight that greeted her. The kitchen was immaculate. The work surfaces were visible. The floor and the sink gleamed. There was the fresh lemony smell of furniture polish wafting in the air.

A scrubbed and polished version of her children, Charlotte and Ellie, were seated at the table, contentedly eating their tea. And on the table between them stood one of her vases filled with fresh spring flowers – garish yellow daffodils with orange centres rubbed shoulders with tight red tulips that strained to keep the weight of their heavy heads upright on inadequately slender stems. It was as if her home had been part of a *Good Homes* makeover. Or that the housekeeping fairy had come and waved her wand over it.

Her husband was wearing an apron which loudly announced – REAL MEN LOVE HOUSEWORK (*or so my wife tells me* . . .) A near-naked hunky man waving a feather duster accompanied the saying. Sophie had bought it for her husband as a joke – and, of course, a strong hint – a few Christmases ago. The hint and the apron had both been steadfastly ignored and it had remained unused in one of the kitchen drawers ever since. Under the apron was a smart shirt and his hair was freshly washed. Tom was bent over the table helping Charlotte to cut up her sausages.

He looked up when she walked in. Sophie's eyes filled with tears.

'Tom . . .' she said.

Tom nodded. 'Sophie.'

'We need to talk.'

'I don't do talking, Sophie. You know that.'

Sophie went towards him. 'Look . . .'

215

'I've always believed that actions speak louder than words.'

'Tom . . .'

He straightened up. 'It's in the past as far as I'm concerned.' He looked at her. 'It *is* in the past, isn't it?'

Sophie, choked, nodded. Tom pulled out a chair for her and she slumped into it.

'I thought we'd get a Chinese takeaway when the kids have gone to bed. And open a bottle of wine,' Tom said. 'A decent one. Use the posh glasses.'

Sophie acquiesced tearfully.

'We could watch a video,' Tom continued crisply. 'Not one of those bloody slushy ones. Something with Arnold Schwarzenegger in it.'

'Fine,' Sophie said. 'Fine. That would be nice.'

'Good.' Tom seemed to be fighting back tears too. 'Good.' He turned back to the children. 'Eat your sausages, Ellie. Before they get cold. There's a good girl.'

And Sophie realised that this was the nearest she'd ever get to telling Tom that she was sorry. And this was the nearest Tom would ever get to saying that he was sorry, too.

Chapter Seventy-Five

I'm in my ratty old, extra-comfort dressing-gown and I am desperate for an early night. All this high-drama with my friend is too exhausting at my age and I need to curl up under the duvet for ten hours straight to recuperate.

All my make-up is scrubbed off and I've even treated myself – and, of course, my peach-skinned, wrinkle-free daughter – to a face pack. And we've had a nail-painting frenzy – pale pink for Poppy so that she might get away with it at school, although she'll normally have bitten it all off in two days. We also painted Connor's finger-nails so that he didn't feel left out. If it's good enough for David Beckham then it's good enough for my boy and it makes me less worried about his tendency to put lipstick on whenever he chances on any lying around. Plus I'd rather it was on his lips than on the walls. I've also put some sort of hot oil treatment in my hair so that it's all shiny like the girls' tresses in the L'Oréal adverts. And I've taken a razor to my stubbly legs – a new one, so no unsightly gouges. I even tried on my new sexy marabou feathered thong to cheer myself up though I doubt it will be tickling anyone's fancy for the foreseeable future. I did take the label off it just in case. Although I now feel all this renewed interest in my appearance is somewhat in vain, since the object of my affections has recently returned to his wife, I don't see why I shouldn't keep doing this for me.

I may have only been back in the ranks of the gainfully employed for little more than a week – and that a rather fraught one, what with the accidental cutting up of food and the weeing incident – but I feel a hundred times better about myself. It is a huge boost to my self-esteem to think that I can cut the mustard along with the majority of the population. And my poor old self-esteem has taken a battering in recent years. The one thing about living on benefits is that it doesn't take long to start to believe that you're not worthy of anything else. Now I feel that I can hold my head high and I can support myself and my own children. If not in high style yet, we will at least be marginally above the poverty line if Nick doesn't decide to sack me. Not all success stories turn out quite like J.K. Rowling's meteoric rise from impoverished single mum to the richest authoress on the planet, but at least I'm trying.

Just as I'm thinking that it's time to lock up, turn off all the lights and hunker down for the night, the door bell rings. Not just one ring, but ring, after ring. An insistent finger is prodding away at the bell. My heart sets up a panicky beat. I do hope this isn't Sophie bearing her suitcase. 'Who the hell is this?'

'It might be Santa,' Poppy suggests hopefully.

'It's March,' I point out. 'Santa's barely packed his stuff away from last time.'

'Oh.' My daughter sighs her disappointment.

As I run down the stairs, the bell rings again several times. 'Coming!'

Ring. Ring. Ring.

'Keep your hair on!'

I'm at the door and it doesn't look like Sophie's figure through the glass. Or Santa's. It's someone taller and thicker set. A man. Nick? My word. He can't see me like this!

After a quick, indecisive nail-chew and two more rings on the bell, I snatch open the door. Before I can stop myself, I gasp out loud. When I find my breath, I say, 'What the hell are you doing here?'

'Hello, Anna.'

The man standing in front of me, looking as large as life and in rude health, is my missing husband, Bruno. He looks tanned and fit and as if he's expecting me to welcome him with open arms. While I stand there in a state of shock, clutching my dressing-gown to me, Bruno grins at me widely and winks.

'Is it Santa?' Poppy yells.

I would have been less surprised if it had been the woolly white-bearded one on my doorstep.

'No,' I manage. But it's another mythical figure who turns up once a year. Except this one never brings presents. And he'd probably eat all the mince pies and drink the sherry put out for Santa. And even do the reindeer out of his carrot if the truth were told.

There's a shout from behind me on the stairs. 'Daddy!' And Poppy runs down, thunders past me in her nightie and bare feet, a look of sheer ecstasy on her upturned face.

'Shit,' is what I think but don't say.

'My daddy!' she cries as she launches herself into his arms. 'It's my daddy!'

It certainly is. This is heartbreaking.

Bruno scoops her up and twirls her round. 'How's my best girl?'

Poppy is clearly in seventh heaven, while I'm distinctly less impressed. My husband lets Poppy slither to the ground, where she clings onto his legs. There are times when I've done that myself in an effort to stop him walking away.

'I'm back, babe,' Bruno states.

My arms are folded and I have the air of a fishwife. I give him my coldest stare. 'Just like that?'

'This time it's for good,' he says. His expression is clear and sincere. And I don't trust him for a moment.

'Oh really?' I stand there like a nightclub bouncer barring a dodgy customer.

'It's cold out here, babe.' My husband shivers for good measure.

Poppy looks at me with pleading eyes. She is clearly terrified that I'm going to say no, that I'm going to tell him to go, that I'll lock the door behind him and never let him over the doorstep again. As I should do.

My daughter starts to tremble in her thin nightdress. 'Please, Mummy,' she says, her eyes filling with tears. 'Please let Daddy come in.'

How can I deny my daughter the chance to be reunited with the only father figure she knows? Even with all his flaws and failings.

'Please, Mummy,' Poppy begs again. I hear myself sigh with resignation, and Bruno smiles. Is it relief or triumph I see in his eyes?

And with the feeling creeping over me that this is a step backwards in my life, I open the door wider. 'You'd better come in then.'

Chapter Seventy-Six

Nick stood in the hall of the house that he and Janine had shared together. His packed suitcase was once again at his feet. Except this time, he hadn't even stayed long enough to unpack his toiletries and stake claim to a part of the bathroom cabinet.

'I can't stand this,' Janine said. Her face was grey with anxiety and she put her hand on Nick's arm. 'You look like Paddington Bear.'

'I'll be fine,' Nick said. 'What about you?'

'Don't worry about me.'

'Phone Phil,' Nick urged. 'Make it up with him. I'd feel better.'

'Perhaps I will,' his wife said. 'But he may not want me back either.' A solitary tear made a wet track over her cheek and Nick brushed it away with his thumb. 'I'm not a grade A student when it comes to the way I treat my men.'

Despite the fact that he didn't bear Janine any malice, he couldn't really argue with that assessment either. 'You needn't tell him that I've been here. Just say that you changed your mind at the last minute. That you made a mistake.'

'I think I made the mistake in letting you go in the first place,' his wife said tearfully.

'Well,' Nick said. 'None of us are perfect. We all do stupid things.'

'Letting my marriage go up in smoke ranks up there amongst one of the most stupid.'

Thinking that they would be able to patch it all up in the blink of an eye was fairly stupid too.

His wife wiped her eyes with the back of her finger. 'You should go,' she said shakily. 'Otherwise I might not let you.'

Nick turned to leave, but Janine clutched him and they hugged each other tightly.

'How did we make such a mess of this?' she cried into his shoulder.

'We didn't do it deliberately,' Nick said. 'I guess it just crept up on us somehow. These things happen.' They happen when you take

220

your eye off the ball. When you're not paying attention and let your guard slip. When you take your relationship for granted.

'We did love each other very much, didn't we?'

Nick kissed her tenderly and eased her arms from around him. 'We did. Once upon a time.'

'Will we stay friends?'

'Of course,' Nick said. 'It would be a waste of our time together if we didn't.'

'I hope it works out with Anna,' Janine said and there was a catch in her voice. 'She's very lucky to have you love her. You're a very nice man, Nick.'

Nice, he thought. There was that damn word again. Nick walked out of the door and didn't look back to see if Janine was still standing there. Nice. Opening the boot of the car he threw his case in. He hoped with all his heart that Anna would think he was more than *nice*.

Nick decided to drive home past Anna's house. He wanted to see her. He wanted very badly to see her and tell her how he felt before he lost courage. His car twisted through the small, winding roads of her estate, bumping over the speed humps, until he recognised her road. Swinging in, he tried to remember the house from the night when he had dropped her off in the taxi after they'd first met up in the FIFTY PER CENT divorced and singles club. Nick slowed down as he approached. He was sure this was the one. The one with her car parked outside. Not rocket science.

He stopped on the road opposite. There was, however, another car parked next to it. Ah. She must have visitors. All the lights were on in the house and there was a cosy warmth emanating from within. He would have liked a bit of cosy warmth in Anna's company right now. Nick fought down his disappointment. Maybe this wasn't the right time to talk to her – not when he was feeling so emotionally battered. He should think about it overnight, decide what he wanted to say. If he was going to declare undying love, then he ought to get it right.

Nick pulled away again. Perhaps he should go and check on Sam – see if his friend had survived the day. Then he looked at the time. No, he should be making tracks to go home. His parents would probably be preparing dinner and he ought to let them know as soon as possible that their house-guest was returning. Besides, he needed a bit of his mother's mollycoddling. He swung his car towards home.

* * *

When his mother opened the door there was flour on her hands and some on her nose. Even when she was cooking she wore her pearls. He didn't think she could have looked more surprised – or more relieved.

'Break out the treacle pudding,' Nick said. 'The Prodigal Son has returned.'

Despite her floury hands, his mother hugged him and ushered him inside. 'You're hurt.'

Nick touched his swollen nose.

'Phil the Butcher didn't hit you?'

'No,' Nick said. 'It was someone else's husband.'

His mother looked shocked. 'Not the mud-wrestler's?'

'I'm afraid so.'

'I won't ask what happened,' Monica said, 'but I take it that you and Janine will be divorcing after all.'

He nodded sadly. 'It didn't work out.'

'At least you tried.'

But he would always wonder whether he had tried hard enough. His mother hugged him again.

'Roger? Roger!' she called. His father was in the lounge watching some gardening programme. The chap on the screen was digging about in his borders, expounding the virtues of root vegetables. Roger tore his gaze away from the television. 'Open the sherry,' his mother instructed. 'Nick's come home.'

Monica took his suitcase from his hand and helped him out of his coat. 'We've got apple crumble tonight,' she said, showing the hands that were no longer floury as it was all over his jacket. 'Your favourite.'

He wasn't sure apple crumble *was* his favourite, but he was in no mood to argue. Instead, Nick allowed himself to be fussed over, surrendering willingly to his mother's excessive ministrations.

His father, as directed, appeared with the bottle of sherry and three glasses.

'I expect you could use a little drink,' his mother said, shepherding him into the sweetly scented warmth of the kitchen.

'Yes,' Nick said. Left to his own devices, he expected he could polish off the entire bottle in a very short amount of time indeed.

Chapter Seventy-Seven

Sophie lay on the bed next to her daughter who was cuddling her teddy bear and crying softly. The bedside light cast a warm pink glow over them both, flattering the tired decoration of the room. Sophie stroked Ellie's hair.

'Shush, now,' she murmured. 'Mummy's here. It was just a little nightmare.'

'I dreamed a dragon had captured you,' Ellie whimpered. 'A big one with black teeth. And he took you away to eat you so that you could never come back.'

'That's because you watched *Shrek* again on the DVD,' Sophie said. 'It's made you think of dragons.'

Ellie didn't look convinced.

'Besides, Mummy's too tough for a dragon to eat.' Sophie smacked her rump. 'Who'd want to chew through that lot?'

Her daughter smiled reluctantly and then snuggled into her. 'I don't want you to go away.'

Sophie felt her throat close. 'I'm not going away, sweetie.'

'Not ever?'

'No.'

'Some mummies do,' Ellie said, her eyebrows drawn down with worry.

'Not this one,' Sophie said. And she meant it. Suddenly, it was brought home to her what it would feel like to be without her girls. Supposing Ellie had been woken by a nightmare and she hadn't been here to placate her beautiful daughter? Would Tom have been able to comfort her in the same way? What if something worse had happened to her children and she'd been off, selfishly cavorting with her lover? Sophie closed her eyes against the horrors that might have been. Next to her Ellie's breathing stopped wracking with small sobs and headed towards the heavy rhythm of sleep once more.

'Night night, Mummy,' she mumbled sleepily.

Sophie opened her eyes to gaze at her daughter, tracing the outline of her eyes, nose and mouth with a gentle fingertip. 'Night night, sweetie.'

Ellie sighed contentedly and relaxed back into the bed. While she slipped her thumb into her mouth and returned to her dreams, Sophie looked round the room. It badly needed decorating. The walls were still graced with the ducks and rabbits of Ellie's baby years. The edges of the wallpaper were grubby and torn. Crayon graffiti covered the lower reaches. The carpet was faded and worn and bore too many traces of dribble, milk and goodness knows what else inexpertly scrubbed away. Her own room was as bad. It was definitely a candidate for *Changing Rooms*. Outmoded curtains and a paper-thin duvet did nothing to enhance the scuffed magnolia that had covered the walls since the builders had last painted it. It was not exactly a palace to passion. Was it any wonder that Tom never felt like making love?

A clean sweep throughout the house might help. She could throw herself into housework and decorating. Scrub and polish, sand and paint until she eradicated all traces of their former life. A new haircut worked for some women. Maybe a new paintjob would work for her. It was worth a try. And to be honest, she had no idea what else they might do. There was no way that Tom would ever go for counselling about the state of their marriage. It was like pulling teeth trying to get him to talk to her, let alone to open up to some 'interfering do-gooder' − as he'd no doubt brand the poor unfortunate counsellor. If they were going to get through this then they'd have to do it alone.

Sophie looked down at her daughter. She'd have to stay whatever happened, for the children's sake. How could she disrupt their lives so cruelly when they'd done nothing to deserve it? Ellie slept soundly − all thoughts of dragons long gone. Sophie clicked off the bedside light and sat in the darkness. If only her major worry was trying not to get eaten by a dragon.

Chapter Seventy-Eight

Bruno and Poppy are sprawled out on the floor playing Bop-It – some hideously noisy game of co-ordination that we bought cheap in Argos last Christmas.

'Bop-It!' Poppy shouts at Bruno, who does Bop-It.

I don't want to Bop-It, I want to Bin-It. I've got a lovely headache developing and I'm not sure that it's entirely the fault of the robotic voice filling my lounge with the endless repetitions, 'Flick-It, Spin-It, Twist-It . . .' et cetera.

Poppy is as close as she can be to Bruno without actually sitting on his lap, and I'm sure it's because she thinks if she turns her back on him for a moment, he'll be off again. She is desperate for him to love her and it twists my insides to watch how attentive he is to her. If you saw a photograph of this scene you'd assume that he was the perfect dad. And they say the camera can't lie? I wonder how long it will last this time before he tires of playing the bountiful father again. Can he not see that he is missing out by not being permanently involved in their lives?

Earlier, I had gone upstairs and changed back into my jeans – Bruno's impromptu arrival banishing all thoughts of an early night for us. After all this time, I wasn't comfortable with him seeing me in my dressing-gown. I needed to think about what I wanted to do, but I couldn't make the thoughts come. My mind seems to have gone into catatonic shock, and my bargaining power has been weakened by the obvious delight my daughter has shown at having her father back at home. Connor, bless, is in his cot sleeping through all this emotion. It was with a very reluctant tread that I went back downstairs to rejoin the homecoming party. Now I sit on the sofa and watch them playing the game and playing their roles – doting father and adoring daughter. For the last few weeks, I feel as if I've really been trying to get my life back together and move on. And I really thought, no matter how small, I had made some progress. Now I seem to be back where I started. Just when I thought I was

225

finally free of Bruno, here he is stretched out on my rug in front of the fire as if he's never been away.

As if he can read my mind, he looks up at me and smiles. It's a very winning smile. Practised long and hard, so even though I try not to be influenced by it, I find it hard to resist. He is such a charmer. But I no longer view charm as a quality in a man. My husband – in name only – is tall and broad-shouldered, his impressive muscles earned from making his living with transient jobs on building sites. He can build walls, install bathrooms, rewire houses. When he puts up shelves they stay there. These are now the qualities I value in a man. The trouble with Bruno is that he's always been reluctant to practise any of his skills in the home environment. His dark hair has grown long since I last saw him and he's sporting a close-cropped beard that makes him look like an ageing member of a boy band. His skin is heavily tanned and looks dry. The wrinkles round his eyes are more pronounced. A few flecks of grey are starting to show at his temples, but in all he looks much younger than his thirty-six years. It's just a shame he doesn't act it.

Bruno pats his flat stomach pitifully. 'I haven't eaten,' he says, giving me a doe-eyed look. 'Be a darling. Knock me something together.'

I heave myself from the sofa. The clock feels as if it's spinning backwards. I'm glad that I have none of Bruno's favourite foods in the fridge otherwise I could be tempted to try to impress him and I really don't want to do that. 'I can probably rustle up some bacon and eggs.'

'Mmm. Wonderful,' he says. 'Just what the doctor ordered.'

Damn. I plod to the door, my feet as heavy as my heart.

'Any nice-cold, ice-cold beer in the fridge?' Bruno calls after me.

'Yes.' I hate to admit it but I bought a six-pack on my last supermarket visit, hoping that on the off-chance, Nick might call around sometime.

My husband winks at me and looks like the cat who's got the cream. Whereas I feel like the mouse trapped by the cat once more.

Chapter Seventy-Nine

Sophie, in a pensive mood, eventually left her daughter to her slumber and came back downstairs. As she did so, her husband Tom, wearing a grim expression, was putting on his coat.

'Is she okay?' he asked.

'Yeah,' Sophie said with a relieved sigh.

'I'm going for the Chinese,' Tom said. 'If there are things you need to do – phone calls and stuff – do them now.'

'Tom . . .'

'I'll be a while,' her husband said gruffly, while slipping the car keys into his pocket. 'You know that place. There's always a queue.'

Sophie nodded and watched Tom as he walked out of the door. She went into the kitchen and watched as he reversed too quickly out of their drive, then stood at the window until the tail-lights had disappeared down the road. It was only then that she picked up her mobile phone and punched in Sam's number. After a couple of rings the answerphone clicked in.

'Hi. This is Sam Felstead. I'm currently out with Gwyneth or maybe Cameron. Catch you later.'

'Sam, it's me – Sophie,' she said. 'If you're there, pick up. I need to talk to you.'

The phone remained unanswered. All she could hear was the whirring of the tape as it wound on. Perhaps he'd gone out on the town with Nick. Drowning his sorrows. Perhaps he'd already decided that she was too much trouble and was out looking for someone to replace her. The thought made her heart contract painfully.

'I don't want to do this over the phone and I don't want to leave a message, but I may not get another chance to ring,' Sophie said. 'It's over, Sam. It has to be. I have to think of Tom, who does love me in his own sweet way. I have to think of the children. I have to think of everyone else except you.' She paused to blink back her tears. 'But you'll be fine. You're young, you're handsome, and most of all you're very, very single.' Sophie laughed tearfully. 'By next week

227

you'll have forgotten all about me. I won't forget you though.' The words 'I love you' stayed lodged in her throat, refusing to be spoken out loud. 'Take care, Sam.'

Sophie hung up. She pulled a piece of kitchen roll from the holder and cried noisily and loudly into it. It felt like absolutely the right thing to do. Her future was here with Tom and with the children. And any lingering thoughts of Sam would fade over time. Sophie screwed up the kitchen roll and threw it into the bin. She'd have to repair her make-up before Tom came back with the takeaway, wipe all traces of her transgressions from her face. Like people who suffered a bereavement, she'd soldier on until that great healer Time could work its magic. But Sam hadn't died – he was alive and vibrant and only living on the other side of the city. It would take ten minutes to go to him. But she couldn't. Never again. She knew that. Sam would move on without her and she'd never imagined that anything could hurt so much.

But it would have hurt more if she could have seen Sam, sitting alone in his darkened room next to the phone, replaying his answer-phone message over and over with tears streaming down his face.

Chapter Eighty

I'm dreading this moment. Poppy is in bed and I have no excuse for lingering here any longer. She's long past the age where she would tolerate me reading a story to her – even to indulge me. And I admit to a pang of jealousy when I see her playing up to her father, the adoring look on her face, the eagerness to please. I never see her displaying these same traits towards her poor old mother who cossets and cares for her every need day-in, day-out. I am not on the list of things to be revered. I am on the list of things to be tolerated – up there with visits to the dentist for regular check-ups, fresh vegetables and a daily shower.

Bruno came up to kiss her goodnight and she was so beside herself with joy that you'd think she'd been visited by the Queen or Gareth Gates – someone for whom she would gladly lay down her life. But then I remember a time, not so long ago, when Bruno had a similar effect on me. Now he's back downstairs and I hear the phiss-hiss as he pops open another can of beer.

'Goodnight, Poppy Possett.' I kiss her on her hot, over-excited cheek.

'Mummy,' she says. 'It's nice that Daddy's come home.'

'Sleep.' I bat her on the end of her nose with my finger. 'Now. You'll be fit for nothing in the morning.'

My daughter gives me a disdainful look. As if to say, 'I could stay up all night and still not be tired.' Whereas I am completely and utterly knackered. Poppy opens her eyes wide and starts to sing an Atomic Kitten number about shagging anything that moves as if to prove a point.

Ignoring the salacious lyrics, I smack her on the bottom through the duvet and repeat myself. *'Sleep.'*

I head towards the door in the vain hope that she might take the hint.

'Mummy?'

'Now what?' There is a worried frown on my child's face.

'Do you think Daddy will stay this time?'

No, I think. But, rather diplomatically, I say, 'Let's talk about it tomorrow.'

'I love it when he's here,' Poppy says, stabbing little shards of hurt into my wounded heart. 'Do you?'

'Yes,' I lie to appease her. 'Now. Go. To. Sleep.'

I close Poppy's door and when I'm outside on the landing, I lean against it and try to concentrate on my breathing to calm myself down. To be honest, I'm not so sure that I want Bruno breathing the same air as me at all.

Chapter Eighty-One

Nick and his father sat opposite each other, both silently tucking into their heaped bowls of Monica Diamond's special apple crumble. Nick had consumed enough sherry to make himself feel relatively numb. In fact, he was so numb that even his parents' choice in florid wallpaper had ceased to depress him. His father, as usual, had stoically avoided any form of conversation with him that might inveigle him into having an opinion on anything. But, again, it had long since stopped bothering Nick that his father would only speak when spoken to.

Monica, still clad in her best frilled, floral apron, popped her head round the door. 'A little visitor for you,' she announced in a sing-song voice.

Nick's heart lifted. Whoever it was, his mother sounded very pleased about their surprise appearance, so it couldn't be Janine.

A moment later, Sam shuffled sheepishly into the room and gave him a self-conscious wave. 'Hi, mate.'

'Mate!' Nick exclaimed. It had been months since Sam had been round to his parents' house. So that was why his mother was looking flushed and flirty.

'Mr Diamond,' Sam said, and shook Roger's hand.

Roger nodded enthusiastically and pumped Sam's hand. It was clear that he'd forgotten the name of his son's best friend.

'Now you sit down,' his mother instructed as she pulled out a chair for Sam. 'Apple crumble?'

Sam put on his butter-wouldn't-melt-in-his-mouth look. 'If it's not too much trouble, Mrs D.'

Monica patted Sam's shoulder. 'Nothing is too much trouble for you, Sam.'

Before his mother finished the sentence she'd conjured up a bowl from somewhere and was dishing out a mammoth-size portion.

'Roger. Roger. Finish up,' she barked at her husband. 'Sam and Nick want to be alone.'

His father hurried up his crumble, but wasn't quite quick enough as his bowl was whipped away from him mid-spoonful. Monica bustled Roger out of the room, closing the door behind them.

Sam and Nick stared at each other. 'We *vant* to be alone . . .' Nick said in the style of Greta Garbo.

'I always thought she said she wanted to be a lawn,' Sam mused.

'You never did understand women.'

'No.' Sam prodded at his apple crumble. 'Do we want to be alone?'

'Looks like neither of us have much choice.'

'Two sad singles again.' Sam exhaled mournfully. 'I went round to your old place. Janine told me you were back here. That didn't last long.'

Nick shook his head. 'It was patently obvious to both of us after about ten minutes that it had been a hideous mistake to think that we could simply pick up where we'd left off.'

'Too much water under the bridge?'

'Something like that.'

Monica popped her head round the door again. 'More custard,' she said by way of explanation and depositing the jug, as discreetly as she was able, departed.

'Custard.' Picking up the jug, Sam inspected its contents. 'The real McCoy too.' His lips pursed in admiration. 'None of that tinned stuff here.'

'Perish the thought.'

His friend looked tired and drawn. Dark shadows circled his reddened eyes and his normally irrepressible twinkle was noticeable by its absence. He was quieter than usual, his natural ebullience suppressed.

'A small glass of sherry, mate?'

'Sherry?' Sam looked suitably surprised. 'Do people still drink that?'

'It's what passes for strong alcohol in this house.'

'Sherry it is then,' his friend said.

Nick stood up and pulling another fancy crystal sherry glass from the silver tray on the sideboard, poured Sam a healthy measure. Another one wouldn't do him any harm either. Nick filled his own schooner.

'Shall we have a toast?'

Sam shook his head. 'Nothing to celebrate, mate.'

'No,' Nick agreed, but they clinked their glasses together anyway and Nick said, 'To us!'

'To us,' Sam echoed, downing his sherry in one. He shuddered away the after-shock of the sweet sticky drink. 'Sad bastards that we are.'

'Sad bastards,' Nick concurred with a slight slur.

Sam put down his glass and tucked into his crumble. 'Wow,' he said, mouth full, smacking his lips in appreciation. 'Heaven.' He stuffed in another spoonful. 'Do you think your mum would let me move in too?'

'Believe me,' Nick advised, 'no amount of home-made crumble is worth it.'

His friend put his head down, eating with grim determination.

'I guess if you're here drinking my parents' sherry and eating apple crumble as if it's your last meal, I should surmise that it's over with Sophie.'

Sam nodded. And Nick suspected that he was using his crumble as a great excuse not to have to try out his voice.

'You okay?' Nick said.

Sam didn't look up. 'Yeah. Never better, mate.'

Nick punched his friend on the arm. Sam looked up and it was the first time Nick had ever seen him so emotional; his heart went out to his friend. He thought Sam had been his usual fickle self when it came to Sophie, but he was clearly wrong. And there was nothing worse than not being able to have the woman that you love. Didn't he know all about it. 'You'll get over it,' Nick assured him.

'Yeah,' Sam said, almost choking on the word. 'I'm fine. Like I said, never better.'

'That's the spirit,' Nick said, vowing to support his friend through his crisis. 'We can go to FIFTY PER CENT again, mate, and break some hearts.'

Sam nodded. And then he put his hands to his eyes and Nick was surprised to see they'd filled with tears.

'Fuck me,' Sam complained with a sniff. 'That sherry makes your eyes water.'

'Then we'd better have some more,' Nick suggested and filled up both of their glasses to the brim.

Chapter Eighty-Two

Sophie was lying stretched out on the sofa, cuddling a cushion and looking subdued when Tom returned half an hour later with a brown paper carrier bag bulging with Chinese delights. As usual, the television played in front of her, but she had no idea what she was watching. Her husband came into the lounge and stood there looking lost.

'Done?' he said.

Sophie nodded. Tom tossed down a DVD next to her. 'They'd no Arnie left,' he complained gruffly. 'I had to get bloody Hugh Grant.'

Sophie smiled a watery smile at him. A white flag if ever she'd seen one. A Hugh Grant film? This was the equivalent of Tom buying her a one-carat diamond ring. 'Tom . . .' she said. 'I'm sorry.'

Tom grunted in response.

She reached out and took his hand. 'I do love you.'

'I'll dish this out then, shall I?' Tom offered.

Sophie grinned. There was no way she was ever going to change this one fundamentally. But there had been a subtle shift which she could work on. 'We'll do it together.'

Tom tightened his grip on her hand and helped to pull her up from the sofa. He put the carrier of Chinese takeaway on the coffee-table and slipped his arms round his wife. 'If the film's crap we could . . . well,' he said. 'We could have an early night.'

'I think that's a wonderful idea.'

'Me too,' Tom said and hugged her to him, burying his face in her neck. His breath was warm on her skin. She pressed into him and there were old, familiar stirrings. 'How hungry are you?' he asked, his voice cracked with emotion.

'Not very.'

She felt Tom shrug against her. 'We could pop the takeaway in the microwave later,' he suggested. 'Reheated Chinese food is good.'

Sophie looked at her husband and her mouth curled up at the corners. 'I've heard that too,' she said.

'We could go to bed now,' Tom suggested.

'I'd like that.'

He took Sophie's hand and led her out of the lounge and towards the stairs. 'You know,' he sighed. 'We should do this more often.'

Sophie nodded.

'We could let the kids stay over at my mum's so that we can spend some more time together.'

Sophie squeezed her husband's hand. 'I couldn't agree more.'

Chapter Eighty-Three

When I go past my bedroom door I see that Bruno has made himself fully at home. He's taken off his shirt and is sprawled out on the duvet, his can of beer on the bedside table. I sigh and lean against the door frame. How can I still be drawn to someone who also has the capacity to fill me with so much revulsion?

'You look comfortable,' I say as tartly as I can manage. It seems strange to see his large frame filling my bed once more.

'I've missed you,' Bruno replies. 'I've missed you all. They're great kids.'

'They are.' I fix him with a stare. 'And they deserve more than you coming in and out of their lives on a whim. *I* deserve more.'

'Don't let's have an argument on my first night here.' Bruno shakes his head. 'I'm back. I've said I'm back.'

I pull my hair away from my forehead and twist it in my fist. 'Perhaps I've heard it too many times before.'

'Come to bed,' Bruno says and turns the full force of his little boy smile on me.

'Don't you think that's a bit presumptuous?'

'You've never complained before.' His voice sounds over-slick and smarmy.

'Well, maybe things are different now,' I say.

'Look,' my husband props himself up on his elbows. 'I want this to work. I do. I mean it. I know we've had our problems in the past . . .'

'That's something of an understatement.'

He ignores my comment and carries on unabated. 'I want to be here for the kids. I want to be here for you.'

'Why the sudden change of heart?'

'Perhaps I've changed as a person,' he offers.

I can't help the disdainful snort that follows.

'I realise now where my priorities lie,' he says sincerely. 'I'm growing up. I know . . .' He holds up his hands. 'And not before time.'

236

That's the words taken out of my mouth. Bruno is the epitome of a POTATO – person over thirty acting twenty-one. 'Where have you been this time?' I ask quietly.

He looks down at his tanned stomach. 'Spain,' he says. 'Marbella. It's nice over there.'

'I wouldn't know.'

'I promise you, Anna,' my hurtful husband says softly. 'This time it's for good. I swear on my daughter's life.'

He's so convincing that I can feel myself weakening. It would be so nice to be a family again. If Bruno could change . . .

'Come here.' He pats the bed next to him. My bed.

'No,' I say. 'It's too soon.'

'But I can stay around?' he asks anxiously. 'I need time to prove myself to you.'

'Yes, you can stay,' I say with an unhappy huff. 'You can even snuggle down in my bed.'

Bruno grins at me.

'But I'm going to sleep on the sofa,' I add.

'You're a cold and stubborn woman, Anna Terry.'

'And you're a cheating, lying bastard,' I counter.

'I love it when you talk dirty,' Bruno says.

It's time for me to leave.

'I still love you,' my husband states.

And I wonder if that is all it takes. Having torn out someone's heart and thrown it to the dogs, having turned their life upside down, having left them bruised, battered and penniless, is it enough to turn up out of the blue and announce that you still love them? Does that make it all right again? Bruno clearly thinks that it does. I look at my husband as dispassionately as I can. He's handsome, relaxed and tanned. He isn't the mass of insecurity and anxiety that I am. He doesn't look like he's struggled alone against adversity for the past months as I have. Just because we still have a piece of paper that binds us, does he have any right to be included in my life again? Each in our own way, we have functioned without the other. And yet I have loved him so fiercely in the past. Could I ever do that again? At one time, I was terrified of life without him. But now I've regained my independence, my self-esteem. And I know that I never want to feel like that again. But there are the children to consider. A divorce is the easiest thing in the world to obtain. A marriage can be snuffed out in seconds. But you can't rub out the small humans you've created between you and who forever bind you together. It's

Connor and Poppy that I'm doing this for. If I didn't have children to consider, and it was simply down to me, I'd be showing him the sharp edge of my tongue and the door, in that order.

Instead, I say, 'Goodnight, Bruno,' and go off in search of my spare duvet.

Chapter Eighty-Four

Nick lay on his single bed, the effects of half a bottle of sherry throbbing in his head, a kilo of apple crumble weighing heavily in his stomach, his failed marriage weighing heavily on his heart. It was time to go back to jolly old Tumley & Goss and set the wheels of divorce in motion once again. Georgie Best sat on Nick's chest and he stroked his soft, furry teddy bear ears for comfort.

His mother popped her head round the door. 'I've tucked Sam up in the spare room,' she informed him with a happy smile. 'It's just like when you were boys together.'

Except when they were boys together Sam stayed over because it was fun to do that sort of thing, not because he was too pissed and, therefore, incapable of driving himself home.

'Is he okay?'

'I think so,' his mother said, 'though he may be at home to Mr Hangover tomorrow morning. I'd better check that I've got some Alka-Seltzer in the medicine cabinet.' Monica Diamond had a wider variety of drugs than Boots the Chemists in her medicine cabinet. They'd been known to phone her up if they were ever running short of something. 'And what about you?'

'Oh, I'm fine,' Nick answered. 'It's a good job you never decided to rent out my room.'

'I'd never do that,' Monica said, shocked. 'This is your home. Where else would you go in times of trouble?'

'Thanks, Mum.'

His mother bent down and kissed him on his forehead. 'Don't worry,' she said. 'This will all be behind you soon. You can move on in your life. That's what you young people say today, isn't it?'

Nick nodded.

'Night night, then,' Monica said. 'I'll see you in the morning.'

'Night, Mum.'

He tossed Georgie Best to the end of the bed and snuggled down.

'You'll find someone else who will love you far better than Janine ever did,' his mother assured him as she closed the door.

Nick folded his arms behind his head and gazed at the moon that peeped in through the gap in the curtains. He let his mind drift, thinking of Anna. With a bit of good luck and a following wind, he hoped that he might already have found that someone.

I pull my spare duvet out of the back of the airing cupboard. It's a bit threadbare and all the filling has bunched up into lumps, but it will do for the time being. There's a fusty pillow stuffed in the corner too and I wrest that out before plodding down the stairs with my bedding for the night. Bruno might insist that he's back for good, but I can't just slip straight back into bed with him as if nothing had ever happened. It would be like having a one-night stand with a stranger. What's more, I don't know what Bruno has been doing while he's been away, but I'm pretty sure that he hasn't been doing it alone. I need time to readjust to this new status quo and decide whether or not it's going to be on a permanent basis.

The television is playing away to itself in the corner of the lounge and a group of minor celebrities shivering in a field appear to be having maggots shoved down their pants in order to further their careers. Is this really a form of light entertainment? Whatever are the television companies thinking of these days? Where did real programmes go? Whatever happened to the heartrending serialisations of books by Catherine Cookson and Jane Austen? There was nothing quite like sitting in front of the television on a Friday night watching some rugged and half-naked man in a bath or a dripping-wet frilly shirt before having his wicked way with some willing female. Why do I now seem to spend most of my nights watching people doing their jobs on the screen? Policemen, firemen, nurses, traffic wardens, airport staff, estate agents, hairdressers – they're all at it. And I'm really not that interested. They might as well come down and film me and Nick at the car yard. I think my life would make a more interesting television programme than half of the stuff that's on – there's certainly more drama in it – but nothing on God's earth would make me want to share it with the great, unwashed general public.

I turn the set off and start to make up my bed. I push the cushions to one end of the sofa and lay out my duvet, patting my pillow into place, and that's pretty much it really. I've forgotten to fetch my nightie from the bedroom, but there's no way that I'm going up

240

there to get it. The central heating has gone off now and the lounge is chilly. I won't have my usual wriggly children to keep me warm tonight and I wonder if Poppy will stay in her own bed. I slip out of my jeans, but keep on my sweatshirt and my socks and slide in under the duvet. The ridges in the cushions of the sofa are in all the wrong places and dig into my hips and my shoulderblades. I've got to scrunch up my knees to fit on at all.

I lie on my side and gaze at the moon through the window, having failed to remember to draw the lounge curtains. Slivers of grey cloud scoot across it, thereby acquiring the mythical silver lining. The wind shakes the trees and I watch as the dead winter leaves are buffeted about. This is not a good start, is it? If Bruno really had turned over a new leaf, *he'd* be lying here all cramped up on the sofa while I was stretched out in my comfy bed.

The lounge door opens and I tense. I do hope Bruno hasn't come to try his luck, since he won't get me to change my mind. But I needn't have worried. In the doorway, Poppy's sleepy figure is framed by the light of the streetlamp outside. 'Daddy's snoring,' she says with a yawn. 'He woke me up.'

'Come here.' I pull back my duvet and my daughter climbs in next to me. 'You're freezing.'

'I went to get in your bed,' she says, 'but you weren't there. I didn't know where you were.' There's a catch in her voice.

'Ssh.' I smooth down her hair. 'I'm here.'

Poppy snuggles down on the spare inch next to me. 'Why aren't you sleeping in the bed with Daddy?'

'That's nothing to do with you, Nosey Miss,' I say, kissing her on the cheek.

Poppy wriggles her bottom around until she gets the lion's share of the cushion. 'I don't think you love Daddy any more,' she says drowsily.

I might be able to fool myself about the state of my relationship, but it's clear that I can't fool my canny ten-year-old daughter. So I lie awake in the dark when I should be asleep and wonder what on earth I'm going to do.

Chapter Eighty-Five

My eyes feel like they've had several pounds of sand poured into them and my eyelids are grating over my bloodshot eyeballs. I'm dressed and ready for work, but I still feel as if I've been dragged through a hedge backwards. The kitchen looks as if it's been the target of guerrilla warfare. The lovely Lorraine Kelly is wittering on from the portable television in the corner and she is getting on my nerves.

'Come on, come on, come on,' I bark at Poppy. 'Eat quicker.' My droopy daughter is eating her bowl of Crunchy Nut Cornflakes one flake at a time. Despite her protestations that she can stay up all night with no ill effects, she can't and now we're all suffering for our late bedtime. Except for Bruno, of course. He saunters into the kitchen wearing jeans and nothing else. His hair is tousled with sleep and his features haven't quite woken up yet.

My husband rubs his hands over his chest. 'This house is freezing,' he complains.

'Put some clothes on then,' I snap.

He leans against the kitchen counter, taking up more room than he should. I bustle around him, flinging dirty dishes into the sink while trying to shove down a piece of cold toast. Connor is banging out a jazz rhythm on his highchair with his spoon. I snatch it from him and my son starts to cry. Bruno looks dazed. 'Why all this activity?'

I look at him open-mouthed. 'It's morning,' I say. 'They have to eat. Poppy has to go to school. I have to go to work. If you want anything, you'll have to sort yourself out. We were supposed to leave *ten minutes ago*.' I glare at Poppy as I spit out my last sentence. She continues to spoon milk lethargically into her down-turned mouth. 'Right,' I say. 'That's it.' And I whip Poppy's bowl away from her and pluck an apple from the fruit bowl. 'Take this for break-time.'

My daughter reluctantly pockets the apple and I notice with some perverse pleasure that she's already ignoring her father.

'Get your coat on.' I hustle Poppy towards the door.

'What about a kiss for your dad?' Poppy ambles towards him and plants a half-hearted kiss on his cheek. Bruno looks quite put out. 'See you later, alligator.'

'Bye,' she mumbles at him. Even the return of her hero can't dent her pre-teen strop.

I unstrap Connor from his highchair. 'We'll be back at about five o'clock.'

Now Bruno looks very put out. 'Since when have you had a job?'

'Since you cleared off and left us to fend for ourselves,' I say over my shoulder. 'Poppy, are you ready yet!'

'When will you be home?'

'I told you – later. Bye.' I can't bring myself to give him a kiss. So I take the long route round the table and to the door.

'You know that I don't like you working,' Bruno says, a dark look spreading across his face.

I laugh loudly and without humour. 'I don't like you disappearing into the night and leaving us without money, but we had to get used to that. You'll have to get used to this.'

Bruno's face relaxes slightly which is not what I'd expected. I was squaring up for a fight and he looks like he's backed down. 'What shall I do all day?' he says.

'I take it you haven't got a job?'

'Not yet,' he admits. 'But I've got a few contacts.'

'You can start with the dishes.' I flick my eyes towards the pile of plates wobbling in the sink.

He doesn't look impressed, but says, 'Okay.'

'There's a mountain of ironing and no food.'

'I'll give the ironing a go,' my husband says in a faintly perplexed manner, 'but I don't know about the supermarket. What shall I buy?'

Despite my best intentions, I soften. 'There's a list on the side.' I point to it hopefully, but I'm sure it will still be there when I come home. 'I'll see you later.' Before I dash out, I hold Connor up to his father. 'Give Daddy a kiss.'

Connor obliges and then high-fives Bruno.

'Cute,' Bruno says. 'Who taught him that?'

'He gets all his bad habits from his Aunty Sophie,' I say. 'Don't you, sweetie?'

'Respect,' Connor lisps and puts out his pudgy baby fist.

Bruno punches his own man-sized fist against it, rather enthusiastically.

I snatch Connor away from him. 'You'll hurt him.'

Bruno lets his hands drop. 'I've missed them,' he says. 'And I've missed you too, babe.' My husband takes my hand and squeezes it. He fixes me with a gaze that looks so sincere. 'I promise you, things will be different from now on.'

'Yes,' I say. 'They will.' And I mean it. If Bruno is going to stay, there's no way that we're going back to the way we were. 'Now I'm late and my boss will go berserk.' Which is a complete lie, because lovely, kind, caring Nick will be as understanding as ever.

Chapter Eighty-Six

I career into Sophie's road and screech to a halt outside my friend's house. Because we were so late leaving, I've had to drop off Poppy at school first which involved a nice circular detour, making me even more late. It's only at this point that I wonder why I didn't think to leave Connor with Bruno. Maybe my mistrust of him runs deeper than I thought.

It's another dismal day. The sky is loaded with unspent rain that it's clearly aching to dump on us. Ominous clouds hang low, like those dreadful festoon blinds that people hang at their windows and which resemble droopy knickers. The trees and grass look weary from the weight of water.

I yank Connor from the car and sprint up the path. Sophie, God love her, is waiting at the door and without preamble I shove my son into her waiting arms.

'Are you sure this is okay?' I nod towards Connor.

'I'm sure,' she promises me.

'Tom didn't murder you then?'

'No.'

'Is everything all right?'

'It's fine. We're fine,' she says with a smile. I notice that her hair is tousled and she's still wearing her dressing-gown. There's a faint flush to her cheeks which is heartening as yesterday she looked as if she'd had the kiss of death.

'Have you spoken to Sam?'

Sophie nods. She lowers her voice before she speaks again. 'He knows it's over.'

I put my hand on her arm. 'I'm pleased,' I say. 'You know that you've done the right thing.'

'I know.' She smiles at me, but there's still an element of regret etched on her face. 'Go on – get a move on. I'll talk to you later.'

'You'd better,' I warn and then fidget on her doorstep when I should be bolting back to the car.

'Spit it out,' my friend says, understanding instinctively that there's more to come. She knows me too well.

'Bruno's back,' I tell her while I chew my lip.

'Oh Anna,' she sighs.

'He turned up out of the blue last night,' I explain. 'I let him stay. He took me by surprise.' Sophie looks at me as if to say that this is clearly an understatement. 'I didn't know what else to do.'

She shakes her head vehemently. 'You *cannot* let that man back into your life.'

I think of Bruno standing as large as life in my kitchen this morning. Bruno back in my bed – albeit without me at the moment. I give my friend a rueful glance. 'I think it may already be too late.'

Chapter Eighty-Seven

Nick paced up and down the office. He'd been awake since dawn and had soothed his sherry-induced hangover with one of his mother's bacon sandwiches. Sam had joined him at the breakfast-table just before seven o'clock, looking worse for wear but seeming brighter in himself. When Monica had finished mollycoddling him for half an hour, supplying him with copious amounts of coffee, scrambled eggs and bacon, Sam left the house with a spring in his step despite the throbbing that was clearly still in his head. His mother might be an interfering nuisance in some instances, Nick thought fondly, but she could always be relied on for tea and sympathy when the situation required it.

It wasn't his hangover that had kept Nick awake, it was wondering what to say to Anna. He'd rehearsed seventy-five different speeches in his head, yet none of them sounded quite right when he said them out loud. He glanced at the clock. Anna was late. This, he had to admit, wasn't unusual. But today he'd wanted her to be early to put him out of his misery.

He had, however, received a telephone call from Mr Hashimoto which had provided a pleasant distraction. Despite Anna's minor indiscretions during the meeting with the business financier, Mr Hashimoto had, nevertheless, made a generous offer of funding to build a new showroom on the current site. The end of Nick's crummy Portakabin days could well be in sight! This was just the news he needed. He'd made an appointment with the bank manager to discuss it as soon as possible, before Mr Hashimoto thought better of it and changed his mind. Things, it seemed, were starting to go his way. He could feel it in his bones, this was a great time to plight his troth to Anna. (Whatever plighting his troth might involve.) Nick glanced at his watch – he was going to have to leave soon whether Anna had arrived or not. He wanted the bank manager on his side, and turning up late for the appointment was not an option.

On cue there was a familiar screeching noise and he watched as she swung into her parking space on two wheels. He realised that he'd been waiting with bated breath for her arrival. It made him smile to himself as he followed the progress of his Executive Assistant and Business Advisor as she bustled across the car yard, smoothing her hair and her skirt and finally bursting through the door.

'I'm sorry I'm late,' she gasped, throwing her handbag to the floor by the desk. 'Extenuating circumstances.' She held up a hand to Nick. 'I'll tell you about it just as soon as I can breathe again.'

Nick rubbed his hands together anxiously. 'Sit down. Sit down,' he said. 'I've got something to tell you.'

'I could kill for a drink.'

'Tea,' he said. 'Right. Tea. The kettle's boiled.'

Anna slipped out of her jacket while he busied himself making her a cup of tea. He hadn't got time for one himself as he'd have to be going in a minute.

Nick handed her the mug of tea and Anna sipped at it gratefully, letting out a welcome sigh.

'You look very serious,' she said. 'Did someone die?'

'No, no.' He sat on the edge of her desk. 'Though I suppose you could say some*thing* died.'

'I haven't broken the computer?' She looked at the offending machine with a feeling akin to terror.

'No, no.'

Anna looked puzzled – as well she might.

'I'm not making a great job of this,' Nick said. 'And I lay awake all night, well nearly all night, apart from the bit where I was asleep because of all the sherry I'd drunk . . .'

'Sherry?'

'I'm back at my parents' house. Back in my old bed.' Nick gave her a sheepish glance. 'Janine and I have finished. For good.'

Anna's eyebrows rose in surprise. 'You've only just gone back.'

'I know,' Nick said. 'And you were right. It was a mistake. A big mistake. I realised – well, Janine realised – that I didn't love her any more. Whatever we had was gone. Long gone. It had well and truly died.'

Anna gave him a sympathetic smile. 'I'm sorry, Nick.'

'No, no. Don't be. I'm not,' he said. 'Because it made me realise something else. About someone else . . .'

His lovely assistant looked very confused.

Nick sagged in frustration. 'I'm making a right bollocks of this, aren't I?'

Anna grinned at him.

He sighed loudly and pressed on. 'What I'm trying to say is that
. . . that . . . I think I might have feelings . . . strong feelings . . . for
someone else.'

She looked at him expectantly.

'For you,' Nick whispered. 'I have strong feelings for *you*.'

'For me!' Anna rocked back in her chair.

'Is it such a surprise?'

'Yes. No,' she babbled. 'Oh, I don't know!' She put her head in
her hands while Nick stood there shuffling his feet. 'Good grief,'
she whimpered. 'This is dreadful.'

He tried a wan smile. 'I didn't think it was quite so terrible myself.'

'Oh, it is,' Anna said tightly. 'You won't believe how terrible.' She
rubbed a hand over her brow which was creased with anxiety. When
she looked up at him her eyes were troubled. 'Bruno came back last
night.'

'Bruno, your errant husband?'

Anna nodded miserably.

'How very embarrassing for me.'

'It's just awful timing,' Anna insisted. 'Awful, awful timing.' She
looked as if she was about to cry, which was the last thing that Nick
had intended. He'd sort of hoped she'd declare undying love for him
too and they would have fallen into each other's arms, et cetera.
Damn and bugger. Why did nothing ever turn out right for him?
Had he been born under the wrong bloody astrological sign or
something? Were all Leos similarly cursed?

'Is he staying?' His voice sounded too flat and too disappointed.

'I don't know,' Anna admitted. 'I wouldn't give him house room
if it was simply up to me. He says he's changed. So I suppose I have
to give him a chance. For the sake of the children.' Her eyes pleaded
for him to understand. And the worst thing was that he did. 'I don't
know what to do for the best. Poppy treats him like some sort of
superhero. She needs a father.'

'She needs a *good* father.'

'He seems different.' Anna sounded defensive. 'He may have
changed this time.'

'Do you really believe that?'

'No.' Anna flopped back in the chair. 'Oh, I don't know.'

Nick looked at his watch. 'Damn,' he said. 'I have to go out. I've
got a meeting with the bank manager. It's important. Mr Hashimoto's
come up with the cash.'

249

'Then I didn't mess up your meeting completely?'

'Far from it.' Nick enjoyed a wry smile at the memory. He was already collecting his coat. Anna looked distressed and he didn't want to leave her like this. He reached out and grabbed hold of her hand tightly. Instantly, she was out of the chair and in his arms. They held each other close, pressing together. She felt tiny in his embrace.

'I love you,' she breathed.

Nick's heart took flight. 'I love you too.' He realised how long he'd been hoping to hear those words from her. Her lips found his and they were warm and honey-sweet. The bland greyness of the Portakabin faded away to be replaced by a field of vibrantly blooming flowers, blue skies and cute bunnies hopping about – a rich and Technicolor hallucination. His legs felt weak with joy. He was drowing, overwhelmed by a giddy wave of sensation. Anna put her head on his shoulder and he kissed her hair. 'I don't want to leave you.'

'You must go,' she insisted. 'It's important.'

'Not as important as this,' he said quietly. His stomach fluttered with anxiety.

'Go,' Anna said. 'Go now.'

He ran his fingers over her worried face. There were tears in her eyes. 'We have to decide what we're going to do. Promise me that we'll talk about this the minute I get back?'

Anna nodded. Nick reluctantly let go of her. 'While I'm gone, do the mission statement or whatever it is,' he said. 'Put in something about us not messing up our lives.' He rushed to the door. 'I'll be back.'

She stood there looking forlorn and he turned back to snatch another passionate kiss. 'I'll be back as soon as I can,' he said. 'Don't go away.'

Chapter Eighty-Eight

The sad thing is, I've already decided what I have to do. I sit and stare out of the window at the newspapers and crisp packets blowing down the road on the spiteful breeze. Tidying the papers on the desk absently, I give a longing look over the tatty, rundown caravan office that I've come to love – almost as much as its owner. It's cold in here and I slip my jacket back on, but it fails to warm me at all. I hug my arms, rubbing them briskly, and I wonder whether I should leave Nick a note.

Standing up, I collect my things and head towards the door. The office is still a mess and I hate to leave like this. But I have to – I know that. It's the right thing to do. And if I repeat it to myself often enough, I may start to believe it.

My time here has meant so much more to me than a mere job; it's been a way out of my old life and into a new one. I'm shocked that I can turn my back on it like this. I'm shocked that I can turn my back on Nick. But I've already explained to him that this isn't about me, it's about the children. Bruno is their father and I can't, at this point, tear them away from him again. I make my legs walk towards the door one step at a time. They're heavy, leaden and I'm shivering all over as if I have flu.

I lock the door behind me, get in my car and somehow manage to drive across the city. Horns honk at me for misdemeanours of which I'm scarcely aware. I should go to Sophie's house, but I can't face it. She would only persuade me to throw Bruno out on his ear and make a go of things with Nick. And that's not what I want to hear. I want to feel that after all I've been through in my roller-coaster of a marriage, that some good can come of it after all. I want to be vindicated in my judgement. To prove that our years together haven't been a complete waste of time and effort.

After a journey that I complete in a trance, I pull into the car park at the Peace Pagoda. It's pretty deserted except for a couple of cars. There's a DHL van parked next to a BT van and the two drivers are sharing a flask of coffee. I swing in next to them for some sort of security, so that my windows won't get smashed while I'm away from my car. Soggy piles of leaves are dotted around the gravel surface and the wispy grey shrubs and dog roses that are so colourful in the summer look cold and bare in this miserly winter light. Despite its bleak appearance, this is always a great place to come and contemplate your life. And I need this solitude to buy some time to think.

I have a thick, waterproof jacket in the boot of my car – I live in constant fear of my poor old heap breaking down and so have an emergency kit to hand. This is one of the few areas in my life where I'm organised. I'm glad of my jacket's warming comfort now, even though it smells slightly of damp car boot and petrol fumes. I kick off my heels and push my feet into the socks and trainers that have seen better days, which also form part of my survival gear. It's strange that I hadn't thought I'd need them in this sort of situation – where *I'm* breaking down rather than the car.

'Want a drink of this, love?' one of the van drivers calls out to me. 'Looks like you could do with it.'

'No thanks,' I say. 'Are you going to be here for a while?'

They both nod.

'Will you keep an eye on my car for me, please?'

'Will do.' Honestly, you'd think it was a top of the range Mercedes the way I fuss over it, but as my only form of transport I don't want any harm to befall it.

I give them a wave and set off on the steep winding path towards the ornate white structure of the Peace Pagoda, which enjoys a panoramic perch overlooking the vast expanse of Willen Lake. The hill is planted with a thousand cherry trees and cedars that came from an ancient village in Japan famous for the beauty of its blossoms. Now the grass needs mowing and it's mottled with clumps of mud, yet the fresh green buds on the cherry trees that are curled tight waiting for the warmth of spring bring some hope to my heart. This was the first Buddhist peace pagoda to be built in the western world, if you believe the local paper, and without seeming to try, it exudes an air of calm serenity. Despite its delicate carvings and fragile flutings, it looks solid and dependable. In a month or so the riot of colour from the blossom will soften its edges, but now it stands stark and proud in the denuded landscape. Its white purity shines out under the dark, glowering sky. I pull my coat around me against the prevailing wind and wish that my emergency kit included a woolly hat too.

Climbing the marble stairs, I circle the base of the pagoda, deep in thought, and then sitting on the steps, flanked by two stone lions, I gaze out over the lake. I can't stay at my job. If things go wrong with Bruno, I must try to work them through. I can't always have kind, dependable Nick there in the background to run to, otherwise Bruno and I will never be able to make a go of it. And heaven only knows why, but I do feel that I need to give my husband one last chance.

The wind is whipping a froth of spray on the dark surface of the lake. Canada geese squawk in complaint as they take to the air, fighting against the elements. I'm completely alone. My fingers are numb with cold and the awful thing is, my heart feels the same. I can only hope Nick will understand.

Chapter Eighty-Nine

M ilton Keynes had got to be one of *the* worst places on earth to park. Nick had trawled round for ages looking for a vacant space, and all the time the minutes were ticking away to his appointment. There were grey meters, blue meters, red meters, black meters – all of them with different tariffs and different restrictions which could only be remembered by someone with a photographic memory or someone with very little joy in their life. And that wasn't Nick today. Today he had lots of joy in his life. No matter that whatever meter he did manage to find would eat his loose change at an alarming rate or that he kept thinking he'd found an empty spot only to see some diminutive vehicle tucked in the back of it – none of it could trouble his soaring spirit. Anna loved him and that was all that mattered.

Eventually, he did manage to park, sprint across Midsummer Boulevard, dodging the lone bus in the specially reserved lane, and still make his appointment with the bank manager on time. His business banker was, by all accounts, a charming fellow. He'd seen Nick through more than one sticky patch with his car yard and it would be nice to reward his perseverance with the business by making a huge success of it. They were even on first-name terms and today, Patrick was being even more chatty than usual. In between discussions about his children, dog, mother-in-law, car – which would soon need replacing – and next year's holiday, Nick had somehow managed to make his pitch for additional funds to put up his share of the finance for the new improved dealership and swanky buildings that it would involve. He had also tried very hard not to look at the clock more than once a minute. Despite the fact that Patrick was very pleasant, today Nick didn't want to waste any time on chit-chat. Today he wanted a quick, rubber-stamped agreement so that he could rush back to Anna's arms and find out what they were going to do with the rest of their lives.

After an interminable period during which he was forced to drink a cup of standard, bank-issue coffee that he didn't want while Patrick phoned someone higher than him for approval of the loan, the deal was done and Nick rushed back out into the fresh air. He clutched the paperwork to his chest. This was it. His dream finally realised. Now, time to concentrate on something that was *beyond* his wildest dreams!

On the way to the car, he dashed into Marks & Spencer's and grabbed the biggest, brightest bouquet of flowers that he could lay his hands on. He even whistled as he queued up to pay.

Back at his car, he handed over his ticket to someone who was scrabbling in his pocket for change so that he could use the unexpired time on Nick's permit – even though this was strictly against parking guidelines. Sod it, Nick thought. Today he felt goodwill to all mankind. He swung out of the car park and headed back towards the car yard with a great deal all signed up in his pocket and a song in his heart.

He should have noticed that Anna's car wasn't in its normal place in the yard, but in his haste to get inside to see her, he didn't. The second hint should have been the fact that the door to the Portakabin was firmly locked, but that didn't register either. And when he burst through the door, making it rock on its worn hinges, he was still shocked to see that the office was completely empty. The papers on Anna's desk had been tidied into neat, ordered piles, which was not a good sign. He felt the colour drain from his face and it was all he could do to stop his knees from buckling and his body sinking to the floor. His heart, that unreliable lump of muscle, was pattering too high and too fast. Anna had gone. And, instinctively, he knew that she wasn't coming back.

Nick picked up the phone and punched in a number. His breathing was ragged and uneven, as if he'd run a marathon and was at the end of his endurance. And perhaps in some ways this was the end. Could he take any more disappointments? Could he really hold onto his dreams in the constant face of adversity?

Sam answered after a couple of rings.

Nick heard himself draw in a shuddering breath. 'Emergency pizza therapy required.'

'Right, mate,' Sam said. 'I'll be there in ten minutes.'

Nick and Sam sat back-to-back in the office. For once, Nick had the privilege of the squishy leather-look executive chair, while Sam perched on the plastic garden chair. It was clear that his friend was pandering to his sensitivities. Each of them had a box of pizza opened on their laps. They both ate with great deliberation.

'Women,' Sam said with a mouthful of hot pepperoni with extra cheese. 'They're like chocolate, mate. The fancier the wrapping, the more disappointing the contents tend to be.'

'True.' Nick sighed over his ham and pineapple.

Sam wagged his pizza at him. 'Married women are definitely off-limits from now on.'

'I could be off women *per se*. This could scar me for life,' Nick confided. He felt sick and not simply because the pizza was greasy and lukewarm. 'I'll be so frightened to commit to anyone else that I can just see myself in ten years' time still going to line-dancing classes with my mum.'

'I won't let it come to that,' Sam assured him. 'I'm your very best friend. We must stick together in times like these.'

'Still, I can't believe it,' Nick said unhappily. 'She came into my life, completely messed up my filing cabinets and left. Just like that.'

'Your filing cabinets will recover,' Sam said. 'And so will you. In time.'

Nick glared at Anna's cup. The one she had left standing half-filled with the tea he'd made her on the corner of his desk. 'She didn't even wash up her cup.'

'Bitch,' Sam concluded.

Bitch or not, Nick thought, he'd miss her desperately. He let out a long, weary sigh and returned to his pizza.

Chapter Ninety

The sunset is magnificent tonight. The sky is ablaze with the colours of a strawberry and blueberry smoothie, flecked with apricot purée. If I was in a different mood this would fill me with joyful awe. As it is, the display of contemporary art by the elements fails to lift my spirits. Although it is making me feel slightly hungry.

I've put this off until the last minute, but now I can't avoid going home. It's still a shock to see Bruno's car in my drive and when I open the front door, it's an assault on my delicate senses to hear the radio is blaring out and my husband whistling tunelessly along. Going through to the kitchen, I throw my car keys on the table. There are bags of grocery shopping piled in the middle. Not my measly Netto nearly-out-of-date bargain shopping, but carriers overflowing with full-priced Waitrose goodies. Bruno has clearly been used to living the high life in his absence.

'Hey,' my husband says, spinning round. He is standing at the ironing board, working his way through a pile of Poppy's school shirts. A couple are already pressed and folded on the draining board – still exhibiting creases – showing his inexperience in such domestic chores. But I'm stunned that he's even trying. His cheeks show a flush of steam and exertion.

'This must be a mirage,' I say.

'Don't knock it,' Bruno laughs. 'I told you – I'm a changed person.' He nods his head at the shopping bags. 'I did a supermarket sweep. But I thought you could unpack it, so you could see what I bought. Plus, I can't remember where it all goes.' He gives me an apologetic look.

'That's fine.' This can't really be happening. Bruno, shopping and ironing? 'I'll take my coat off and put it away.'

'Tea?' he asks as I shake off my emergency anorak. I nod my grateful thanks. I need something to thaw out my chilled bones. My husband even remembers to turn off the iron as he moves seamlessly onto tea-making duties while I delve into the contents of the shopping bags. There seems to be a large ratio of alcohol to food, but other than that he has done a good job so I say nothing and start to find homes for the various tins and packets.

'I didn't expect you so soon,' Bruno says, handing over my tea.

I try to avoid his gaze. 'I've had a few problems at work,' I say, busying myself arranging a row of baked-bean cans. 'I thought it was better if I left.'

'Problems?' Bruno's brow darkens. 'Do you want me to go round there and sort it?'

'No.' I give him a wry glance. 'I don't want you to "sort it".' I am well aware what Bruno's idea of sorting it would be. 'And I thought you said you'd changed?'

'I don't want anyone causing you problems.'

'You are the root of all my problems,' I say and Bruno doesn't realise how true that statement is.

He comes to me and wraps his arms around my waist and I try not to stiffen at his embrace. 'Not any more,' he says flatly. 'Those days are over.'

My look must give away my scepticism because he bends and kisses me on the end of my nose. 'I promise,' he adds. 'I want us to be a family again.'

'Why have you come back now?' I ask. 'After all this time?'

'Because I love you,' Bruno says. He finds my lips and crushes them in a fervent kiss. And I hope, in time, that I'll be able to say the same.

Chapter Ninety-One

The reams and reams of paperwork for the new dealership franchise had been completed swiftly and relatively painlessly. Yet it had taken three months to finally get the money through from Mr Hashimoto and the bank for the new dealership building. Then another three months of hassling the local Planning Department to get the drawings approved. However, when the diggers moved in and broke ground in the middle of summer, it did mean that said ground wasn't sodden with rain, and a particularly fine spell of glorious weather had allowed the builders to crack on with a vengeance. Soon, a brand new range of Japanese cars would grace the resulting forecourt.

Nick stood and viewed the footings of the new building and the sleek, grey brick walls which were now nearly at waist height. Perhaps not too impressive at the moment, but eventually it would dwarf the jaded Portakabin standing next to it. The finished showroom would be a fine architectural example of glass and steel. The muddy patch where the cars now stood would be transformed by the miracle of block-paving into a work of art graced with row upon row of gleaming Hivanti vehicles. Bronzed, bare-chested builders swarmed over the structure like worker ants. Mr Hashimoto, smart in a black linen business suit, smoked a cigarette with the anxious fervour of the Japanese, sucking the smoke in rapid gasps into his lungs. Nick's new business partner stared at the building and grunted in appreciation as the midday sun beat down on them both.

'This looks good.' Mr Hashimoto clapped Nick on the back and waved expansively at the building site in front of them.

'It'll be great,' Nick agreed proudly.

'Another few months and you'll be different man,' Mr Hashimoto suggested.

'You're right.' Even now a flash of Nick's legendary misplaced loyalty surged in him. Who would sell the population of Milton Keynes reliable if ageing vehicles now he was moving on to bigger and better things?

Mr Hashimoto glanced at his watch. 'I must go,' he said and they both turned, heading back towards his gleaming Jaguar. 'This will be a very good move for you.'

It had already proved to be a good move. For the last six months he'd been busier than ever before, which had gone some way to ensuring that not all of his waking moments were filled with thoughts of Anna. The sleeping moments were still something of a problem though.

They were at Mr Hashimoto's car. 'No lovely assistant today?'

'No,' Nick said. 'Lovely assistant unfortunately moved onto pastures new.' He gave Mr Hashimoto a philosophical smile.

'That is unfortunate,' the small Japanese man said. 'She was a lot of fun.'

'Yes,' Nick said.

'I hoped she'd be working for us in the new dealership.'

'Me too.'

'I want to make the showroom female friendly. Young, trendy ladies should be buying our cars. Anna would have been ideal to put that in place.' Mr Hashimoto shook Nick's hand and, with a little bow, slid into his car. 'You should give her a call,' he suggested. 'Offer her a job.'

'Maybe I will,' Nick agreed.

He waved as Mr Hashimoto purred off into the distance then plodded back towards the Portakabin. Maybe he should call Anna. He could do as his business associate suggested and offer her a job. What did he have to lose? It had taken him months to get the filing back in its rightful place in the cabinets and the mission statement still lurked in the computer, woefully incomplete. But wouldn't it be worse to have Anna working beside him every day knowing that she was beyond his reach? They say that time's a great healer, but people who spout that popular belief clearly haven't been cut too deeply. He'd gone down several routes to healing – strong drink, blokish nights out with Sam, long hours at the car yard – but nothing worked. Even the last resort – line-dancing with his mother – had failed miserably. He still missed Anna just as much.

Yes, he decided, he would give her a call – to be sociable, nothing more. Was there any harm in that? As he headed to the office, a car pulled up and a bald man with a pot belly and his skinny wife climbed out.

'Hiya, mate,' the man said. 'I need a car for the wife.' He flicked his thumb at the careworn woman by his side.

Nick considered making a joke about not taking wives in part-exchange, but thought better of it. 'What sort of price range are you looking at?'

The man turned to a row of cut-price Corsas. 'Something like this.'

'Fine,' Nick said. 'This one runs well. Shall we take her out for a spin?'

The couple agreed with enthusiastic nods.

'I'll just get the keys,' Nick said. And as he strode purposefully back towards the Portakabin, he realised that he'd narrowly avoided making a fool of himself all over again.

Chapter Ninety-Two

I lie on my front on the checked picnic rug watching Connor and Bruno playing with the football. My son is trying to cling onto my husband's legs while he expertly dribbles the ball.

'Get it! Get it!' Bruno shouts his encouragement while Connor shrieks with delight and works himself up into a lather.

My cardigan and Poppy's have been pressed into service to form the goal mouth which my daughter is currently guarding. 'Shoot! Shoot!' she shouts even though she has no idea what she's talking about. A longing for David Beckham is the nearest Poppy has ever come to an appreciation of football.

I kick my bare feet in the air and pull absently at the clumps of long grass nearby, selecting a piece to nibble on. I'm surrounded by remnants of half-eaten picnic, but can't quite summon up the energy to tidy it away yet – but I must do so soon as it's all starting to wilt in the heat.

This has been another long hot summer flying in the face of traditional British weather and, as a family, we've taken every advantage of it. We've had breakfast out in our sunny little garden at the weekends, picnic lunches, dinners *al fresco* too – enjoying a brief glimpse of the Mediterranean way of life. Perhaps it's because we've had this space to expand, this air of cheerfulness that good weather brings that Bruno and I have found it relatively easy to slot back into our relationship. If we'd been cramped up in the house during a long wet winter I wonder would we have rubbed along so well?

I watch one of the colourful longboats move by on the cool green depths of the Grand Union Canal. Its bright red paintwork, scattered with the gaudy traditional flowers of the waterways, is perfectly framed by the blue colourwash of the sky. Willows weep, tentatively dipping the delicate tips of their leaves in the water. Birds sing, butterflies flutter by, bees buzz busily. And it all seems so idyllic, doesn't it?

Bruno scores a goal and falls to the ground, kicking his legs in the air in celebration. The children pile on top of him and pummel him until they're all wrestling in a heap and, once again, I feel like an observer, on the outside of this joyous scene. I'm floating above, watching it all like an out-of-body experience, detached and not quite here. I wonder when this will all start to become real to me again.

My husband fends off his assailants and scoops up Connor, carrying him over to me. He deposits my wriggling son on the picnic rug whereupon Connor, with renewed gusto, sets about the cocktail sausages once again.

'Hi,' Bruno says, leaning over to plant a kiss on my lips. His face is red from the sun and too much lager. He's panting hard. 'I'm exhausted. Couldn't we have brought them up to be less energetic?'

And there it is, right on the surface again – the urge to correct his version of life, to tell him that it wasn't *we* who brought them up, it was *me*. I'm the one who struggled with them alone while he was off with who knows who, doing who knows what. Having said that, Bruno has been a perfect husband since his return – well, almost. It's as if he's read a textbook on how to be the ideal spouse and is trying it on for size. And I still can't decide whether it fits him or not, so I bite down the comment and store away my hurt. But I can't help thinking that we're still skirting round the edges of the dance floor. I look at my husband as he lies down and stretches out on the rug. The dance of anger is a very potent one and the steps aren't easily forgotten.

Bruno catches hold of my hand. 'Happy?' he asks.

'Yes.' I make myself smile broadly. There seems to be some sort of smokescreen obscuring the picture, blurring my eyes so I can't see the truth. And I wonder if the process of peeling back the layers of our love is simply revealing the hard, unyielding scar tissue that lies beneath.

I've slipped back into my role as Bruno's wife and I do feel as if it's a retrograde step. I don't work now, because my husband doesn't like me to, and I've quietly retreated into being a housewife and mother once more. I don't see much of Sophie either as she's no longer looking after Connor for me, so there isn't the obligatory twice-daily download. Also, since time began, my friend and my husband have been sworn enemies. She sees through Bruno more easily than I do – or used to. Frankly, it's easier if they are kept apart, so Sophie hasn't called around much recently. And I miss her. I miss her bossiness and our girly chats and her sense of fun.

Looking over the family tableau in front of me – Bruno snoozing gently, Connor finishing the remains of the picnic, Poppy chasing butterflies on the banks of the canal amid the buttercups and daisies – I wonder how long the façade can last. I don't love Bruno as I used to. I don't light up when I see him. I don't ache when he's not around. But if there aren't the highs that we used to have, then maybe there won't be the lows either. And the lows are something I could definitely live without. Other than that, we go through the motions of family life pleasantly enough. Bruno and I make love, but not with our old abandon. It was the one thing we were always good at and there was always plenty of 'making up' sex. Now it's perfunctory and there's a tension in my body that I can't ignore. I'm holding back and I know it. I can't give everything to him any more. I suspect Bruno knows it too.

I try not to think about Nick very often and what might have been. Bruno is out at work all day – doing what, I'm not exactly sure. Building work is the catch-all term. But he spends fairly long hours at it and it's paying well – perhaps too well, but I haven't the strength to dig any deeper. Partly because I'm not sure that I want to know, and with a certain amount of ignorance, I can more easily brush off my misgivings. So on the surface all is lovely. What more can I ask for?

I'll admit that there have been times when I've very nearly picked up the phone – just to see how Nick is. I hated walking out like that and I just . . . well, it would be nice to talk to him again. But Sophie has had to wean herself off Sam and if my friend can do it then so can I. It doesn't stop me from feeling slightly sick when I think that this is my life for the foreseeable future. Poppy is spinning round and round, carefree. Connor is wiping his sticky fingers down his T-shirt. I do hope my children will thank me for this decision in years to come.

Wasps start to circle round the oozing quiche. The sky is darkening ominously. 'I think we should be making tracks,' I say.

Bruno opens his eyes and pushes himself up. 'If you want to.'

It's too hot and I'm getting a headache. Perhaps there's thunder in the air. We're due a storm, I think.

My husband helps me to pack up and we load the car. The children complain that they don't want to go home and Connor cries because he's over-heated and over-tired and I hope he doesn't throw up his excess of sausages. It's going to be hell getting him to sleep tonight in his stifling bedroom.

'I'll drive,' I say.

'*I'll* drive.' Bruno is insistent.

'You've had too much to drink.'

Bruno ignores me, gets into the driver's seat and starts the engine. I get in next to him, my hands clenched on my lap.

In silence, Bruno steers the car homewards. Within seconds Connor is fast asleep in his car seat and Poppy is entertaining herself by singing rap songs courtesy of Eminem, complete with all the 'f' words and a good majority of the 'c' words too. Where's Postman Pat when you need him? Somewhere under one of the seats, I suspect. I let my head drop back onto the head-rest and try to get my mind to go into free-flow. With the heat through the window and my general level of exhaustion, I'm just getting nicely drowsy, letting the motion of the car lull me into sleep when Poppy cries out. 'Look!' she says.

My eyes pop open. My daughter is pointing out of the window. 'There's Uncle Nick!'

I turn my head to follow her finger. And she's right. We're passing by the car yard and there, standing in the middle with a customer, is Nick. It's the first time I've been this way since I walked out on him, as I've always taken care to find a circuitous route to avoid just this scenario. Nick looks tanned and well. He's chatting animatedly and smiling – his nice, honest smile. My heart starts a heavy thud and my palms have gone cold and clammy.

Bruno removes his eyes from the road and takes in the scene. Poppy has wound down her window. 'Uncle Nick!' She's shouting at the top of her voice. 'Uncle Nick!'

'Poppy! Wind up that window,' I snap.

My daughter, her euphoria sharply curtailed, sullenly winds up the window as instructed. 'I only wanted to say hello,' she complains.

My husband's face has darkened. 'Uncle Nick?'

'That's my boss. *Was* my boss,' I correct.

'*Uncle* Nick?'

'He took the kids and me on a day out to London,' I explain. 'A long time ago.'

'He's lovely,' Poppy pipes up as if she's talking about Gareth Gates and I could gaily throttle her even though she is blissfully unaware of her culpability.

'Is he?' Bruno asks tightly.

'He's a very nice man,' I say. 'He was kind to us when we needed it.'

'Anything more?' Bruno is holding the steering wheel in a death grip. His knuckles are white. And I think that my face is.

I lick my lips nervously. 'No.'

We're leaving the car yard behind and I resist the temptation to turn my head. Poppy has no such qualms and watches Nick until he disappears from our sight. It seems my daughter misses him too and that makes me even sadder.

My hands are balled up in front of me and, as I avoid looking at Bruno, my old fears return. If you love someone, you shouldn't live in constant dread of them. If you love someone, you shouldn't spend your life tiptoeing round the outskirts of their unpredictable moods. I've just seen a glimpse of the old Bruno and it seems as if the dormant volcano has started to simmer once more. How long will it be before there's an almighty eruption?

Any trace of a smile has faded from Bruno's face and the sun suddenly goes behind a threatening black cloud. It looks as if the fine weather is over.

Chapter Ninety-Three

'I have organised a date for you,' Sam said.

'No, no, no.'

'Yes, yes, yes.' Sam drank from his bottle of beer. 'A blind date.'

'She'd have to be blind to want to go out with me.'

'Big Gemma's a lovely lady. Just your type.'

'Big Gemma?'

Sam mimed with his hands which particular part of Gemma was big. And it didn't appear to be her brain.

'She's one of your cast-offs, isn't she?'

Sam didn't meet his eyes. 'I have road-tested her for you, if that's what you mean.'

'Oh man,' Nick complained. 'I'm a secondhand car dealer, I don't want secondhand girlfriends too.'

'Has anyone ever told you that you're very picky?'

They were in All-Bar-One in Midsummer Boulevard and it was quiet before the usual evening crush, but that didn't stop Sam from eyeing up the few lovely ladies who were lurking there. Nick wished that he could be like Sam and simply turn his attentions to someone else, but he didn't work that way. He wasn't sure that his friend did either – Sam was just better at hiding his misery.

'We're meeting them at FIFTY PER CENT.'

'No,' Nick said.

'Yes. This is the alternative to going line-dancing with your mother and her star-spangled, septuagenarian friends.'

Nick didn't need blind dates. He needed someone to talk to. Someone to restore his battered self-confidence. Being dumped by two women in one year was more than any man should have to bear. But male friends, Sam included, were hopeless at providing reassurance. Nick had hoped that now they'd both been rejected by the women they loved – plural in his case – they would find some common ground for emotional discussions, but no such luck. If he'd told Sam that he was feeling vaguely suicidal and that driving a car very fast into a big tree was, on some days, quite an appealing thought, Sam would have tutted his sympathy and said, 'Women, eh? Is it my round?'

Maybe that was doing Sam a disservice. But Nick wanted to talk about Anna, he *needed* to talk about Anna, he needed to know that he wasn't a complete failure and that one day, preferably before all his hair and his teeth fell out, someone else would come along to love him. He wanted to share his insecurities and his heartaches with his best mate. Instead, Sam had fixed him up with Big Gemma.

It was easier for women. The minute anything went wrong in a relationship legions of friends turned up on the doorstep armed with tissues, bottles of vodka, girly bonding DVDs featuring Orlando Bloom or Johnny Depp and boxes of chocolates. They'd cluck phrases like, 'He wasn't worth it anyway!' and, 'Once a bastard, always a bastard!' and gleefully pick over every lapse in his sexual technique. Whenever there was a crisis a dozen people were a text message away, ready to offer completely biased sympathy. If all that failed there were a dozen different magazines women could turn to that offered pages and pages of solace from the sisterhood. It just wasn't the same with blokes. If you were a dumped bloke, you were on your own. And yet everyone, particularly other women, seemed to expect you to shrug your shoulders and skip gaily down to the pub to eye up your next conquest. He looked over at Sam who was doing just that. Nick sighed.

'Come on,' Sam said, downing his beer. 'We'd better not keep the girls waiting.'

'I want to tell you now that I'm doing this under the utmost duress.'

The bar was starting to fill up with scantily clad women and sharply dressed men who were clearly out for a good time. Sam and he fitted in just fine. He couldn't stand going out 'on the pull' – it had always been a deeply humiliating experience for him. Even when he got lucky he wasn't the type who could jump straight into bed with someone, and that seemed to be expected these days. If that was going to happen he'd have to start paying more attention to his toenails and nasal hair, eat less of his mother's calorie-laden puddings and hit the gym more often. The thought of getting naked with a stranger filled him with terror. He seemed to be going through some sort of sexual numbness. If he couldn't be with Anna, he simply wasn't interested.

'I'm not going home with anyone,' Nick stated firmly as he followed his friend out of the bar. 'I want to get that straight now.'

Sam winked at him. 'When Big Gemma gets hold of you, you might not have any choice.'

Ageing Dolly Parton lookalikes in fringed cowgirl outfits were sounding more attractive by the minute.

Chapter Ninety-Four

Connor has been spark out for hours and I go into his room to check on him, watching him as he dreams contentedly. When was the last time I had such untroubled sleep, I wonder. I smooth his wispy blond hair and kiss his forehead. He wriggles and pushes his thumb further into his mouth. Even though he's wearing just a nappy, his cheeks are pink with the heat and I open his window wider to let in some of the still night air, but there's no hint of a breeze to cool him down. Not that it seems to be troubling Connor.

In Poppy's room it's a different story. She's wired, agitated. Her duvet and the ever-present and slightly disgusting Doggy have been kicked to the floor and she's chasing herself round the bed, huffing and puffing. I pick up the duvet and fold it tidily, placing Doggy jauntily on top of it.

'What's he doing here?'

'I thought he might be lonely.'

I sit down next to her. 'Okay?'

'I'm too hot.' My daughter's hair is damp against her forehead. Her windows are already open as wide as they will go. There's a faint buzz of traffic from the nearby main road. Out there, somewhere across the city, Nick is going about his life.

'There might be a thunderstorm,' I warn her.

'Cool,' Poppy says, but I know it's bravado as she's frightened of thunder just like I was as a child. I realise why Doggy has been purloined from her brother and that, despite her best efforts, Poppy is still my little girl. Now, with my advancing years, I know that life holds much more terror than the mere showy clashing of clouds.

'Try to settle down to sleep,' I say. 'If you stop fidgeting you won't get so hot.' I turn off her bedside light.

'Mummy,' she says in the darkness. 'Will we never see Uncle Nick again?'

My throat closes. 'Possibly not.'

'Why?' she asks. 'He was very nice. Funny. I liked him.'

270

'So did I,' I confess quietly.

'Is this one of those complicated grown-up situations?'

'Yes,' I answer. 'Very complicated.'

'Sometimes I don't think that I want to grow up,' Poppy whispers.

'Sometimes I don't want you to either.' I kiss my daughter's hair and hope that she has a simpler life than I have. I hope she finds someone wonderful to love and cherish her, and that her experience of love is free from pain. I hope she loves well and not unwisely. And I hope that when she's older, I can talk to her about these things and prevent her from making the same stupid mistakes as her mother made. I sigh and kiss her again before I leave.

As I open the door to my own bedroom, I see that Bruno is pacing the floor. He's been drinking since we came home from the picnic and now he's looking rather the worse for wear. 'I thought you'd gone to bed,' I say.

'So what's with this *Nick?*'

'Nothing.' My insides twist into knots of anxiety. Bruno's face is dark with anger and it's an expression that I recognise only too well. Crossing the bedroom, I go to the tallboy and open a drawer to get a clean T-shirt to sleep in. 'He's a nice man,' I say calmly, but notice that my fingers tremble. 'He was very good to the kids.'

'*My* kids.' Bruno's tone is menacing.

'Only when it suits you,' I say over my shoulder. Which is a mistake.

Bruno flashes across the room. Pushing me away from the drawer, he grabs it from my hands and throws it onto the bed, scattering the contents. The marabou-trimmed thong, as it would, lands on the top of the pile. Its feathery nonsense stands out like a sore thumb, cheap and tarty amid my sensible, over-washed granny pants.

Bruno picks it up, waving it between his fingers. 'Did you buy this for Nick?'

'Don't be ridiculous.' And I should remember that when Bruno is in this sort of mood, it's best not to antagonise him. It's best to keep quiet, say nothing and take what's coming. But as he's been playing the perfect husband for the last few months, my guard is down.

Before I can stop him, he's on me and has slammed me up against the wall. His face is inches from mine, contorted and ugly. '*Ridiculous?*' he spits, rubbing the marabou thong roughly across my face. I feel it graze my cheek, cutting into the skin. 'Has he been fucking you?'

'No.'

271

The husband that I know so well presses his body forcibly against my ribs: the pain is excruciating. He clutches a handful of my hair and pulls at it with all his strength. Strands are tearing away from my scalp. 'Tell me.'

'There's nothing to tell you.' My voice is shaky and cowed. How did I think this man could have changed? After last time I vowed that I'd never let Bruno intimidate me again, and yet here I am, back in a situation that's been played out over and over, like a recurrent nightmare.

I summon up all my strength and knee Bruno in the balls. I don't know whether it's because I make good contact or whether this is the first time I've ever fought back, but a look of surprise crosses his face. His hands go to protect himself and I take my chance to push him off me. But as I move away from him, Bruno recovers and grips my arm, swinging me round like a rag doll. I land with a hefty thump on the floor. Instantly he's on top of me, pinning me to the floor, his weight crushing me.

'Do you think you can make a fool of me?' he says, spittle spraying my face. His hands are around my throat and then he punches me hard, rocking my head sideways. A gurgling noise is starting in my throat, but I can't cry out, I can't stop him from throttling me. Black and red lights swim before my eyes and my eardrums feel as if they're about to burst.

Suddenly I hear Poppy. 'Mummy!' she shouts.

'Get away!' Bruno snarls and I hear a thump.

'Leave her alone! Leave her alone!' She's screaming hysterically and Bruno's hands leave my throat.

The blackness clears from my eyes and I see Poppy beating Bruno with Doggy with all her might, while he's trying to hold her at arm's length.

'Get away from my mummy!' she cries.

I push myself up from the floor. I've no strength left, as if every limb in my body has been crushed. 'Poppy!' My attempt at a shout comes out as a croak, but she hears me and runs to me, cannoning into me, putting her arms round my neck. She's crying and I rock her against me. 'Ssh. Ssh.'

Bruno is staggering, his anger spent. I look at him and feel nothing but hatred. He heads for the door. 'I'll be back,' he warns me.

Poppy turns round and I never, ever want to see that look of fear in my daughter's eyes again. We hold each other as Bruno stamps down the stairs and we both flinch as the front door slams.

'It's okay now,' I say soothingly. But I know in my heart that it isn't. It will never be okay until I get this man out of our lives for good. My throat is burning and I can barely speak. 'It's okay.'

Doggy has parted company with his head. His stuffing leaks out of every conceivable gap and as I pick up his ruined body, it almost breaks my heart.

'Don't worry, Mummy,' my daughter says, her voice wavering. 'You can fix it. You can make it all better.'

'I will, sweetheart,' I promise. 'Doggy will be all right.' I stroke her hair which is plastered to her head with sweat. 'And we'll be all right too.'

'Don't ever let Daddy come back,' Poppy begs through her tears. 'I don't like him. He frightens me.'

I squeeze my daughter against me. He frightens me too. And for the final time, the house of cards that is my fantasy life comes crumbling down.

Chapter Ninety-Five

'This is the master bedroom,' the estate agent said. It was actually the *only* bedroom, but Nick didn't feel moved to correct her.

Lauren Baker from Ketley & Co gave him a wide grin. 'Just the thing for the man about town.'

For that read 'sad, lonely and heartbroken divorcé'. But Nick didn't correct her about that either. And the bedroom was incredibly macho. There was a grey Indian slate wall behind the kingsize bed, that was spread with dark red covers. The radiators were stainless-steel retro – like the ones that had been in his classroom at school – and there was some sort of embarrassingly erotic modern art on the wall featuring a couple copulating in a rather athletic position. He noticed that Lauren too was tilting her head to try and work out which way up they were. They smiled at each other shyly with the sudden realisation that they were both doing the same thing.

'It's a great room,' Nick said. If this didn't get him feeling like a Love God then nothing would.

'Shall we look at the rest of the apartment?' Lauren asked.

'Lead on.' And Nick followed her into the bathroom. More slate, more sexy guy stuff. A shower that would fit six people in it. Just two would be nice.

The apartment was in Sam's block, the next floor down from his best mate. It was smaller and with a worse view of the park, but nevertheless, it would be a fabulous place to live. Infinitely better than his cramped childhood bedroom in his parents' house. Living here would give him a sense of worth and independence again. It was expensive – what wasn't these days? – but his broken spirit felt like it needed a lift and his bank manager, very agreeably, had seen fit to approve the mortgage. All he had to do was put in an offer for the flat – or 'desirable bachelor pied-à-terre' as it said on the front of the agent's brochure.

Lauren was doing her best sales spiel, but Nick wasn't really listening. His mind was made up. He deserved this. He deserved a bit of comfort and luxury in his life. And if he didn't look after himself, who would? There didn't seem to be a rush of willing females to his door to do it for him. With the possible exception of his mother, of course.

Monica, he was sure, would be distinctly unimpressed with his decision to move out of the clutches of her tender loving care, but he was in severe danger of being cosseted to death. He wanted to re-establish his grip on his own life once more. As a start, he'd taken to spending hours in the gym simply to regain control of his waist-line after months of his mother's calorific assaults. He rubbed what would very soon be his six-pack and noticed that Lauren's eyes travelled to his stomach. Being a typical bloke, he sucked it in.

'The kitchen,' she said helpfully when they arrived in the kitchen. It was sparse and gleaming and could go a long way towards nurturing his culinary skills, which had also been somewhat curtailed since he'd moved back home.

Nick ran his hand over the work surface. Granite – reassuringly expensive. A small table, just big enough for two, stood in front of the large picture window. He could have some very romantic nights here. Home-cooked food, good wine, romantic lighting, pleasant company.

'This would be a lovely place to entertain,' Lauren suggested as if reading his thoughts. She shifted the clipboard in her arms. 'Do you have a partner?'

'No,' Nick said truthfully, before he could think of a better answer.

'Oh.' Lauren smiled at him again. She was tall with long dark hair. Slim. Pretty. Just Sam's type.

Nick wandered away from her and looked out of the window over the lush green expanse of the park. Children ran around the playground area, laughing and shouting. Mothers pushed babies in prams. Toddlers with their fathers fed ducks by the small pond with the over-sized fountain. A pang of longing twisted his insides. Would he ever feature in such a scenario? Nick still felt emotionally drained. Would he ever have the necessary energy to start a new relation-ship? Wasn't it the same with most newly divorced men? Didn't everyone groan inwardly at the thought of having to go through the whole damn process of finding yet another soulmate? The whole process of meeting someone, sifting through their baggage, having his *own* baggage sifted through, filled him with dread. He'd have to tell all his old, tired stories all over again. There would have to be introductions to his parents. That was enough to put anyone off. Then you go through all the game-playing that a new relationship inevitably involves only to discover after three weeks that you really have nothing whatsoever in common other than that you are both human and breathing. Or you could spend months having your affections toyed with, thinking you were onto a winner, only to have it all crumble to a heap of dust before your eyes. He wished that relationships were like CDs – you could skip the first three duff tracks and get straight into the good stuff.

'Have you seen enough?' Lauren asked.

'Yes,' Nick said. Enough to last him a lifetime, really. 'Sorry to keep you.'

'That's okay.' Lauren tucked her hair behind her ear. She was very cute in a crisp, professional way. 'Are you interested in the apartment?'

'Very. I'd like to offer the asking price.' Negotiating had never been one of his strong points either and he knew that a place like this was likely to have a raft of people chasing it.

'Great. I'll put a call in to the vendor as soon as I get back to the office.' Lauren handed him a business card. 'I hope you don't mind,' she said coyly, 'but I've put my personal telephone number on the back.' There was a faint flush to her cheeks. 'Maybe you'd like to give me a call sometime. Go out for a drink?'

Nick turned it over and examined it. He'd managed to escape the clutches of Big Gemma relatively unmolested, but someday soon he was going to have to force himself back out into the world and begin socialising again.

'Thanks,' he said and smiled back at her. She was lovely. Very lovely. He'd be mad not to ring her. 'Thanks.' He slipped the card into his pocket. Someday soon he'd begin socialising. But not just yet.

Chapter Ninety-Six

'And how's Poppy now?' Sophie asks.

I'm sitting snivelling in the familiar surroundings of my good friend Sophie's kitchen.

'Traumatised,' I say. 'I took her to school this morning, but she looked dreadful. I've never seen her with such dark shadows under her eyes but I thought it was better if she was out of the way. I spoke to her teacher, Mrs French, and asked her to keep an eye on her.'

Connor, bless him – who is blissfully unaware of the domestic upheaval in his life – has been despatched to Sophie's mum's house for the day. Although I felt like clinging onto my son and never letting him go, my friend persuaded me that I needed a quiet day to think about my lot. And quiet days and Connor don't go hand-in-hand. So here we are, just the two of us across the kitchen table once more.

Sophie gives me a rueful look. 'I won't say "I told you so".'

'You can if you like.' I blow my nose noisily. 'Because you did. Time and time again.'

After Bruno left last night, I locked and bolted the front door and stacked the dining-room chairs across it just in case – barricading us in our own home. Poppy sat on the stairs shivering and crying the whole time, and you don't know how wretched that made me feel. I know that I have to do something as I can't expose the children to this kind of danger. What sort of role model does it make me if my daughter sees me letting my husband use me as a punch bag?

This, of course, isn't the first time it's happened and that's not something of which I'm proud. No matter how many times people tell me that it's not my fault if Bruno is incapable of controlling his temper, it doesn't leave me feeling any less ashamed when it happens. It's as if the bruises highlight a weakness in me too. Everything hurts this morning, but nothing more so than my pride. I'm sporting a livid bruise and a graze on my cheek. My neck is mottled with red blotches and it's agony to swallow. I choke down my tea which Sophie has insisted on putting sugar in – even though I don't take sugar. Despite the fact that it's tooth-rottingly sweet, it's making me feel a lot better.

'You need to go to the doctor and let him look at your throat.'

'Yes,' I say, even though I've no intention of going. How would I explain how it had happened? You can walk into doors by mistake, but you can't accidentally try to strangle yourself.

I lay awake all last night, cuddling my sobbing child and dreading any sounds that would signal Bruno's return. But he didn't come back and when we left the house this morning there was still no sign of him. I may not be in a rush to get the doctor involved but I did phone a locksmith first thing to ask him to come and change all the door locks and add some extra window locks downstairs for security. He's also fitting a chain and bolt on the inside of the door. I'm going to be making a return visit to Tumley & Goss as soon as is humanly possible to divorce Bruno. Better late than never, I suppose.

'I don't know what possessed you to take him back,' Sophie says with a shake of her head.

'I did it for the kids,' I say. 'I thought it would be better for us to be a family again.'

'I'm not sure that living with an alcohol-fuelled pugilist is better than struggling along as a single parent.'

'I did love him,' I point out.

'You're too trusting of people.'

'Yeah,' I agree. 'And the one person I should have trusted I treated badly.'

'Do you regret that?'

'Daily,' I tell her with a lightness I don't feel. 'But I had to give Bruno one last chance.'

'Why? He blew all his other chances.'

I shrug and it makes me realise that my shoulders ache too. 'Isn't love about accepting someone even with all their flaws?'

'Doesn't it help if they overlook your flaws and imperfections too?' Sophie takes hold of my hand and squeezes it. 'Breaking your ribs if you look at them in the wrong way doesn't sound to me as if the love is reciprocated.'

'You're right,' I say. And Sophie has spent many a long hour in the past, waiting in the local Accident and Emergency department while I've had some bit or other of me X-rayed and set in plaster.

'If someone loves you, shouldn't you feel like a better, happier person when you're with them rather than a shadow of your former self?'

Sophie nods. 'Like you did with Nick?'

'Don't go there.' I rub my hands over my throbbing forehead. 'That's what started the argument. We saw Nick outside the car yard and that aroused his suspicions, then Bruno found the marabou-trimmed thong we bought in the sex shop. He put two and two together and came up with about ten.'

'Oh gosh, I'm sorry.' Sophie grimaces. 'That's my fault.'

'Yes, it is,' I say. 'And it's a good job you make great tea otherwise I'd never forgive you.'

We both laugh even though mine comes out rather more tearfully than I would have liked.

'I've missed you,' Sophie says.

'I've missed you too.' I go and give her a hug, wincing as I crush my ribs against her.

Sophie is tearful too. 'I feel terrible,' she says. 'I was contemplating leaving my husband because I was bored with him in and out of bed – and here's you hanging onto an abusive relationship due to some misguided sense of loyalty to the children.'

'I took my marriage vows seriously.' And I did, even though it seems too feeble an excuse now in the light of the latest developments.

'Well, the sooner you break them the better, in my opinion.'

I've learned a lot about love in the last year and it's been a painful lesson in more ways than one. If you love someone, you should give them as much room as possible to fulfil themselves. I think that's the only way of keeping someone close to you. I don't expect my life to be full of beaming smiles, endless sunny days and flower arranging, but I do want someone who will help me to grow as a person and not stamp me down the minute I try to move.

Sophie lets go of me and, catching sight of her kitchen clock, I say, 'I have to go back.' Even though it troubles me to do so. 'The locksmith's due any time now.'

Sophie picks up her handbag. 'I'll come with you.' And for once I don't argue with her. At the moment, I need all the support I can get.

My friend puts her arm round my shoulders as we head towards the door. 'You'll be fine,' she says. 'Just give it time.'

'Yes.' I nod and try to ignore the fact that all the dreams that I dared to dream really didn't come true.

279

Chapter Ninety-Seven

When we pull up at my house, I'm relieved to see that Bruno's car is nowhere in sight and the locksmith's van is parked patiently outside.

'I was just about to leave you a note, love,' the man says. 'I thought there was no one home.'

'Sorry,' I say.

'No harm done.' He's trying not to stare at my bruises and I turn my face away from him.

My friend takes control. 'She wants the door-lock changed,' Sophie instructs him. 'A chain put on. And security locks on the windows too.'

'Fine, love,' the guy says. 'I'll get on with it.'

Unlocking the door, I see that the dining-room furniture is still in disarray from functioning as our temporary barricade. I can tell that Bruno's not here, but I feel like I'm in one of those horror films where the unwitting female is going from room to room, aware that somewhere there's a baddy lurking, waiting to spring out on her. I should be dressed more skimpily and have a jagged knife in my shaking hand.

'Hello! Anyone at home?' Sophie calls out and makes me jump.

Sensing my discomfort, she says, 'Come on, we'll check all the rooms. Let's start upstairs.'

She hooks her arm through mine and leads me determinedly up the stairs. My knees are weak with fear. In the bedroom, it looks like we've been burgled. All the drawers are out of the cupboards, contents strewn on the floor. The wardrobe doors are open and my clothes, ripped to tatters, lie in a heap. Bruno, clearly, has been back.

'Jeez,' Sophie breathes.

But the one thing in this that makes my spirit lift, is when I notice that my husband's clothes have gone. All of them. Every single last item. 'He's gone.'

'Good riddance to bad rubbish,' my friend says. She's picking up the drawers, briskly folding the contents and putting them back inside. 'It won't take long to get this back to normal.'

'No.' It might take a bit longer for me though. My wits seem to be as scattered as my clothing.

We tidy up as best we can, and scooping up armfuls of my ruined outfits, carry them downstairs to be put in black bin bags ready for the council rubbish tip.

'He's done you a big favour,' my friend says lightly. 'Some of your clothes were *so* last season!'

I laugh even though I want to cry as we stagger into the hall under the weight. Scrubbing the entire place with carbolic soap or bleach also seems like a good idea, as I want to remove every trace of that man from my home.

The locksmith is working quietly and purposefully, turning our house into Fort Knox. I wish he could put locks on my thoughts and emotions as easily.

'You look worn out,' Sophie says.

'I am.'

'I'm going to come and sleep here tonight,' she announces. 'You can't stay alone.'

I don't have the energy to protest. At the moment I'd like one of those gargantuan, eight-feet-tall, eighteen-stone bodyguards that Britney Spears has. It's nearly time to collect Poppy from school and I don't want to be a minute late. Terrible thoughts about Bruno trying to snatch her are going through my head.

As I pick up my car keys, I notice that my special tea tin is out on the work surface. The special tea tin where I keep all my money. I take off the lid and sure enough it's completely empty.

I sigh loudly. 'There was a hundred quid in there.' How will I pay the locksmith now?

Sophie comes and puts her arm round me. 'Believe me,' she says, 'it's a bloody bargain if it gets *him* out of your life.'

And I know that she's right.

Chapter Ninety-Eight

Christmas had rolled round again, as it was prone to do, with monotonous regularity. The Diamond household was kitted out with all manner of festive accoutrements – tinsel was draped on every possible surface, tiny silver bells hung from the mantelpiece and every light fitting. A faded 'real fir-effect' Christmas tree struggled vainly in the corner under the weight of several dozen smiling Santas, flying angels, jolly snowmen and, his personal favourite, chocolate coins – which, of course, Nick's mother had bought especially for him. Carols drifted out of the kitchen radio accompanied by the smell of freshly baked mince pies.

Outside, the ground was coated with a light sprinkling of snow – just enough to make a seasonal improvement, but not enough to be dangerous underfoot. Nick's father Roger had been pressed into decorating the cherry trees with twinkling lights and there was some sort of twig sculpture in the garden which his mother assured him was supposed to be a reindeer. Still, it could have been worse. The Browns across the road were home to a twelve-foot blow-up Santa tethered to the roof.

In the lounge, a religious Christmas card from Janine and Phil the Butcher wishing 'joy to all mankind' graced the windowsill, but Nick had received nothing from Anna. It was almost a year since she'd walked out of the office and he'd had no contact with her since. The only indication he'd had that she was still alive was a request for a character reference from an office in Milton Keynes. He'd completed the application form in ridiculously glowing terms and hoped that Anna had got the job – but not as much as he hoped that one day he would see her again. If you were without your loved ones at Christmas, it really was the most bloody depressing time of the year.

'We're going to be late, Nicholas,' his mother said.

He was not the one faffing about with last-minute preparations. 'I'm ready,' he said, jingling his car keys to prove it.

Monica fluffed her hair and shrugged on her sturdy winter coat.

It was the St Stephen's line-dancing Christmas social and Mrs Diamond was wearing a scarlet cowgirl outfit trimmed in white fur in celebration. Mrs Santa does Dallas, thought Nick. He'd been pressed into escort service again, simply because he couldn't think of any good reason not to go – other than the fact that he would hate every minute of it.

'Roger. Keep away from those mince pies,' his mother warned. 'I've counted them all.'

She'd got another tin of home-baked goodies secured under her arm for the refreshment table, so at least Nick had something to look forward to. He ushered his mother out into the cold air and then the chilly enclosure of his new car, a top of the range model, which their warm breath steamed up immediately.

While they waited for the windscreen demister to melt away the fug, his mother fussed with her seat belt and keeping her mince pies upright. 'How's the flat coming along?' she said.

'Good,' Nick replied. Lauren Baker was trying to move the chain of buyers along to completion but it was a torpid process and he could detect a certain amount of tension between them as he had never followed up on her invitation to call her. 'I should be moving out in the next week or so.'

'You don't have to move out at all,' his mother noted.

'I know.' He put the car into gear and they set off. He'd be lucky if everything was in place by Christmas, but that was okay. The new building at the car yard was progressing well and that, too, would also be ready – not a moment too soon – for occupation sometime in the next few weeks. He had a big, official launch planned for January. His last winter in the mangy Portakabin! Which was just as well, as his ankles hadn't reached normal body temperature for months.

'We'll miss you.'

'I'll miss you too.' And in a strange way he probably would. Recent surveys had shown that single men experienced the worst state of mental health in the country. Single men who lived with their mothers, he was sure, experienced the most rapid deterioration.

'Still,' his mother said, 'you have your own life to lead.'

They pulled up outside the hall which was decked with fairy-lights swinging in the breeze. As they got out of the car, she added, 'You never know, you might be spending it with someone special.' And she winked at him, which with hindsight should have set alarm bells ringing.

★   ★   ★

283

'Brenda!' His mother air-kissed a woman who was similarly, though not so festively, attired. Monica gave up rearranging her mince pies for the third time and pulled him forward by the arm. 'This is Mrs Washburn. Brenda, this is my son, Nick. He's divorced.'

'Oh my,' Brenda said. 'Pleased to meet you.'

Nick forced a smile. The sort of sickly smile that babies give when they've got wind. Mrs Washburn, in turn, pulled forward a young woman who was lurking sullenly behind her and Nick knew that he should have seen this coming.

'This is my daughter, Cassie. She's divorced too!'

'What a coincidence!' both scheming mothers trilled.

Cassie looked suitably humiliated.

'Yes. What a coincidence.' Nick tried to glare at his mother but she was too busy exchanging a smug look with her co-conspirator, Mrs Washburn.

'Why don't we leave you two young things together?' Monica suggested. 'I'm sure you don't want to hang around with us old fuddy duddies!'

Nick felt like reminding her that the only reason he'd agreed to come was to hang around old fuddy duddies. 'Achy Breaky Heart' started out on the ancient turntable. Was there an EU directive which stated that line-dancing could only be done to the hits of Billy Ray Cyrus? Brenda and Monica bustled onto the dance floor.

Cassie turned towards him. 'We've been had,' she remarked.

'Would it go against the grain in this season of goodwill for us to strangle them with the fairy-lights?' Nick asked.

His fellow embarrassed divorcée shook with laughter. 'What a piece of work they are.' She looked down at her checked shirt, jeans and cowboy boots. Her ill-fitting Stetson slipped forward over her eyes, causing more giggles. 'I only agreed to wear these because I didn't think there'd be anyone remotely fanciable here . . .' Cassie ground to a halt when she realised what she'd said. 'What I mean is,' she continued shyly, 'I was convinced any men here would have false teeth and comb-overs.'

Nick bared his teeth and raised his Stetson. 'No comb-over,' he said. 'So, how long have you been divorced then?'

'A year,' Cassie said. 'I just can't face getting back into the social scene.' She shrugged sadly and caused her Stetson to wobble. 'The thought of it terrifies me.'

'Me too,' Nick admitted.

'How long for you?'

'Same sort of time,' Nick answered, although he didn't admit he'd had his heart broken again since then. 'I thought it would get easier with time.'

The heel-clicking geriatrics were in full flow. His mother and Cassie's mother Brenda kept throwing surreptitious glances in their direction.

'We're being watched like hawks,' Cassie noted.

'We could avoid having to join in the dancing by going to get a drink and a mince pie,' Nick suggested. 'My mother, despite her many, varied and extremely irritating faults, does make good mince pies.'

'That would be nice.'

He took Cassie's elbow and steered her towards the bar, carefully avoiding the mistletoe. His mother might spontaneously combust if they lingered too long under that. Nick ordered them both a drink and they leaned against the wall trying to avoid looking at their mothers.

'Thanks for being understanding,' Cassie said. 'My mother has tried to fix me up with a whole range of men ever since Patrick left me.' She sipped at her tepid white wine. 'First I was thrust upon an accountant at her Golf Club. Terrible body odour, but loaded. Then someone short, fat and bald from the Bridge Club.' Cassie looked up at him from beneath her cowboy hat. She looked quite cute in it really. 'My mother has appalling taste in men. Present company excepted.'

'Thanks.'

'You're almost normal,' Cassie noted.

'Nice is the most commonly used word to describe me,' Nick told her. Not sexy, not hot in bed, not rolling in it, not well-hung. Just nice.

'There are worse things to be than nice,' Cassie said. 'Has your mother fixed you up with a range of unsuitable women too?'

'No,' he said. 'Not until now. Not that you're unsuitable.'

Cassie laughed.

'Far from it,' he added. My word, in his own hideously tongue-tied way, he was flirting! How had that happened? And it felt good – as if a weight had lifted from his heart. Taking Cassie's drink from her, Nick put it on the bar. 'Come on,' he said. 'Let's show these old biddies how it's done.'

Nick took her hand and they exchanged a shy glance as they hit the dance floor. Not wanting to demonstrate his intrinsic lack of finesse to the whole world, he headed towards the back of the rows of dancers. As they passed his mother, she took hold of his sleeve and whispered in his ear, 'Now tell me that Mother doesn't know best?'

He grinned at her and wondered to himself whether Monica might not, for once, have a point.

Chapter Ninety-Nine

The shopping centre is packed to the gills with people indulging in a festive outpouring of retail excess. Mind you, the place does look wonderful. We're in the main hall, which has been transformed into some sort of magical Arctic land, complete with miniature models of Eskimos, igloos, huskies and polar bears. All unbelievably cute. Poppy has been pressed into coming along and is pretending that she's too cool to care about something so stupid and childish – her words, not mine. She's hoping that no one from school sees her. Particularly not someone called Charlie Brooks on whom she has a crush.

Connor, in contrast, is in raptures. Which is just as well as we've got a good half-hour of standing in a queue waiting to see Santa – who'd better not turn out to be some raddled old drunk with a cheap greying beard and naff presents. If he is, there'll be trouble.

Oh yes. Trouble is now my middle name. No longer the doormat of the world, I've been on an assertiveness training course for the last few months and I know all about getting my rights in a calm and controlled manner. I've also got myself a new job. I'm working in a small printshop in the even smaller admin office staffed by just two of us – Mary and myself – who take it in turns to job-share, sorting out the hours between us. There's no rancid Portakabin, no draughts whipping round my knees and, unfortunately, no Nick.

Still, you can't have it all. And at least most of my life is back on track. The pay is good and I can have all the free photocopying I'll ever need. Bruno and I are a couple of weeks and a signature away from being divorced. This I view as a positive step. Tumley & Goss were able to track him down in order to serve the papers and I didn't even ask them where he was living now, because I don't really care. All my wounds are long healed – and even the ones that people can't see are doing quite well. I am turning my life around big-style. My wardrobe now contains a few sharp statement items rather than retro charity-shop finds and, even though I say it myself, I'm looking pretty cool.

Poppy and I, with a little help from Sophie, have redecorated the house from top to bottom, non-drip glossing and Fresh Parchmenting Bruno out of our lives. Some of our more shabby furniture has been replaced by cheap but trendy stuff from IKEA. I disposed of all of my bedlinen – somehow a cathartic move – and now everything is cheerfully colour co-ordinated in the style of home makeover magazines.

The other, even more startling thing I've done is to contact Steve – my first husband. Without too much effort, I managed to track him down through friends and we met up for coffee a few weeks ago. The new fearless me shook like a leaf before he turned up. However, in the intervening years since our divorce, Steve seems to have turned into quite a decent bloke. He's remarried now and has three-year-old twin boys. He said that becoming a father again had made him realise exactly what he'd missed out on, and he was full of regret that he'd never met Poppy. He also said that, although he'd wanted to, he hadn't dared contact me for fear of my reaction. Yeah – me the scary woman. If only he knew.

I want him to meet Poppy and to get to know her. He is, after all, her true father. I haven't told her yet that I've contacted Steve. I want to make sure he isn't a maniac too – one in her life was more than enough. He also has to be committed to making a proper relationship with her as I don't want him coming back into our lives only to drift out again a few months later. Steve's doing well in his carpet-fitting business, it turns out, so he's going to make maintenance payments for Poppy, which will certainly help our cash-flow situation. It may be belated, but it's nice that he offered rather than me having to beg for help. I feel hopeful that this will all turn out well. I've invited Steve and his family to visit us in the New Year and, I guess, we'll take it from there – slowly, slowly, one step at a time.

I have done all this because I want to make my daughter proud of me. I want to make *me* proud of me. And if it wasn't for the fact that I'm building up to my usual pre-Christmas stress and I still miss Nick more than I care to admit, everything in my garden would be very rosy.

Mary has come in early today, so that I could sneak off and take Connor to meet Father Christmas for the first time. Sophie, of course, has been roped in for this too and is waiting, less patiently, beside me with Ellie who is swinging on her arm. My friend jiggles her youngest daughter, Charlotte, backwards and forwards in her buggy. Connor is transfixed by a display of a round-faced Eskimo driving a silver dog-sled with four impossibly white huskies. My child is standing with his face pressed up against the bars of the jolly picket fence, making barking noises. Fake snow drifts down from the ceiling, making us all look like we have severe dandruff.

'Uncle Nick would like this,' Poppy declares out of the blue. My jaw drops and I notice that Sophie's does too. Nick hasn't been mentioned in our house for months. 'He likes kids' stuff,' she continues. 'You should have asked him.'

'I didn't think of it,' I admit.

She looks at me as if that isn't a surprise. 'Can I go to Claire's Accessories, please?'

'Yes.' I'm still a bit shell-shocked. 'But come straight back here to meet us afterwards. Keep tight hold of your purse. And don't talk to any strangers.' Not everyone sees this as the season of goodwill. 'And don't be too long. We need to get a move on once we've seen Santa. Aunty Sophie's got a movie première to attend tonight and I'm having dinner with Russell Crowe.'

'Get a life, Mum,' my daughter advises me and then flees before I can change my mind.

'Well,' I say with a sigh. Sophie and I haven't spoken about Sam or Nick for months. They've become taboo subjects between us. Probably because they both signify how badly we messed up.

'Russell Crowe?'

'It's a nice thought,' I say.

'You okay?' my friend asks.

I nod.

Sophie gives me a wry smile. 'It's been an interesting year. All things considered.'

'Yes.'

She huffs expansively. 'This time of year always makes me melancholy.'

I take up position on the fence next to her as we inch forward in the queue. 'I guess we both have regrets.'

'One or two. But I try not to think about them otherwise I'll get all bitter and twisted.'

'Things are all right with you and Tom though?'

'I'd like to say that he now appreciates me for the hot-blooded woman that I am, and that he does realise how close he came to losing me, but in truth, life has continued pretty much as before.' She twists her mouth in what might be regret. 'There's been a subtle shift rather than any great improvements. I get a cup of tea in bed every morning now and something a bit more exciting once a week. Does that mean everything's all right?'

'That's better than it was.' This is my new positive outlook on life.

'The only thing I've learned is that we're not such different creatures. Despite what the self-help books say, men are from earth and women are from earth – we've just got to live with it.'

I smile and wonder if she is right.

'I still miss him, you know,' Sophie says quietly. 'I nearly sent him a Christmas card.'

'But you didn't?'

'No,' she says. 'It was a close-run thing though. I got to the point of choosing one.'

I arrange a pile of fake snow with the toe of my boot. 'I nearly sent Nick one too.'

'There's no reason why you shouldn't,' Sophie points out. 'You're young, free and sort of single.' She casts an eye at my son. 'Nick is too.'

'I was rooting through the personnel files yesterday – in a purely professional capacity,' I add, in case she thinks I was just nosing about to see what was lodged in my manilla folder. Which, of course, I wasn't. Not really. 'I saw the character reference that Nick supplied for me.'

Sophie raises her eyebrows.

'He gave me a glowing reference. I read through it and barely recognised myself,' I grin. 'I sounded great.'

'That's because he thinks you're great,' my friend says. 'Clearly he bears you no ill-will for your stupid ditching of him at a crucial moment.' I love it when Sophie is at her straight-talking best, and if it wasn't for my assertiveness training I'd be shrinking beneath her gaze. 'Why don't you call him up and thank him?'

'I will.'

'Which means you won't,' Sophie observes.

'I wouldn't know what to say.' I haven't got to the part in the assertiveness course yet that deals with the winning back of abandoned potential boyfriends.

Miraculously, we're at the front of the queue and hand over our cash in exchange for a ticket granting an audience with Santa. We

290

shuffle through a sparkly igloo that makes Connor, Ellie and Charlotte wide-eyed with excitement, and through more festive scenes of baby polar bears and cartoon penguins. And, finally, there he is – the white-bearded one. Connor shrinks in terror and tries to hide behind my skirt.

'Merry Christmas,' Santa booms in a very Father Christmassy voice and holds out his hand to Connor. I peel my son off my leg and usher him forward. The children don't sit on Santa's knee any more, because these days Santa might well turn out to be a paedophile and would enjoy it far too much. 'And who do we have here?'

My child is rendered speechless with a mix of ecstasy and fear.

'This is Connor,' I say.

Santa gives him a kindly smile. 'Have you been a good boy?'

Connor stuffs both of his fists in his mouth and nods.

'And what do you want for Christmas, Connor?'

'Uncle Nick,' Connor breathes through his spitty fingers.

Sophie and I exchange a puzzled glance.

I kneel down next to Connor. 'This isn't Uncle Nick,' I say. 'This is Santa. Tell him what you'd like for Christmas.'

Connor turns to me and there are tears in his little eyes. 'Me want Uncle Nick,' he insists.

Eager to avert any more distress, Santa has a quick root in his sack and pulls out a fab fire engine. 'Now then,' Santa says. 'What about this?'

Connor is immediately won over and grabs the fire engine, clutching it to his chest. Well done, Santa. You obviously have a degree in Child Psychology. If in doubt, distract with a large bribe.

I, however, am less easy to distract. 'Say thank you,' I instruct as I move Connor away.

'Thank you,' my son mumbles, still intent on examining his new toy.

Ellie the fearless steps forward and reels off a list of gifts that she's decided she can't live without.

'Wow,' I say to Sophie, still open-mouthed with shock at Connor's statement. 'What do you think brought that on? I didn't think he could even remember Nick.'

'Well, it looks as though he does.'

'Maybe it was just because Poppy was talking about him?'

Sophie shrugs. 'Who knows what goes on in their brains.'

Maybe my children are trying to tell me something. Perhaps they feel their lives would be better with Nick around too. I have to do something about this. It's an unresolved issue, as my assertiveness skills teacher would say.

'Promise me something,' my friend says over her shoulder. 'If fate does offer you a chance to get back with Nick, you will grab it with both hands?'

And it should be so easy to pick up the phone, apologise for acting like an arse and say that I'd like to give it another go. How hard can that be? But it is. We've all been there.

'And what would you like for Christmas, darling?' Santa says to me.

I stare at Santa's jolly smiling face and the old perv gives me a lascivious wink. I've tried to be a good girl. I wonder, if I asked nicely, would he be able to bring me Nick for Christmas?

Chapter One Hundred

The fine sprinkling of snow was now about an inch deep – bringing, as always, utter chaos to the British roads. What was it about a few snowflakes that sent even the sanest of drivers into a blind panic?

Nick stared out of the window, transfixed by the somnambulant effect of the drifting snow. At least the shell of the new dealership building was complete, which meant that the workmen could retreat inside out of the elements and still continue with their work. All his days were now accompanied by the faint ring of hammers and the buzz of power tools as the men put the finishing touches to his masterpiece of patience and planning. He toyed with the piece of paper in his hands, the one on which Cassie Edmonds – Mrs Washburn's lovely divorced and line-dancing daughter – had written her telephone number. And the really weird thing was that he, Nick Diamond, had actually plucked up the courage and the necessary enthusiasm to ask for it.

What a difference a day makes. He was here watching his new, improved empire take shape, with the phone number of a really attractive woman who he was planning to call and a strange appreciation for the joys of line-dancing classes. There was a lightness in his spirit that he hadn't felt in a long time. It was going to be the last winter he spent in a Portakabin. And it was eleven o'clock and he hadn't thought of Anna once. Well, not until now.

It was time to move on. Enter the New Year with a changed attitude. Cassie was funny and pretty. So what if they'd been thrown together against their wishes by their meddlesome mothers? In the end, it had served a good purpose and his mother would crow over her success for days, months – no, years. Even he could see himself and Cassie sitting together round a dinner-table with friends in the future laughing about how they met at a line-dancing class they'd been coerced into attending by their respective parents. Nick frowned. But then again, maybe not. Perhaps they could invent something more romantic than that, should the occasion arrive. He rubbed his hands together, not just to ward off the cold, but in excited anticipation. There was no way he was going to be lonely this Christmas. He'd thought of a great place to take Cassie for dinner – a little romantic candlelight, a little festive spirit and who knows what could happen.

Just as he was about to pick up the telephone, he spotted a shaven-headed youth hanging round one of the cars. Nick's heart sank. It was a few days until he could shut up shop for Christmas and he wanted to spend them quietly pondering the wonder that was going to be his new life. He didn't want any aggro from a tattooed skinhead.

Nick stood up, pulled on his North Face jacket and headed out into the freezing yard. The youngster was now peering in the window of a sporty and rather ageing VW Golf GTI. The car all boy racers saw as their heart's desire. He was wearing just a T-shirt and had his hands stuffed in his pockets, but he was still shivering in the cold.

'Can I help you?' Nick asked.

'I'd like a test drive, mate.'

Nick looked at the grey sky and the flurries of snow. The young man looked rather pathetic and more like he was interested in getting out of the snow than exploring the driving dynamics of the GTI. In all honesty, he didn't even look old enough to drive. 'A test drive?'

'My dad's giving me some dosh for Christmas.'

'Oh. Okay.'

The youth shivered some more.

'I'll go and get the keys,' Nick said. 'Won't be a minute.'

Nick plodded back to the Portakabin. He could bring the guy a jacket – there was a spare one in the cupboard. But then that was the sort of thing his mother would do. If he was stupid enough to come out without a coat, then let him freeze. Nick grabbed the keys.

'Test drive,' he muttered to himself as he headed back out into the falling snow. The lovely Cassie Edmonds would have to wait.

Chapter One Hundred and One

Connor is already strapped into his car seat. 'Come on, come on,' I snap at Poppy. 'The excitement that is Morrisons waits for us.'

My eldest child is slithering about on the snow outside the house in her good boots. She won't do her coat up either even though she'll probably catch her death of cold. This I could do without. I'm in full pre-Christmas harassed mode and am best not crossed. Any minute now, I can see myself turning green and ripping my clothes off. And that would not be a pretty sight.

When we come back I'm going to see if I can penetrate the depths of the junk in the garage to find the spade and clear the snow away. In a couple of days it will be grey slush with dubious brown and yellow patches due to next door's dog.

'I don't want to go food shopping,' my daughter points out, rather too petulantly for my liking.

'Neither do I,' I say. 'But we all have to eat. And Connor isn't old enough to con into going by himself.' His time will come though. As will Poppy's.

'It's boring.'

'Yes, but life is like that. Two per cent interesting, ninety-eight per cent tedium.'

'What's tedium?'

'Being a working single mother with two whining children.' I have to say that describing myself as 'working' gives me a buzz.

'Stephanie Fisher's mother doesn't make her go food shopping.'

'That's because Stephanie Fisher's mother has a very wealthy husband and doesn't work and, therefore, has countless leisurely hours stretching ahead of her to fill by going to the supermarket alone.' Just after her session in the gym and shortly before her manicure appointment.

'When I grow up, I'm going to marry a rich husband.'

'You're not,' I say. 'You're going to work hard at school, go on to university and achieve everything by your own merits.'

My daughter looks at me as if to say, 'Fat chance.' Despite my exasperation at her premature teenage outbursts, I'm glad that she's back to her normal stroppy self. For a month or so after Bruno left, she followed me about the house like a shadow and I was terribly worried about her. Now I'm just constantly annoyed at her and she hates me, so I think the status quo has been successfully re-established.

The reason she is being particularly awkward is that I have just spurned her Christmas List Mark Ten which, despite my telling her that no way would Santa bring her these things in a million years, still lists A Pierced Belly Button, A Dolphin Belly Ring and A Mobile Phone as her top three items. She wants to grow up too quickly, too soon. Whereas I don't want her to grow up at all. I may be a working mother now, but I still don't plan to indulge her.

'Come on, come on,' I urge her again. My patience is wearing thin. 'I've got an hour to whiz round the shops and then I have to drop you at Aunty Sophie's before I go to work. Make life easy for me.'

Reluctantly, Poppy gets in the car. I jump into the driver's seat and we hurtle off down the road – even though the driving conditions do not favour hurtling.

Chapter One Hundred and Two

Nick waved the keys at the shivering youth. 'Shall I put it through its paces?'

'No, mate.' The young man shook his head. 'I'll drive.'

As Nick threw the keys to him, a smirk crossed the youth's face which did nothing to reassure Nick of his driving skills. And with a certain amount of reluctance, he lowered himself into the passenger seat.

The engine burbled into life and the youth – who Nick was beginning to think of as more of a young thug – revved it round to six thousand on the clock. Oh no, another nineteen year old who thought he was Formula One ace, Jensen Button.

'Steady on,' Nick advised. Even to his ears his voice sounded worried. 'Let's take it slowly.'

The youth floored the accelerator and they shot out of the car yard with the wheels spinning wildly in the gravel. Nick grabbed the dashboard. So that's how it was going to be. He made sure his seat belt was nice and tight, sat back in his seat and tried to appear as calm and in control as possible.

The windscreen wipers clack-clacked away the falling snow as they careered down the dual carriageway at a breakneck speed.

'As you can see,' Nick said in measured tones, 'the accelarator is in perfect working condition. Perhaps you'd like to try the brakes for size?'

The hooligan laughed at him.

Nick closed his eyes as they came up on a lorry far too quickly. 'Perhaps not.'

He should have known that anyone who didn't wear a coat in this freezing weather had to be insane. At the end of the dual carriageway the road narrowed and wound its way through a residential area. And Nick had to admit that the hooligan did slow down to a speed that was positively dangerous rather than outright reckless.

They rounded a corner far too quickly, scattering pedestrians on a pelican crossing. The hooligan laughed hard. Nick looked behind him terrified, hoping against hope that there were no dead bodies lying in the road. The hooligan laughed harder, but it had a hollow ring to it and he too, alarmingly, looked behind him to assess the damage.

'I think you seriously ought to consider slowing down,' Nick said and regretted that the car didn't come with dual controls.

As they both looked back to the road in front, a car turned out of the side road just ahead. Nick and the hooligan screamed in unison.

'Brakes! Brakes!' Nick shouted. 'Hit the bloody brakes!'

The hooligan braked. Hard. But the crash was inevitable. He'd managed to shrug off some speed, but they slid inexorably towards the other car. There was a huge, grinding noise and an unhealthy thud. They were both rocked in the impact. Nick put his head in his hands.

The hooligan looked at him, slightly chastened. 'The brakes are good.'

Nick sighed.

Then there was a second, almighty crash as another car hit them in the rear, shunting them further up the road.

'Yes,' Nick said. 'But, unfortunately, his aren't.'

Chapter One Hundred and Three

If I wasn't so dazed, I'd be furious. I turn to Connor and Poppy. Miraculously, they seem to be unhurt, as do I. The side of the car, however, is mangled.

'Are you both okay?' I ask anxiously.

Poppy nods, but does look slightly shaken. Connor's lower lip is trembling. I give him Doggy to cuddle.

'Stay here,' I instruct. 'I'll be right back.'

I get out of the car, slam the door and stomp over to see what sort of idiot has managed to completely total my poor ageing car.

The driver is some tattooed yob who doesn't look old enough to have passed his test. He's standing in the road shouting at the man who ran into the back of *him*. Bugger. What a mess. My front wing is crumpled and my headlight is hanging out on its wires like a horror-film eye. The traffic is backing up already and there are horns honking, but frankly, I don't give a shit. I just want to give these lunatics a piece of my mind. Watch this for assertiveness! Don't they know that there are kids in my car?

The front passenger door opens and a man staggers out, looking the worse for wear. I'd know that long, gangly frame anywhere. For a moment, I stand there frozen and then his name comes out as a breathless blurt. *'Nick.'*

As I rush towards him, Nick's head snaps up. His face is white, drained of blood. 'Anna,' he says. His breathing is also uneven. He frowns at me anxiously. 'You're not hurt?'

'No.' I shake my head. 'But it's no thanks to that twat!'

Nick rubs his forehead. 'That twat is on a test drive.'

And despite the fact that my car is probably unfit to move, I have to smile. 'Oh.'

'I can get that fixed for you,' he offers.

We both look at my car and realise that it is beyond redemption. The pine air freshener that hangs from the rearview mirror is probably worth more than the whole car. It's really only fit for the knacker's yard.

'It doesn't matter. I should get a new one soon.' What am I saying? A new one? What with? My brain must have been shaken in the impact. 'I'm sure my insurance will cover it.'

I'm actually sure that my insurance company will tell me to push it off the nearest cliff.

'The new dealership will be open soon.' There's a flush of pride on his face despite his obvious discomfiture.

Now we're both a bit embarrassed. Several drivers have joined in the fray at the back of Nick's car. Traffic is stopped in both directions. Out of the corner of my eye, I see the skinhead driver hit one of the other motorists, who falls to the ground. A couple of the other men pile in and a full-scale scuffle breaks out.

'Well, I hoped I'd bump into you again,' Nick says, trying to add levity to the situation.

'But not quite in this way.'

'No,' he agrees.

I smooth my hands down my jeans. Punches are flying now in the major free-for-all that's developing behind us. I gaze at my lovely ex-boss. He looks well. Fit and happy. 'How are you?'

'Fine, fine,' he says. 'I'll probably have a stiff neck tomorrow.'

There's the sound of a police siren and a squad car pulls up on the other side of the road. Traffic grinds to a halt in their wake. Two tall young policemen jump out and try to separate the hooligan and the other driver who are now pushing and shoving each other and throwing comedy punches.

'Not this.' I gesture at my severely bent car. 'I meant everything else. How are things with Janine?'

'Oh,' Nick says. 'Fine. They're fine. Well — we're divorced. It went through a couple of months ago. All very amicable. She's gone back to getting free meat from Phil the Butcher. And I'm back at home, temporarily.'

I have no idea what to say to this news.

Nick pats his stomach and continues quickly, 'I need to move out before my mother turns me into Billy Bunter. I'm buying a whizzy apartment in the same development as Sam.'

'Nice.'

Nick fidgets. 'How are things with you and . . . whatsisname?'

'Bruno?'

Nick nods. The policemen are trying to push everyone back into their cars and are failing. There's another screech of brakes and a car travelling in the other direction hits the police car.

'Good,' I say. 'He's gone – for good.' And, of course, Nick is unaware quite what that means to me.

'Oh.'

I glance back at the kids in the car.

'They're not hurt?' Nick's face is creased with concern.

'No,' I say. 'They're fine. They bounce at that age.' What a stupid comment. I study the tarmac. 'They both miss you.'

'Oh. That's good. Well no, I suppose it isn't.'

This is my one big chance. Fate has brought Nick back to me and Sophie made me promise that I would grab any opportunity that presented itself with both hands. And I'd love to, but I have no idea what to do. Instead, I'm standing here being tongue-tied and pathetic – even though I could blame it on shock.

'So,' I try the light-hearted approach too. 'How's the filing?'

'I've done my best,' Nick says. 'But it's still a bit of a mess.'

My courage is firmly grasped. 'Maybe . . . if you'd like me to, I could come back and sort it out for you.'

Nick looks serious. 'The thing is, Anna, I don't know if I could cope with you coming back, pulling the entire contents out all over again and then just leaving. I've only just managed to get it all together.' His eyes are sad. 'So, if it's all the same, I'd rather manage without you.'

'Oh.'

We stand awkwardly, neither of us able to move. The chaos is still going on around us and in a minute, as soon as they've stopped all the brawling and questioned the man who hit their car, the policemen are going to be coming over and asking what our part is in all this. My moment will be past. I have to do this.

'What if I promise that I won't leave?' I offer. There's a hint of panic in my voice and my eyes are filling up with tears. 'What if I promise that I won't ever leave? That this time I'll stay and see it through.'

Nick looks at me, but I can't read his expression. I smile tearfully and move towards him. 'Nick?'

Absolute mayhem surrounds us, but I don't care. The shouting, the fighting and the honking horns fade away. And then the two policemen, notebooks in hand, stride over towards us. Nick's attention flicks away from me. My moment has gone.

'Now then, love,' the burliest one says to me. 'Is this your car?'

And he leads me back towards my crumpled wreck. Nick, similarly, is escorted back to his car. I look over my shoulder and Nick is gazing back at me.

301

'Are the kids okay?' the policeman asks, peering in the window.
'Yes, yes.'
'And you?' he asks. 'You're not hurt?'
Yes. I am hurt. Deeply hurt. 'No. I'm fine, thank you.'
But I'm not fine. I'm not fine at all.

Chapter One Hundred and Four

'You are a wanker, you know,' Sam said.

'Yes.' Nick leaned back on the sofa and shivered in the cold. 'I had also come to that conclusion.'

The sofa had been a purchase from eBay. Black leather. A sexy bloke's sofa. And he and Sam were sitting on it in the back of the transit van he'd borrowed to move the few possessions he'd acquired for his new home. The van was parked outside the curving block of the apartment building that was – in a very few minutes when the estate agent arrived – to become his home.

'So you told Anna, when she so generously offered, that you didn't want her to come back and now you're missing her desperately and have realised rather too late in the day what a twenty-four-carat plonker you can be.'

Nick nodded succinctly. 'That just about sums it up.'

'It's a shame when you're so handsome that you possess a brain the size of a pea,' his friend observed.

Sam was right. But how could Nick begin to explain to his friend that he had been so scared of losing Anna that he couldn't take the risk of getting involved with her again? His heart was a delicate and bruised flower that needed to be protected. And Anna had taken him completely by surprise: if she'd given him a few days to think about it, maybe he would have come to a different conclusion. Maybe? Of course he would have come to a different conclusion! He might be bruised and battered, but he certainly wasn't whole without her. And surely it was a risk worth taking to fill that void?

'I don't know what to do.'

'You could just ring her,' Sam advised.

Nick tutted impatiently. 'How can I do that?'

Sam held up his mobile phone. 'It's an amazing piece of technology. You push the right buttons, Anna answers and then you speak.'

'You make it sound so easy.'

'It is, my friend. It's you who's making a mountain out of a mole-hill.'

Nick tried to ignore him.

'The worst thing she can say is no.'

'Just like I did?'

'I'll phone her for you, if you like.'

'No,' Nick said. 'I don't like. The last thing I want is you interfering in my love-life.'

'Can I point out to you that you don't actually *have* a love-life for me to interfere in.'

'You know what I mean.'

'I do,' Sam said with a sigh. 'And that's why I'm worried about you.' He put his phone away. 'I know what you're going through, mate.'

'You don't.'

'I still miss Sophie,' Sam admitted quietly. 'Just because I don't talk about it every ten minutes, that doesn't mean I feel it any less than you.' He punched Nick on the arm. 'I might appear to be an insensitive bastard sometimes . . .'

'Most of the time.'

'But I've had to accept that this is the way it's going to be. I've moved on. I've had to. You, on the other hand, are stuck – despite fate handing you the most wonderful opportunity to put it right.'

'I can't equate a ten-car pile-up with "wonderful".'

Sam ignored him and ploughed on. 'You don't want to go back and yet you're unwilling to move forward.'

'Perhaps I'm just not ready yet.'

'And in the meantime your life and a fantastic chance of happiness are slipping slowly away from you.'

'I am painfully aware of that,' Nick said, sighing into the cold air and making a cloud of unhappy breath.

Before they could discuss it further, at the appointed time, Lauren Baker from Ketley & Co drove up in her company BMW.

'Here she is,' Nick said and they got up from the sofa and jumped out of the back of the transit van.

Lauren Baker strode towards them, clipboard in hand. There was no doubt that she was a very attractive woman, but Nick had never taken up her offer to call her. He was ashamed to admit that he hadn't ever phoned the lovely line-dancing Cassie Edmonds either. His heart just hadn't been in it and he couldn't bear to string anyone along or to sit and pretend to be having fun on a date, when the likelihood was that he wouldn't be. It looked like he was destined to spend his life turning down the few offers he got from eligible women. His mother, however, had been distinctly unimpressed that her matchmaking attempts had all been in vain. She wasn't that impressed that he was finally moving out of his old bedroom either, but it felt like a huge weight had lifted from Nick's shoulders. He could now start to regain his waistline and his independence.

Lauren Baker dangled his new front-door key in front of him. 'Congratulations,' she said, smiling at him coolly.

It was clear she bore a grudge about his lack of personal phone calls, although she'd been very professional in her business dealings regarding the sale of the apartment.

He took the key from her and it felt like a momentous occasion. 'Thanks.'

His friend nudged him out of the way. 'Sam,' he said. 'Nick's friend. I'm helping him to move in.'

Sam shook Lauren's hand – holding it, of course, for a moment too long. Nick could feel a gooseberry experience coming on.

'Hi, Sam.' Lauren Baker's smile suddenly warmed up. 'I'll come up to the apartment with you to check everything's okay,' she said and walked ahead of them into the building.

Sam fell into step next to Nick. 'This is the one who gave you her phone number?' he mouthed silently.

Nick nodded.

Sam's eyes widened in shock and he hissed under his breath, 'And you didn't call her?'

Nick shook his head.

'Are you fucking nuts?' his friend said out loud. Very out loud.

Lauren turned and pouted sexily at Sam.

The apartment looked bigger and brighter than when he had viewed it, but that was probably because there was no furniture in it. He was trying to hide it – in true British style – but he felt quite emotional. This was his home. His new home.

Lauren completed her brief survey of the place.

'It all looks to be in order,' she said. 'I hope you'll be happy here.'

Nick did too. And he was sure he would be – the place was fabulous.

Sam leaned casually on the wall by the door, turning the full force of his smile on Lauren – who, it seemed, wasn't immune to it. 'I live one floor above this.' Sam tilted his head towards the ceiling. 'The penthouse suite.'

That wasn't a strictly accurate description, but it was bigger and better than this apartment, so Nick allowed Sam some leeway.

'Really?' Lauren Baker found this news enthralling.

'You could come up and look at it, if you like. Perhaps give me a professional valuation.'

'I didn't know you were thinking of moving . . .' Nick's words trailed to nothing. Of course, Sam wasn't thinking of moving.

'We'll be ten minutes,' Sam said, steering Lauren towards the door. 'Maybe fifteen.'

He'd be lucky if Sam remembered to come back the same afternoon. 'I thought you were supposed to be helping me move in,' Nick mouthed silently behind Lauren's back.

'I am!' Sam mouthed back. 'I'll be half an hour. Max!'

Sure. His friend slid his arm round Lauren's slender waist and eased her out of the door. His only hope was that Lauren was busy and couldn't stay for long.

Nick sat down on his oak wood floor in the space where his romantic table for two would eventually go and wondered how he was going to move a sofa up two flights of stairs alone and how he was, without further ado, going to get Anna back into his life. He looked at the space where the table for two was destined to go and wondered if a table for four would fit.

Chapter One Hundred and Five

'**A**ny idiot could see that he was mad about you.' Sophie gave me an exasperated look. 'Except you, of course.'

This does not make me feel better. I am round at my best friend's house recounting the details of my rather close encounter with Nick and his front bumper for possibly the seventh time, and picking over his subsequent refusal of my offer to throw myself back into his arms. 'Nick wasn't interested, Sophie. He made that very clear.'

'You hurt him very badly,' my friend says as if I don't realise this. 'Give the poor bloke a chance.'

'I might never be able to make it up to him. What then?'

'At least give it a chance. You'd just had a car crash and done a hundred-and-eighty-degree turn in your emotions. He was probably in a state of deep shock. You know what blokes are like.'

He did look a bit dazed and confused. 'I'd better get going,' I say. 'We've nothing to eat tonight and I need to feed this pair.'

'Stay for dinner,' Sophie says. 'We've got home-made spaghetti Bolognese. Not a jar of Dolmio in sight. Followed by lemon drizzle cake – also baked by my own fair hands.'

'My word,' I say. 'This *is* the new improved Sophie. I hope all your efforts are being appreciated.'

My friend shrugs. A noncommittal sort of shrug.

'How are things going?'

'Okay,' Sophie says. 'Not wonderful, but not dreadful either. I don't suppose miracles happen overnight, but little by little it's getting better.'

'I'm pleased to hear it.'

My friend hugs me. 'I just wish you'd get it together with Nick then I feel it would all be worth it.'

'You can't say that I didn't try.'

'But maybe I could say that you didn't try hard enough.'

★　　★　　★

307

I finally manage to coerce Poppy and Connor back into the car, which does rather look like some crazed maniac has taken a tin-opener to it.

My daughter has been deeply embarrassed to be seen out in said vehicle during the hours of daylight since the accident. Not surprisingly really. I think I should be embarrassed to be seen out in it too. I remember my parents had a bright orange Austin Princess that I was mortified to be seen in. I dreaded anyone that I knew – particularly of the male species – recognising me while I was in the passenger seat. So I do have empathy with her. I used to take a book everywhere with me and pretend to read, even though it made me car sick. Poppy shrinks down in the front seat and holds her school bag up to her face. 'This car is a death trap, Mummy.'

'No, it isn't.' Actually, it is. The headlight is taped back in with that horrible brown parcel tape that sticks to everything and that is not ideal in anyone's book. I'm not even sure it would be legal to drive, but I'll cross that bridge when I come to it. 'What you mean is, as well as all the rust, it's sadly lacking some sort of designer status and there's no CD-player or heater or air-conditioning.' Other than the holes made by the rust, of course. Despite my child's concern I know that she's far more occupied by style than safety – she is, after all, her mother's daughter. And I realise in this car we have neither. 'I know that all of these things would make your life worth living, but we can't afford it. The very meaning of your existence isn't reliant on Will Young blasting out through speakers with perfect bass balance.'

My daughter doesn't look convinced. 'But you're working now, Mummy. You can do anything.'

I swing into the car park at the supermarket and as I rattle into a space, a little light bulb goes on above my head. She's right. My daughter has a point. There's no way it's going to be economical to repair this heap of jaded metal. I could get a new car – just about. I couldn't afford to buy it outright, but who does these days? Aren't we all living on the never-never? We can afford a small deposit and with a regular salary coming in, I could make the repayments on a loan. I'd need a good deal, but – the thought warms my toes – I know just where I could get one.

I feel a smile spread across my face and I pull Poppy towards me and hug her.

'What?' she says belligerently.

'I have just decided to make an investment in our future,' I say. And I'll do it tomorrow before I lose my nerve.

Chapter One Hundred and Six

There's no sign of the dilapidated Portakabin that was once our office – and in some ways, I'm sad about that. But what is in its place is bigger, better and brand new. The mud and puddles have gone too, replaced by acres of smart, granite block-paving. Rows of spick and span cars line the spacious forecourt. I feel slightly breathless. Nick's new dealership is swish with a capital 'S'.

I've put a suit on to come here. It's a smart, tweedy Chanel one that I bought cheaply at an Oxfam shop – my only concession to charity-shop purchases – and it makes me feel rather like Audrey Hepburn. I've abandoned the kids at Sophie's house, as always, and now I'm standing clutching my handbag like Connor clings to the newly patched up Doggy and I feel as if I'm transported back to another place in time when I first arrived here for my interview. My stomach is just as acidic, my nerves are just as shredded, my confidence is just as low.

I am a different person now and remembering all the things I have learned on my assertiveness training course, I take a deep breath, stride up to the revolving glass door of the showroom and spin myself inside.

The climate-controlled interior is an oasis of calm and efficiency. A few strategically placed, white Christmas trees acknowledge with understated taste the festive season. Shiny new cars are displayed like trophies, turning leisurely on pedestals: visions of twinkling loveliness in gleaming red, blue and silver, with not a dent in sight. Bliss.

Standing in the middle of the showroom, it feels wonderful that I have a legitimate excuse to be here. I am a genuine buyer. I can afford a new car. I am without a shadow of a doubt a punter.

In my excitement, I run my hand over the wing of the nearest car and it feels as smooth as new painted gloss – no lumps, bumps or stippling of rust. It has a proper radio aerial, not a bent coat-hanger. It's chic and stylish – just like I am now. This car would suit me down to the ground.

A couple with a new baby sit proudly in a People Carrier; two older children squabble in the back while the saleswoman runs through her spiel. Tucked away in a corner, far from the gleaming paintwork of the cars, there's a children's play area. There's also a busy service desk and a place where waiting customers can sit and have coffee, dispensed from a state-of-the-art espresso machine. I take it that Nick doesn't make the tea and coffee any more.

There're no knackered filing cabinets, no ancient kettle, no fungus growing anywhere. It's quite a transformation and I'm so pleased for Nick that he's managed to achieve all this. He must be very proud of himself. I cast my mind back to the embarrassing food-cutting-up incident at Nobu with Mr Hashimoto and it seems like a lifetime ago.

A young, fresh-faced salesman comes over to me. 'Can I help you?'

'I'd actually like to speak to Nick Diamond if he's available, please.'

'Certainly,' he says. 'Can I take your name?'

'It's Anna,' I reply. 'Tell him it's Anna.'

And with that he bustles away.

For lack of anything better to do, I open the door of the car next to me. It happens to be one of the smallest cars in the Hivanti range and, as such, within my price range. I lower myself into the driver's seat. Mmm. It feels nice and I think even my hard-to-please daughter would approve of this.

After a moment, the passenger door opens and Nick slides in next to me. 'Hi,' he says rather shyly.

We both close our doors and are cocooned in the car, cut off from the rest of the showroom.

'This is a bit flash,' I say. Nick is a bit flash too. He's wearing a dark grey suit and a trendy tie. 'You look every inch the boss.'

'I've gone up in the world since my Portakabin days,' he says with a smile.

'I can see.' I let my hands drop from the steering wheel. 'It's good to see you.'

He turns towards me. 'It's good to see you too.'

'I'm here to buy a car,' I say chirpily. 'I'm exerting my newfound wealth and independence.'

'That's good.'

'Plus Poppy said if I didn't get rid of my old heap, she'd disown me as an unfit parent.'

'In that case, your daughter mustn't be disobeyed.' Nick's eyes take in the Hivanti. 'Is madam interested in this particular car?'

'I might be,' I say. 'I had an unfortunate crash in my current vehicle and it's now worth about fifty pence. And only then if someone took pity on me.'

'Were you all okay afterwards?' Nick asks. 'By the time I'd finished with the policeman, I looked round and you'd gone.'

I don't say that I didn't think there was anything to hang around for.

'I should have called to find out how you were . . .' His voice tails off.

'We were all fine,' I say. 'But since then my car has steadily dropped to bits. I think it's fairly terminal now.'

'So you really are looking for a new car?'

'Yes.'

'Oh,' he says. 'I did hope that you might have come in just to see me.'

'Maybe a little bit of that,' I admit, 'but I do also want to buy a car.'

'Then you've come to the right place,' Nick says.

We exchange a glance. 'I rather hoped I had.'

'I have to say though, I'm not in a tearing hurry to take you out on a test drive,' he continues. 'I'm still suffering from post-traumatic stress syndrome after the last time.' Nick shakes his head. 'I am sorry about the crash.'

'It wasn't your fault,' I say.

'That doesn't stop me from feeling guilty.'

'So some things don't change then,' I tease.

'No,' Nick admits. 'I'm still a soft touch.'

And I wonder if his heart has softened towards me.

'I couldn't have stood it if anything had happened to you. Or the kids.'

I don't know what to say to that.

'And I miss you in the office too,' he admits quietly and my pulse rate goes into overdrive. 'I've got a new assistant, but she's not like you.'

'I thought that would have been a plus point.'

'She's marvellously efficient.'

I feel a nip of jealousy.

'And has a face like a bagful of spanners.'

I laugh.

'Fewer distractions,' he confesses. 'I recruited her specifically. I can't afford my attention to wander now that I'm in charge of all this.' He gestures at the showroom outside our cosy little bubble.

'It looks fantastic.'

Nick flushes with pride.

'I'm working too,' I say. 'And I've got that filing thing licked once and for all.'

'And the computer?'

'There are days when it still wins, but I'm getting better.' I can't meet his eyes. 'I've changed. I've sorted out my life. I know what I want now and I'm going for it. I love my new job – not quite as much as my old one,' I give him a rueful smile, 'but I've got my independence back.' My pride and my self-esteem too.

Nick takes hold of my hand. 'To be honest with you . . .' he looks into my eyes 'I miss you even more outside of the office.'

This is what I've wanted to hear. 'Really?'

'But I could never mix business with pleasure again.'

'Never?'

'No,' Nick says. He pulls me towards him and kisses me tenderly. His mouth is soft and warm against mine. I feel like I've come home. This is where I'm meant to be, right here with Nick.

The couple getting out of the People Carrier stop what they're doing in shock. The mother covers her children's goggle eyes.

'Would you like me to demonstrate some of the wonderful features on this car?' Nick asks. 'The automatic recline feature on the front seats is particularly useful.'

I grin at him. 'I think that would be nice.'

Nick presses two innocuous-looking buttons by the gear lever and we gently tilt back together. He pulls me towards him as we lie on the seats, face to face.

'Are you sure that you want a shiny new model?' he asks. 'Wouldn't you rather have one that's a bit bruised and battered? One that has a few miles on the clock. One that's endured a few dents and knocks, but is still totally reliable. One with character and charm to cruise down life's highway in. One that desperately needs some tender loving care.'

'Are we still talking about cars?'

'No.'

'Then, yes.' I reach up and stroke Nick's face. 'I'll take that one please.'

'You don't know how happy that makes me,' he says. 'So happy, that I might just throw in a new car for you too.'

'I love you,' I say, laughing.

'And I love you too.' He kisses me gently, tentatively, on the lips.

There's a clunking noise in the car.

'Central locking,' Nick says as he takes me in his arms. 'Another very useful gadget.'

'You don't need that to keep me here,' I say. 'I'll be a very careful new owner.' I touch my finger to his lips. 'I promise that I'll never, ever trade you in.'

'That's all this old wreck has ever wanted to hear.'

Nick turns on the radio and some thoroughly sentimental and smoochy love song drifts out. We settle into each other's arms. The seats in this car are very comfortable and I'm glad because I think we'll be here for a very long time.